33 A.D.

By

DAVID McAFEE

COELACANTH PRESS

Coelacanth Press
P.O. Box 27792
Knoxville, TN 37927-7792
CoelacanthPress@yahoo.com

ISBN-10: 0982630700
ISBN-13: 978-0-9826307-0-9

Visit David McAfee on the web at mcafeeland.wordpress.com

10 9 8 7 6 5 4 3 2 1

This book is lovingly dedicated to my wife, Heather, for all the love and support she has shown me over the years.

I love you, Hon.

Author's Note

33 A.D. was very much inspired by *Violent Sands*, a book written by Sean Young and published by Breakneck Books (now an imprint of Variance Publishing). After reading Young's wonderful depictions of ancient Jerusalem and its people, I started to think about how vampires would have fit into society during those days leading up to the Crucifixion – vampires being the subject I seem to come back to most of the time. Thus the concept for 33 A.D. was born.

That said, please note this is a work of fiction, and as such it should not be taken seriously as anything other than entertainment. The story in your hands should in no way be considered as an indicator of my beliefs nor those of anyone associated with the production of this book.

Lastly, I would like to point out that I tried to make this novel as historically accurate as possible, however in a few places I was forced by the needs of the narrative to take a minor liberty here or there. Some people more familiar with history and/or the Bible than I am will no doubt spot these right away. For those that don't, well...I'll leave it a mystery.

All that said, I certainly hope you enjoy reading 33 A.D. as much as I enjoyed bringing it to you.

Thank You,
David McAfee

CHAPTER ONE

Jerusalem, 33A.D.

Ephraim darted around his modest wood-and-mortar home in the Upper City, grabbing as many of his possessions as he could carry – mostly clothing and a few personal items – and shoving them into a large burlap pack. Every now and then his brown eyes shifted to the door, waiting for a knock. Or worse, no sound whatsoever. The latter worried him the most because it would mean the servants of the Council had found him. A Psalm of Silence only carried for about twenty paces, so if the world around him went suddenly quiet, he would know those who hunted him were very, very close.

As an Enforcer, or at least a former Enforcer, Ephraim knew the inevitable result of breaking the laws of his people, a race not known for mercy. Now, as he packed, he couldn't help but wonder why he'd felt the need to tell the Council about his indiscretions. Bad enough he'd defied them, but he also gave them all the information they needed to punish him. And for what? A strange feeling in his heart? A pang of consience? Was he mad? In retrospect, it seemed possible, but he couldn't do anything about it now. His elders wanted him dead, and unless he hurried they would get their way.

A worn, woolen tunic hung halfway off his bed. *I'll need that*, he thought as he reached for it. He couldn't afford to leave a single piece of clothing behind. He stuffed the tunic into his bag and turned to regard a large chest on the wall opposite the bed. He reached down and flung the lid open, breaking one of the hinges in the process, and started grabbing more clothes. *I'll need that. And that.*

Then his fingers closed on something small and hard. He didn't have to look at it to know it was his ceramic wolf's head figurine, a symbol of his former rank. *I won't need that.* Ephraim tossed it over his shoulder, where it shattered on the hard floor. He didn't pay it any attention as he picked up a short, fat bladed knife. *I'll need that, too.* It joined the many tunics in his bag. Just as he picked up a pair of worn breeches, a noise outside his door caught his attention.

What was that? Ephraim froze, craning his ears and trying desperately to catch the elusive sound. He stood silent and still for sixty long seconds, muscles tense and booted feet nailed to the floor. The breeches hung from his fingers like a mouse in a raptor's claw. He eyed the sickle-shaped sword on the opposite wall, ready to spring over and grab it if necessary. Although the sword was very old, he kept it sharp and in perfect balance, not easy to do with a *khopesh*.

When the noise didn't return, he shook his head. *The wind*, he told himself, and returned to the task at hand. He had to hurry. They were coming.

He couldn't allow himself to be captured by the Council's minions. They would make him talk, and that would be bad. Not just for himself, but for his newfound friends, as well. The elders of the *Bachiyr* race had many methods by which to extract information, even from one of their own. All of them brutally effective. If they caught him, they would find a way to make him talk. Sooner or later Ephraim would tell them anything they wanted to know, the only real question was how long would it take to break him.

As he packed, his hand brushed against a small figurine of a lamb from the shelf above his bed, knocking it off and sending it toppling through the air. "Damn!" He reached out to catch it and missed, but his fingertips brushed the delicate figurine just enough to alter its course so that, instead of following the wolf's head to the hard floor, the lamb plopped down amidst the soft linens on the bed. Ephraim breathed a sigh of relief when the delicate figure didn't break, and reached down gently to pick it up. He didn't miss the irony that he, the predator, had thrown away the wolf figurine and kept the lamb.

Former predator, he amended, shaking his head. *I am not like that anymore.* He stared at the lamb for several precious seconds, remembering what it symbolized and making sure, in his heart, he'd made the right decision. Satisfied, he placed the tiny item into a small velvet bag and tied it shut, then placed the bag into his pack, stuffing it between the folds of a coarse brown tunic. He tied the pack closed and set it on the floor in front of him.

Ephraim then stepped over to the far wall and eyed his ancient *khopesh,* which he had wielded for over a thousand years, though the style of blade had largely gone out of use eight centuries ago. He reached a tentative hand up to the sword, but his fingers froze before they touched the handle. Ashamed, he pictured the faces of his many victims, heard again their anguished screams, and saw their mouths stretched wide in agony. The smell of their blood returned to him, sending an unwelcome rumble through his belly. Far from the pleasure these memories once brought, Ephraim now felt only shame. *How many?* He wondered. *How many have I killed with this very blade?* He had no idea, but the number must surely be huge.

"So great is my sin," he whispered. He could not shed tears, none of his race could, but his face felt hot and flushed, nonetheless. He drew his hand back, unwilling to touch the ancient sword, his most trusted companion for centuries, now too poignant a reminder of who he used to be. With a sigh, he turned from the wall and walked over to the bed, determined to leave his past at his back.

Now ready to go, he just had to wait for his friend to come and help sneak him out of the city. Ephraim sat on the edge of his bed, waiting for Malachi's knock. He hoped it would not take long.

Please hurry, Malachi, he thought. *Time is running out. They are coming.*

Above Ephraim, crouched amidst the pressed oak beams that supported the structure's ceiling, a single pair of eyes looked down at the one-time Enforcer. The Council's agents were not *coming,* as Ephraim feared. They – or rather, *he* – had already arrived. If he had looked up, he might have seen the dark shadow hiding among the lighter ones in his ceiling, but he never so much as glanced upward. His visitor thought lack of sustenance to be the cause of Ephraim's inattentiveness, and he shook his head in disbelief. From his dark vantage point, he watched the scene unfold, memorizing the layout of the room for future reference.

Earlier that evening, before he had left the Halls, the Council told him what to expect. Even so, he hadn't wanted to believe that one of their own, particularly one with as glorious and faithful a history as Ephraim, could be capable of such treachery. Until he witnessed Ephraim's hurried packing and the incident with the wolf's head – an article of rank sacred to the *Bachiyr* – he'd hoped to discover his superiors mistaken. The longer he waited on high, however, the more he came to realize they were right, and the angrier he became.

They are always right, he thought to himself. *I should have known better than to doubt. Just because he's a friend—* he stopped himself there, not wanting to diminish his readiness. He couldn't waste time thinking of past friendships and obligations. He had a job to do, and reminiscing would only make it harder and might even cloud his judgment, which could not be allowed. He had to be clear-headed and alert for the next few minutes.

Long enough to kill Ephraim.

First, however, he had to wait and observe a short while longer. The treacherous dog would die, certainly, but not before his visitor discovered who he'd betrayed them to. Ephraim's message to the Council had been vague in that regard; most likely a deliberate omission. To that end the watcher held himself in check through his growing anger while his thick, sharp nails dug furrows into the wooden beams. He held still, relishing the tantalizing scent of fear that emanated from his former friend, and waited for the knock that would signal Ephraim's allies had come to save him. On that, the Council's orders were very clear. *We must know who the traitor is in league with. That is of utmost importance, Theron.*

Theron had never failed the Council before, not once in over nine hundred years, and he didn't intend to start now. As much as he wanted to drop from the shadows like an evil beast from a child's tale, he waited. *Patience,* he counseled himself. *Not yet.* Waiting was the essence of his craft. He was a professional. If you wanted to put a fine point on it, he was *the* professional. The Lead Enforcer for the Council of Thirteen, albeit newly appointed. These days, that mostly meant he acted as their primary assassin, although every now and then the Council sent him for capture rather than elimination. But those occasions were few.

And this wasn't one of them.

So until Ephraim received his visitor, Theron would sit, out of sight, and wait for the sound of knuckles on the door. However long it took. But once he had his information, then… well, *then* the fun would begin.

He didn't have to wait long. About five minutes after Ephraim finished packing a loud knock thundered through the house, violating the silence with a hollow boom. Ephraim jumped at the sudden sound, but Theron had heard the visitor's boots crunch on Ephraim's gravel walkway and was expecting it. He smiled as he watched his intended victim's face go from terror to joy.

"At last!" Ephraim said. "You certainly took enough time to get here." He walked over to the door and grasped the handle. Then, just as he was about to raise the wooden latch, the relief fled his face, replaced by a look of wariness and renewed fear. "Who's there?"

"Ephraim, you dog. Open the damned door. We don't have time for this."

"Malachi! Thank the Father you've come." He released the latch on the door and swung it inward.

Malachi the butcher? A human? Theron had expected another *Bachiyr* to be behind Ephraim's treachery. But a human? What in the Father's Name was going on?

Malachi stepped in, ducking his head and twisting a bit to the side in order to maneuver his broad shoulders through the doorway. He wore his shoulder-length brown hair tied back with a leather thong, leaving his craggy, olive-skinned face exposed from forehead to chin, and he didn't look pleased. He fixed his stern features squarely on the much smaller Ephraim. "Thank 'the Father,' Ephraim? Why would you offer thanks to a demon? Have you learned nothing these last few weeks?"

"My apologies, my friend. Old habits can be difficult to break."

"Indeed, they can," Malachi said. "That you are trying at all says much about your progress." The butcher's face relaxed. He reached his hand out and clasped Ephraim's. "So what is the news?" Malachi looked around the room at the mess of Ephraim's frantic packing. "Are they coming?"

"Yes." Ephraim sprang into motion, grabbing his pack off the bed and hoisting it over his shoulder. "I'm sure of it. We have to leave."

"How did they find out?"

"You want to waste time on explanations? Didn't you hear? They are coming. Let's go and I'll explain on the way." He started to go around the larger man, and Theron tensed. He could not allow the pair to leave, which meant he would have to kill the human first and deal with Ephraim, by far the more dangerous of the two, afterward. He readied himself to spring as Ephraim tried to squirm his way around the huge man.

But Malachi would have none of it. He reached down and grabbed hold of Ephraim's shoulder. The thick, corded muscles on his arm twitched as he casually tossed the smaller man back into the room. He then placed his bulky frame between Ephraim and the door, folding his thick arms across his chest.

"How did they know, Ephraim?" Malachi asked again.

Ephraim glared at the human and chewed his lip, as though trying to decide how much to tell. It surprised Theron that the man handled Ephraim with so little trouble. Either Ephraim's lack of feeding weakened him more than Theron had expected or the butcher was extremely strong. Probably a bit of both. He made a mental note of Malachi's strength; he'd need to be wary of it soon enough.

After a moment or two spent in tense silence, Malachi spoke. "If you don't trust us by now, Ephraim, I can't help you." With that, the giant turned his back to Ephraim and started to walk out of the house.

"I told them!" Ephraim cried. "I'm sorry. I told them. I thought they would be pleased, I… I thought they would see as I have seen. I wanted them to know the truth."

Malachi turned to face him, his face a mask of rage and disbelief. "You *told* them, Ephraim? Dear God, what were you thinking?"

"I didn't tell them everything. Just that I couldn't serve them any more. I thought they would understand." Ephraim's voice cracked on the last syllable. "I thought I could *make* them understand."

Malachi closed his eyes. His massive chest swelled as he took a deep breath. The look of anger washed away from his face, replaced by one of sorrow. When he opened his eyes Theron noted a hint of moisture around the edges. "They do understand, my friend. They understand all too well. That's why they will kill you now, and him too."

"No," Ephraim shook his head, his eyes wide. "No, Malachi. Me, certainly. But him? Why? He's done nothing to them."

"Do you truly think they will care?"

Ephraim didn't answer, but he didn't need to. In the shadows above, Theron could have answered the question for him. Of course the Council wouldn't care. The Council *never* cared. One of their own had betrayed them, and thus he must die. Ephraim would be executed, along with any co-conspirators, be they human or otherwise. Theron's very existence proved that. After all, why would a forgiving Council need Enforcers?

Malachi sighed, his face troubled but resolute. "We must get you out of here, Ephraim. There's a merchant caravan going out with the first light. We can put you in a strong box so the sun will not touch you. The driver's name is Paul. They are heading west to Lydda. There you will find shelter and solace, as much as can be given one of your kind."

Ephraim stood, his face brightening with renewed hope. "Thank you, Malachi. I can never repay you."

Theron had heard enough. "I can," he said as he dropped from the rafters. He positioned himself between the entrance and the room's two surprised occupants. In one fluid motion, he kicked the door shut behind him and pulled his sword from his sheath. Not a *khopesh* like Ephraim's, Theron's sword was of a more modern, almost Roman design. The straight, thick blade, relatively short for a sword, was designed more for piercing than cutting, though it was certainly capable of both. He hadn't planned on using it when he left the Halls earlier, but Malachi's strength and size presented a very real threat. Since he would need to face Ephraim, as well, speed was a primary concern. That meant using the blade. Theron hadn't become Lead Enforcer by taking chances. The human would die first, then he would deal with the traitor.

Malachi reached for the hammer at his belt, but although large and strong, he was not fast. By the time he got his fingers around the handle, Theron had already spun a circle in front of him, blade first, and cut open his throat in a precise line from one side of his jaw to the other. Malachi sputtered and tried to speak, but his severed vocal chords failed him. The fingers on his right hand started to twitch, and the hammer fell from them and hit the floor with a dull thump. He brought his left hand up to his neck in a futile attempt to stem the flow of his life's blood, then he followed his weapon to the floor. The big human didn't seem angry or bewildered, as Theron might have expected, but content. His face softened into a peaceful expression the Enforcer found somewhat odd. Before he could puzzle it out, however, he would have to deal with Ephraim.

Theron whirled to face him, fully expecting to be bowled over in a mass of teeth and claws. But Ephraim stood in the same spot as before. He hadn't moved at all during Malachi's death, and had not plucked his infamous *khopesh* from the wall. Theron thought he knew the reason. *He knows it won't help. He already knows how this must end.* He stepped closer. Malachi's blood dripped from his blade, leaving a thin trail of small red puddles on the floorboards.

"Theron," Ephraim said. "They sent you?"

"I'm the best. Of course they sent me." Theron gave a mocking bow.

"Are you the Lead Enforcer now, my old friend?"

"Someone had to take your place. Who better than me? But you are no friend of mine, traitor." He spat at the other's feet, barely missing Ephraim's dusty leather boot.

"Don't be so quick to choose, Theron. You should hear what he has to say."

"I don't need to hear what he has to say. I still serve our people. The rambling words of a deranged rabbi will not show me my path. The Council's laws have protected our people for over four thousand years. You," he pointed an accusing finger, "have violated them."

"His words would save you, my friend," Ephraim said, so softly Theron almost didn't hear him.

Theron laughed. "Save me? As they saved you? You are a handful of seconds away from death, and you would presume to save *me*?" In that instant, Theron determined he would make Ephraim's death as unpleasant as he could manage. He threw his sword to the floor and willed his claws to grow. In a few moments his fingernails grew long and thick. The brief but intense pain in his fingertips was worth it. He would rip the traitor's head from his shoulders. "You should worry about saving yourself, *old friend*."

"I did," Ephraim replied, just before Theron leapt at him.

It was over quickly; Ephraim didn't fight back. When Theron grabbed Ephraim's head between his clawed hands, the traitor only stared at him with a sad, wistful expression on his face. He didn't speak, not even to beg for his life, which was a bit disappointing. Ephraim didn't flinch at Theron's touch, and he didn't scream, not even when Theron drove his clawed fingers through the flesh of his throat and began to twist, rending tendons, tearing muscle, and sending a spray of blood all over the wall. Once the head rolled off onto the floor, it was over. Theron felt let down. It was too easy.

A quick search of Ephraim's body turned up a rolled piece of parchment. Theron noted the red wax seal, which matched the *E* on Ephraim's ring, and snapped it in two. He unrolled the letter and read every word, but it didn't tell him anything he hadn't already surmised. It was only a letter to Malachi. Apparently Ephraim had wanted the butcher to be prepared in the event of his death, but in the end it proved too little, too late. Now both lay dead, and Theron had his answers. He dropped the paper onto Ephraim's headless torso and went to the back of the house to find a shovel. He would need to bury the bodies so they would not be found, at least not before he completed his business in Jerusalem.

It took a long time to bury Ephraim and Malachi. The hole had to be deep enough to keep any stray dogs from smelling the bodies and digging them up. Due to Malachi's tremendous girth, it also had to be wide and tall. Theron spent the better part of four hours digging the hole, rolling the bodies into it, and covering them up. He also tossed in Ephraim's last letter to Malachi. He wouldn't need it to convince the Council; he had proof enough already.

Afterward, he carefully replaced the layer of grass and sod to better hide the corpses, though the telltale bulge of the earth would be a dead giveaway if anyone came looking. By the time Theron finished the arduous task, dawn loomed a mere two hours away. That didn't leave much time to make his way through the city, but he thought he could manage it.

He walked away from the house, carrying his macabre prize in Ephraim's burlap sack, which he carried slung over his shoulder. Ephraim's head, which bounced and jostled along inside the bag, wore neither fear nor malice on its lifeless features, instead the dead vampire's expression seemed... peaceful. Theron didn't care. The job was done; the Council would be pleased. What's more, he had the information they sought, for Theron now knew the identity of the person to whom Ephraim had betrayed his people. It could only be one man, the same man who'd acquired followers from all across Israel over the last few years. The very man Malachi swore his life to protect only a month ago.

Jesus, they called him. Jesus of Nazareth.

CHAPTER TWO

Theron walked the dusty streets of Jerusalem with his sack slung over his shoulder. His sandals whispered against the cobbles, making no more noise than air passing over an owl's wing. The wood and stone buildings on either side of the street faded to the same dirty gray in the dim light of pre-dawn. At this hour, they all looked the same.

He had to be careful to steer clear of any legionaries. Theron didn't fear them, but if any soldiers found him walking the streets they might mistake him for a thief and question him, perhaps even demand to look into his bag. He couldn't allow that to happen, of course, because then he would have to kill them. Although it would be easy enough to do, he ran the risk they might raise an alarm before he could finish. A contingent of Roman soldiers scouring the city would hamper his movement, and thus his ability to report back to the Council. Better not to be noticed at all.

Theron kept his eyes and ears trained on his surroundings. He could not afford any surprises this close to his goal. He slipped from shadow to shadow, as one with the night blanketing the city, and managed to keep out of sight of any legionaries. The few patrols he saw were too far away to notice him, and the clip of their sandaled feet on the cobblestones revealed their presence long before they came into view.

He'd been traversing the Upper City, where Ephraim kept his home, but his way to the Council lay through the New City, which required him to pass through the Middle Gate. He threaded his way softly through the darkened streets, passing the massive Palace of Solomon and the Temple, neither of which impressed him in the least. As he approached the gate he heard voices, and swore under his breath. He stopped at the edge of a potter's shop and peered around the corner. Sure enough, two red cloaked legionaries stood watch at the gate, their steel breastplates glinting dully in the moon-light. Theron couldn't tell if they were posted there or if they just happened to stop for a break. Either way, their presence was damned inconvenient. The threat of dawn lingered less than an hour away, which meant he didn't have much time to wait for them to move on.

As the two legionaries settled into a comfortable conversation, one of them produced a set of dice, much to the delight of the other. They soon hunkered down in front of the gate and lost themselves in a game. Several times Theron heard one of the men whisper a harsh curse when the roll didn't go in his favor.

He huddled back into the shadows to consider his options. He could circle back and try another route, but he didn't know the city very well and worried he might get lost. If that happened he would be forced to take shelter from the day in a stranger's house. Since killing the stranger in his bed might rouse the neighbors, it was not an ideal prospect. The thought of lying helpless in bed while a group of armed Roman soldiers surrounded him didn't appeal to Theron. As such, he would wait a while and see if the two patrolmen moved along on their own.

Twenty minutes later, the first light of day threatened to break over the horizon, and the soldiers still hadn't moved. Theron could wait no longer. He checked his attire to make sure everything looked fine, even retrieving fresh dirt from the street and smudging it into his face. The peasant who had "donated" his clothes earlier in the evening hadn't gotten any blood on them, so he felt optimistic his disguise would hold. If the guards questioned him, he would tell them he was on his way to one of the wheat fields outside the city to begin the workday. If they believed him and let him go, good. If not he would have to kill them fast and run like a demon. His path set and his list of options short, he strode from the shadows and walked toward the legionaries, trying to look as though he belonged there.

He was only ten feet away when one of the men looked up from the dice and spotted him. The soldier nudged his fellow on the arm and they both stood to face the newcomer.

"Hold," one of them commanded, and Theron, remembering he was supposed to be a peasant, stopped in his tracks.

"Yes?" He asked.

The soldier looked him up and down, taking in his clothes, his face, and the bag he carried over his shoulder. "A bit early to be going to the fields, isn't it, friend?"

"Begging your pardon, sir, but it's never too early to start an honest day's work, is it?"

"Indeed," the soldier fixed him with a doubtful gaze. "Which of the landowners do you tend for?"

"Jared," Theron pulled the name from memory. Jared owned several fields just outside the city, and was well known in Jerusalem for his high quality wheat and barley. "For ten years now. You can ask him, if you like."

"Don't be flippant. There's been a great deal of zealot activity of late, and the centurion has ordered us to keep the streets safe for the law-abiding citizens of Jerusalem."

"No offense meant," Theron bowed his head in respect. "It's just that I'll be leaving the field early today on account of a personal matter, and I thought to go in early so as to not miss my wages."

The soldier gave him a second look, taking in his posture and his stance, both of which Theron had worked hard to cultivate in order to portray himself as nothing more than he appeared; a poor farm hand, beaten down by the life of a peasant and tired with age. After a cursory examination, the legionary waved him through the gate.

"Thank you," Theron said, and proceeded to walk through. Just as he exited, he felt a strong hand grip his shoulder.

"Do all Jared's hands wear a sword to work?"

Damn! Theron looked at his waist, where the hilt of his sword poked from a flap of coarse brown cloth. He'd done his best to hide it in the folds of his clothing, but the peasant garb was not well suited to such a deception, consisting as it did of a simple coarse shirt and a pair of baggy trousers, and he'd been forced to make do. The large ruby and trio of emeralds mounted in the hilt didn't help.

His mind raced frantically for a suitable lie. All was not lost; he might still be able to—

"Claudius, look at his bag. It's spotted with blood," the other soldier said.

Claudius and Theron both looked at the bag. It was true. Theron had spent too much time waiting for the soldiers to disperse, and Ephraim's blood – which, like that of all *Bachiyr*, didn't coagulate – soaked through in places. He scrambled to think of a suitable excuse. A sheep, maybe, or something for Passover.

But with his very next breath, Claudius ended any chance of avoiding a fight. "Open the bag."

Theron's shoulders slumped. So much for discretion. "No," he said. "I don't think I will."

Claudius's eyes narrowed to slits. "I knew it. He's a zealot. Take him!" Both soldiers drew their swords and the masquerade was over. *Fools*, Theron thought. If only they'd let him pass unmolested through the Middle Gate. Now he had to kill them, and fast.

He didn't have time to reach for his sword, so he swung the bag containing Ephraim's head with all his strength. As Claudius swung for Theron's shoulder, the bag slammed into the legionary's face. Theron smiled at the satisfying crunch of bone as the soldier's nose shattered.

Claudius fell backward into the street, but he was only stunned. Soon enough he would scream for reinforcements. That meant Theron had only a few seconds to kill the other soldier and then turn his attention back to Claudius. He spun to face his other opponent just in time to avoid a roundhouse swing that would have severed his head had it connected. He ducked under the blade, but not before it opened a gash on his shoulder. Theron kicked out with his left foot, connecting solidly on the soldier's torso and sending him crashing into the dusty stone wall behind him.

Theron took a second to examine his wound, noting the lazy flow of blood. He scowled and returned his attention to the legionary. This time, he didn't feel the sting as the nails on his hands grew longer and thicker. In half a heartbeat they were three inches long and strong as bone. He threw the bag to the side and leapt at the horrified legionary, who pressed his back into the wall and watched, eyes wide as dates, as death found him.

"What are you?" the Roman asked.

In answer, Theron struck the unfortunate soldier in the throat with both hands, letting his fingers sink all the way through until the newly lengthened nails poked out the other side. He then turned his palms outward, curling his fingers before spreading his arms wide. The sound of rending flesh and the spray of blood in the air invigorated him as he tore the head from the legionary's body. Theron's eyes followed it as it flew through the air to land a few inches from Claudius's left foot.

Theron turned to face Claudius, a smile on his lips. He raised his right hand to his face and ran his tongue along the length of his bloody index finger. The dead soldier's blood covered his face and his clothes. The smell of it filled the air and assaulted his senses. He felt the familiar hunger building inside him, burning his discipline away with the promise of more. Theron forced himself to remain in control, promising his primal side he would feed when he returned to the Halls.

Behind him, he heard the sound of the body as it hit the ground. He feared he'd waited too long; that Claudius would scream the alarm to every Roman Soldier in the city, and Theron would be forced to run into someone's house for the day.

But the injured legionary said nothing, perhaps *could* say nothing. Claudius's eyes never left Theron's claws as he approached. The man tried to speak, but no sound came from his lips. Theron's nose wrinkled as he caught the acrid odor of urine, and noted the puddle spreading beneath the fallen legionary. He would have to make this quick. Theron started to use his claws again, but thought better of it. It would be best for the Romans to blame this on the zealots. He willed the nails back into his hands and instead pulled out his sword.

The sound of metal sliding against leather and the sight of the claws disappearing seemed to wake Claudius from his stupor. The legionary drew in a breath, perhaps to scream, but Theron was too fast.

He drove the point of his sword through the soldier's breastplate, piercing the man's heart and silencing him. As Claudius looked down at his ruined chest, he brought one hand up and clutched the sword in a feeble attempt to pull it out. Theron twisted the sword in his hand and watched as Claudius grimaced. The sharp crack of the man's sternum and his sudden intake of breath were the only sounds to be heard.

The dying legionary looked up at Theron from the dirt, his eyes squeezed nearly shut and his lips peeled back from his teeth. The ruin of his nose painted the lower half of his face the same color as his bloodied chest. A single tear formed in his right eye and rolled down his cheek as he shuddered his way through his final breaths.

"You should have just let me through," Theron said.

Claudius slumped over, and Theron pulled out his sword. The whole encounter had taken less than two minutes, and neither of the men made a sound louder than a whisper. He wiped the blade on the dead man's uniform before putting it away, not having time to give it a more thorough cleaning. The sight and smell of so much blood made Theron's hunger bubble to the surface, but he could not indulge it. If he fed now, it would leave an empty body in the streets of Jerusalem for the next patrol to find. That, in turn, would raise questions; questions his superiors would not like raised. He turned his back on the men, shaking his head. He would just have to wait.

He picked up his bag and noted a great deal more blood on it than before. Theron recalled the sound Claudius's nose made when it cracked and his smile returned. He was glad he'd come this way and run into the two soldiers, after all.

On this mission alone he killed a traitor and three humans, four if you count the peasant from whom he'd taken the clothes. *It's been a good night,* he thought as he set out once again for the New City.

CHAPTER THREE

A t that same moment, half a city away in an alley between a tailor's shop and a butcher's, another meeting was taking place. While significantly less violent than either of Theron's encounters, it was just as secret. A tall Roman legionary with an uncommon mane of shoulder-length blonde hair and the raven haired daughter of a middle class Jewish merchant met in the inky darkness between the two buildings. They embraced, and shared the stolen pleasure of a kiss which would be denied them any other time of day.

"I missed you, Taras," the woman said when she finally pulled away.

"I missed you, too," he replied.

Her eyes twinkled. "Your Hebrew is improving."

"I've been practicing." He reached up with his right hand and twined his fingers through her hair, staring into her olive-skinned face. "I haven't seen you on my patrols the last few days, though I look for you every day."

She looked away from him, hiding her face in his shoulder. "My father has been keeping me too busy during the day to get out much."

"Do you think he suspects?"

She nodded. "I'm sure of it. Two days ago I left the house to run an errand at the market, and he insisted Zechariah accompany me. He's never done that before."

He continued to stroke her hair, which slid through his fingers like strands of satin. "It could be due to the recent increase in zealot activity. Last week, Prefect Pilate ordered every legionary in the city placed on extra alert. With the coming of Passover and the greater numbers of people in Jerusalem, Pilate fears the zealots will become even more aggressive."

She looked at him then, and he noted the moisture rimming her eyes. "No, I don't think that's it."

"But you don't know for sure."

"Yes I do," she said firmly, and pushed him back to arm's length. "He knows you by sight, somehow. I see the way he looks at you when your patrol goes by. He watches you, and his face... I've never seen it like that. It's like he's made of stone."

"He is probably just watching the patrol. Your father, as I recall, is none too fond of Rome and her legionaries. I've had to step in on his behalf to prevent the Centurion from taking action against him several times already."

"I know." She smiled, and brushed the fingers of her right hand against his clean-shaven cheek. "But it isn't the patrol he watches when your unit walks by, it's you. I overheard him speaking to mother several nights ago. He even mentioned you by name."

"What did he say?" Taras asked.

Mary shook her head, and by her posture he knew she would never tell him. She could be very stubborn at times. But her hesitation did tell him one thing: whatever her father said about him, it was not good.

It didn't surprise him that her father would feel such animosity. Taras walked on dangerous ground by continuing to see her. Men in Jerusalem had been killed for less than the short kiss they shared only moments before. When Rome's forces took control of the city such executions became illegal, especially on a Roman soldier, but that didn't mean it never happened. The zealots loved any excuse to make the Romans' lives miserable, and Taras knew for a fact Mary's father, Abraham, had strong connections to zealot circles. If Abraham took a mind to, it would be easy enough for him to try and have Taras killed in what would likely be seen as just another zealot uprising. The threat of her father's ire forced Taras to walk a very fine line with their budding relationship. For the time being, it could not become public knowledge.

Still, one look at her face, and he knew he would walk that line as long as it took. The risk was a small price to pay for the pleasure of her company. He longed for the day he could do better by her. Her father would never be persuaded to let him marry her by any normal means, of course. But there were always alternatives.

"Taras?" her voice was soft, hesitant, "What do you think of when your face gets that way?"

Taras shook his head, trying to clear his mind of the thoughts he'd been entertaining. "What do you mean?"

"Your eyes...sometimes when we talk, especially about father, they become so hard."

He pulled her close. "It's nothing. Just something I will need to discuss with the centurion later. As for your father, he is only trying to protect you from the great evils of the Roman Empire."

"Evils like you?" She asked.

"Exactly like me," he replied, unable to suppress a grin.

She returned his smile, and the two shared another kiss. This time it was Taras who broke it, albeit reluctantly. "I have something for you. A gift."

Her smile widened, and although she protested such a thing was unnecessary, he reached into his pocket and withdrew a small wooden box. "It's not much. Beautiful as Rome is, she does not pay her soldiers as well as I would like." He held it out to her.

Mary took the little box in both hands and gently opened the lid. Her eyes widened when she saw what lay inside. She reached her fingers into the box and came away with a gold ring. A single ruby sat inlaid into the gold, surrounded on either side by two triangular onyx panels. Taras had saved his salary for months to pay for it, but the delight in her deep brown eyes was worth every copper. She slipped it onto her finger and looked up at him, moisture brimming in her dark eyes.

"Do you like it?" He asked.

"I love it, Taras." Mary threw her arms around his neck. "And I love you."

Taras pressed his face into her dark, curly hair, reveling in the scent of her perfume and the soft feel of her skin. She shuddered in his arms, and he thought his heart would burst. "I love you, too."

They stood in the alley, locked in their embrace, for a span of several heartbeats. If he could have his way, they would have stayed there the whole night. But Taras knew if she didn't get home soon her father would discover her missing, and knowing Abraham, he would rouse half the city to look for her. With a sigh, he pulled away.

"You should go. It would not be good if you were caught out so late. Your servant might not be able to keep herself quiet if you are gone too long."

"Elizabeth will not say a word, of that I'm sure," Mary said. "But you are right. Father told the all servants he wanted to wake early to make the preparations for his trip to Bethlehem. If he rises and I'm not there, she will be hard pressed to find an excuse."

She leaned forward and gave Taras one last kiss. "Will I see you tomorrow evening? Father will be on the road and will not return for several days, and he will have to take Zechariah with him."

"Of course. I will meet you at your front gate tomorrow evening after my patrol is finished."

She favored him with a nod, then turned and walked away down the alley. He watched her go with a mixture of love and frustration. How he ached to share more than a kiss with her, and he knew she felt the same. He could feel it every time they were together in the shudder of her arms and quickening of her heartbeat. But her father hated him, and Jewish law forbade her to marry without her father's blessing. Even if Abraham were more amenable, that same law would not allow a Jewish woman to marry a Roman. A Jewish man could marry anyone he wanted, but a Jewish woman must marry a Jewish man. Not even Pilate would dare to bend that rule, not for a single legionary of no discernable rank. The outcry of the locals would be incredible.

The only way to circumnavigate that law would be for Caiphas himself to authorize an exception, but the High Priest would never do such a thing, at least not without a very large donation to the Temple (or to Caiphas' personal coffers). Taras didn't know how large a sum it would take, but he did know it would be far more than he could offer on a legionary's pay. He blew out a frustrated sigh as he fingered the hilt of his sword, wondering what sort of persuasion it would take to change the old man's mind. He pictured himself standing over the portly priest, sword in hand. How long would it take for the man to give in? Would he ever? If it came to it, would Taras have to kill him?

He jerked his hand away from the sword, surprised at his own malice. As much as he would like to, killing the old Sanhedrin wouldn't do him any good; he would just have to deal with the next High Priest, who would likely be every bit as stubborn as Caiphas. He sighed as he looked at the bronze hilt sticking out of his leather scabbard.

I'll just have to find another way, he thought. Then he, too, left the alley, headed for the barracks and a few hours' sleep before the morning report to Marcus, the Centurion.

CHAPTER FOUR

Theron carried his macabre burden through the streets of the New City. He walked with haste through the long shadows, his only refuge from the sun now that it had begun its ascent. He finally stopped in front of a small, unimpressive house not far from the Damascus Gate. There he dropped his burden to the cobbles and searched his pockets, taking from them a small gold key. He grabbed the bag containing Ephraim's disembodied head and lifted it over his shoulder, then inserted the key into the lock and stepped through the door.

Inside the house there was no light, but Theron didn't need any. His sharp eyes, more adapted to night than day, could make out the gradient walls in perfect detail in even the poorest illumination. In addition, he'd been here often enough in his long years that he could find his way blind. He walked down a narrow hallway to another door; a heavy oaken monstrosity adorned with a carving of a wolf, and pushed his way through. Light poured from the doorway and into the hall, casting aside the prior darkness and bathing the inside of the house in a soft glow, revealing numerous bas-relief images of wolves and the moon carved into the walls.

The carvings were exquisite; the work of true masters whose time and skill had been bought and paid for with their very lives centuries before. The poor souls worked diligently for years to bring this hallway into its present splendor, only for Theron to kill them when the work was complete so there would be no witnesses.

Theron chuckled at the memory. *How they begged me to spare them. How they cried and screamed.* He hadn't spared any. Not one. He couldn't. The Council ordered him to kill every last one of them. By that time Theron's hands were so covered in blood he no longer cared if he added more. He reached out with his right hand and traced the contours of a wolf's head carved into the wall, relishing the feel of the smooth stone beneath his fingertips.

A voice from the room interrupted his thoughts. "Don't linger in the doorway, Theron. Come inside and report."

Theron turned and entered the room, closing the door behind him. Inside, the stone walls gave way to a deep, varnished wood that glowed in the restless light of several lamps, which burned from all four sides of the room. Theron wrinkled his nose at the acrid scent of lamp oil. He'd never cared for lamplight, preferring the dancing light of a torch or, even better, his enhanced night vision.

On the walls, portraits of various sizes depicted the thirteen members of the Council. Small statues stood like miniature sentinels upon a shelf on the back wall. From Herris' brassy, chiseled features to Algor's twisted and misshapen profile, every member of the Council of Thirteen was represented here, in the Council's Jerusalem Receiving Room.

In the center of the room stood a large granite desk, the top of which lay strewn with sheaves of papyrus and various other writing materials, most notably a vial of human blood with a quill dipped into it. A psalm placed on the vial kept the blood from coagulating, making it perfectly suitable as ink for the Council's steward, who sat behind the desk eyeing Theron with curiosity and excitement.

"You're a mess," the clerk said.

Theron frowned and looked down at his clothing. Rust-colored splotches of dried blood stiffened the fabric and plastered his hair to his scalp. He could feel the stiffness around his face from the layer of dirt and yet more blood. His hands and arms, too, were covered with the stuff. All in all, he resembled the wall of a slaughter pen. He looked up from his torso and shrugged. "Sometimes my work is messy, Simon."

"Did you get him?"

"That's a foolish question." Theron hefted the bag containing Ephraim's head, making sure to point out the stains where the blood soaked through the burlap. "Of course I got him. I always do."

"That you do, Theron. That you do. That's marvelous. May I?" He stood and walked over to the Enforcer and pointed at the lip of the bag. Theron sighed and opened it so Simon could have a look.

"Dear Gods!" Simon said after he peeked inside. "Did you actually *rip* off his head? The wound is not from any sword." He peered at the Enforcer, wearing an expression halfway between fear and envy.

"No, it's not."

Simon waited, obviously expecting more, but when Theron didn't elaborate, he turned back to his desk and sat in his chair. He pulled a sheaf of parchment from a drawer on his right, took the blood-dipped quill from the vial and recorded the information. The sweet, heady scent of blood wafted up from the paper and teased Theron's nostrils, giving him a pointed reminder that he needed to replenish himself as soon as possible. The quill moved across the parchment with an itchy sound that never failed to make Theron's skin feel like it was being stretched over a washboard. The combination of smell and sound made him eager to leave the room and enter the Halls.

"Did you discover the identity of the person or persons assisting the traitor?" Simon asked without looking up.

"I did."

"Who was it?"

"That information is for the Council, Simon, not you."

Simon ceased writing and glared at Theron, who pretended not to notice as he examined several of the paintings in the room. Simon was just a steward, after all. Theron owed him no respect. Besides, he'd just killed one of his oldest friends for betraying his people. That, combined with his growing hunger, put him in a sour mood. He had no intention of catering to the inflated ego of a lowly clerk, who'd never done anything more strenuous or dangerous for the Council than drawing up a dissertation or penning a letter. "Are you going to announce me, Simon? Or should I stroll into the Council Chamber and hope they are all seated in their proper places when I arrive?"

Glowering at Theron, Simon reached behind him and pulled on a thin rope that hung from a hole in the ceiling. The faint peal of a bell sounded from somewhere in the Halls, summoning whichever Lost

One was assigned to assist Simon. Before the sound died away the door on the back wall opened.

The temperature of the room dropped twenty degrees before the Lost One even stepped through the doorway. Clad in the tattered black robes of its station, it floated through the room like the specter of Death. Hordes of squirming larvae feasted on its person, roiling and undulating like miniature waves on a lurid ocean. The curse of a Lost One meant there would ever be just enough flesh on its bones to keep the larvae fed and itself animate, and no more. As Theron watched, a fat green grub perhaps an inch long chewed a hole in the decayed skin of the creature's left forearm and loped upward to the elbow, where it met with more of its ilk and burrowed beneath the gray flesh once again.

Theron detested the Lost Ones. The horrid things prowled the Halls of the *Bachiyr*, the ancient home of Theron's race, tending to the needs of their masters and waiting for either salvation or death, whichever came first. They were once like him, but they had run afoul of the Council and paid the ultimate price. Their bodies no longer held the power to keep the flesh from rotting away, and they were not permitted to feed. As a result the grotesque things spent their time in excruciating pain, their hunger twisting inside them like a viper. Their presence served as a constant reminder to others of the hefty price the Council exacted from those who broke their laws. It was not a price Theron wanted to pay. Ever. Death would be better, he was sure of it.

Simon handed the Lost One a rolled sheet of parchment. "Take this report to Headcouncil Herris. Hurry, now. The Council will be eager to hear the *Lead Enforcer's* news." He said "Lead Enforcer" with a noticeable sneer. Theron didn't care. What was the opinion of a clerk to him? Nothing. When the Lost One departed back through the doorway, he cinched up the sack and followed behind, not even glancing at the steward on his way through. Theron thought he heard Simon mumble something just before the door closed, but he paid no attention.

The Lost One led him through the meandering hallways that were as much defense as anything else. From the outside, the old building appeared to be nothing more than a modest, slightly worn down house, much like many others in the city. It had been designed not to attract notice. The inside, however, told a different story. Halls and passageways far too long and wide to fit inside the structure roamed freely about, unconcerned with the limits of time and space. Chambers large enough to hold half the city of Jerusalem appeared here and there, along with many smaller rooms. This was made possible by the fact that the Halls of the *Bachiyr* didn't exist in Jerusalem, or Judea, or even Israel. Few knew the actual, physical location of the structure. Only Theron, the Council of Thirteen, and a handful of others were privy to such knowledge. Even the many individuals who worked inside the immense structure had no idea where in the world they were.

Access to the Halls was granted via a network of portals, which were spelled to allow entrance from anywhere. Nearly every major city in the world had one, and from these gateways Theron's people could enter the Halls for purposes of petition, judgment, or, like Theron, to report on various tasks that had been completed. The passages that led to the Council's main chamber twisted and turned in a preposterous myriad of directions, making navigation without a guide impossible unless one knew the way.

After centuries of traversing the hallways, Theron knew the way. Thus when he came to the passage that led to his personal chambers, he broke off from the Lost One and headed for his rooms. He didn't want to appear in front of the Council looking like a muddy rat. The Lost One would not be able to assemble all thirteen members of the Council quickly, anyway, which should give him just enough time to clean up. On the way, he intended to stop by the Larder to feed, hoping he would find clean humans there for a change, rather than the more common unwashed variety the staff usually captured. But Theron's hunger gnawed at his insides; he would feed on whatever humans waited in the tiny room, clean or otherwise.

╫ ╫ ╫

When he arrived in the Council Chamber, twelve torches flared to life around a large, U-shaped obsidian table. Between the legs of the U, a small dais waited, just big enough for one person to stand on. Theron stepped into the room, noting as he did so that one of the torches sat dark in its bracket. The unlit torch signified the absence of one of the Councilors. Theron didn't need to ask which one was missing; it would be Ramah, The Blood Letter. Ramah often spent months, even years, away from the Halls on some errand or another. The Council relied heavily on him as their primary assassin, sending him out to take care of any troublesome individuals none of them wanted to deal with; a task very well suited to his ruthless nature.

But the world grew larger every day, and Ramah could not be everywhere at once. Thus the Council formed the Enforcers, an elite unit which policed the populace, enforced the laws of the *Bachiyr* race, and punished those wayward individuals who broke them. Individuals like Ephraim, who not only had befriended a human, but had apparently sworn allegiance to one, as well. Theron didn't think the Council knew about that last part, but they soon would.

The dancing torchlight caused shadows to flit and canter around the room like leaves in the wind. The tiny crags and nooks in the gray walls flirted with the patches of light and dark, making an eerie pattern that waved as he watched. The reassuring smell of pitch from the torches and the feel of the familiar setting lent him comfort as he walked into the chamber where the most powerful of his kind waited for his report. He strode up to the dais in the middle of the chamber and stepped onto it.

"Councilors," he said, "I have found and punished Ephraim, as you commanded."

"Where was he hiding, Theron?" Headcouncil Herris asked.

"Jerusalem, Headcouncil." Theron heard the murmurs from those gathered around the table. He understood their reaction. Very few of his people lived in or even visited Jerusalem, or any other part of Israel for that matter. The many Jews in Israel, with their strong faith in God, made hunting there uncomfortable. Of late, the Roman influence had helped to diminish the problem, but all in all it was simply easier to feed elsewhere. "I found him packing his things for a trip. As the Council commanded, I waited until I knew who was involved."

"Well, don't keep us waiting, Enforcer," Lannis said, her dark eyes blazing. "Who was it? Was it Baella, as we feared?"

"No, Councilor Lannis. It was not Baella. In fact, Ephraim didn't betray us to one of our own at all."

"Are you telling us he was innocent?" Algor asked.

"No, Councilor Algor. Not at all. He just didn't go to a renegade *Bachiyr*. Ephraim betrayed us to the humans."

It took a moment for that to sink in. The Councilors all looked stunned, as well they might. The *Bachiyr* race, better known by the common term 'vampire,' relied on secrecy for their very survival. To violate that secrecy was to put the entire race in danger. In their four thousand year history, only twice before had one of their own intentionally revealed their existence to the humans. In both cases the Council captured those responsible and turned them into Lost Ones as a warning to others.

It was Herris who recovered himself first. "The humans? Are you sure?"

Theron nodded.

"Damn," Herris' face hardened. "How many, Theron? How many of them know?"

"I don't know, Headcouncil. I executed Ephraim, as ordered. I didn't interrogate him. The human who came to his room spoke of others. A man named Paul was to drive Ephraim to Lydda in safety. It is safe to assume there are more."

"And you didn't investigate? You simply left without hunting them down?" This from Mattawe. Always quick to anger, that one.

"Begging the Council's pardon, but dawn was approaching. I thought it best to return to the Halls and report this immediately."

"Yes, Theron. That was the proper thing to do," Herris said, fixing Mattawe with a glare, all but daring him to argue. Mattawe sank back into his seat and looked sullenly at the Enforcer. Theron had to be careful around that one. Lannis, Algor, and Mattawe were always eager to punish failures. That made the next part of his report much more difficult. He'd been saving the hard part for last, but he wasn't sure how to broach the subject.

Herris noted the look on his face and saved him the trouble. "Is there something else, Theron?"

"Yes, Headcouncil. I'm afraid there is. It wasn't just any human. Ephraim joined a group of them who follow one man, a man whose teachings attract more followers every day. If he knows about us, then it will not be long before many, many humans are aware of our existence."

The faces of the Councilors grew dark as Theron spoke. All present knew what would happen if their secret were revealed to the rest of the world. The humans would be relentless in their hunting. Though far stronger and much more dangerous than the average human, the vampire race was vastly outnumbered; they would have no chance against a widespread genocide perpetuated by the race of Man.

"Who is it, Theron?" Herris asked. "Who did Ephraim betray us to?"

"The man's name is Jesus, Headcouncil."

"Jesus?" Mattawe spat. "The young rabbi from Galilee? I think you overestimate his influence."

"No," Algor said, "he doesn't." He glanced at Herris as he spoke and raised his eyebrows in a gesture whose meaning did not escape Theron. It was enough to cause Herris' face to darken further, and when he next spoke, his normally strong voice sounded troubled.

"Theron, thank you for bringing this to us. You are dismissed. Do not leave the Halls. We will be calling for you shortly."

Theron bowed and stepped off the dais. As he grasped the handle of the door, he overheard Lannis' voice.

"Is he the one you told us about, Algor?"

"He is," Algor replied. Any other words the Councilor might have said were lost as the door closed behind him.

Theron wasn't concerned about missing the rest of the Council's conversation; he had a feeling they would call for him soon enough.

‡ ‡ ‡

The discussion in the Council chamber soon grew heated, and it centered on a single question: was Jesus dangerous? Headcouncil Herris needed to know the answer, and soon. The safety of his people was at stake.

"He's nothing!" Mattawe said, "Just a rabbi with a few sheep. Even the Jews distrust him. How can he be a danger to us?"

"You're wrong, Mattawe," Algor said, "Unlike you, I've been to Israel and heard the people talk about him. Many of them love him and follow him blindly. He gains more followers every day. There are even those who have taken to calling him the Messiah."

"Fools, Algor." Mattawe banged his ebony hand on the stone table. "Only fools would believe that of him. And only fools would follow him. Are we supposed to be afraid of a band of fools?"

"An army of fools is still an army," Algor replied. "Would you stand your ground, Mattawe, as ten thousand armed fools descended upon you? Who, then, would truly be the fool?"

Mattawe opened his mouth, doubtless to issue a stinging retort, but Herris silenced the argument with a raised finger. "What do the Romans think of him, Algor?" Herris asked.

Algor's misshapen features eased. "The Romans do not think much of him at all, actually. They have their own gods, and as long as the taxes in Judea are collected they are content to let the people of Israel have their God, as well. But the Jews are another story. Many love him, as I said, but many of them also fear and distrust him; they claim he is a charlatan out to steal their money or property. Still others believe he is insane."

"You see, Herris?" Mattawe said, "Even among his own people he's an outcast. He is not a threat to us."

"Are you counseling that we do nothing, Mattawe?"

"Of course not! Our secret has been breached, but—"

"Then why are we arguing? This Jesus knows about us. He must be dealt with. If he has any followers who also know, they must be dealt with, as well."

"Agreed," Mattawe said, calming down now that a decision had been made. "Shall we send for Ramah?"

"No, the Blood Letter is in the northlands. There is no telling when he will return. We will send Theron. He should be able to take care of this with little trouble. Unless anyone has an objection?" Herris looked over the gathered Council. When no one objected, he continued. "It is settled, then. Theron will leave tomorrow night for Jerusalem. Once there he will kill Jesus."

Around the room, eleven heads nodded in response.

CHAPTER FIVE

Taras awoke with the sun. Though his trip into the city had left him only two hours to sleep, he woke refreshed and alert.

Years ago, as a new recruit, his commander drilled into Taras and his classmates the idea that nothing in battle is guaranteed. Thus, a good soldier takes what food and sleep he can get, when he can get it. As a result Taras was rarely awake more than five minutes after his head hit the pillow, and he woke fully alert and ready to work or fight, as the situation dictated. This quality served the legionary well in the field, but was even more valuable in the city, where death was stealthier and far more treacherous. Jerusalem was an environment perfectly suited to a man of Taras's skill.

That skill was death; Taras was an assassin. A rather important one, at that. No one in Jerusalem, or even Israel, for that matter, knew his position except for his Centurion, the Centurion's Second, and the Legate. To everyone else, even Pontius Pilate himself, Taras was just an ordinary legionary. This level of secrecy was necessary for him to be effective in his work, especially since Rome could never acknowledge his existence in any capacity other than that of an ordinary soldier.

But whenever Rome needed someone killed – a foreign official, or a recalcitrant Senator, perhaps – or information gathered in Judea,

Marcus invariably called Taras first. When called, he did his best to serve his country in an unknown capacity, doing things for Rome she could not admit to having any part in. Men of his station had been integral in the conquest of dozens upon dozens of nations, including Israel. Masters of infiltration and stealth, they excelled at the silent kill: poisons, the quick turn of the blade across the throat, a crossbow bolt to the lungs, and many others. Taras, and others like him, had one simple job: prepare the arena.

Ceasar and the Legate often called the centurions the backbone of the mighty Roman Legion. If so, Taras and others like him acted as its fingertips. Always touching, exploring, and discovering the weaknesses of Rome's enemies beforehand so her army could battle them with greater efficiency.

He did not always enjoy doing the things his country asked of him. Sometimes the Legate called on him to make examples of innocents, an act for which he, unlike many of his hidden brethren, had never acquired a taste. But Taras's love of his adopted homeland overcame his misgivings. The greater good must be served, and when Rome needed his services, he obeyed without question. To do otherwise would be a slap in the face to the empire that had given him a home. Taras would die before so dishonoring his country.

Outside the barracks window, roosters called a hoarse greeting to the new day. Taras stretched and rose from his cot. As usual, he was the first in his barracks to wake up. Typical. Many of the legionaries stationed in Jerusalem owed their presence there to the fact that the Legate could think of no other place to send them. There were a few notable exceptions, such as the Centurion and even Taras himself, but they were the minority. The majority of soldiers sent to occupy the outer provinces were a sorry lot. Leave it to the Legate to send soft men into a hard city like Jerusalem; the man never visited the province, so he had no real idea how dangerous Judea could be. The zealots took advantage of the slow and overweight members of the Roman Legion whenever the opportunity presented itself, often with mortal results.

Taras frowned. He buckled on his sandals and his belt, making far more noise than necessary in the process. Not a single man stirred from his bunk, though one sleeping soldier grunted, then emitted a vile noise from his rear. The gassy fellow then reached around and scratched an itch on his bottom, and soon fell still as sleep reclaimed him.

Taras looked around at the group of snoring, oblivious men and shook his head. Small wonder Mary's father disliked the Romans so much, with such examples of slovenliness to be seen. The Jews of the outer provinces were, by and large, an industrious lot, and they tended to look poorly on laziness. No wonder the zealots and the people of Jerusalem held little respect for the typical Roman soldier. They rarely saw the real Legion; the hard, disciplined men who fought and died while spreading Rome's glory across the world. If those soldiers occupied Israel, things in Jerusalem would be much different. But what did Israel get instead? Fat, gassy men who could not be roused before breakfast.

He scowled. Sooner or later, the Legate would have to deal with Judea, and Taras hoped he would still be around to help bring the Jews into line.

With that last pleasant thought, he snapped his helmet into place and left to gather the information he would need in order to make his morning report to Marcus, Taras's only real friend in the city. On his way out he kicked one of his comrade's cots, breaking the leg and sending the surprised legionary to the floor with a yelp.

✠ ✠ ✠

A young baker named Matthew, who had only arrived in Jerusalem two days prior to spend Passover with his family, was the first to find the bodies of Claudius and his friend in the early morning hours. Terrified by the sight of a headless corpse in the middle of the street, he sprinted to the barracks to report his find. But before the morning ended the unfortunate man found himself face to face with Pontius Pilate, much to his dismay.

Several citizens witnessed Matthew running from the spot where the two soldiers were murdered. Those people reported this to the nearest legionary, who in turn reported it to the centurion. When Matthew finally managed to find the barracks he was quite surprised to learn an order for his arrest had been issued. Despite his pleas of innocence, he was a stranger to Jerusalem and thus not to be trusted. The centurion, none too pleased about being faced with the murder of two soldiers before he'd even had breakfast, wasn't taking any chances. He ordered his soldiers to shackle Matthew hand and foot, and then he and his men dragged the poor fellow before Jerusalem's Prefect.

✟ ✟ ✟

Pontius Pilate, despite the claims of the zealots, was not a stupid or cruel man. He was, however, coldly practical and held no love for the Israelites. Upon interviewing the young man, Pilate knew in his heart Matthew was innocent. That meant the real killer was still loose. If the people of the city learned of this, it would make his job much more difficult. Pilate was under a great deal of pressure from Rome due to the constant harassment of the zealots. To allow the people of Jerusalem to believe a man could murder two Roman soldiers and get away with the act was unthinkable, so he pronounced Matthew guilty and had him thrown into stocks to await execution for the murders. It didn't matter that the man was innocent; Matthew was just another Jew, after all. What mattered to Pilate was keeping order in a city that trod along the edge of rebellion with a reckless indifference to Rome and her glory. To that end he would sacrifice a hundred innocent bakers. More, if need be.

But executing Matthew, while it would save face with the Jewish citizenry, didn't solve Pilate's problem that someone in the city had murdered two of his men. After the guards marched the prisoner to the dungeon, Pilate called Marcus, the centurion, to his side. "That man didn't kill anyone this morning," he whispered.

Marcus nodded. "I have come to the same conclusion, Prefect."

"How so?"

"The man is a baker, not a warrior. He could barely lift a heavy blade, let alone swing it hard enough to remove the head from a trained Roman legionary and stab another through the heart. And not only that, there is no blood anywhere on him. If he's our killer, then I am a Jewish rabbi."

"That you are not, Marcus," Pilate said, a slight smile on his face. Pilate wasn't surprised at his centurion's reasoning. He'd chosen Marcus for his intelligence and discipline, and the man had grown into as fine a centurion as could be found anywhere in the Legion. He'd proven an asset more times than Pilate could count.

His smile didn't last long, however. "You must learn the identity of the real killer, but do not let anyone know what you are doing."

"Yes, Prefect."

"When you find the man responsible, Marcus, kill him quickly and quietly. Then take the filthy bastard's body out to the desert so no one will know."

Marcus blinked. "You don't want me to bury the body, Prefect?" In Rome, all bodies were treated to the respect of a proper burial, even the slaves and the criminals.

"No, not this one." Pilate could not hide the anger in his voice. "This killer will receive no consideration from me. Not even after death. Let his soul wander the world forever. Understood?"

"Yes, Prefect," Marcus said, saluting. Then he left the Prefect's chambers to carry out his orders.

╬╬╬

Prior to his meeting with Pilate, Marcus had ordered a dozen of his best men to stand guard around the two bodies and prevent any of the city's inhabitants from disturbing them. This meant traffic through the Middle Gate had to be routed elsewhere, which caused no end of trouble in Jerusalem, especially with travel through the city already choked with visitors during the Holy Week. The hordes of visiting Jews mixed with the other inhabitants of the city, and all of them jammed together, elbow to elbow, and complained loudly about the delay to any who would listen. But the grumbling of the people didn't concern Marcus. It was only a temporary detour, after all, and the mild inconvenience it posed to a few hundred civilians meant little compared to the murder of two legionaries. He wanted the area around the deceased to be as preserved as possible, and to the Abyss with anyone who didn't like it.

Of course nothing of the sort happened. The streets overflowed with armies of the Jewish faithful who'd come to celebrate Passover. While the crowds made way for the centurion and his armed escort, albeit grudgingly, they could only go so far, and Marcus often found navigation through the city entailed a great deal of shoving and pushing through the masses. When he finally arrived at the scene he had to elbow his way through a thick ring of spectators who had gathered to gawk and stare at the two bodies. Several times, he heard men comment about how the soldiers deserved their fate, but he could never identify the speaker among the throng. Once through the crowd, he posted soldiers at the fringes of the clearing to give himself space to breathe.

Upon his arrival, he learned his guards had arrived at the scene too late to prevent the local thugs and thieves from tampering with the corpses. He saw evidence the dead soldiers had been kicked, robbed, and even spit on after their murder.

"The gods take them," he muttered to a nearby soldier, who nodded his agreement. Now it would be impossible to distinguish the killer's tracks from the many others in the vicinity. He silently cursed those who'd violated the dead, and hoped they fell victim to some unfortunate disease or another. Still, there wasn't much to be done about it, and complaining would not help matters. *I'd better have a look, anyway.*

The first thing he noticed was the smell. The scent of blood and body fluids hung like a thick cloud in the vicinity of the bodies. Flies zipped about, swimming through the air with their incessant buzzing and generally making a nuisance of themselves. They lighted on the gory parts of the dead and attempted to lay eggs in the red, swollen flesh. Still others hovered around Marcus's face. Having served in the Roman Legion for three decades, Marcus had long ago grown accustomed the smell of blood, as well as the many insects it brought. He swatted a few of them away and stepped up to examine one of the corpses.

Marcus recognized the first victim as Claudius. No great loss there. Claudius had always been a bit of a coward, and a very poor soldier. That's why the Legion sent him to Judea rather than to the front for active duty. For some reason the Legate believed the provinces were safer than the battlefield. Marcus could have told him otherwise, but the Legate was a stubborn sort; the man would never listen. That was the problem with the officials in the Roman Legion; they always underestimated the determination and spirit of a local population in the grip of religious fervor. While most legionaries would fight for Rome and claim they loved her with all their souls, the zealots had gone so far as to give their souls over to their cause. It was only the sheer strength of Rome's might and numbers that kept the zealots from overthrowing Roman occupation and pushing Pilate and his soldiers out of Israel for good. He'd tried to explain as much to the Legate numerous times, yet the man continued to send him soldiers like Claudius.

Marcus knelt next to the body and examined the wound in his chest. Right away he noted the cracked sternum and ripped flesh, which indicated the killer twisted the sword prior to removing it. Interesting. That meant the culprit had wanted more than just to kill; he'd wanted Claudius's death to *hurt*. But why?

A good question, which led to another: had Claudius known his killer? It seemed possible, even likely. The type of wound and the malice with which it was delivered hinted at something personal; a vendetta, perhaps. Marcus looked up from the body.

"You," he pointed at the nearest legionary, "go back to the barracks. Get the names of every person Claudius has been spending time with. I want to know who his friends are, and I want to know where they were last night. Go."

The soldier gave a crisp salute and left, winding his way through the crowd. Marcus watched him go, marveling at how young the man was. *No more than seventeen,* he thought, *Just a boy, really.* His face softened as he recalled his own investiture in the Legion thirty years before. Now, at forty six, Marcus had lived about as long as could be reasonably expected, and he'd given himself over to the Legion with every breath. He'd never taken a wife or fathered any children. Although he loved his country and never regretted his decisions, sometimes when he looked at the younger recruits he thought of himself all those years ago. Just a boy, with no idea of the things he would see and do in the next thirty years.

He longed to tell the younger recruits not to make a life of the military. *Serve your years and get out,* he would say. *Find a woman and start a family.* He could never bring himself to say it, though. Having ignored such advice himself, he would feel like a hypocrite.

Marcus shook his head and focused on the task at hand. He had one legionary dead with a gaping hole in his chest, and another body yet to inspect. He stood and walked to the next corpse, and when he reached it he couldn't help his sudden intake of breath. Not because the head was missing – he'd known about that – but the manner in which the head had been taken baffled him. The torn and shredded flesh of the neck could not be the work of a sword, at least not one Marcus had ever seen. The man's head looked to have been ripped from his shoulders. He knelt next to the body, his knee digging into the blood-soaked dirt, to get a closer look at the stump of the neck.

Eight wounds, he noted. The tear in the neck had been started by eight punctures roughly an inch wide. They were too jagged to be the work of knives, but he had no idea what else they could be. It seemed to Marcus whoever killed this soldier had stabbed him in the throat, then pulled the skin and muscle apart. But who would do such a thing? More importantly, who *could* do it? And how?

Marcus looked up from the body and noticed something else that struck him as odd. He stood and studied the wall behind the headless soldier. A great spray of coagulated gore seemed to track upward from about the height of the dead man's neck, but there was none below it save for a few spatters and random droplets. Marcus looked down at the body again and noted the large pool of dried, rust colored blood that soaked the earth under him. *So much blood.* He turned back to the wall, and it hit him. *The man was standing right there, by the gods!* He must have been standing with his back to this wall when the killer tore off his head. He'd most likely been facing his attacker. Why didn't he fight back?

Marcus checked the dead legionary's body, wanting to see if his sword remained in his sheath. It was gone. A cursory look at Claudius's body confirmed his sword, too, was missing. That could mean the two did fight back and lost, or it could mean the crowd looted the bodies before he arrived. His lip curled at the thought, which was all too likely. Sure enough, a quick check told him both of the dead men's sandals were missing. He didn't bother to ask if either had been found with their purses, knowing the answer would be no. Of course, no honest Jew would steal from a dead man, and Caesar's currency would be useless to most, but Jerusalem played host to all sorts of people: Jews, Romans, Greeks, and many others. Even a handful of merchants from the Far East called the city home. Truly, a myriad of people inhabited the city, not all of whom were devout. Any number of unsavory elements could have robbed the corpses; there simply was no way to tell.

With no way to track the killer's steps thanks to the hundreds of people milling about the scene and no way to know if the two men died fighting, Marcus tried to think of a way to question the locals without letting them know the murderer remained on the loose. He would have to be circumspect; maybe plant a few soldiers in the city. He would order a squad of men to cease shaving immediately. It would take a few weeks before they could blend in, if even then, but at present their clean-shaven features would mark them as legionaries as clearly as their uniforms.

With the beginnings of a strategy in mind, he left the bodies and walked to the nearest living soldier. "Who is the other man? Has he been identified?"

The blood drained from the man's face, and he lowered his eyes to the dirt. A tear squeezed from between his eyelids. "Centurion, I'm not certain. I…I think it's…"

"Out with it!" Marcus didn't have the patience for blubbering. If the man had lost a friend to the sword, so be it. Death and the Roman Legion walked hand in hand, and many soldiers lost friends every day. If this man could not handle it, he was of no use to the centurion, especially in a city like Jerusalem.

"I think, sir…that is, I heard—"

"Well?" Marcus glowered at the young man, surprised at how weak he was. *How did he get to be in the Legion at all? He's a sniveling—*

"Centurion," said a new voice behind him, "you should come and see this."

Marcus turned from the young soldier and saw Gordian waving him over. He fixed one last glare on the weeping legionary and promised himself he'd see the man sent to the farthest reaches of Judea before the week was out, and good riddance, then stepped over to his Second. "What is it, Gordian?"

"The head, Centurion. It's over here."

"Bag it and bring it back to the barracks. Someone is bound to know who he was."

"But, Centurion I…I really think you should come and have a look." Marcus took a better look at Gordian and he noticed for the first time the man seemed shaken and worried. Marcus had known Gordian for fifteen years and had never seen him look troubled by death, not even when they'd been captured by Germanians eleven years prior and forced to watch as several members of their group were drawn and quartered. Gordian's own twin brother had disappeared that day, and it was widely believed he'd been killed. For as long as Marcus had known him, Gordian's rock-solid presence could be counted on to help maintain order in the worst situations. If he was shaken up, then perhaps Marcus did indeed need to look at the head lying in the dirt twenty feet away. He started toward it.

"Who is it Gordian? Do you know him?"

"Yes, Centurion," Gordian's voice cracked, and Marcus noticed moisture building in his eyes, too. "So do you."

"So do I? Just tell me—" His breath stopped short as he arrived next to Gordian. Now he could make out the features on the dead man's face. They were features he'd seen nearly every day for most of his life, easily recognizable despite the dirty imprints of several boots upon it. The dark hair, the strong chin and cheekbones, the wide nose with the small scar from a childhood accident, and the dark brown eyes that looked much like Marcus's own. Except where the centurion's eyes would still sparkle in the sun, a milky glaze obscured those in the severed head as they stared sightlessly up at nothing. A single fly landed on the left iris, and when the lid didn't blink and no hand shooed the thing away, Marcus nearly fell to his knees. As it was, he swayed on his feet and only Gordian's strong, steady hand on his shoulder prevented him from tumbling into the street.

"Didius," Marcus whispered. He somehow managed to keep the choke out of his voice, but he couldn't stop the tear that broke free as he stared down at the lifeless face of his younger brother.

CHAPTER SIX

Theron didn't have to wait long; the Council called for him a few hours after his report. He was easy to find, as he hadn't left his chambers since. The Lost One who came to get him didn't even have to knock; Theron sensed the thing approaching and, not wanting to let the creature into his chambers, stepped out into the hall to meet it. He stared at the writhing, slithering mass and shivered. He couldn't help it; the damn things unsettled him, which didn't happen often.

"I know the way to the Council Chamber," he told it. "You are excused."

The Lost One gave a slight bow of its head. The white of its skull showed through several patches of gray, worm-eaten scalp, dotted here and there with a few strands of long, sickly hair. Then it turned around and walked back up the hallway. Theron paused a few moments to give the thing plenty of time to get far ahead, and then he, too, turned toward the Council Chamber and started walking. He didn't rush, there was no need. He already knew what they were going to say.

Theron would be back in Jerusalem before nightfall.

† † †

"Enter, Theron," Herris called from inside the room. Theron didn't have to ask how they knew he was at the door. They always knew. No ordinary vampire can begin to comprehend the vast power wielded by the Council of Thirteen. Although Theron was far from ordinary, comparing his powers to that of Herris would be akin to comparing a pebble to a fortress. He shuddered to think of the awesome forces at the command of the original thirteen vampires. In secret, Theron hoped he might enjoy such power someday; although he knew it wasn't possible. Still, even a dead man can dream.

Inside the chamber, the twelve ancient vampires once again sat behind the U-shaped table. As was customary when facing the Council of Thirteen, Theron walked out onto the raised dais in the center of the floor and bowed his head. "You sent for me, Headcouncil?"

"Yes, Enforcer. We have another task for you."

"Of course, Headcouncil. What do you wish of me?"

"You will return to Jerusalem and find the human rabbi known as Jesus. Once you locate him, you are to kill him."

Theron bowed from the waist, he'd expected as much. "As you command, Headcouncil. Will that be all?"

"No. You must also find out who among his followers knows of our existence. They must die, as well."

"Yes, Headcouncil."

"Also, and this is very important, you are not to drain him. His body must be found so everyone knows he is dead. We do not want him to simply disappear and leave room for speculation in the eyes of those he leaves behind. There must be no doubt what happened to him."

"Yes, Headcouncil," Theron agreed, although he wondered why they were going through all this trouble. The Council never cared before if Theron's victims disappeared. Not as long as he didn't leave any empty bodies for people to find. But he knew the Council had their reasons, even if they didn't share them with him. They never did anything without a reason.

"You may go." Herris dismissed Theron in much the same manner as Theron had dismissed the Lost One.

"Yes, Headcouncil." Theron bowed again and stepped from the dais. While privately annoyed at such offhanded treatment, he would never think to express such feelings aloud, not as long as he wanted to continue living. Theron turned and walked to the door. He'd just wrapped his fingers around the handle when Algor spoke.

"Enforcer?"

Theron turned. "Yes Councilor?"

"Make sure his death is especially unpleasant, even brutal. We want his pain and suffering plainly evident to those who find the body. And if possible, try to make it appear the zealots are responsible."

"Yes, Councilor," he said, smiling. Unpleasant? Even brutal? The assignment might be fun, after all.

╬╬╬

"The zealots?" Mattawe asked after Theron had gone. "Why the zealots, Algor?"

"Because," Algor replied, "the zealots have harassed the Roman legionaries to no end of late, as well as any non-Jewish inhabitants of the city, but for the most part they have left the rest of the Jews alone."

"And?"

"And if the Romans believe the zealots are turning on rabbis and killing them, not to mention the rabbi's followers, it would give Pilate a reason to crack down on them even harder. And if the people of Jerusalem can be made to believe this as well, they will be more likely to side with the Romans, and such a thing can only help us in Israel. Even Tiberius will be forced to address the deteriorating situation in Judea if it seems the zealots have taken to murdering the general populace."

"You think the Romans might use this as an excuse to ban the worship of the Jews' One God and try to force them into following the Roman faith?" Mattawe asked. "Shift them to the belief in the pantheon of gods?"

"Why not? If the Romans can convince the Jewish population the zealots are evil, then it would be a natural progression to suggest they abandon the faith shared by such criminals," Algor replied. "Caesar might even give Pilate permission to outlaw the Jewish faith altogether. It wouldn't be the first time the Roman Empire declared a religion illegal. Rome would simply impose a death sentence on anyone practicing another religion."

"Will the people abandon their faith, do you think?" This from Herris, who for the first time seemed interested in Algor's plan. "Many of them are quite strong in their beliefs."

"I think," said Algor, "that given the choice between not believing in God and being sent to meet him face to face, most of them will choose the Roman pantheon."

"And those who refuse?" Mattawe asked.

"Those who refuse to convert will not be a problem," Lannis said, seemingly catching on. "The Romans will see to that."

Algor nodded. Lannis had a quick mind and agile wit. He liked that about her.

"I still don't understand why you didn't tell Theron about Jesus," Taluk said. "Theron is our Lead Enforcer, and quite valuable. He should know the details of his mission."

"What details, Taluk? We have no details. Rumors only. That is what we have. Miracles performed in the name of God? Jesus making blind men see and lame beggars walk? Ludicrous! Why bother Theron with such things when they have no bearing? Better that he not be sidetracked with such ridiculous claims. Killing Jesus will be difficult enough as it is."

"I see your point." Taluk conceded.

Algor smiled. Alone among the Council, he'd known all along what to do with the knowledge that Ephraim had betrayed them to the rabbi from Nazareth; it was just a simple matter of getting the rest to agree. He'd been planning to kill Jesus for several years, ever since he first heard rumors of miracles. Some people claimed he was the Messiah. Others called him the Son of God, sent from Heaven to free the Jews. Ridiculous, of course, but faith had a way of doing strange things to the human mind, especially when that faith was strong. *Let's see how strong their faith is when their "Messiah" is brutally murdered.*

CHAPTER SEVEN

T hat night, while Marcus stormed his way through the barracks demanding to know who was the last to see his brother
alive and where they'd been, a dark shadow broke from the
doorway of an innocuous-looking house and made its way to the
Damascus Gate. Theron didn't know of Marcus's rage, nor did he
realize one of the soldiers he'd killed was the younger brother of the
centurion. Simon could have told him, but Theron had walked by the
clerk's desk without saying a word. Simon, still miffed by Theron's
earlier treatment of him, hadn't acknowledged him, either.

In truth, he would not have cared. Another dead human was
another dead human as far as he was concerned. The only real
shame of the encounter was that Theron couldn't drain the bodies, or
even hide them as he did Malachi and Ephraim. He'd been too long
into the night to take the time to cover up his deed.

He threaded his way through the crowds of people, mostly Jews
visiting with family for the Holy Week, and shoved and jostled his
way to the Damascus Gate. The sheer numbers of the Jewish faithful
who found their way to Jerusalem each year staggered him. Even at
this late hour, a horde of sweaty, noisy people choked the streets.
Most were on their way to wherever they would spend the night.
Two or three hours after the sun went down the streets of Jerusalem
would be all but deserted, which suited him just fine.

The swell of people ebbed and flowed around him. Hundreds of them. Thousands, even. All of them moving, talking, and bustling about and generally getting in the way of the soldiers who worked so hard to keep order in the city. A myriad of colors swirled around him as people, some bedecked in finery and some not, faded into and out of his view only to be replaced by more of the same. And the noise! The maddening din of the crowd reminded him of the neverending rumble of ocean on the rocky coast of Spain; one long, loud noise, all the individual sounds and voices lost in the general din. The musky smell of so many bodies packed so close together stung his sensitive nostrils, spurring him toward the gate in an effort to free himself from the masses as soon as possible.

As he walked past the overworked and irritable guards at the Damascus Gate, he overheard snippets of a whispered conversation between two who stood off to the side. No doubt they thought their voices low enough to ensure their conversation remained secret, and to their credit, no human would have overheard them. To Theron's hypersensitive ears, however, their words came as clear as though he stood right next to them.

"...the centurion is furious."

"I heard it was the zealots."

"Of course it was the zealots. Who else would it be?"

"I've never known a zealot who could rip off a man's head, have you? That's not a human, that's an animal."

"You think a wild, dangerous animal is running loose in the streets of Jerusalem? How could something like that go unnoticed?"

"I'm just saying..."

Theron missed the other man's answer because he had moved on by that point. The two soldiers, for their part, didn't even glance at him. Their primary concern was to guard entry through the gates, not to prevent people from leaving, at least not when no alarm had been raised in the city. Since Theron wasn't doing anything more suspicious than walking about in the early evening, the guards let him be. Theron, for his part, didn't care much either way, although he was glad he'd listened to their conversation.

So the ruse worked. The centurion thinks it was the zealots. Perfect. He smiled and wondered whom the zealots would blame. As he left the city and began his walk to the Mount of Olives, where Jesus was said to be staying in the Gardens of Gethsemane, he realized it didn't matter. *Tonight will be the last night you draw breath, rabbi,* he promised. So intent was he on his goal that it never occurred to him he'd been walking with his habitual silent tread. Likewise he didn't notice the slight breeze that ruffled his clothing.

If he'd been paying more attention, he would have noticed as one of the guards, one of those *not* involved in the conversation at the gate, left his post and ran back into the city.

⧾⧾⧾

"I didn't think you would be able to come tonight," Mary said as Taras walked to her front gate. "With the death of the two soldiers this morning, I thought you would be very busy."

"I am never too busy to see you," Taras whispered, careful not to let anyone overhear his words. He longed to reach over and take her in his arms, to kiss her as he'd done last night. More than that, he wanted to pick her up and carry her into the house behind them, up the stairs and into the master bedchamber. But of course he could not.

Unlike their rendezvous in the alley the previous night, this time they had met in a public place. They stood surrounded by people, most of them Jews, coming and going as they were all over the city. Far too many would see them, especially if they engaged in any illicit activities. For now, he was just a soldier speaking to the lady of the house in her father's absence. Nothing at all suspicious there, considering her father happened to be one of the more prosperous merchants in the city. But one touch, one overheard word, would change all that. He dared not even hold her hand, although he could not suppress a smile as he noticed the familiar gold and ruby ring on her finger.

"What did your father say when he saw that?" Taras asked.

"Nothing."

"He didn't care?" Taras found the notion difficult to believe.

"He hasn't seen it," she said. "I hid it in my dress until he left for Bethlehem." She looked away, her cheeks reddening. "I couldn't let him see it, yet I couldn't bear to be without it."

The smile on Taras's face grew.

"Is it true what they say?" Mary asked, switching topics. "Was the wrong man arrested for that horrible crime?"

"How did you—?"

"My father is wealthy, remember?" She smiled at him. "We hear much from our sources in the Upper City."

"Did your sources happen to say who the real killer is?"

"So it *is* true," she replied. "How could Pilate do such a thing?"

"Pontius Pilate is charged, by Tiberius himself, with keeping peace in Jerusalem. He will do so at any cost."

"Even if that cost is the life of an innocent man?"

"One man, compared to how many others? If the zealots thought Pilate's resolve was slipping, how many others would die?"

Mary looked away, her shoulders slumped. After a moment she nodded her understanding. Taras's heart ached to see her so upset.

"It still doesn't seem right," she said. "Maybe you could talk to him."

"Pilate won't listen to me, but he will listen to Marcus. The baker would be set free if Marcus could bring him the real killer before the execution. You can help him, if you know something. Did your father's contacts name the killer?"

"No. At least not to me."

"Your father, then?"

Mary sighed. "I don't know. He doesn't tell me everything." She turned her neck to face her large, well apportioned house. "He tries very hard to protect me."

"A smart choice," Taras replied. "If Pilate thought your father knew anything, they would not hesitate to arrest him. And if he thought you knew something..." he trailed off, unwilling to finish the sentence.

"I know," she replied, turning back to face him. "It is a hard world we live in, legionary." She favored him with a wan smile.

"No, not a hard world, Mary. Just a hard city," he said. "Most of the world is softer, much more forgiving." He thought of Rome as he spoke. Not the city proper, which could be just as dangerous as Jerusalem, but of the outlying countryside: the vineyards and olive orchards, the endless expanses of fertile green farmlands, and the peaceful fields where cows and horses spent their day leisurely cropping the grass. Taras pictured the small farmhouses where families some four and five generations deep dwelled, as they had since time out of mind. He'd passed through such places many times in his service to Rome, and more than once he thought it would be nice to retire there. Find a woman, raise a family. Maybe plant a small vineyard of his own, which his children could help tend. His family would produce the best wine in the Roman Empire, favored by the Caesar himself.

It was a beautiful dream, and he longed to share it with her. If only the laws of the Jews would bend. Taras thought again of sneaking into the Temple at night to pay Caiphas a visit, wondering what he would have to do to win the old man's consent.

"Why do you look so hard, Taras?" Mary asked. "The look on your face could grind wheat."

"It's nothing. I—" Taras stopped, struck by a sudden thought; while it was certainly true they could never gain permission to marry in Jerusalem, Rome had no such law.

I wonder…

The idea was just beginning to take shape in his mind when a shout from down the street drew his attention.

"Taras! There you are. By the gods, I've been looking all over the city for you."

Taras jumped, and abruptly stepped back from Mary, to whom he'd been unintentionally leaning a little too close as his thoughts progressed. Snapping his mind back to the present, he turned to see Gordian running up to him. Taras flashed the senior officer a fast salute.

"Yes, sir?"

Gordian took a moment to catch his breath, then he nodded to Mary. "Pardon the interruption, Lady," he said. Then he turned to Taras. "You must come with me. It's urgent. Centurion's business. I will explain on the way."

"Of course," Taras replied. He turned to Mary "If you will excuse me, Lady?"

"Certainly," she replied. "I should be going inside to check on the house and make sure it is ready for Passover." She turned to Gordian. "Good evening," she said, and went back into the house.

When she was gone, Taras fell into step beside Gordian and followed him to the Damascus Gate.

"Continuing to see her is dangerous, Taras," Gordian observed. "Her father is a ruthless man. He would not hesitate to have you killed if he ever came to suspect."

Taras nodded his agreement. Gordian wasn't telling him anything he didn't already know. Thankfully, the man didn't push the issue. Taras didn't want to explain himself or his plan to the Centurion's Second before he had the opportunity to talk to Marcus himself.

They walked in silence for a short while, but finally Taras could stand it no longer. "So what is this about, Gordian?"

"The killer," Gordian replied, smiling. "We may have found him."

Taras stopped in his tracks. "Already?"

Gordian nodded. "I believe so," he said, but didn't stop. Taras was forced to run in order to catch up with him.

Taras thought of his good friend Marcus, and the pain in his eyes as he told Taras the news of Didius's murder that morning. Didius was a fine young man, and a good soldier. His wife, Adonia, was nothing short of beautiful and their three children likewise. Didius's death was a blow to everyone, including Taras. Could they really have found his killer in only a day?

Gods, he hoped so. He smiled as he ran alongside Gordian to the Damascus Gate, thinking of the many ways he would repay the unfortunate zealot for his treacherous act.

⚜ ⚜ ⚜

Marcus sat alone in his private chambers, cradling his head in his hands and nursing a headache that threatened to render him unconscious. He'd spent the ten hours since the morning's grisly discovery questioning each and every soldier under his command, and more than a few who were not. No one had seen anything unusual. Claudius had very few friends, and although Didius was well-liked among the other soldiers, no one had seen or heard from him for several hours before the discovery of his body. The men on patrol were supposed to check in with each other frequently throughout the night due to the recent increase in zealot activity in the city, but they'd been lax. The last time anyone could recall seeing either of the two men alive was at least three hours before their bodies were found, possibly as many as five.

That left plenty of time for someone to come in, kill the two soldiers, and leave. It also left plenty of time for some of the city's more dissident residents to rob and abuse the bodies. Marcus recalled the dirty footprints on his brother's face. His fist clenched and the muscles in his jaw tightened to the point where he thought his teeth might break. *If I ever find the person who kicked Didius's head around the street I will personally strap them into the rack. I will make their loved ones watch while I stretch them out for weeks.*

He sat with his elbows on the desk and enjoyed a brief fantasy of making the mystery kicker scream while he pulled the handle as slowly as he could, one notch at a time, until his voice grew too hoarse to scream. A grim smile spread across his face, but it didn't last long. A few moments into the daydream a loud and urgent knock shattered the morose silence of his chamber.

"Centurion," came his Second's voice through the door, barely audible above the pounding.

"Leave me alone, Gordian." Marcus had to raise his own voice to be heard. "I already told you I have no desire to drink tonight."

"Centurion, please. I have news. A stranger was spotted leaving the Damascus Gate."

"Many strangers have left the city tonight, Gordian." He'd left orders at every gate to report anyone leaving at night that looked like they didn't belong. Unfortunately, that description was ambiguous at best. He'd been inundated with reports of suspicious people leaving the city all night long. From the Damascus Gate alone he received twenty different reports in the first two hours. Marcus had already chalked the order up as a fool's errand, especially with the multitude of people going in and out of the city for Passover. "This cursed city is full of strangers who want to leave, and I don't blame them."

"This one is different, Centurion."

"How?"

"The guard said the man made no sound at all upon leaving, for one thing. Stealthy, like an *assassin*."

Marcus lifted his head from his hands and stared at the door. A man would have to be extremely quiet to kill two Roman legionaries and not alert anyone in the vicinity. Very few people could walk the cobbled streets of Jerusalem, or any city in Judea for that matter, without making any sound at all. Such a skill was beyond most people, and few would train in it. The purpose of such movement is stealth, and the purpose of stealth is to not get caught or to surprise someone. Someone like a soldier standing guard at the Middle Gate, perhaps? Gordian was right, this *was* different.

"Centurion? Are you there?"

Of course I'm here. Where else would I be? Marcus stood and walked to the door. He unbolted the latch and admitted his Second into his chambers. "Sit down." He pointed to the chair opposite his own on the other side of his desk. After Gordian took his seat, Marcus followed suit. He leaned forward over the desk, his face only a foot from the other man's. He didn't want to miss a thing Gordian said. "Was there anything else?"

"Yes, sir. The man had a sword."

"Lots of men have swords."

"But how many try to hide it? The guard at the gate would never have known about the sword at all if a slight breeze hadn't blown the stranger's cloak up just enough to reveal a brief flash of the hilt. Also, the man dressed like a peasant, in coarse, dirty clothes, yet the sword had several jewels in it. Lastly, how many men wear sandals with small spatters of blood on them."

Marcus leaned back in his chair, digesting the news. *Well, now. That* is *interesting.* Several bloody footprints had been found in the street surrounding the bodies that morning, indicating the killer must have stepped through the gore while it was still wet. Marcus would have cleaned his sandals first thing, but not everyone would think to do so, and it would be easy to overlook a spot or two.

Still, it proved nothing. The man could have been a shepherd after slaughter. Jerusalem was in the middle of Passover, after all, and lambs were being killed by the dozen. Even so, it was the closest he'd gotten all day, and after hours and hours of interrogating his own men with nothing to show for it Marcus wasn't about to let this lead, small as it might be, slip away. "Who reported this?"

"Lurio, sir."

"Where is Lurio now?"

"I sent him back to the Damascus Gate to continue the watch. There are only a handful of men stationed there, and it would not do for—"

"Yes, yes, Gordian. I'm aware of the reasons we need a guard."

Marcus toyed with his Centurion's Seal while he thought about his next course of action. "Have the man followed. I want to know where he goes tonight. Send Taras, I don't want this stranger to know he's being observed."

"It is already done, Centurion. Taras left the Damascus Gate half an hour ago."

"You sent Taras after the man without consulting me first?"

"My apologies, sir," Gordian offered. "Time was of the essence, I knew you would want the stranger followed, and who better to do so than Taras?"

Marcus mulled it over. Gordian was right. He did want the stranger followed, and they would have lost too much time if Gordian had come to the barracks to get orders from Marcus. One of the reasons he chose Gordian as his Second was the man's ability to think on his feet and act accordingly. Once again he'd proven himself a good choice. "Good. Very good. Thank you, Gordian. You may go."

Gordian stood and walked to the door, he was just about to close it when Marcus thought of one last question. "Wait."

Gordian poked his head back into the room. "Yes, Centurion?"

"Which direction did the stranger go?"

"West, toward the Mount of Olives."

"Probably going to the Gardens of Gethsemane," Marcus mused. "Isn't that where the rabbi from Galilee is staying? What's his name?"

"Jesus, sir?"

"That's the one. Is he staying at the Gardens?"

"I believe he is staying with some of his followers in Bethany, but he can often be found in the Gardens, preaching to any who will listen."

Marcus rubbed his chin with his fingers. *That's intriguing.* Jesus was known for speaking of love and forgiveness; it would be interesting to discover if one of his followers had gotten the message wrong and slaughtered two Roman legionaries. Such a thing would not bode well for the Nazarene.

"Thank you, Gordian. You may go. Alert me the moment you have more news."

Gordian bowed and left the room, closing the door behind him. Now alone, Marcus got to his feet and walked over to the fireplace. He leaned an arm against the wall, stared into the embers and thought about his younger brother. He thought of his brother's wife and children. They would probably be in a panic right now, wondering when Didius would be home, if they hadn't heard the rumors on the street already.

That thought brought him upright. *Dear gods! I still have to tell Adonia she is a widow!* His vision blurred as he imagined the look on her lovely face when he broke the news to the family. Teeth clenched, he gripped the handle of his sword, wanting nothing more than to run someone through with it. At that point, it wouldn't have mattered who. He just wanted to lash out at someone. Anyone.

With a growl, he swept the bust of the god-like Caesar from the mantle, taking a small amount of satisfaction in hearing the clay shatter. He would have to clean that up before anyone saw it, lest he face charges himself, but it could wait. For now he was alone in his chambers, and it felt good to break something. Soon, he promised himself, he would be able to take out his anger on his brother's killer. He hoped it was the man the guards saw leaving the gate, the stealthy man headed for the Gardens of Gethsemane. This train of thought soon turned to the other notable man currently staying in the Gardens, and the strange rumors that surrounded him. Ridiculous stories about healing and miracles that only a fool would believe.

"Are you involved in this somehow, Nazarene?" Marcus asked the empty room.

He didn't know, but by the gods, he was going to find out.

CHAPTER EIGHT

Theron left the road and its throngs of people behind, opting instead to traverse the rocky scrubland to the north. He threaded his careful way among the rocks and pebbles, trying to be as silent as possible while he approached the Gardens of Gethsemane from the northwest. He didn't want anyone to hear his steps. He had long ago perfected the art of walking in silence, and after centuries of practice it just came naturally. Most of the time he didn't even realize he was doing it.

As he drew nearer to the Gardens, he heard a man speaking. The voice carried loudly, and every now and then when it paused, the space between his words filled with murmurs and rumblings from what sounded like a large group of people. He nodded to himself. *The shepherd is addressing his flock. This is good.* Theron would have the opportunity to view his target, and also to get a good look at many of his followers. His orders from the Council were not only to kill Jesus, but also those of his followers who knew the truth about Theron's race. Since Theron couldn't be sure which devotees would have such knowledge, he had already determined he would kill them all. Better to be safe than sorry.

As he rounded a corner he caught his first glimpse of the group, and right away he realized his mistake. The crowd of people who stood listening to Jesus as he spoke was not large; it was *huge*. All through the Gardens of Gethsemane people of all types stood, sat, or squatted in the grass, listening to the words of Theron's next target. He'd been expecting a dozen, or perhaps a score of people to be present, but there were many, many more. *By the Father, there must be hundreds of them!* He doubted he could kill them all, at least not in a timely manner. The throng was so large it spilled into the street running in both directions.

Some of the people wore the coarse, earthy linens of Jerusalem's poor. Others stood about in fine, colorful silks and satins. Here and there Theron even caught a glimpse of vibrant purple, a color made from such rare and expensive dyes only the wealthy could afford to wear it. He even spotted a few legionaries in attendance, their bright red capes fluttered in the cool breeze while their polished steel breastplates glinted dully in the flickering light of many torches.

And almost everyone in the crowd was focused entirely on Jesus of Nazareth. They stared at him in rapt attention, some in open-mouthed astonishment. He spoke to them of forgiveness and love, of being kind even to those who have wronged you, and helping those in need. His words were not inflammatory, as Theron would have expected of a Jewish Messiah, but calm and peaceable. Even sedate. He didn't call the Jews to war, he called them to faith.

He called them to God.

By the Father, he's undoing everything we've worked for in Israel! The *Bachiyr* had long sought to sway the Jews from their faith, even going so far as secretly aiding the Roman occupation of Judea in hopes of spreading the belief in Rome's gods through Israel. But this man, through the mere weight of his words, would undo all that. By the Father, he could set the *Bachiyr* influence in the region back hundreds of years. He had to be stopped.

Theron needed to get a better look, so he waded into the crowd. He still had not seen the so-called Messiah's face. He needed visual identification in order to know who to kill. He wasn't going to try anything while surrounded by hundreds of people, of course. But later, when the rabbi slept, Theron would find him. He would go to him while he lay in his bed, or on his pallet, or wherever he spent the night, and take his head from his shoulders as he'd done with Ephraim and the legionary in Jerusalem.

No, he thought. *It must look like the zealots did it.* He put his right hand on the hilt of his sword, remembering Algor's request. He would make sure the Nazarene died brutally, but he would use a blade to do it. After all, his sword could remove a head just as well as his claws. Better, even, since he kept it very sharp.

As he walked among the followers, he watched the faces of those in attendance. Not everyone, it seemed, was swayed by the young Nazarene's words. Here and there Theron spotted an occasional angry face, and more than once his keen ears picked up the words "blasphemy," and "heresy." This was good news; it meant Jesus's credibility wasn't total. Some still questioned his words, and it would be those people who would make the strongest arguments against him after his murder. They would unknowingly help Theron and the Council to further establish their race in Israel. Theron thought it fitting. Pawns behaving as pawns. He grinned at the idea.

His smile faltered when he came to a break in the crowd and got his first look at the speaker. He stopped short and stared at Jesus in surprise and awe, his *Bachiyr* eyes picking up on something none of the humans in the crowd could see, and he cursed under his breath. Killing Jesus had suddenly become much more complicated. Not because the man was strong or powerful. Quite the opposite; in build and stature, Jesus was largely unimpressive. His simple linen robe swallowed his thin, spare frame. Theron would have thought him weak, even by human standards.

The problem lay in the fact that Jesus literally glowed with the strength of his faith. The kind of faith that only comes from a strong belief in a wise and benevolent God. It formed a halo around him Theron could see all too clearly, and it was exactly the kind of faith the Council wanted to keep from spreading, because it was the only thing in the world that could save a human from a vampire. That was the Council's biggest obstacle in Israel. The Jews were so strong in their faith – though thankfully very few were strong enough to glow from it, as was this man, Jesus – and their collective strength weakened the power of Theron's people a great deal. Things had improved with the arrival of the Romans and their archaic beliefs in the pantheon of gods, and the Council had long hoped to someday build on that success.

But this man could ruin everything. With just his words he could strengthen the weakening resolve of the zealots. He could bolster the confidence of the Jewish populace. He could— *damn it all!* There were too many ways Jesus could thwart the Council's will. Just standing in the man's presence made Theron feel a little weaker, and he was nearly thirty paces away. He knew what would happen if he approached closer. His strength would flag until he would not be able to stand on his own legs. Then perhaps he would crawl, at least until he could no longer accomplish that much. In the end he doubted he would be able to get within five paces of his intended victim. No wonder the Council wanted Jesus dead, the man was dangerous. Killing him would prove immeasurably profitable for his people.

But how was he to do it if he couldn't get close? Of course, there were many ways to kill a man from a distance: spears, arrows, even a sling. However, the Council wanted Jesus's murder to be brutal, and Algor wanted it to look like the work of the zealots. Granted, the last part was not a direct order from the Council, but Theron liked to please them. Algor was especially influential. If Theron could find a way to earn the misshapen councilor's favor, he would make every effort to do so.

He stood in the midst of the crowd for a long while watching the rabbi from Galilee. He devised plan after plan, but none of them would bring the desired effect. His frustration led his mind into broad circles, but no suitable option presented itself. Theron's fists were clenched at his sides, his eyes narrowed to slits as he pondered ways to kill the Nazarene. With so much at stake, he could not fail. He had to find a way.

Jesus had to die a horrible death.

‡ ‡ ‡

Taras caught sight of the dark stranger with the blood-spattered sandals shortly after leaving Jerusalem. The man headed straight for the path that led to the Gardens. A short distance from the Damascus Gate, he left the path, something few travelers dare to do during the night, and walked directly to the Mount of Olives and into the Gardens of Gethsemane. Taras followed him the whole way.

Privately, Taras marveled at the man's ability to traverse the roads and then the scrubland in complete silence. Not once along the way had Taras heard a single crunch of gravel or broken twig. Very few indeed were the people who could tread so lightly; it was not an easy skill to learn. It had taken Taras the better part of a decade to learn it himself, at least to the point of mastery required of Roman legionaries in his particular field. That his quarry showed signs of being similarly well trained was both obvious and unsettling.

Taras watched the stranger enter the mass of people and work his way to the front of the crowd. At first he didn't want to follow into the throng, fearing he would stand out. But as he looked around he noted several other Romans in attendance, including a handful of legionaries. Since they didn't seem to generate any extra attention, he decided to risk going in. Taras swore under his breath as his quarry disappeared into the crowd. He needed to know how deep Didius's murder went. He had convinced himself the man he trailed was indeed the killer. The sneaky bastard was far too stealthy, far too careful, to be anything other than an assassin. Which left only one question in Taras's mind: Was Jesus involved? He would not return to the city until he found the answer. Taras checked the blade at his side, reassured by its heft at his waist, and stepped into the crowd to relocate the stranger.

It didn't take long. Taras spotted his man seconds after shoving his way into the gathering. He was weaving and twisting through the mass, threading his way closer to Jesus. Despite the stranger's ragged clothes, to Taras's eyes he stood out among the peasantry with his fluid bearing and feline grace. The rest of the people didn't seem to notice him, so intent were they on Jesus's speech.

Taras hung back about twenty feet, watching as the object of his attention stared at Jesus. The stranger seemed deep in reflection, paying rapt attention to the rabbi and his words. *Aha! So he* is *a follower of the Nazarene, probably a recent arrival from Galilee or some such place.* One thing Taras knew for certain, even from where he stood; the man was no novice to battle. The confident way the stranger carried himself and the easy manner in which he wore his barely concealed blade spoke volumes about the man's experience and skill.

In the flickering, dancing light of the many torches scattered about the gathering, the stranger always seemed to stay in the shadows. Yet another indication the man made his living dealing in death. Taras could relate; he preferred the shadows, himself. When a man spends a lifetime hiding from one shadow to another, it just becomes natural. The darkness has a way of etching itself into a person's soul.

After a few minutes spent observing the stranger, Taras decided he could do nothing for the moment. So he left the crowd to find a suitable spot to sit and wait. The man would probably not take the main road on his way back to the city, so Taras found a spot where he could watch the most likely routes unobserved. Away from the torches, he had to rely on the moonlight to see where he put his feet. As luck would have it, the night was clear and the moon full and bright. He had little trouble navigating through the Gardens and back into the scrubland.

Once there, he hunkered down behind a large boulder and waited. The thick grass on the lee side grew several feet high, more than tall enough to conceal his body from view. Perfect. Sooner or later the stranger would return. And when he did, Taras would take him.

While he waited, he thought of Mary, and the idea that had struck him earlier. Tomorrow, he would ask Mary to come to Rome with him. Once there, they could marry without fear of her father's dis-approval. The reach of the zealots was long in Israel, but it didn't extend into Rome. He would retire from the Legion and buy a small plot of land in the country. Then he and Mary would raise a family of their own. It was a beautiful dream, and he knew in his heart she would say yes.

Once he finished this business with the zealot assassin, Taras would speak with Marcus. He had no doubt the Centurion would approve his resignation; there were times when Marcus talked of it himself. It would be painful to leave his good friend behind, espe-cially after the death of Didius, but if it meant he could finally be with Mary, openly and without fear of reprisal, then he would do it. Marcus would understand.

Taras smiled as he waited in the dark, his mind on the green fields of the Roman countryside. He could almost smell the tall wheat and the blossoms on the grapevines as they twined around the supports. The bees would buzz from one flower to the next, ensuring a fine crop, which he would turn into as fine a wine as could be found anywhere. By this time next week, he and Mary would be on their way to a new life together, and Abraham and his narrow-minded beliefs would be far behind them. Theirs would be a life of earth, wine, and olives, of children and laughter, of love and family. There would be no more death for Taras, no more killing. Perhaps more important, there would be no more sneaking around at night and hiding his love like a shameful thing. Finally, he and Mary would be free.

But first, he had one last job to do for Rome.

CHAPTER NINE

When the crowd started to disperse, Theron knew the time to leave had come. He'd stayed at the Gardens pretending to listen to Jesus for over an hour because he feared he would draw too much attention by leaving early. He spent the entire time trying to think of a way to accomplish his mission, but with no success. By the time the crowd began to thin, he'd almost resigned himself to using a bow or a spear.

He turned around and walked back toward Jerusalem, still unsure how to go about his task. Since it seemed he would have to strike from a distance, it meant Jesus's death would have to be quick. He could not afford to merely wound him and thus risk an escape. His best bet would be a poison-tipped arrow. The Council wouldn't like that at all; it was much too easy a death. So even though they'd told him to make Jesus's death brutal, Theron was going to have to disappoint them.

The thought wormed its way into his mind and stuck like a thorn. *I'll have to disappoint them.*

In his nine centuries of service, Theron had never disappointed the Council of Thirteen. He'd spent his existence making himself useful. Killing wayward vampires, capturing humans who knew too much, and all in all doing anything and everything he could to please his rulers in hopes they would one day accept him into their ranks. He knew that was unlikely, but one could only guess what would happen should one of them die. By ancient law passed down from the Father himself, the Council must have thirteen members. It wasn't unthinkable to imagine that, should anything happen to one of them, they would put another in the empty seat.

It never happened, of course. No force known could destroy a Council member. But Theron had always clung to the belief that just because it had never happened before didn't necessarily mean it *couldn't*. He would just have to be there and make sure they knew he was available if it ever did. As Lead Enforcer, he would be the logical choice.

But now the Nazarene would ruin his standing. He would have to go back to the Council and explain to them that he could not get close enough to Jesus to give him the brutal murder the Council so desired. Less than a week at his new title and he'd already failed. He could picture the looks on their faces; the disappointment, the pity. Worst of all would be Algor's smug, contemptuous expression. That would be the hardest to bear.

Theron put his fist an inch deep into the trunk of a nearby acacia as he passed, taking out his irritation on the tree since he couldn't take it out on the Nazarene. There was a sharp crack, and he pulled his hand back immediately, taking a quick look around to make sure no one saw what he'd done. No one did; they were all too engrossed in Jesus's words to notice him.

By the Father, his claws itched to reveal themselves and shred someone. It didn't matter who. It could just be some stranger who'd wandered off the road. He didn't care. He just needed an outlet for his pent up frustration. Not here, though. Too many witnesses. He would wait until he was out of the vicinity of the Gardens, then he would vent his anger on the first person he met on the road back to Jerusalem.

He had just rounded a large boulder and started looking for an unfortunate soul to play his victim when he felt a sudden explosion of pain on the back of his head. It was enough to knock him off his feet, but mostly because it caught him off guard. He fell face-first into the dirt and lay there a moment, quietly assessing the situation. Someone had ambushed him. He could feel the wetness of his blood as it flowed in a lazy trickle from the wound. His mouth, only an inch from the dirt, widened in a smile. This was just the opportunity he had hoped for. *You don't know how bad a mistake you just made, friend,* Theron thought. *But you will soon find out.*

He was just about to stand up and slaughter his attacker when he saw the person's feet. Sandals. Legionary's sandals. That surprised him. He'd expected a robber, or a band of them, but not a soldier. Why was a legionary ambushing people on their way to Jerusalem? Not that it mattered. The man would die either way, but despite his anger, Theron's curiosity was piqued. The Romans were not known for being friendly, of course, but he'd never heard of legionaries ambushing civilians in the road before. Rome tended to frown on such activities, especially when committed by her soldiers. More than a few legionaries were put to death in Israel during the early years of the occupation for stealing trinkets from the Jews. Today, few soldiers were willing to risk public execution for the meager possessions of the average Jewish citizen, so why would this one? Perhaps he'd seen Theron's sword and decided it was valuable enough to risk his life for.

Theron's curiosity got the better of him, and rather than kill the fellow right away, he decided to wait a few minutes and see what he could learn. He groaned softly, pretending to be coming out of a dead faint.

The legionary stuck his knee into the small of Theron's back and grabbed his arms. When he felt his hands being tied, Theron had a twinge of momentary panic. He almost jumped up and killed the man then and there, but he forced himself to remain calm. He could escape any time he wanted. The ropes would never hold him, and he still wanted to find out what was going on. To do that, he would have to go along with this for a little while.

"Stand up," the man ordered, and yanked Theron to his feet with a sharp jerk.

"What? A... a legionary?" Theron asked, attempting to sound woozy. He swayed on his feet and blinked several times. "Have I done something wrong?"

"Marcus would like a word with you."

"Marcus? The centurion?" So this wasn't a random incident, the centurion wanted to see him. But why? Theron was more curious then ever. "What does he want with me? I haven't done anything."

"Nothing, you say?" The soldier reached under Theron's cloak and pulled out his sword, which still had a smear of blood on it.

Theron hadn't cleaned it as thoroughly as he should have because he'd been too excited about bringing his news to the Council.

"Then what is this?" the soldier asked, pointing to the blood.

For answer, Theron hung his head and gazed at his feet, saying nothing.

"No matter," the soldier said, apparently realizing no response would be forthcoming. "The centurion will have the truth from you. Now walk."

Theron felt something very sharp and hard poke him in the back. The legionary had jabbed him with his own sword.

So, the centurion wants to see me? This is interesting. No doubt it has something to do with the two legionaries I killed this morning. I wonder if he knew them? Theron tried to remember what he knew of the political situation in Jerusalem, but for all his research before coming to find Ephraim, he could not remember anyone of importance named Claudius. He didn't get the name of the second soldier at the gate, but it didn't matter much. The centurion would be angry at the murder of any of his legionaries, friend or otherwise. He would move swiftly to find, capture, and execute their killer. Theron knew – he'd seen it happen to a pair of hapless zealots not long ago. Centurion justice had a swift and merciless quality he admired.

Theron smiled, but kept it hidden from his captor. *Too bad I am going to have to disappoint Marcus.* That thought reminded him he was going to have to disappoint the Council, as well, and his anger flared anew. He would enjoy tearing this human to pieces for the indignity of binding his hands. True, he'd allowed it, but that didn't matter. The soldier would pay for the offense with his blood, which Theron would be sure to take very, very slow.

Just before he moved to break his bonds and sink his teeth into his captor's throat, an idea occurred to him. Maybe he wouldn't have to disappoint the Council, after all. Maybe this could work to his advantage. As the plan formed in his mind, he almost nodded. *Yes*, he thought. *Yes, it could work.*

The second time the soldier poked him in the back, Theron did as the soldier commanded and started walking back toward the city. Along the way he finalized his plan, turning the angles over in his mind, checking them, making sure he saw them all. It was perfect. Flawless. The Centurion would never suspect a thing.

He now had his course of action, and all it required was a little acting on his part. No doubt the centurion would be eager to punish the zealots responsible for the murder of his men, his animosity would take care of the rest. Theron sent a silent prayer of thanks to the Father that his captor walked behind him and couldn't see the smile on his face.

He allowed himself to be taken into Jerusalem. He glanced up at the night sky to make sure he still had time to do what he needed. There were still several hours until dawn. Plenty of time. His plan hinged on the hope that the centurion, in his anger, would come deal with him right away rather than wait until morning. He felt certain that if Marcus deemed his arrest important enough to send men after him at night, then he would also want to speak with him as soon as possible. If not, Theron would have to escape before dawn and return to the Halls. He didn't doubt his ability to do so, but it would mean abandoning his plan, which was not an option he wanted to consider.

Once they arrived at the city and passed through the Damascus Gate, several legionaries jostled their way through the crowds of people and joined the one holding the sword to his back. They flocked around him like carrion birds at a fresh carcass. His captor, however, remained at his back.

"What's this, Taras?" One of the men asked.

So his name is Taras, is it? Theron committed the name to memory. He would have need of it later.

"A zealot," Taras replied. "I'm taking him to the dungeons."

"A zealot, eh?" the first soldier replied. "Probably knows who killed Claudius and Didius, too, I'd wager."

Didius? So that was the other soldier's name. It sounded familiar, but Theron couldn't place it.

Taras said nothing, but the group of soldiers began to tighten around the pair. Several called to Theron, taunting him, calling him a filthy Jew and a whoreson and just about anything else that crossed their minds. They ignored the angry shouts from the many Jewish men and women nearby, who took offense to the insults hurled at their faith. One of the soldiers, perhaps emboldened by Theron's bonds, went so far as to strike him across the face, which brought more jeers from the gathered citizenry. Seeing the actions of their comrade, several more legionaries stepped in, their fists raised to dish out some punishment of their own. For a moment Theron thought he would have to abandon his plan then and there, lest the legionaries rip him to shreds before he ever got to see the centurion.

"That's enough." Taras stepped in front of him, and Theron got a brief glimpse of his captor. Tall, muscular, and blonde, he sure didn't look like a typical Roman legionary. Typical or not, Taras pulled his sword and pointed it at the soldier who'd slapped Theron. He jabbed it into the surprised man's forearm just enough to draw a thin line of blood. The injured soldier yelped as he yanked his arm back, then fixed Taras with an angry glare.

"What did you do that for?" the surprised legionary asked.

"Don't assault the centurion's prisoner again, soldier," Taras said, his stance not wavering in the least.

The many voices dropped off at once as Roman and Jew alike stared, wide eyed, at the tiny sliver of red on the tip of Taras's sword.

"How dare you, Taras," the man said when he regained himself enough to speak. He reached to his belt and wrapped his thick fingers around the hilt of his sword.

Taras snapped his blade up to the man's throat so fast Theron barely registered the movement. "I wouldn't, Filius. The centurion has questions for this one, and he will not be pleased if the prisoner is in no condition to answer them upon his arrival." His cold, low voice carried an unspoken promise even Theron, who knew a thing or two about the centurions, could hear. No one would be allowed to molest the zealot, at least not until Marcus got the chance. The punishment for those who tried would be swift and severe.

The soldiers, one and all, stepped back and out of Taras's way. Most eyed him with a mixture of confusion and fear, while a few muttered curses under their breath that only they and Theron, with his superior ears, heard.

Though his face stung and he was furious at the soldier who struck him, Theron didn't say anything. Inwardly he smiled. This was going to be much easier than he'd anticipated. These people hated the zealots. *Hated* them. Even more than he'd imagined. It would take almost nothing to move them to violence; their distrust crackled like dry twigs underneath kindling. One tiny little spark from Theron and his mission would be accomplished. He wouldn't even need to fan the blaze.

When it was obvious the men would make no further moves against them, Taras moved back to his post behind Theron, and again poked his sword point into Theron's back. "Move, zealot." Theron obeyed without hesitation, but he glanced back one last time at Filius, who stared hard at Taras's back with a look that might as well have been a blade. Theron committed Filuis' face to memory; he would want to find him in a few days to repay him for the slap.

╬╬╬

Taras jabbed and prodded Theron through the barracks and down the dank stone passageways to the dungeon. The pair stepped through a stout wooden door into a small, dark room carved into Jerusalem's bedrock. The only illumination came from a torch in the hall they'd just left, and the weak, feeble light might as well have not been there at all. To Theron's eyes, however, the cell was lit as bright as a full moon. Moss and lichen discolored the rough stone walls, and the steady *drip, drip, drip* of water somewhere nearby did nothing to drown out the moans of the other prisoners. Theron was impressed; the Romans could certainly build a secure cell.

Taras shoved him into the room and put him in the stocks. After ensuring the locks were securely fastened, Taras stepped around to the front of the stocks and removed his helmet, giving Theron his first good look at the man who captured him. Theron took in the large, muscled frame, stern face, wheat colored hair, and ice blue eyes that identified Taras as hailing from the cold lands far to the north of Rome. He wondered what such a man was doing in the Roman Legion, but it wasn't important. What Theron wanted then was to memorize the man's face. He would need to find him again when his business with the centurion was completed.

"Marcus has been waiting for your arrival," Taras said. "I am sure he will be anxious to get started." Then he turned and left.

Theron was glad to hear the centurion would come soon, just like he'd planned. After the door closed, he allowed himself a smile, and even let out a chuckle. He quieted immediately. It wouldn't do for any guards who might be standing just outside the door to hear him laughing. He steadied his emotions and his mind and waited in eager anticipation. If everything went well, he would be leaving this cell soon, anyway. Released by the Centurion himself.

Best of all, he would still be able to please the Council, and Marcus was going to help him do it.

CHAPTER TEN

It had been a long day for Marcus, one that saw his only brother murdered, along with another legionary, and the apparent escape of the zealot who'd killed them. Throughout the day, he'd been forced to wear a straight face and hand out orders as though the grief of Didius's death were the farthest thing from his mind. And the worst part was yet to come. He still had to visit his brother's wife and officially deliver the news of the tragedy that had befallen her family. He should have done it hours ago, but in the frenzy of the immediate investigation he'd been unable to break away. And, if he was honest with himself, he was afraid of this duty, afraid to be the one to hurt her so badly. He knew he had to do it, and soon, but he just couldn't force himself out the door and down the street.

He slammed his hand on the desk. Damn the zealots! Damn all of them! His anger helped. By focusing on his hatred and letting it work its protective magic he was able to conceal the anguish that threatened, at any moment, to wear him down and leave him a help-less old man.

But for now, in his chambers, with the lamp low and nothing but his memories for company, Marcus could let go if he wanted. He could let his tears fall to his desk and wet the stack of papers that sat upon it. He could choke out a sob or two, although he'd have to keep them quiet, lest someone overhear them. Marcus was free to feel and express his grief without fear of judging eyes that might think him weak and unfit to lead.

But he didn't. No tears fell from his face, and his lower lip didn't tremble as it tried to hold back. His hazel eyes were dry, though bloodshot, and his thin lips drew a straight line across the lower half of his face. His hands lay at his side, balled into tight, trembling fists, the nails digging bloody furrows into his palms. He longed to put those fists to good use on Didius's murderer. *I will find you,* he promised. *I will find you, and when I do I will strap you to a cross and display you at Golgotha, but not before I hurt you. You will bleed from a hundred, no, a thousand wounds before I allow the legionaries to crucify you.*

"Make peace with your God, zealot," Marcus whispered to the ceiling. "I am coming."

Exhausted, he laid his head in his arms, thinking to rest for a moment. He had just begun to doze off when a loud knock at the door woke him. He sat up with a start and reached for his sword out of instinct, wondering what had happened. In his state of near sleep, he temporarily forgot about Didius and Claudius, and for a brief moment he feared the zealots had attacked the barracks. Again.

"Damned zealots," he said as he jumped to his feet, his honed body responding to danger even though his mind had not yet cleared. Years of military training and experience carried Marcus from his bed to his door with his sword in his hand before he'd even realized he was awake.

Slowly, as though hearing it through a thick fog, a voice on the other side of the door began to penetrate into his mind. At first he thought it was Gordian, but then the voice came again.

"Centurion! Are you there?"

No, not Gordian, Marcus realized, but Taras.

Taras!

Memory hit him like a physical blow. The stranger with the sword. Of course! "Taras!"

Marcus grabbed the latch on the door and flung it back, breaking the mount and stabbing his finger on a sharp metal edge in the process. He never noticed the pain or the blood that trickled from his hand as he yanked open the door to find Taras standing alone in the hallway. Without preamble, he shot his bloodied hand out, grabbed the legionary by his tunic, and pulled him inside. Then he slammed the door shut and turned to face the newcomer.

"Did you find anything?"

"Yes, sir. I followed the man with the blood on his sandals to the Gardens of Gethsemane. As you suspected, he is a follower of Jesus of Nazareth."

"Are you certain?"

"When the man arrived, he went straight into the crowd, nearly to the front. Once there he stood and listened intently to the Nazarene's words. He didn't leave until Jesus finished speaking and the rest of the crowd began to disperse. There is little doubt he is one of them."

"And? Did you capture him?"

"Yes, sir. I captured him as he left the Gardens."

"What did he say?"

"I didn't question him, sir, but he had this on him." Taras pulled a sword from his belt, pointing out to Marcus several spots of blood still present on the jeweled hilt, as well as a smear of it on the blade. "And his sandals were bloody, just as the guard said."

Marcus took the sword from Taras and examined it closely. To his surprise it was similar in design to his own sword, but it was not of Roman make. The jewels in the hilt, though beautiful, were not practical as befitted a legionary. The polished steel blade, however, was balanced to perfection and held a wickedly sharp edge. The work of a master, without doubt. Such a weapon would be worth a fair sum, much more than a peasant in Jerusalem could afford. The thought gave Marcus pause. Just how far did the Nazarene's influence stretch? "You didn't interrogate him?"

"No, sir. I thought you would prefer to do it yourself."

Marcus looked up from the sword to find his friend smiling, and he couldn't help but grin, as well. Taras knew him too well. Marcus did indeed want to talk to the prisoner. Doubtless the man would deny any involvement, and Marcus hoped he would continue to do so for a long, long time. In the end, however, Marcus meant to have the truth from him.

"When would you like to question him, Centurion?" Taras asked.

Marcus turned the sword over in his hands, looking at the tiny drops of blood on the hilt. He brought a hand up to the blade and touched his finger to a red-brown stain about the size of his smallest fingernail. Didius's blood, perhaps? "I will see him right away."

"I thought you would," Taras replied, still grinning.

✠ ✠ ✠

The door to Theron's cell opened and two men stepped in. After being in the darkened dungeon, the light from the doorway was so bright he could not tell who had entered the room. Then the door closed, taking away the light from the hall and plunging the place back into welcoming darkness. As the light faded, Theron saw his two guests were Taras and Marcus, the centurion.

Ah, he thought, *now the fun begins.* A good thing, too. His back was starting to ache from being held in the stocks.

Theron could sense the seething anger boiling inside the centurion. It rolled off the man in waves like the heat of the sun. Good. Anger would make him easier to manipulate. Outwardly, however, the centurion appeared calm and in control. His cold, distant stare reminded Theron of the way a sparrow looked at a grub. Theron did his best to appear weak and afraid, knowing the Roman would pick up on that fear and try to use it against him.

"Are those secure?" Marcus pointed at the locks.

"Yes, sir. I checked them myself just before I came to see you."

"Very good, Taras. You may go."

Without another word, Taras bowed and stepped out of the room. Theron caught a glimpse of the man's face as he left, and noted his smirk. *You will not be smiling for long, friend. I will see you again.*

Marcus walked around the stocks without uttering a word. Theron heard the clop of the centurion's sandals circle behind him, out of sight. Theron recognized the tactic; the gesture was supposed to create tension in his mind and increase his fear. If he couldn't see the centurion, then he would have no idea what the man might be about to do. Fear made prisoners easier to control, to interrogate. It was the same reason Marcus had yet to address him. He wanted to make Theron nervous enough to speak first, which would mean the centurion was in control of the conversation. Theron played along.

"Why am I here?" he asked. "I have not done anything wrong."

Marcus stepped from behind the stocks and regarded Theron with a look so openly hostile Theron could almost feel it burrowing into his skin. By the Father, the man took the death of his men seriously! Theron was beginning to think the centurion would simply move to kill him while he was in the stocks without questioning him. He didn't fear for his life. The centurion couldn't kill him, but it would certainly hinder his plans. *No, he won't do it. He can't be sure I did anything yet.*

Theron was right. After a prolonged silence Marcus spoke. "Do you know who I am?"

"You are Marcus, the centurion."

"Yes. What is your name?"

"Ephraim. Ephraim of Sepphoris."

"A Jew?"

Theron said nothing, allowing the centurion to draw his own conclusions.

"Well?" Marcus asked.

"Yes, Centurion."

"Have you heard of the zealots?"

"Of course I have, Centurion. Everyone in Israel knows of the zealots."

Marcus turned quickly and brought the back of his gloved hand hard into Theron's face. It stung, but Theron was expecting it. So far, things were going exactly as he'd planned.

"That's for your insolence." Marcus spat. His face flushed, he reached his hand back, and Theron thought he was going to strike him a second time. But Marcus's expression calmed, and he lowered his hand to his side.

He's unsteady, Theron thought. *Good.*

Marcus, having apparently regained control of his anger, continued. "Do you know of the recent zealot activities in Jerusalem?"

"No, Centurion," Theron put what he hoped was just the right amount of fear and pain in his voice. "I am new to the city."

"So my guards tell me. They say they have never seen you here before." Marcus squatted on the floor, bringing his face right in front of Theron's. "Why are you here?"

"I followed a rabbi from Galilee."

"Jesus?"

"Yes."

"So you are a follower of the Nazarene's?"

"No, Centurion."

"Don't lie to me, Ephraim. You just admitted to following him here." Marcus raised his hand as if to hit him.

"No, Centurion. I *was* a follower of Jesus, but not any longer."

"You were captured just outside the Gardens this very night." Marcus struck him again, and Theron had to give the man credit; the blow hurt. "My agent saw you there. You were listening with rapt attention to every word the Nazarene spoke. Don't deny it."

Theron felt a warm trickle on his chin, and he licked his lips. Blood. He was bleeding. The centurion split his lip open. He would pay for that later.

"No, Centurion. I do not deny it. I have decided this very night not to follow Jesus anymore. When your soldier attacked me, I was on my way here, to Jerusalem, to get my things. I planned to return to Sepphoris with the morning light."

"Tell me why."

Theron shook his head.

"Tell me." Marcus raised his hand for another blow.

"I... I don't like the things he talks about, Centurion."

Marcus frowned, "My men tell me he talks openly of love and forgiveness. Mercy and compassion. You do not like those things?"

This is it. Theron thought. Now was the time to get into the centurion's head. He sent out half a dozen mental fingers. He pictured them reaching out toward Marcus and wrapping around his mind. He had to be very careful not to let Marcus know he was there, if he got the slightest notion Theron was manipulating his thoughts it would break the spell. With skill honed from centuries of practice, Theron sent a tendril of thought into the centurion's head. It wasn't much; the thought had to appear to be the centurion's own. Theron wasn't going for total control; just trying to implant a suggestion.

Marcus blinked, and his hand dropped a few inches.

Ha! Theron thought, *I have you now!*

Marcus regained himself quickly, then glared down at his captive. "Why are you silent, Ephraim? Answer me." He drew his hand back again as if to strike, but Theron noted the troubled look that flitted across his face. "Do you not like love and forgiveness? Would you not wish to receive mercy and compassion yourself at this moment?"

"Yes. Yes, of course I do, Centurion. But Jesus does not speak of such virtues."

"So my men are liars, then? Is that what you're telling me?" Marcus hit Theron a third time, but the blow did not have as much force as the previous two, and Marcus didn't look as sure of himself as he had only a few minutes before. "Do not lie to me again."

"He only talks about those things when he knows the Legion is listening. He is a tricky one, Centurion. He has scouts all over the

Gardens and along the roads leading into and out of the city. When legionaries are spotted, he talks of those worthy ideals. But when only Jews are present to hear, his words are very different."

"Explain."

"He talks about conquest, Centurion. Rebellion. Even war. He speaks openly against Rome and her legion. He talks of driving the Romans from Israel in blood. He tells the people he is here to free Israel, and that he is the Messiah. He… he even…"

Marcus's hand had dropped to his side as he stared at Theron. His eyes were wide and his mouth hung open. Theron guessed part of the man's reaction was shock, but some was the result of Theron's mental fingers at work inside Marcus's mind.

"Yes? He what?" Marcus asked. This time he didn't raise his hand.

"He tells the people that he is the Son of God. What is worse, they are starting to believe him. Many will follow him anywhere, even to war with Rome."

Marcus didn't look entirely convinced, but he didn't accuse Theron of lying, either. He stood and walked to the door, which he pulled open and spoke to someone waiting outside. Probably Taras. Whoever it was, they handed Marcus something long and metallic. Marcus closed the door and brought the item over so Theron could get a look at it. Theron recognized his own sword, and was prepared for the next question.

"Is this yours, Ephraim?" Marcus asked.

"No, Centurion."

"Yet you carried it to the Gardens of Gethsemane," Marcus noted, a dangerous tone creeping back into his voice.

"Yes, I carried it." Theron said quickly, "And I guess it *is* mine, now. But it only recently came into my possession."

"Explain."

Theron dropped his eyes to the floor and didn't answer. *Let him get angry again. His anger will only aid to convince him.*

He felt a sharp pain in the back of his neck and knew the centurion had cut him. Not badly, but enough to draw blood. In a mortal man it would have been a serious cut that would require stitching, but to Theron it was only a painful annoyance. He cried out anyway, just for effect.

A strong hand grabbed his jaw and forced his gaze upward. Theron found himself looking directly into the eyes of a very angry

Roman. A sharp point poked into his throat, and he knew Marcus had the sword poised to stab him through the neck, possibly with the intention of severing his head.

The entire time Theron had been making plans, it never occurred to him that the Centurion might simply cut off his head. He'd figured on the stocks and the beating, but decapitation was another matter entirely. That would put an end to him for good. Not even vampires can heal a severed head.

He fought back the instinct to smash open the stocks and attack, to rip through the centurion and tear his way from the dungeon. Instead he channeled his very real fear into his next lie. The lie that would finish the ruse.

"I…I killed a man with it last night! I'm sorry! I didn't mean to!"

"I knew it! It *was* you! You killed the two legionaries outside the Middle Gate!" The point of the sword fell away from Theron's neck, and he felt relieved. When he looked up, however, he saw Marcus holding the sword high above his head, ready to bring it down in a blow that would surely take Theron's head from his shoulders.

"You killed my brother." Marcus's voice was cold, empty.

His brother? His brother! *Of course. That's why he's so angry.* The eyes staring down at Theron shone with anger and grief, and he knew in that instant Marcus would do it. He would cut off his head. No trial, no fuss, just private justice carried out in a dank cell somewhere below the streets of Jerusalem.

The Centurion's eyes blazed, the muscles in his arms tensed.

The sword started to come down…

CHAPTER ELEVEN

"Wait!" Theron screamed, feeling a trace of genuine fear for the first time since the night began. "I murdered no legionaries last night. It was Malachi I killed!"

"Malachi?" Marcus checked his swing just in time, but kept the sword resting on Theron's neck. "The butcher?"

"Yes, that's him. I killed Malachi the butcher. But he attacked me first. I swear."

Marcus knelt in front of the stocks and brought his face level with Theron's. "He attacked you? Why?"

"He knew I was thinking about leaving Jesus's faithful." Theron tried his best to appear frantic, but inside he started to calm down. He'd cast the line, and despite a slight hitch, Marcus had taken the bait. Theron just had to pull him in. At least he didn't have to pretend to be rattled; the Centurion's sword had come far too close to his neck. "Malachi was also a follower of Jesus, and he came to me in my home last night. He said he knew I was thinking of leaving Jerusalem. He told me Jesus would not allow me to go. I asked him why, but he refused to say. Then he pulled his sword and tried to kill me."

"Yet according to your story you killed him, not the other way around."

"Yes. At first, when I saw the blade, I thought he was making a jest. But then I noticed a few spots of dried blood on it and I knew he would do it. He would really kill me if I let him. His mind had been poisoned by the Nazarene.

"I threw myself on him. He was a big man, so I knew I had to get the sword away if I was to have any chance of defeating him. I managed to wrestle it from his hands, but not before he cut me on the shoulder." Theron cast his eyes to the shoulder that had been wounded the night before, now glad he hadn't yet thought to heal it. "Then, when I had the sword, I told him to leave me be. But he pulled out that hammer of his and came at me a second time. I couldn't let him kill me. I did what I had to do. I opened his throat with his own blade before he got close enough to crack my skull."

"If that is the case, and Malachi attacked you, why did you go to see Jesus tonight? If you knew he wanted to kill you, why didn't you just leave?"

"I only had Malachi's word it was Jesus who wanted me dead. And that only after he tried to kill me himself. I had no way of knowing if it were true or if Malachi simply made excuses for his own desires. I had to see for myself."

"And did you?"

"Yes. I decided to go at a time when Jesus would be surrounded by many others and thus unable to attack me, just in case. When I arrived at the Gardens, I walked near to the front. I didn't fear for my safety because several legionaries were there; Jesus would not dare do anything with your soldiers present. But when I neared him, he saw me, and I knew it was true. The way he looked at me… it's hard to explain. His eyes stared at me, into me. It made me feel like I was dead already, and just didn't know it."

Marcus turned the sword over in his hands, fingering the hilt and examining the spots of dried blood on the blade. "You say this was already bloodied when Malachi came to visit you?"

"Yes, Centurion. That is how I knew Malachi meant it. He really would have killed me if I had not acted."

Marcus went silent. He looked into Theron's eyes and the vampire had the distinct feeling he was being tested. *Don't… even… flinch.* He told himself. *Make this look good.* He did a quick check to ensure the mental fingers he'd placed in Marcus's mind still held.

Satisfied, he willed himself to be patient. *Trust your skill. You have him. It's only a matter of—*

Marcus stood, and Theron noted with some relief the centurion replaced his sword in his scabbard. "Where is Malachi's body?"

"I buried it. In my garden."

"You will take me there and show it to me. If you are telling the truth, I will set you free. If, however, you are lying to me…" Marcus let the implication hang in the air.

"I will take you. Yes, I will take you. Thank you! Thank you, Centurion." Theron did his best to prostrate himself while still locked in the stocks. He looked to the ground and said "thank you" over and over again until Marcus finally told him to be quiet, at which point he snapped his mouth shut.

Marcus went to the door and tapped on it twice. The lock turned, and Taras opened the door and stuck his head into the room. "Yes, sir?"

"Find Gordian. Have him assemble six legionaries who are wide awake and still sober at this hour without pulling any from the watch. Tell him to send the men here. As soon as you have delivered my orders, come back to this room. Once all six men are present, you will unlock the stocks and let our friend, Ephraim, out. He is going to take us on a little trip this evening."

"Yes, Centurion," Taras said, and stepped out. Theron heard the lock on the door turn. Marcus was not taking any chances. But it didn't matter, his ruse was set. Once he led the centurion to Ephraim's garden and dug up the body of Malachi, his story would be confirmed. Theron didn't know much about brothers, but he knew anger when he saw it, and Marcus seethed with it. *His rage will blind him, and he will see exactly what I want him to see.* Theron smiled at Marcus's back. Less than an hour since his arrest, and he'd already succeeded in making the Centurion into a tool of his plan.

Soon Marcus would hunt Jesus himself.

╬╬╬

"There it is, Centurion. Just as I said," Marcus's prisoner said from inside the hole. He'd been digging for nearly half an hour. "Right where I said it would be."

"Stand aside," Marcus ordered, and shoved the dirty man aside to look in the hole. Sure enough, there was Malachi's body, complete with a deep cut from one ear to the other, just as Ephraim had said.

Marcus stepped back from the hole and whispered a prayer to Pluto, the god of the dead. He looked at his prisoner once again. "Why did you not report this?"

"I am new to the city, Centurion. Had I come to you with this last night, would you have believed me?"

"I am not certain I believe you now," Marcus replied. "Still, if what you say is true, there is a good chance this is the man who murdered my brother."

Marcus tried to recall everything he'd ever heard about Malachi, which was surprisingly little. In a city the size of Jerusalem, there were plenty of butchers. But he did recall seeing the man's name once or twice in connection with Jesus of Nazareth. He imagined the huge man coming at him with a hammer and wondered what he would do in Ephraim's place. It took him only a fraction of a second to realize he would do exactly the same thing.

He looked from the shackled prisoner to Taras, and after a few moments worth of consideration he made his decision. "Remove the leg irons."

Taras moved quickly and without question to the prisoner and unlocked the shackles around his ankles. "Shall I give him back his weapon, sir?"

"No," he said. Then he turned to his former captive, "Ephraim, the sword belonged to Malachi. And while Malachi gave you the right to take his life when he attacked you, he didn't give you the right to rob his corpse."

Ephraim at least had the decency to look ashamed. His gaze dropped to the dirt and he fidgeted with his tunic. "It is a fine sword, Centurion. I had thought... that is... it is a long way to Sepphoris, and..." His feet shuffled back and forth like a child who'd been caught stealing a sweet before supper.

"So you thought to protect yourself?"

"I wish I could say yes, Centurion. But it was nothing so noble as that. I would need supplies for the trip and—"

"And so you planned to sell it. Is that it?"

The man nodded, but didn't raise his eyes from the street. "What will happen to me now? Am I to be arrested?"

Marcus shook his head. *You'd think he'd have caught on after I had the leg irons removed.* Some of the folks from the outer provinces were so... simple. "No, Ephraim. It's not a crime to defend yourself. You're free to go."

The man smiled gratefully, then turned and shuffled down the street, going away from his house, which Marcus thought a bit odd. Certainly if he'd had a night like Ephraim's, he would want to go to bed and rest. Maybe Ephraim thought a walk around the city would settle his nerves. Or, more likely, he craved a drink after his ordeal. Marcus couldn't blame him for that; he wanted one himself.

As he watched Ephraim walk away, something nagged at him, but he couldn't quite put his finger on it. The man's story checked out, and he appeared to be nothing more than an ordinary Jew. He certainly didn't speak or act in any way odd that Marcus could think of, but for some reason he still didn't quite trust him.

Then, as he watched his men walking around the site, gathering shovels and clinking and clacking in the cobbled street, he realized what it was that bothered him about Ephraim: his walk. He didn't walk like a peasant from the outer provinces. His back was too straight and his bearing too... authoritative. Even now, shuffling away, Marcus could barely hear him. The whole way to the house he made hardly a whisper of sound, as though he had long ago grown accustomed to sneaking around. Marcus recalled Gordian had said as much when Lurio first spotted him leaving the Damascus Gate.

Still, he couldn't shake the belief that Ephraim had told him the truth. Marcus knew how to read men; it was part of being a centurion, and he liked to think of himself as a good one. When he looked into the man's face after nearly severing his head, he'd seen the truth of his words, however odd they seemed. Yet there was something in the back of his mind he couldn't quite place. Not a lie, exactly, but somehow he doubted Ephraim had told him everything.

"Centurion?" Taras asked, "Are you well?"

"I'm fine."

Taras looked down the street at their departing ex-prisoner. "You don't trust him, do you?"

Marcus shook his head, not the least bit surprised his friend had been able to read him so easily. "Do you?"

"Not as far as I could throw him. Something about that man just isn't right. He moves too quietly, too easily to be a simple peasant from Sepphoris."

Marcus nodded, glad he wasn't the only one who thought so. "Did you find anything in his house?"

"Nothing to indicate he is lying. Just some worn furniture and a few writing instruments: parchment, a quill pen, a personal seal, that sort of thing." Taras held up the seal he'd taken from Ephraim's desk; a dark piece of wood about five inches long and one inch in diameter. The steel tip bore a stylized *E*. "Nothing unusual."

Marcus looked at it. Taras was right. Nothing out of the ordinary. Still, his unease bothered him. "Follow him, anyway. I want to know where he goes in the city before he comes home. If he tries to leave Jerusalem, arrest him. But be careful," Marcus looked down the street to where he could just see the outline of Ephraim as he walked silently away. "There's more to our friend than he shows."

Taras nodded and set off to follow, but then he stopped and turned back to face Marcus. "Centurion?"

"Yes?"

"I have a request to make of you, sir."

"Of course. What is it, Taras?"

Taras hesitated. He looked over his shoulder in the direction Ephraim had gone. He seemed unsure how to proceed. Finally he sighed and turned back to Marcus. "It will keep until later, sir. Tomorrow, morning, perhaps?"

Taras was holding on to something, or perhaps he was letting go of something. Marcus knew his northern friend had been courting a Jewish maid of late. He also knew her father would never allow such a union. Marcus smiled, feeling true warmth for the first time since finding Didius's body in the street. He thought he had a good idea what Taras's request might be.

"Very well, Taras. Tomorrow, then. After you give your morning report?"

Taras nodded. "Thank you, sir." Then he turned and sped down the street after Ephraim, making no more noise than Ephraim had. Marcus watched him go. He felt a stab of regret that he would soon be losing his closest friend. But if it meant Taras would get out of the Legion and spend the rest of his days in the country with a wife who adored him and a family, then he considered it a good thing. If Marcus had any brains, he would have long ago done the same.

The sound of sandals on gravel reminded him there was work to do. He turned away from Taras's departing back and pointed to one of the legionaries. "You. Find my scribe. If he sleeps, wake him.

Tell him I will meet him in my chambers in one hour's time." The legionary saluted and went to do as Marcus bid.

"You," Marcus pointed to a second man, "Find the undertaker and bring him here. This body must be moved and given a proper burial." The second legionary saluted and sped off to find the under-taker.

"And you," Marcus said to a third, "You remain here and keep watch. I don't want anyone to disturb the body before the undertaker arrives."

"Yes, sir," the soldier replied.

Marcus turned to the remainder of the gathered legionaries. "The rest of you men are dismissed. You may go about your business."

As the group dispersed, Marcus thought about his upcoming meeting with the scribe. Ephraim could not be trusted, that much was obvious. Yet despite these misgivings, Marcus knew in his heart Jesus was the cause of his brother's death. He didn't have any real evidence, but he wouldn't need any. Not when the people had taken to calling Jesus the Messiah. He smiled as he walked away from Malachi's body to meet with his scribe.

"The son of God," he mused. "No, Nazarene. I won't need any evidence of your treachery to see you brought to justice. Not when you have provided so much else I can use to snare you."

He had a message for the Sanhedrin.

A short while later, much too short for Marcus's liking, he found himself talking to a comely young woman and her oldest son as the three of them sat on thin cushions in a modest house in the Upper City. Their eyes grew bright with moisture as they listened to the news every soldier's family fears will one day find them. The man of the house had been slain. Not just killed, but murdered in cold blood by those who sought to overthrow Rome though treachery and guile rather than honorable combat. The zealots made life difficult not only for the Romans and their families, but for all the law abiding people of Israel who only wished to live their lives in peace. Now they had taken something irreplaceable, not just from Marcus, but also from Adonia and her four children, the three youngest of which were currently playing in another room.

"He was killed by a zealot named Malachi, a butcher who also followed Jesus of Nazareth." Marcus said. "I believe the Nazarene is behind it. I've received reports that he's trying to incite the Jews into an uprising. Didius…" he still had trouble saying his brother's name out loud, "Didius didn't do anything at all. He was only in the wrong place at the wrong time, and for that Malachi killed him."

"But I know Malachi, Marcus. He is not a zealot," his sister-in-law said. Though her eyes were red and puffy, she had yet to break into tears. In looking at her face, however, Marcus knew she was close.

"Yes he was, Adonia. You can never tell with them. They are masters of hiding and spineless warfare. Cowards, every one."

"But I've been to the Gardens on nights when Jesus was there, and I've heard him speak. He's never said anything about rebellions and war. He talks about peace and forgiveness for your fellow man, and also of love for the Jews' lone God."

Marcus shook his head. "Was Didius with you?"

"What do you mean?"

"Was Didius with you when you heard Jesus speak? Or Opilio?"

"What difference could that make?"

Opilio, fifteen years old and already wiser in the ways of politics than his mother could ever be, answered for him. "He doesn't speak of rebellion in front of Romans, mother. He does so when only Jews are present. Is that what you are hinting at, Uncle Marcus?"

Marcus nodded, proud of his nephew. "He knows when Roman soldiers are within hearing range. He has spies everywhere."

Adonia shook her head. "But why would they murder Didius? He was nowhere near the Gardens of Gethsemane last night."

Marcus sighed, and leaned back in his chair. "I believe Malachi wanted to get through the Middle Gate, and one of the soldiers questioned him. Malachi was large, strong, and skilled with a blade. He was a butcher, after all. For that matter, he might have had friends with him who helped. Who can say for sure? Malachi is dead. I have seen the body. A pity, too. I would have liked to question him."

"I would have liked to help, Uncle."

Marcus looked at his nephew, startled by the harsh tone of his voice. Upon reflection, he realized he shouldn't be too surprised. Opilio was a fine, strong young man. Passionate and honorable, just like Didius. In fact, he was the spitting image of his father. The boy's voice carried not a trace of hysteria or depression, only a calm, smoldering anger. Marcus thoroughly approved of this; glad he didn't have to worry about a reckless youth out for revenge. He'd lost a brother already; he didn't plan on losing any more family to Jesus and his ilk. He nodded to Opilio, and returned his eyes to the patch of floor between his feet.

"What of the other man?" Opilio asked. "Ephraim. Was he also involved, uncle?"

"I can't say. There is something he's not telling me, that much is certain. But I have no idea if he is involved with the zealots or if he, like your father, was simply in the wrong place at the wrong time. I spoke to several people in the area, and they all confirm that he is new to the city. Several of them have told me they heard him say he was born in Sepphoris. Every one of them, however, feels there is something odd about the man."

"Are you having him watched?"

"Of course I am having him watched. I was not made a Centurion because the uniform complements my appearance, Opilio."

The boy cringed, and right away Marcus felt a pang of guilt. He hadn't meant to be so harsh, but he wasn't going to let a fifteen year old boy question his ability to do his job, no matter what dreadful news he'd brought. Confused and frustrated, his gaze slid back to the pale wood floor and he said nothing else.

"So what happens now?" Adonia asked, breaking the silence that had settled over the three of them.

Marcus looked up. "I am going to arrest the Nazarene tomorrow morning. The Sanhedrin will accompany me and they will present their case to Pilate. As it is, I have no evidence of Jesus's treachery. But the Sanhedrin will demand his execution based on the claims that he is the son of their God. The Prefect might be reluctant, but once I fill him in on my suspicions, he will go along with it willingly enough. He trusts my instincts, and as long as the temple priests are pressing for it, he won't need evidence. Not even Tiberius would want Pilate to offend the Sanhedrin unnecessarily."

"So what will happen to him?" Opilio asked.

"He will most likely be crucified."

Opilio nodded. "I want to be there."

"Of course. In fact, half the city will be there, I'm sure."

"No, uncle. I want to be close. I want to see the look on his face when they flog him. I want to smell his blood. I want to watch as the cross is raised and he realizes what his actions have cost him. I want to watch him die."

Marcus, stunned by the vehemence in his nephew's voice, could only stare at the boy in silence as he tried to find a reason to tell him no. Less surprising was the realization he couldn't think of a single one. Opilio deserved no less than what he asked for. Marcus had reluctantly presided over several crucifixions already, an unfortunate fact of his station, and he knew how unpleasant they could be for the spectators as well as the condemned. In this case, however, he thought he might enjoy the spectacle for a change. Opilio should have that opportunity, as well. Didius was his father, after all, and the Nazarene would die whether the boy was there to watch or not. "Very well, nephew. I'll see to it you have a good spot."

"Marcus, no," Adonia said. "He's too young—"

"Too young to have his father killed in such a cowardly fashion by enemies of Rome?" Marcus interrupted. "I agree, Adonia. I don't like it, either, but the boy deserves justice, and I will not be the one to deny it to him."

Adonia lowered her eyes and nodded. Marcus's heart nearly broke when he saw the tears finally fall from her cheek to land on the floor. The news that her husband was murdered hadn't pulled the tears from her eye, but the idea of her son witnessing a crucifixion had done the job. He disliked having to hurt his sister-in-law like this, but he reminded himself that life sometimes hurts. There were times when the best you could hope for was to stand up and keep moving. That's what Adonia needed to do now, and Opilio, too. If watching the execution of the man responsible for his father's murder would grant the boy a measure of peace, then so be it. In any case, Marcus had only spoken the truth; Opilio deserved Justice. So did Adonia. So, too, did Marcus. He would not be swayed.

"I must see to the other children," Adonia whispered. She stood on shaky legs and walked to the next room, where Opilio's younger siblings waited to learn the purpose of their uncle's visit. Adonia pulled the door open, and for a brief instant Marcus saw the curious but worried face of little Prisca as she stared through the doorway. Ordinarily her pretty face would light up at the sight of her uncle, but not today. Today her jubilance seemed muted, subdued somehow, as though she already knew something was wrong even if she didn't know what it could be. Marcus wanted to give her a reassuring smile to let her know everything would be all right, but he just couldn't do it. The harsh truth of the matter was it *wouldn't* be all right, perhaps never again, and Marcus knew it. Then the door closed and he was left alone with Opilio, who remained silent.

He heard Adonia's muffled voice. He couldn't make out the words, but by the screeching of seven year old Prisca that followed, he figured she'd just been given the news of her father's death. As the other two children joined in the sad chorus, Marcus felt his own eyes grow damp. He stood and paced through the small room, his anger like a boiling cauldron. He hated this. Hated hurting his sister-in-law, hated having to tell her that the man she loved was dead. He hated having to show his young nephew the more brutal side of the Roman Legion. He hated hearing his nieces and nephews in the next room cry for their dead father. Most of all, he hated that his brother was gone, taken from him by a man who spoke so often of love and forgiveness in one breath while ordering the deaths of Roman citizens in the next.

He looked at his nephew again, wanting to see how the boy would stand up to the sound of his siblings' reactions and wanting, as well, to be ready to offer comfort if it was needed.

Opilio's eyes filled with tears. After a short time spent listening to the sound of his brother and sisters crying in the other room, he stood and ran through the front door. Marcus started to stop him, then thought better of it and let the boy go. Opilio would need time to sort through the emotions churning inside him. Marcus knew this because he had yet to sort through his own.

Marcus had never seen the Nazarene, but as he stood in his dead brother's house he pictured a hooded man standing in the Gardens spouting his treason to all who would listen, poisoning the souls of those foolish enough to heed him. He thought of the man telling the zealots to kill any legionaries they found alone; men with wives and children who only wanted to do their jobs and make the streets of Jerusalem safe for everyone.

"May the gods damn you," he said to the image in his mind. His fist clenched at his side, and the entire room took on a reddish cast as his rage built to a raging maelstrom inside him. He would catch the Nazarene, by the gods, and Opilio would get his wish. Marcus and his nephew would both watch as Jesus died, and if Marcus had his way, the Nazarene would die very, very slow.

CHAPTER THIRTEEN

Taras followed Ephraim through the city, taking care to always stay just far enough behind to keep from being seen or heard. Taras was as skilled as anyone at threading his way silently through the shadows, his occupation as one of Rome's elite secret killers demanded it, but even he could not help but be amazed by the stealth of his subject.

Only a few hours ago, he would not have been able to move through the city streets without jostling and shoving his way through a never ending throng of people. Now, at this late hour, he found the city all but deserted. While the odd person could still be seen here and there, running through the city on whatever errand had him up and about in the wee hours, overall Taras and his quarry had the streets of Jerusalem all to themselves.

Once Ephraim was far away from Marcus and the other soldiers, his odd shuffling gait ceased and he began to walk on the balls of his feet in absolute silence. In addition, he kept to the darker shadows on the sides of the city streets almost as if by habit. As though he'd learned long ago to stay hidden. More than once, Taras – a skilled tracker – thought he lost his quarry only to see him emerge from a shadow further down the street, leaving Taras hard pressed to catch up while maintaining his own silence. Taras could appreciate such skill, of course, but it only confirmed what Marcus suspected.

Ephraim was dangerous. From what Taras could see, he was *very* dangerous.

Where are you going, Ephraim? Taras had already determined the man's path through the city was too direct to be the random wanderings of a man who simply needed to clear his head. As they passed through the Middle Gate, where Didius's blood still clung to the wall like rusty moss, the man paused to look at the stain. Taras could not quite make out Ephraim's face in the darkness, but he had the impression the other was smiling. Then the man was off again, and Taras had to wonder if his feelings were legitimate or just the result of his suspicion.

He soon realized Ephraim was heading in the direction of the Damascus Gate, and he recalled Marcus's order that the man not be allowed to leave the city. *He's off to warn Jesus, no doubt,* Taras thought. *He's in league with him, I'll wager.* His anger started to boil. Jesus and his band of followers were turning out to be nothing but trouble. Cutthroats and brigands, every one of them. He prepared to arrest the fleeing zealot as he left the city, as Marcus ordered. *Why did you really kill Malachi?* Taras wondered. Not that he cared. Let them all kill each other. Rome, and Judea, would be far better without them.

Taras broke from his concealment and drew in a breath to shout for the guards at Damascus Gate to arrest the stealthy peasant, but Ephraim surprised him. Rather than head for the gate, the man stopped in front of a small wooden house just inside the walls.

Taras froze. He stood exposed in the middle of the street with nowhere to hide. If Ephraim turned around he would surely be spotted. He ran several stories through his mind as to why he was there, then realized he was overreacting. As a legionary, a soldier in Rome's great army and part of the occupying force in Jerusalem, he had every right to stand wherever he wanted. He would not make excuses for his presence. He straightened his posture, squared his shoulders, and waited for the man to notice him.

But Ephraim didn't. Instead, he fished a golden key from his pocket and used it to unlock the door. Then he went inside. Taras didn't see any light inside the building when the door opened, but a few seconds afterward light flared from under the doorway, then faded. After that there was nothing at all. Just a slightly run down, seemingly harmless house on the outskirts of the New City.

Taras walked over to the door and pressed his ear to it, straining to hear any noise coming from inside, but there was nothing. Only cool, rough wood against his cheek. But he did catch a whiff of something coming from the building that caught his attention. A smell every soldier comes to know if they have spent any time behind their shield: the coppery, earthen scent of blood.

Marcus had told him to find out where Ephraim went, and report back to him. But Marcus had probably not guessed he would go to another house in the city. The centurion had likely thought Ephraim would either leave the city altogether or just walk around for a while and return home. Taras could go back to his commander and report the location of this house and no one would say anything at all. As far as all involved were concerned, he would have done his job to the letter.

But he smelled blood. And that didn't bode well. By the time Marcus returned with a group of soldiers, who knew what Ephraim would have done? Better to learn as much as possible. His mind made up, he straightened, keeping his eyes on the street. He looked around the area to make sure no one could see him. He heard the conversation of the guards at Damascus Gate, but just barely. Either they hadn't noticed him, or they had recognized him and decided to leave him be. The important thing was, for the time being, no one was paying any attention to him.

With his right hand, he thumbed down the locking mechanism on his scabbard, freeing his blade. He drew it out just an inch to keep the device from latching again. He would probably need to pull the sword out in a hurry very soon. With his left hand, he reached down to the door handle and snaked his fingers under the cool brass.

Besides, what if he leaves while I am searching for Marcus? What would I tell the centurion if he came all this way only to arrest an empty house? And we did take away the man's sword, so he should not be able to fight back once I get inside. The faulty logic didn't make him feel any better. Ephraim could very well have a house full of swords or armed reinforcements on the other side of the door, but Taras had decided on his course of action and he meant to see it through. And so, with the faint smell of blood mixing with the loamy scent of earth and the dust from the street, he pulled on the handle.

It was locked.

"Gods take it," he swore, and let go of both the sword and the door handle. He took another quick survey of the street to make sure he was still alone, and knelt in front of the door to examine the lock. *I can open this,* he thought after a cursory examination. He reached into a pouch on his belt and pulled out his tools. Like all men of his trade, he'd been thoroughly trained on locks and how to pick them in Rome. There was not a lock made, not even those on the great Caesar's abode that Taras could not compromise in under a minute, and this one was rather simple. It would be easy enough to bypass it and gain access to the building.

Just as Taras put a slender metal pick into the lock, he felt the temperature of the air around him drop. Unconcerned, he worked the tool into the mechanism, shoving the thought of the increasing cold to the back of his mind. It wasn't important. *Focus.* Only the lock mattered. Patience and concentration are the most important tools in any assassin's arsenal, and life doesn't show mercy to those of his occupation who never learn them. So although the air around the door felt like it had dropped to below freezing in a matter of seconds, Taras's attention remained fixed on the lock, even when his breath began to fog in front of his face and his flesh pebbled with the chill.

Almost there...

The lock gave with a light click, and the door moved inward a fraction of an inch. Taras sighed and sat back, now able to refocus on his surroundings. The first thing he noticed was it had gotten much, much colder than he'd thought.

A light scratching noise, similar to the sound a dog's paws make when it scrapes them against a wooden door, drew his attention back to the house. He thought perhaps his sword might be rubbing on the wood, but it wasn't. In fact, no part of him was even close to the door except his hand, which still grasped the handle.

He felt a chill creep into his bones that had nothing to do with the cold. His spine prickled and the fine hairs on his arms and the back of his neck stood on end as he realized that someone, or something, was on the other side of the door, separated from him by perhaps an inch of wood. A sense of malevolent evil flowed from under the door and floated upward like a chilly mist, and with it came the cloying, putrid smell of decomposing flesh. It swirled around his face like a tendril of fog, and as he breathed it in he knew a fear so deep it nailed him to the street and released his bladder.

The warmth of the fluid down his inner thighs went unnoticed as the handle moved. Taras jerked his hand away, but he could not bring himself to stand up. He could only watch as the door creaked open and a dread creature from his darkest nightmares emerged into the moonlight.

It stood as tall as a man, but where its flesh should have been were only writhing, pulsing insect larvae, wriggling here and there upon the specter's person. Empty eyes bored into him from beneath a tattered black hood. It made no sound as it reached for him with a decrepit, grub-covered arm. Taras watched the approaching fingers, and he knew it meant his end. Fear and despair wormed their way through his veins like poison, and still he could not bring himself to move or even speak.

Taras had seen many things during his time with the Legion, but nothing compared to the apparition before him. The sight of the thing and the smell of decay that surrounded it made him gag. As he looked on in a dark kind of fascination, he knew he was about to die. He forced his mind away from the thing in the house and thought of Mary, remembering her laugh and the scent of her perfume. He used those memories to blot out the image of the creature, wanting Mary's beautiful face to be his last thought in this life. He braced himself for the thing's touch.

"You there, legionary. Are you all right?"

At the sound of the voice, the worm-eaten hand paused. The clop of sandaled feet approached from the direction of the Damascus Gate. As they drew closer Taras, too numb to feel relief or amazement, watched as the creature retreated back into the house and pulled the door closed. A bar slid into place on the other side. Taras heard it as if from a distance, and he had a vague impression of hands on his shoulders just before the world grew dark.

CHAPTER FOURTEEN

Taras woke with a start as icy water splashed over his face. Cursing and sputtering, he sat up and wiped the fluid from his eyes so he could look around.

He lay in the street a few yards from the house where the worm-eaten creature almost grabbed him. Nearby, the two guards from the Damascus Gate stood anxiously discussing what to do about him. One of them wanted to carry him to the infirmary right away. The other held a dripping bucket in his hands and looked ready to run for more. The one with the bucket eyed Taras with a worried look on his face. "Are you all right, soldier?"

Taras tried to stand, but his rubbery legs failed him, and he fell backwards onto the street. Embarrassed, he tried again, this time willing the muscles in his legs to hold. With an effort, he was able to bring himself upright and face the two men.

"What happened?" he asked, still a bit groggy.

"You fainted," the guard with the bucket said.

"I know that." Taras's patience hadn't returned with his muscle control. "I meant what happened to that thing? Did you capture it?"

"Capture what?"

He gaped at the two men, for the moment unconcerned that he was supposed to be an ordinary legionary. "That thing! The creature. Don't tell me you just let it go?"

The two men looked at each other, then back to Taras. By the looks on their faces, they thought he was still a bit dazed. One of them stepped closer and offered a steadying hand, while the other – the one with the bucket – took a step backward.

"There's nothing there, soldier," the first one said. "You were kneeling in front of that door," he pointed a thumb in the direction of the house, "and then you fell into the street. We came right over, and Iovinus here ran to get a bucket of water. When he returned, we poured it on your head. You were out for two minutes, at most."

Taras forced himself to calm down. He noticed his hands were shaking, and he willed them to stop. He needed to regain his composure. He reminded himself these two men didn't know who he was, and thought of him only as another legionary. They couldn't know he possessed intincts much sharper than theirs, and they obviously hadn't seen the thing that tried to attack him. "Of course," he said, forcing steadiness into his voice. "I must have hit my head. Thank you, Iovinus, for reviving me."

"You should let me look at your head," Iovinus said. "You might have an injury."

"No, thank you. I'll be fine. I think I'll just go and lie down for a while."

Iovinius eyed him, his skepticism clear on his face. "Be careful. Head injuries can be serious."

"I will. Thank you." Taras turned and walked away from the two guards without looking behind him. As he walked, his head finally began to clear. He hadn't been seeing things. A hideous creature lived in that house. And Ephraim led him right to it. In fact, Ephraim even had a—

Taras stopped in the middle of the street, too stunned by his latest thought to keep walking. Ephraim had a key! He and that… thing… must be in league together. Marcus never should have trusted him.

So, you were planning to leave Jesus's followers and go back to Sepphoris, eh? Taras scowled, remembering how keen Ephraim had been to see the blame for Didius's death placed on Jesus's shoulders. It was so obvious! Why, that son of a whore had probably never even met Jesus. Most likely he…

Taras froze as the implications of this new train of thought sunk in. Then he swore loud enough that the soldiers at the gate heard him and turned to stare. He paid them no attention and sprinted for the barracks, his only thought being to get back and stop Marcus from arresting and executing the wrong man.

⳨ ⳨ ⳨

From his hidden vantage point atop a small shop across the street, someone else watched as Taras broke into a run. In the moonlight, the newcomer's face split into a wide grin, revealing twin canines that were much too long and far too sharp to be human.

You have erred, Theron, the vampire thought. *You led a human right to our door, and even let him see a Lost One. The Council will not be pleased.*

He turned and walked to the other side of the building, then checked up and down the street, looking for any potential witnesses. Once assured he would not be seen, he arched his legs out over the side and jumped from the roof, landing lightly on the cobbled street some thirty feet below, then started walking.

The newcomer had a plan. One that would ensure his rise to the top of the Council's esteem. No more debasing himself for Theron, that arrogant bastard. Finally, after many years of insults, he would get the respect he deserved. If all went well, soon he would be an Enforcer, maybe even Lead Enforcer. And Theron, if the Council let him live at all, would be a Lost One.

He laughed at the thought. The high and mighty Theron forced into servitude and reduced to playing host to thousands of insects as they feasted on his flesh for hundreds of years. It was too good to be true. He felt like dancing through the streets of Jerusalem.

Before he could see to Theron's fall, however, he had to make sure his plan was carried out. He couldn't just tell the Council how Theron had led the human to their domain. While that information would certainly get Theron in trouble, it would do nothing to help his own ascent to power. No, in order to facilitate that, he would need to succeed where Theron failed.

He would have to kill Jesus first, before Theron could complete his mission. The first step to reaching that goal was to make certain Taras didn't get a chance to tell Marcus what he'd seen.

CHAPTER FIFTEEN

When Taras reached the entry to Marcus's chambers, he found his way blocked by four armed legionaries. As he approached, the four closed ranks in front of the thick oak doors, crossing their spears to block the doorway.

"Let me pass. I have important news for the centurion."

"Move along, soldier," one of the guards said. "No one is permitted to see the centurion tonight, by his own order."

Taras glared at the legionary who'd spoke, but the man never flinched. He looked around at the other three, and realized he didn't know any of them. They looked like fresh recruits. They would not know who he was, and even then, they would only know him as a fellow soldier. There were times when the need to keep his position secret could be damned inconvenient. Looking at the firm set of the guard's face, he would not get in to see Marcus, so he turned to go. Before he got more than a few steps away, one of the men called out to him.

"Wait," the man said. Taras turned around to see the speaker. A young legionary eyed him from top to bottom, his eyes finally settling on Tara's shoulder length wheat-colored hair. "Is your name Taras?"

"It is."

"In that case, I have a message for you: the centurion expected you sooner. He finally had to retire, but he instructed me to give you this." The soldier held out a rolled piece of parchment, sealed with Marcus's symbol.

"Thank you," Taras said as he took it. He examined the tube, wondering if he should read it now or take it someplace private. One look at the eager expression on the guard's face and his decision was made. Marcus had sealed it for a reason, therefore, Taras would take it someplace where he could read it in solitude. He turned around and, without offering anything in the way of a parting greeting to the four soldiers, walked away from the centurion's chambers and out into the barracks.

Most of the legionaries were long asleep by the time he made it outside and into the moonlight. Their snores echoed through the halls of the barracks, a deep vibrato coming from behind every door. The two guards stationed at the entrance were not much better off; they stood mute guard, leaning on the doorway and almost asleep on their feet. Taras coughed loudly as he passed by, startling them to attention as he walked away from the compound and stepped out into the moonlit night.

He gazed about the city, wondering about the thing he'd seen earlier. It had to be a demon of some sort, because it clearly wasn't human. He shivered as he recalled the fat grubs crawling over the creature's skin. The sense of fear it inspired could still be felt in the slight trembling of his hands whenever he remembered it. If his suspicions were correct, and Ephraim was in league with that hideous apparition, the centurion needed to know.

Gods! He needed to talk to Marcus. But he couldn't very well kill four legionaries to do it. He looked around at the empty street, as though it could provide him with a solution. It didn't. Taras sighed. He would just have to stop by Marcus's office in the morning before he left to arrest the Nazarene. Although come to think of it, he was certain Marcus would want him along, anyway, in which case it would be easy enough to give his news to the centurion in time to stop the arrest.

That decided, he eyed the rolled-up sheaf of parchment for a moment, then broke the seal and unrolled it. As he expected, it was a letter from Marcus. Taras sat in a doorway on the side of the street and read his commander's instructions.

Taras,

The guards are in place to prevent anyone from waking me, even you. Before you take offense to this, I remind you that tomorrow will be a very important day, and we must all be rested for what is to come. This includes you. I suggest you retire soon after reading this, as I will require your presence tomorrow morning for a trip to the Gardens of Gethsemane. We will accompany the Sanhedrin and arrest Jesus of Galilee. I expect there to be a great deal of trouble from his followers. I have already sent word to the temple.

Before you sleep, however, I have one last task for you. Return to the home of our friend, Ephraim, and see to it that the dog Malachi is exhumed properly. I have left instructions for the undertaker to give him a proper burial, but that was only for the men. I want you, Taras, to take the man's body outside the gates and leave it for the animals. I will not grant the murderer an honorable service, and he deserves none.

Do this last task, then return to the barracks and sleep. I will speak with you again in the morning. I do not think I have to tell you to talk of this to no one.

M.

Taras rolled the letter up and put it into a pocket of his tunic. Marcus had deliberately left his name off the document just in case. He had a feeling the four guards at his door would be reassigned to the farthest reaches of Judea in the next few days, just to make sure no one could connect the centurion to the request to dump a body in the middle of the desert rather than give it a proper service, a thing unheard of in Roman society.

He's right, though. I do need to rest before morning. So Taras headed over to Ephraim's house to see to Marcus's command, and then he would get some sleep. The odds were good he would need it for the day to come.

Taras saw the soldier running toward him just as he rounded a corner onto Ephraim's street. It was Gordian, the centurion's Second and the only other person in the barracks that knew Taras's secret. The last Taras had seen of him, Gordian was on his way to bed. What was he doing up and out at this late hour? No matter, Taras was relieved just to see a familiar face.

When Gordian saw him, his eyes grew wide, and he ran all the faster.

"Taras," the man panted for breath. "Hurry. You must see this."

"Gordian, I'm in the middle of something for Marcus. I'd come with you, but this is pretty important."

"You'll want to see this, Taras" Gordian said, still struggling for breath. "I guarantee it." Then he turned around and ran back up the street.

Taras said nothing, but he broke into a run and followed Gordian, trusting his judgment. Before long he found himself back at Ephraim's house, which is where Marcus wanted him to go, anyway.

"Here?" Taras asked.

Gordian nodded and led Taras around to the back, where the body of Malachi lay facedown in the dirt, loosely wrapped in a coarse blanket. The smell of freshly turned soil filled the area, along with the beginnings of decay. Taras wrinkled his nose as he rounded the rear wall. He expected to see the undertaker, but no one else was near the house. "Where is the undertaker?" he asked.

"I dismissed him," Gordian said. "The other soldiers, too. I thought it best to keep this a secret until Marcus could be told."

"Keep what a secret?"

"Look over there." Gordian pointed into the pit where Ephraim had dug out Malachi's body earlier. He expected a sword, or perhaps more evidence of the man's crime, and was not quite able to keep from giving a start when he discovered a second body. As with Didius, the new body had also been beheaded. Taras bent over to get a closer look at the flesh around the neck. Bits of skin and other tissue hung from the ragged stump. The wound looked very familiar. *Just like Didius,* he thought.

He stood and looked at Gordian. "Recognize the injury?"

"Yes. Just like the centurion's brother," Gordian replied. He looked to the ground and shook his head. "Malachi was busy last night."

Taras almost told Gordian his suspicions, but he kept his doubts about Malachi's involvement to himself until he could talk to the centurion. After that, if Marcus wanted Gordian to know, then Marcus would tell him. If not, then so be it. Gordian didn't need to know everything. However, this second body posed several new questions.

"Have you found the head?" Taras asked.

"No," Gordian replied. "Just the body."

Taras nodded. He'd expected as much. "So who is this? And why was he killed?"

"I don't know who he is, not yet. But I have two men trying to find that out right now. As for why he was killed, I don't pretend to understand the minds of men who are capable of such things, Taras. Perhaps Malachi killed this man, as well, and buried him before Ephraim arrived and killed him."

"Perhaps," Taras admitted, but he wasn't convinced. Something about the whole story had seemed off from the beginning, and the discovery of a second decapitated Jew, in the original suspect's garden, no less, did not ease his concerns at all. Had Ephraim killed this other man? If so, why? And why would he bring the centurion to the site at all and risk it being discovered? It didn't make sense.

Unless Ephraim hadn't killed the man, and Gordian's suspicion that Malachi had done it before Ephraim arrived was correct. But that didn't make sense, either. Why would Malachi kill a stranger and bury the body here, then wait for Ephraim? Taras couldn't think of a single reason.

He stepped out of the hole and took in the surrounding area, looking for a clue. Any clue. "Did you search the body?"

Gordian hesitated a moment before answering, "No, Taras. Why would we?"

Taras snorted. *Why, indeed?* Though normally quite intelligent, there were times when Gordian could be a bit dense. He knelt down and searched through the corpse's pockets, but found nothing. He checked the dirt around the body and that's when he noticed a small bit of what looked like parchment sticking up from the dirt by the dead man's foot. "What is this?"

Taras pulled out a rolled piece of parchment. Two small pieces of red wax fell from the roll as he raised it to his eyes. Probably the seal. Ignoring the shocked look Gordian gave him, Taras unrolled it and began to read.

Malachi,

I write in haste because time demands it. The Council of Thirteen, those I told you about, have sent one of my own to destroy me. In case I am unable to escape I wanted you to know, so you do not waste any time searching for me.

You must warn him, Malachi. I spoke of him to the Council, thinking I could sway them. While I did not tell them his name, they may still try to find him. Above all, he must be kept safe. I know you can do this.

I must pack. I pray to see you again, but if not, please remember this letter and inform Jesus of what has befallen me.

Ephraim

There it was, proof that Ephraim and Malachi were involved with Jesus, and that Ephraim had lied about wanting to leave the Nazarene's followers. *I knew we shouldn't have trusted you, Ephraim.* Taras couldn't wait to see the treacherous bastard again. He would die a horrible death, as befitted a traitor to Rome.

As damning as the letter was, it still didn't explain why Ephraim killed Malachi, or tell Taras who the other body belonged to. Perhaps it was someone sent to kill them both. There was no way to know for sure. And what of this Council of Thirteen? Who in the blazes were they? And what interest did they have in Jesus? There were too many questions.

He looked up from the letter and saw Gordian staring at him wide eyed, the shovel clutched in his hands.

"It's just a letter, Gordian."

"Of course. What… what does it say?"

Taras handed it to him. "Here, read it yourself." Then he bent down and resumed his examination of the body.

After a few more minutes' digging failed to turn up anything else of interest, he was about to step out of the hole and tell Gordian good night when he noticed something shiny on one of the headless body's fingers. *A ring?* He cursed himself for not even looking at the man's hands, an oversight if ever there was one. It just showed how exhausted he was.

He knelt in the dirt, thinking that after he took the ring off the man's finger he was going to follow Marcus's order and get some sleep. Gordian could see to the disposal of Malachi's body. He slipped the ring off and examined it. It wasn't much, just a simple steel ring, but there was a single filigreed letter *E* engraved into the top. The design looked familiar.

"Wait, I know this symbol..." He scrambled around in the dirt, looking for the broken pieces of the wax seal from Ephraim's letter. When he found them, he put them back together, and there in the wax was a stylized *E*. Taras compared it to the ring in his hand. A perfect match. The ring even showed a few red wax flecks in the grooves of the *E*. It had obviously been used to seal the letter.

But that didn't make sense. If this was the ring used to seal Ephraim's letter to Malachi, then how did this person get it? Did he steal it? Or something else? What if...

"Ephraim," Taras breathed. "By the gods, *this* is Ephraim! But then who did I follow to the house by the Damascus Gate?"

The answer was simple: a killer. Probably the same man who'd killed Didius, Claudius, Malachi, and apparently Ephraim, as well.

He had to tell Marcus right away. This time the guards at his door would let him in even if he had to force them to do it. He started to rise but a blinding flash of pain on the back of his head knocked him back into the hole. He fell face-first to the ground and lay next to the real Ephraim's body.

"Very good, Taras." Gordian's voice, but it sounded hollow, like it came to him through a pipe. "You weren't supposed to figure that part out. That damned ring! I should have thought to remove it."

Taras lifted his head, trying to get a better look. He put his hands under him and was surprised to feel not dirt, but a soft, rubbery substance. Some of the soil fell away as his scrabbling fingers disturbed it, revealing the pale, waxen face of Archarius, the undertaker.

Another blinding flash of pain exploded on the back of his head, and Taras's world went dark.

CHAPTER SIXTEEN

A thousand miles away from Jerusalem, in a chamber buried deep within the earth and secured by centuries of secrecy, Algor, Fifth of the Council of Thirteen, held a private meeting with his fellow councilors Lannis and Mattawe. As the rest of the world slept, the trio discussed their plans for the Nazarene.

"Jesus will be arrested in the morning," Algor said.

"That is not what Theron was sent to do," Lannis pointed out.

"True, but it will suffice."

"But Algor," Mattawe said, "You instructed him to make it seem as though the zealots killed Jesus."

"That I did. An error on my part, actually. I hadn't realized he wouldn't be able to approach the Nazarene. My own fault, I should have known Jesus's faith would protect him. But with his pending arrest, it does not matter. The Sanhedrin will demand he be crucified for blasphemy, and faith will not protect him from them. He will die soon enough, and the Romans will still connect him to the zealots."

"But will that be enough to enrage Rome to the point of forcing the pantheon on the people of Israel?" Lannis asked. "That was your objective, if I recall."

"No need for such disrespect, Lannis. Even if the death of Jesus in this manner does not force the emperor's hand, we have other things to gain from it."

"What are you thinking, Algor?" Mattawe asked.

"We cannot pin a crucifixion carried out by the Romans on the zealots, it is true. But Jesus's death will still serve us. Look how many have fallen under his sway with his talk of the one true God. If nothing else, his death in such a brutal fashion can only diminish the number of people who believe in him. In addition, many in Rome, including Caesar, already believe he is linked to the zealots. If the people of Jerusalem can be made to believe the same – and I've no reason to doubt they can – so much the better. Jesus's influence in Israel will die soon after he does."

"But what about Theron?" Lannis asked.

"What about him?" Mattawe asked. "He's just the Enforcer."

"He's been sloppy. Look at what he did this evening. He led that northern legionary right to our door. The man tried to break in. He even saw a Lost One. He was all but running to tell the centurion where to find us."

"The legionary has been taken care of," Algor said. "He will not be able to tell anyone about Theron's lapse."

"Is he dead, then?" Lannis asked.

"Yes," Algor said.

"Are you certain?" Mattawe asked.

"Very. I received word from my agent only a few minutes ago. Taras, who by the way is no ordinary soldier, has been dealt with. He is no longer a concern."

"But what about Theron?" Lannis asked, sticking to her point. "Don't forget, he is the one who led Taras to our house in Jerusa-lem."

"Yes." Mattawe added. "New at his position or not, he has made too many mistakes. I can't fault him for not being able to kill Jesus himself, but he has given far too much away and endangered us all with his reckless confidence. He will need to be punished."

"He will," Algor assured them. "After Jesus is crucified, we will turn Theron into a Lost One."

In a similar chamber a great deal closer to the city, Taras, very much alive, was having a difficult time deciding if he was glad of that fact or not. Strapped to the rack, his muscles burning and his joints on fire, he almost wished he wasn't.

The room around him was lit by a handful of flickering torches, as well as an open furnace on one wall that cast an evil red glow around the chamber. Embedded in the coals of the furnace were a number of steel brands. Their tips glowed red hot and they looked eager to taste flesh. Taras studied the various instruments of pain scattered around the room and moaned, knowing sooner or later he'd probably experience most of them.

A tall, obese soldier chuckled from underneath a black hood as he pulled the rack's tension lever. A flab of fat under his arm jiggled with the movement. He was dressed in a sleeveless leather vest and loose breeches, but no armor, and he carried no sword that Taras could see. Taras only knew the man to be a legionary by the bright red cloak he wore, so out of place among his other accoutrements. Because of his size and the heat in the chamber, the rotund fellow's skin glistened with sweat despite his sparse attire.

"Scream, Taras," the man said, his voice like gravel in a flower pot. "If you scream I'll ease the tension, just a little."

Taras clamped his jaws shut, determined not to give him the satisfaction, but even he knew it was only a matter of time. Sooner or later he would not be able to hold back any longer. Then the screams would come in force. But he would endure the pain as long as he could before giving in. Besides, he doubted the bastard would keep his word and ease the pull, anyway. He shook his head.

The soldier laughed. "Do you know where you are, legionary?"

Taras remained silent.

"You are underneath thirty feet of solid earth, about five miles east of the Damascus Gate. Do you know what that means? When you do finally scream – and you will, do not doubt it – no one will hear you. Except for me, of course."

Wonderful. Taras still didn't speak, but his heart sank. He hadn't had much hope of rescue, but if the man spoke the truth, Taras was done for. Worse, if his torturer could indeed act without fear of Taras's screams attracting notice, his death was likely to be very long and unpleasant.

"What do you want?" Taras asked, hoping to stall him.

"What do I want? I thought I told you; I want a scream. Are you going to give me one, now?"

Taras shook his head again.

"Good," His captor said, and even though Taras couldn't see the man's face he had a feeling there was a broad smile underneath the mask. "It's much more satisfying if I have to work for it. Motivation is important, wouldn't you agree? Of course you would. Now, let's see if I can't change your mind."

He gave the lever a sharp jerk. Taras's joints, already stretched to the point they felt like they would tear in two, pulled apart a little further. His muscles screamed at being thus treated, but he could not hear them over the rush of blood to his ears. Taras, ever the soldier, held his scream back as long as he could. But eventually he could take it no longer.

He couldn't help himself. He gave the man what he wanted.

‡‡‡

Gordian finished reburying the bodies of Ephraim, Malachi, and Archarius. It was difficult to get them out of the city without being recognized. He'd had to load them onto a wagon and drive through town as quietly as a stubborn burro could be made to travel, all the while dressed in the coarse garb of a Jewish peasant. The guards at the gate hadn't recognized him, or they might have wondered what the Centurion's Second was doing dressed so poorly and driving a cart in the middle of the night. They hadn't detained him long once he handed them a few silver pieces each. After that the way became much easier, at least until he got far enough away from the wall and had to stop and dig again. He hadn't wanted to bury the bodies at all. He'd much rather leave them for the desert fauna, especially Ephraim's, which would burn away in the sunlight anyway, but his brother's instructions had been explicit.

The bodies must never be found, Gordian. The Council of Thirteen does not forgive mistakes. Gordian had nodded, the thought of Theron's upcoming punishment fresh in his mind. A Lost One. Just the thought made Gordian shudder. Far better to be dead than to be turned into one of those things. Gordian, battle-hardened as he was, could almost feel sorry for Theron.

But Theron had failed to maintain the secrecy of the vampire race. He'd led Taras right to their front door. He might as well have invited the legionary in to have a look around. Not Gordian, though. He would not fail. No one would ever find the bodies of Malachi, Ephraim, Archarius, or Taras. They would disappear forever into memory, and he, Gordian, would reap the rewards of his brother's people.

As he tamped down the last of the soil over the bodies, the shuffle of boots in the dirt behind him caught his ear. Fearing he'd been discovered, he whirled around, holding his shovel – which still bore a few drops of Taras's blood – in front of him. He was somewhat relieved to see his twin brother behind him, watching as he finished his work. "It's you," he said. "You scared me, brother."

"My apologies, Gordian," The newcomer replied, "I just wanted to see how everything was coming along."

Gordian lowered the shovel to the ground and walked up to his brother. "All is going well. Taras is in the Hole, tied to the rack and very likely screaming like mad at this very moment."

His brother frowned. "He's in the Hole? Why? He was supposed to report to Marcus that he'd discovered Jesus was indeed involved in Didius's murder, as we planned."

"Taras discovered the truth. He saw Ephraim's ring and figured it out. I was forced to improvise. I hit him with a shovel and snuck him out of the city."

"You couldn't think of anything better than hitting him with a shovel? Something that wouldn't jeopardize my plan, perhaps?"

"I panicked," Gordian admitted.

"All right, but why did you put him in the Hole? Why didn't you just kill him? We can't afford any careless mistakes, Gordian."

"I owed Octavius a favor, so I left Taras in his care. Don't worry, brother. I assure you, Octavius is skilled at his work. Taras will be dead by morning. As for his report, I can deliver the news to Marcus myself; we don't need Taras for that. "

His brother nodded. "Go on."

"The bodies that would have proven Theron lied to Marcus are buried, so no one will ever find them, which will ensure Theron's punishment remains a Council matter. Marcus will march with the Sanhedrin in the morning to arrest Jesus of Nazareth. He will most certainly be crucified, and the Council's worries of his influence will be as dust."

"You forgot one thing."

"What's that?"

"Passover is coming. Tradition demands Pontius Pilate pardon one condemned prisoner. What happens if he chooses Jesus?"

"He won't. I overheard some men in the street talking about that very thing on my way to the gate. A few of the city's inhabitants, those sympathetic to the zealots, have been calling for the prisoner Barabbas to be released. We will use that to our advantage. Also, there are rumors of Jesus's involvement in the zealot movement, and he has been implicated in a plot to overthrow Rome."

"Implicated by whom?"

"By some of my own men." Gordian had to keep his face neutral, lest his twin discover the lie. He would not tell his brother it was Theron who'd actually planted that idea into the Centurion's head. Let him think Gordian was clever for a change. "Marcus is convinced the Nazarene is attempting to overthrow Rome, and Pilate will never release him under such strong suspicion from his favorite centurion. Rest assured, Jesus will walk to Golgotha with a cross strapped to his back."

"Very good," his brother said, nodding.

"Don't forget," Gordian said, "You promised to share your gift with me when this is over."

"I won't forget," his twin replied. "You just make sure you do your part. Jesus must die. No excuses. That fool Theron can't seem to do it without letting the entire city know about us, but once my plan is complete the Council of Thirteen will see who truly deserves their confidence."

The tone of his voice raised the hairs on Gordian's arms. His twin brother had been a vampire for eleven years, and Gordian still hadn't gotten used to the way he behaved. Sometimes he was the same brother the legionary had always known. Other times – like tonight, for example – he was someone else. Someone dark, and evil. He shuddered to think what malicious course his twin's mind traveled.

Still, he couldn't pass up the promise of immortality. When his brother had offered to share his gift and make Gordian a vampire, too, he had accepted gladly. It would be like old times. They would do things together, and have long conversations, and maybe they would both be awarded positions within the Halls for their efforts in Israel. It all seemed so wonderful.

But at times like these, looking at his brother's half mad, twisted visage, Gordian had to wonder if he would become the same dark, hateful creature his brother had turned into. He thought, and not for the first time, that perhaps he'd made the wrong decision.

Much too late, now. There would be no backing out of the deal at this point; he'd already seen and done too much. The Council could never let him live, not with everything he knew. Gordian looked up into the sky and his eyes found the moon. *I'd better get to know her,* he thought. *The moon and I will be seeing a lot of each other.*

"I have to go," his brother said. "Dawn is only a few hours away, and I will be needed in the Halls. You should go as well, brother. You will need to be ready for when Marcus marches to the Gardens of Gethsemane in the morning. I would suggest you go home and get as much sleep as you can."

With that, the vampire disappeared into the night. Gordian watched him go, then climbed back into the wagon and urged the stubborn burro forward. Marcus would rise with the sun, as always, and would be ready to march less than an hour later. And although Gordian doubted the Sanhedrin could be roused so early, he knew Marcus would expect him to be awake and ready at the same time as him. That meant Gordian had about three hours before he had to wake up. It wasn't much, but it would have to do.

As he recalled the look in his brother's eyes and the sound of his voice when he'd talked about Theron, Gordian doubted he would be able to sleep, anyway. Fortunately, the events of the day to come would be unnerving and exciting enough so that he should be able to stave off exhaustion until after his brother had kept his promise, and by then it wouldn't matter anymore.

Gordian would be a vampire, too.

CHAPTER SEVENTEEN

Marcus stood, fuming, at the door to the barracks. He'd been awake for over an hour and had been ready to move for half that. Taras was late, and that wasn't like him. *Where is he?* Normally, Marcus was a very patient man, but this morning he had an appointment with the Sanhedrin he didn't want to miss. They would go to the Gardens of Gethsemane and arrest the man responsible for Didius's murder, and the attempted murder of another man, Ephraim.

If he was telling the truth. It wasn't the first time Marcus heard the thought echo inside his head. Ever since he'd gone to bed the night before he couldn't help but wonder if he'd been right to let the man go, even though he sent Taras to follow him. Now that Taras could not be found, Marcus heard that same thought buzzing around inside his head over and over again in a steady, annoying cadence. The doubt gnawed at his nerves.

But the body was right where he said it would be. If he was lying about his reason for killing Malachi, why would he show us the body? It doesn't make sense.

"None of this makes sense," he said aloud.

"Pardon, Centurion?"

Marcus whirled around, startled, and was considerably relieved to see his Second. Gordian had long ago stopped commenting on Marcus's habit of talking to himself. "It's nothing, Gordian. I am only thinking out loud. Has Barrius returned?"

"Yes, sir. Only moments ago, in fact."

"And?"

"He found no sign of Taras, either. It is as if the man simply left Jerusalem and never looked back."

"Damn the delay. He's probably off somewhere asleep." Marcus didn't believe that. He'd known Taras a long time, and the man was as solid and dependable as they come. He wouldn't miss an event this important, at least not voluntarily. Something had gone wrong.

"Why don't we go without him, Centurion?"

"I would, Gordian. But Taras is the only person I trust who has actually seen the Nazarene. I don't want to get to the Gardens and arrest the wrong man just because half the people in attendance claim to be Jesus themselves in an attempt to protect him."

"But surely *some*one else can identify him."

"No."

"But, Centurion—"

Marcus's patience, stretched thin already, wore out. His hand seemed to shoot out of its own accord. He grabbed his Second by the throat and shoved him against the wall, drawing stares from several passers-by as well as the handful of legionaries who stood with the Centurion. He paid them no heed, focusing all his attention on his Second.

"Let me be perfectly clear on this, Gordian," Marcus growled, "We are not leaving without Taras. That is final."

"Yes, Centurion," Gordian replied, his eyes wide with shock and a trace of fear.

Marcus held him a moment longer, wanting to leave no further doubt about his position, then released his grip.

"Good," he said. "Now, go and see if Jacobo found anything. He should be back by now."

"Yes, sir," Gordian saluted, then went to find Jacobo. Marcus watched him go. Something was definitely not right. Gordian had never pressed Marcus's authority in such a bold and blatant manner before, and certainly not in front of the men. Every soldier under Marcus's command knew he didn't tolerate any questioning of his orders. The Gods knew Gordian should have been more aware of that fact than most, having been a frequent witness to the punishment meted out for such violations.

He hadn't told Gordian the whole reason he waited, of course. Gordian only needed to know so much. Marcus was beginning to think he'd acted rashly when he wrote to the Sanhedrin. A nagging voice in the back of his mind insisted he'd been misled, and it hadn't left him alone all morning. Now he started to wonder if Jesus could really be part of all this. It was certainly possible Ephraim had lied to him, although Marcus interrogated the man personally. He hadn't appeared to be lying, but...

...But where is Taras?

Marcus reached into a pouch and pulled out a roll of parchment, which bore his personal seal and had Taras's name written on the outside. He'd written it up last night and planned to present it to his friend this morning before they went on to the Gardens. He stared at it for a long moment, then replaced it in the leather pouch at his belt, wondering again where Taras could be.

He shook his head in frustration and went back into the barracks. He'd skipped breakfast in hopes of getting an early start, and now his stomach informed him that it didn't appreciate being left out of the day's preparations. *I'll get something to eat,* he thought. *With luck Taras will have returned by the time I finish.*

Marcus headed for the kitchens muttering under his breath. "Taras better have a good reason for this."

† † †

Had he been able, Taras would have told the Centurion he had a very good reason for being late. As it was, however, he was having difficulty enough just staying alive. His torturer had worked him on the rack for hours, bringing him to the brink of unconsciousness, then letting up only long enough for Taras to regain his senses, at which point the rotund legionary would start anew. By the time the knock came to the chamber, Taras felt like every joint in his body was on fire. He tried to open his eyes to see who had come, but his vision blurred from a combination of pain and exhaustion.

"What do you want?" his torturer asked. "I'm busy."

"There's been a change of plan." The voice sounded familiar, but Taras couldn't quite place it. He strained to listen, hoping it might help him escape.

"What do you mean?"

"He's become too dangerous. You can't toy with him any longer. He must die, and soon."

"But why, Jesus?"

Jesus! That must be why the voice sounded so familiar. He'd heard Jesus speak in the Gardens. So the Nazarene was part of this, after all.

"Because he knows too much. We can't risk him escaping somehow. The centurion is starting to have second thoughts, thanks to a few words from some of our friends in the Legion. The word now is he might not come to arrest me, after all. We must keep building on that doubt in order to keep the Sanhedrin at bay for as long as we possibly can. Your prisoner knows all about the traitor Ephraim's death. He knows about Malachi and Archarius, and he knows about the demon near the Damascus Gate. If he escapes and finds his way back to Marcus, the centurion will find out about us for certain. If that happens we are finished. I don't want Rome to know what is going on in Israel until it is too late for her to fight back."

"As you command, Jesus," came the reply, then Taras heard the door close.

Friends in the Legion? Dear gods! How deep did this go? Taras needed to get word to Marcus, somehow. *Gordian is involved, too.* He nearly wept as he realized that knowing the truth and being able to do something about it were two entirely different things. The harsh reality was that Taras remained securely tied to the rack, and had no hope of escaping his dingy little cell to warn the centurion of Gordian's treachery. In fact, he would probably never leave this room alive.

The shuffling sound of the fat soldier's feet as he walked back across the room bolstered that assessment. "You heard the Nazarene, Taras," the man chuckled, and Taras heard him walk around the machine toward the lever. "How would you like to die? The sword? An axe? Beheading? You should be grateful. I have been ordered to make it quick."

Even weak, Taras had strength enough to tell him what he could do with his gratitude.

"Not terribly complimentary, Taras," the man said after he'd stopped laughing. "Still, I guess I can't blame you. We should take advantage of the straps while we have them. They will ensure you don't flinch and make your death longer than necessary. I'd better check them."

He walked around the table, making a show of checking Taras's bonds. On one of them, he stopped. "What's this? Looks like this one is loose. Let me fix that."

He bent over Taras's arm and made a slight adjustment. It didn't matter; Taras couldn't feel anything in either arm, anyway. "There. That should hold you. Now then, I hate to kill on an empty stomach. I think I'll go get something to eat. You should take a moment to commune with your gods before I send you to meet them. Would you like me to bring you something?"

"Your black heart on a plate, perhaps?" Taras replied, though just speaking the words hurt his chest.

"Such venom, Taras. Not very civil. Well, I suppose I can't blame you, given the circumstances. I'm off. Don't wander off."

With that, the fat man left. Taras heard the clank as the cell door shut and listened to his echoing laughter as it faded down the hall.

He fought the instinct to try and pull his arms free. He'd already strained against his bonds while the rack stretched his limbs, and all he'd managed to do was rub his wrists raw and bloody. The thirsty leather straps soaked up his blood and sweat and only grew tighter. Finally, they'd gotten so tight they cut off his circulation, and now Taras couldn't feel his hands at all; he only knew they were still attached because he could see them.

Gordian the traitor had blindsided him with a shovel and put him here, may the gods damn the bastard's black soul. The fat man's, as well. Both of them. But most of all, Taras hoped the gods felt his anger and passed some of it along to the Nazarene. Gordian may have put Taras in the stocks, but it was Jesus who'd started this mess. Gods take them all. Traitors, every one of them. In his mounting rage, he shook violently, and soon he thrashed in fury like a fish on land. His wrists burned and started to bleed again.

His energy lasted only a few seconds before his flagging strength ebbed away altogether, and he lay back down on the rack while the fingers of his right hand tingled. He promised himself he would see his killers again in the netherworld. When that time came, he would make them pay.

"May the gods damn you all," he said aloud, and chuckled in spite of the pain. "Now I'm talking to myself, like Marcus."

He closed his eyes and wept softly. Not for himself, death was a danger all legionaries faced, but for his friend. Once Jesus had his rebellion, he would have no use for the centurion. Doubtless he would have Gordian kill Marcus in his sleep. It made sense. Gordian was the only one besides Taras and the centurion himself who had complete access to Marcus's chambers.

Then he thought of Mary, with her dark, curly hair and olive skin. He could almost smell her hair. She would be wondering where he'd gone. Worse, once the zealots succeeded in killing Marcus there would be no one left who could tell her the truth of his demise. Would she believe he had left her?

Tears flowed freely from his eyes as he imagined the pain she would bear for him. She would never know about his plan to give up his life as a soldier and take her to Rome to be his wife. She would likely marry some man her father chose for her and live out her days thinking Taras had abandoned her.

Taras had never been a praying man, but as he thought about Marcus and Mary, he sent up a prayer to whatever of his gods might be listening. "Please help Marcus," he said. "Help him see the truth of the Nazarene's scheme before it's too late. And please help Mary to—ow!"

The tingling in his fingers had turned into painful spasms. It felt like someone had rammed needles into the ends of his digits. *Gods, that hurts!* He grew angry as he realized he wouldn't even have the satisfaction of praying. The pain in his fingers was too distracting. He couldn't even...

My fingers! He realized. *I can feel my fingers.* He wiggled them experimentally, and although they hurt, he was able to move them. He looked up to his right wrist and discovered the bond was loose. He thought back and remembered the torturer adjusting it just before he left. The fat bastard must not have secured it properly.

Now, at least, he had a chance. He used his fingers to work the catch on the buckle. After several agonizing minutes, it came loose and his right hand swung free. Working as quickly as his stretched and aching joints would allow, he reached over and undid the catch on his left hand, also. Once that was done he attempted to sit up, but his body would have none of it. His lower back protested with a white-hot flash of pain.

Taras fought back a scream and looked for something to use as a bit. Finding nothing he could reach, he bit down on his tongue and tried again. He did his best to ignore the pain in his back, but by the time he'd succeeded in sitting up he could taste blood in his mouth. He spat a wad of crimson to the side of the table and set about freeing his ankles.

With his feet now free he swept his legs slowly over the side of the platform and lowered himself to the floor, standing for a moment on shaky legs. When he could be sure he would not simply fall over he took an unsteady step toward the door, which he noted, was not locked. And why should it be? He'd been strapped to the rack. No one would have thought he could escape.

Taras smiled. The fat man should have paid more attention.

Taras's things lay piled into a corner by the door. His uniform, his shield, his sword and armor gleamed dully in the weak, flickering torchlight, begging him to take them and use them to exact revenge.

Later, he promised them. Right now he couldn't even lift them, let alone fight with them. As much as it galled him to do so, he would have to leave his things behind. At least he still had his tunic and sandals.

Taras walked to the door as fast as his abused joints and muscles would allow. He pushed it open just enough to poke his head into the hallway, the whole time expecting to hear an angry voice shout for him to stop. When no such command came from the hall, he stepped into it and looked around.

The stone hallway stood empty in both directions. Doors were positioned on either side, which he assumed opened into other chambers similar to the one he'd just left. He heard men whimpering from behind several of them, but he was far too weak to help them. He could barely stand and walk as it was.

How do I get out of here? What was it the fat man said? The chamber is thirty feet down, about five miles from the city. If Taras could find his way to the surface, he should be able to find his way back to the city of Jerusalem with ease. He just had to get up there.

With no better means of making a decision, he picked a random direction and started walking. The shakiness of his steps gradually stabilized as renewed hope lent him strength and purpose.

Behind the door to another cell, Gordian watched Taras leave with a sardonic smile. He clutched a piece of parchment to his chest as the wobbly soldier made his way down the hall. He hated to let Taras go, but Marcus had made it quite clear that he would not move to arrest Jesus without him. Of course, now that Taras knew all about Gordian's involvement, letting him go meant Gordian could no longer show his face in Jerusalem, but once Jesus was dead, his brother would make good on his deal to turn him into a vampire. When that happened his standing in Jerusalem would no longer matter. Then he, Gordian, the former Second to the centurion, would kill Taras and Marcus both. Who would stop him from coming and going as he pleased, then? No one. Not even Pilate would be able to hurt him once his brother fulfilled his promise. Best of all, he would be able to spend time with his twin again.

Go, Taras, he willed the departing legionary's back. *Find Marcus and repeat everything you heard.* He looked down at the piece of parchment in his hand and smiled. Gordian dropped it and watched it flutter to the ground in a clumsy spiral. Then, when his former prisoner had gone far enough that he was certain he would not be overheard, he stepped out into the hallway and followed Taras. He needed to make sure the injured legionary left the dungeons alive; his revised plan depended on it. As he passed through the halls, Gordian went over his new plan in his mind, turning it over and examining it from all angles, checking for any weaknesses. His smile broadened. He could not find a flaw.

‡ ‡ ‡

In the now empty cell, the piece of paper lay face up on the floor. If anyone had been in the room, they would have been able to read the large words scrawled across it: *Octavius,* the paper read, *Call me Jesus, and do the opposite of what I tell you.*

CHAPTER EIGHTEEN

Taras followed the tunnel through a seemingly endless series of chambers before finally coming to a stairway. Remembering what the fat man said about his cell being thirty feet down, he climbed the stairs, gritting his teeth with each step, and was relieved to see a small room at the top. A door stood closed in the far wall of the room, outlined by bright light. Taras hoped it meant the door led outside; the light seemed bright enough. But in his pain-fogged state, it could just as easily be another torchlit chamber like the one he'd just escaped. Still, he didn't have much choice. He could either go forward into the unknown, or backward to the fat man's waiting hands. He limped over and pushed the door open.

Taras stumbled out into the bright midday sun. He shielded his eyes with his left hand and steadied himself against the door with his right while his vision adjusted to the sudden wall of painful sunlight. After a while his eyes stopped burning and he could see. He lowered his hand and took a look around.

Scrubland surrounded him in every direction. Small bushes crawled over low, rolling hills, while fields of patchy, tough grass waved in the soft breeze. Acacia trees dotted the landscape, their sinister outlines guarding the entrance to the dark passages he'd just left behind. A handful of wild olive trees could be seen, as well, their blossoms just beginning to flower in the spring air. Here and there, patches of pale green brush poked up from the rocky ground, battling the grass for sunlight and moisture. On the horizon, tall gray mountains pointed accusingly into the sky as though they, too, longed for escape. Standing in the open air, sweet and untainted by sweat or blood, Taras felt his heart race. He was free.

He took a few steps away from the door and almost fell, but caught himself on the trunk of a nearby acacia. A low hanging branch poked its thorns into his arm, but he didn't notice. He squinted and looked toward the horizon, but he could not see the walls of the city. He recalled the fat man saying they were about five miles east of Jerusalem.

Taras shoved his body off the acacia with a grunt of pain and put the gray mountains at his back. Facing west, he scanned the horizon, but he could not see the city. Taras looked to the sky, trying to gauge the time of day by the position of the sun, then he set off, hoping he would live long enough to make his way to the Damascus Gate. If he had his bearings correct, the road to the city must be nearby, but he thought better of searching for it. Gordian – and probably Jesus – would be looking for him soon enough. No sense making it easier for them by being out in the open. Let them track him through the brush.

He did all right for a while, but a long night of hunger, thirst, and pain soon overwhelmed him. Before Taras had walked more than two miles he fell face first in the dirt. He picked himself up and staggered a few more steps toward his goal before falling a second time. A small cloud of dust rose up to choke him, and he coughed, sending spasms of pain through his ruined body. Three miles to go. He would never make it. He raised his head and squinted toward the horizon. There, barely visible over the low hills and scattered trees, was the Damascus Gate. He'd found it, but was too weak to reach it.

Taras lay panting on the ground, eyeing the stone walls of the city through the sparse patches of grass and brush. The city was so close. A trivial stroll on a normal day, but far beyond his reach in his present state. He tried to yell for help, but his dry throat could only manufacture a hoarse croak. His muscles and joints felt like they were on fire, and it was only a matter of time before Gordian or another of Jesus's cronies found him.

"Help…me," he rasped. His voice was not even loud enough to scare a field mouse that hopped into view beside him. Gods, he needed a drink! "Help…"

It was no use. He was too far away from the wall; no one would hear him. Taras laid his head in the earth and waited for death, certain it would be along shortly.

"Sorry, Marcus," he whispered.

╬ ╬ ╬

Epidius was a new recruit, a mere three months into his time of service, but eager to do his part to serve his country. Unfortunately for men new to the Roman Legion, doing one's part often meant running errands for older soldiers who'd been there far longer. This happened most often when the task in question included something unpleasant such as night duty, or helping in the kitchens, or even standing outside in the sun for hours on end, as it did today. Earlier that morning, an older soldier handed him a bag of coins and gave him the name and description of a man, then ordered him to meet the man on a trail outside the city. Gavros, the soldier who passed the job to him, was a large, muscular brute of a Roman. The smaller and woefully outranked Epidius hadn't had much choice.

Now he muttered curses as he stood in the midday heat several miles outside the city. His instructions were to wait for the man on a small path well off the main road. He recalled Gavros' words: *Take this bag and leave the city through the Damascus Gate. A mile outside the city, look for a path that branches off to the left. Follow it to a clump of bushes next to a big rock with a drawing of an asp on it and wait there for a mousy little man, smaller than you, with dark curly hair and brown eyes. He will be dressed in simple traveler's clothes, and he will be looking for you.*

Then the bastard pushed Epidius out of the room. The raucous laughter of every soldier in the room followed him as he was shoved through the door like a rejected suitor. His face flushed, but there was nothing he could do about it; Gavros outranked him by several tiers. So he consoled himself my mumbling obscenities about the man who'd sent him outside. *Confounded, mule headed son of a whore. How am I supposed to know who I am looking for?*

What Gavros failed to mention was the description he'd given could have fit any of a hundred thousand travelers in Israel. Dark curly hair and brown eyes? To Epidius, the Jews all looked alike. How was he supposed to know one from another? *I'll probably be out here all day waiting. And for what? To give away a pittance!*

Epidius had looked inside the bag shortly after having the job thrust on him. It contained silver. While he didn't make a physical count, he estimated the amount at somewhere between twenty five and thirty five pieces. Not a life altering sum, to be sure, but enough for a few glasses of ale and an interesting night in certain sections of the New City. He'd much rather pocket the silver and tell the Jew to go to the Abyss, or wherever it was they believed they went when they died. Epidius could never remember the silly customs of these people.

Only one god. Ha! As if a single god could have created the world or would have the time to run it. Blasphemy! Everyone knew Jupiter reigned in the heavens with his consort and a host of lesser deities. Scores of them watched over the world of Men, guiding or destroying them as whim demanded. Together, the Gods had forged the earth and brought the seasons to the world so Man could live there. The idea that only one god sat in attendance over the universe seemed ludicrous. How would anything get done with only one supreme being to do it all? *Crazy Jews!*

Still, as much as Epidius would like to take the money and leave, he knew enough of what the military did to thieves to not even dream of taking a single piece of silver from the bag. Odds were good he'd not live long enough to spend it. Or if he did, he would wish for death long before he received it. No, better to just find the man, give him his silver, and be done with it.

He sighed and stared out into the field. He'd found the path and the rock with the asp painted on its side with no trouble, and now he had nothing to do but wait. He sat on the rock, partially shaded from the midday sun by an acacia tree, and settled in for the duration. He hoped the fellow would be along soon.

He kicked at a loose rock and swore under his breath, wishing he were stationed in Carthage, or perhaps Caesarea, instead of this gods-forsaken place. Judea was, without doubt, the lowest point of the Roman Empire. The absolute worst of the provinces. Jerusalem. Pah! He would rather be in Athens than here.

After a time he grew bored, and decided to count the silver, after all. Thirty pieces. All Roman mint. Tiberius's profile stared off to the right as though lost in thought. Epidius thought he looked very wise on the coin, even if he didn't deserve to be Caesar. But then, what was the opinion of a lowly legionary worth? Much less than the silver in his hand, to be sure. He spat at the ground, cursing the Jews, Gavros, Tiberius, and just about anything else he could think of to blame for his being stuck out in the wilting sun waiting on some man he didn't even want to see. What was his name again? Jadas? Jipsus? Something like that. *How should I know? I should just give this money to the first Jew I see. Then I could—*

Epidius stopped short as he heard a noise from somewhere to his right. It sounded like a crow. He peered through the brush and, sure enough, he saw a couple of the black feathered birds bouncing around something in the dirt. Probably a dead animal. He stood and headed toward them, thinking to at least relieve his boredom for a short while by finding out what kind of animal it was. When he saw one of the birds come away with a shiny bauble, he realized the carcass was probably human. The thought made his heart beat faster.

It was probably just some drunkard who wandered too far from the walls and ended up prey for roving bandits. But a dead body out here in the scrubland, far away from the city walls, would certainly give him a good excuse to abandon his wait and go back to town. Not even the centurion would discipline him for breaking orders in such an instance.

The birds took flight as he approached, and Epidius got a good look at the body. He realized with a shock he'd been mistaken. *That's no Jew!* Epidius had only been in Jerusalem a short time, but he'd seen the man before. He recognized the large, muscular frame, blond hair, and northern features of a soldier from his own barracks.

"Taras!" he yelled, his boredom forgotten. "Taras, can you hear me?" He knelt in the dirt next to the body and put his hand in front of the fallen man's mouth, checking for breath. It was there, but very faint. *He's alive!*

Epidius stood and examined Taras as best he could. The crows had gotten a few bites on him. Here and there were pocks of broken flesh, oozing lazy crimson in the noonday sun. But the carrion birds hadn't been at him long enough to do serious damage.

He knelt back down, grasping the unconscious legionary's chin in one hand and reaching for his waterskin with the other. He thumbed the top off the skin and held Taras's face up to the lip. "Drink this."

At first, the precious liquid dribbled from the dry, cracked lips to pool in the dirt. Epidius pinched Taras's nostrils closed and tried again. After perhaps thirty seconds, Taras sputtered and gulped in air. Epidius let go the man's nose and poured water into his mouth. This time the fallen legionary drank greedily, gulping as much of the fluid as Epidius would allow, which wasn't much.

"Slow down, you'll get a cramp." He looked around and saw there was still no sign of the Jew he was supposed to meet. Then he looked back at Taras, who still hadn't opened his eyes. *To the Abyss with Gravos and his silver.* "I have to get you back to the barracks," he said.

Taras mumbled something, but Epidius couldn't make it out. He leaned in, placing his ear right next to Taras's mouth. "What, Taras? What did you say?"

"Marcus…" Taras whispered. "Must tell Marcus… Jesus." He broke off in a fit of coughing.

"Easy, Taras," Epidius said. "Save your breath. I'll get you to Marcus." He reached for Taras's wrist, realizing for the first time how raw and stripped the skin appeared. Epidius had been around the military long enough to know what that meant; someone bound him. Someone had bound a Roman soldier's hands. Probably left him out here to die, too. Zealots, most likely. Damn those bastards. Why couldn't they just accept the fact that Israel was part of the Roman Empire now? He grasped Taras's forearm, careful not to rub the injured wrists, and hauled the body over his shoulders so the top half hung over Epidius's right shoulder, and the bottom half over his left. He secured his burden by putting both arms behind him and over Taras's back.

"Oof! You're heavy." He looked in the direction of the Damascus Gate, partially obscured from view by low hills and scattered trees. He wasn't sure if he could make it, but he intended to try.

He hadn't gone fifty yards when he realized that, unless the guards at the gate saw him and came to his aid, he would not be able to carry his fallen comrade the entire way. He stumbled more than once, and each time he did Taras groaned. He hoped he could at least get close enough to attract some assistance, but first he needed to get off this path and out onto the main road. *Just a short walk*, he thought. *I can do this.*

He took a deep breath and forced his feet into motion, one in front of the other. He didn't stop to catch his breath, and he didn't slow his pace. If Taras was to have any chance at all, Epidius needed to get to the infirmary as soon as possible. He half-walked, half-jogged through the scraggly brush for what seemed like an hour, but finally emerged onto the road with his burden. He started walking toward the city, now only a mile distant, but was stopped by a voice from behind, coming from the direction of the path.

"Do you need some help?" The voice asked.

He turned to see a gangly man with olive skin and short, curly black hair standing about twenty feet behind him. He'd been making so much noise carrying Taras he hadn't heard the stranger approach. The man's thick accent, as well as his features, clearly marked him as a Jew. *Probably one of the ones who did this to Taras. Well, you aren't going to finish the job while I am around.* "No, I don't," He said curtly. "Leave us."

"But I just thought you might… you looked like you were having trouble. Is… is he dead?"

The man's face twisted in anguish, and he wrung his hands nervously at his waist. He looked guilty. Guilty and sad, as though he'd just done something terribly wrong and the gravity of it was just starting to catch up to him. Epidius wanted no help from such a man. The fool was fortunate Epidius hadn't arrested him yet. He could do it, too. He wouldn't even need a reason; he could make up a charge and no one would question it, not with all the recent zealot activity in the city. Luckily for the newcomer, Epidius had bigger problems.

"I said be gone, Jew. I don't need help from the likes of you."

The man's face reddened, and for a moment Epidius thought he was going to offer a stinging retort, but he didn't. Instead he dropped his gaze to his shoes.

"Very well," he said sadly, "I guess no one needs my help. I'm just useless. That's me. Useless Judas." He turned to walk away.

Judas? Why does that name sound familiar? Epidius searched his memory for a moment, and then it hit him. *Judas,* he thought. *The silver!*

"Wait," he called. "Judas Iscariot?"

"Yes." Judas turned to face him. "That's me."

"I have something for you." Epidius laid Taras gently back onto the ground, grateful for the respite. He reached into his pocket and pulled out the bag of silver, which he tossed to Judas. "From the Sanhedrin," he said, remembering Gavros' instructions. "You are to come to them after sundown tomorrow."

Judas watched, wide-eyed, as the small bag flew through the air. He made no attempt to catch it as it sailed toward him and landed on the ground by at his feet with a metallic clink, spilling silver pieces in the dirt and on his sandals. Judas's face tightened. He didn't look like a man who'd just been given thirty silver pieces; he looked horrified. He stared at the coins lying on the ground with an expression of fear and loathing. Then, with a sigh, Judas bent over to pick up the money. The tears in the man's eyes surprised the legionary.

Epidius turned to look at the Damascus Gate. One of the guards had noticed him and was running his direction. *Good, I can get some help.* He turned back to Judas, but the man had already walked away. Epidius stared at his back as it grew smaller and smaller. He could swear the man's shoulders bobbed up and down, like a child overcome by sobs. He watched for several minutes until the strange man disappeared around a bend in the road. *Good riddance*, he thought. Now to get Taras to the city, and the sooner the better. He would be glad to get off this road and back behind the gate.

Since setting Taras down and catching his breath, Epidius had the odd sensation he was being watched from the brush. The feeling raised gooseflesh on his arms and made him uneasy. He attributed it to a soldier's sixth sense, an animal instinct that kept men alive in the field. He'd thought it must be because of Judas, but now Judas was gone, and he hadn't made a single move toward Epidius or his fallen comrade. Yet the feeling persisted. He spat on the ground where Judas's footprints lingered, and chalked it up to nerves.

Jews. He shivered, rubbing his hands on his arms to calm his screaming nerve endings. *The gods take them all.* He turned to meet his fellow legionary, who was now only twenty or so feet away. "This is Taras, he's a legionary under Marcus," he said, pointing at the prone soldier. "He's alive, but only just. Help me get him to the infirmary."

The guard said nothing, just grabbed hold of Taras's legs behind the knees, circling his arms around and underneath them. Epidius snaked his arms under Taras's shoulders and hefted him off the ground. Together, the two legionaries carried their fallen comrade back into the city.

⚯⚯⚯

From his hiding place behind a stand of acacia trees, Gordian watched the two soldiers carry Taras away with a mixture of relief and triumph. Until the other soldier arrived, he'd thought he would have to send a message to the guards himself. Octavius had taken too much out of Taras. Or perhaps Taras was not as strong as he thought. Either way, until Epidius had come along, Gordian thought Taras would die before he could speak to Marcus, and that was no good.

No fear of that now. Taras would make it to the infirmary, and Marcus would most certainly visit him there without delay. Gordian smiled. Taras would tell Marcus it was Jesus who'd had him tortured, and then he would also tell him the Nazarene planned an open rebellion against Rome. Those two charges would ensure the centurion's swift departure for the Gardens of Gethsemane and seal the rabbi's fate. Gordian's only worry was Marcus would be so enraged by what he heard that he might execute Jesus on sight, rather than waiting for Pilate to give the order. It was a risk, but not much of one. Marcus had spent his whole life in the military; he knew how to follow orders. Iron discipline would keep his sword in check. And if it didn't, then so what? Jesus would die, anyway. Sooner was just as good as later as far as Gordian was concerned. In fact, sooner would be better for him, because his brother would get what he wanted early, and thus Gordian's new life could start sooner than expected.

He would have to kill Taras, of course. He couldn't let anyone know about the tunnels below the fields. The door was hidden in such a way that, unless you knew it was there, you would never find it. If Taras tried to backtrack, he might be able to remember the door's location. Gordian couldn't have that. His brother would not like his secret halls revealed to the Roman Legion, or anyone else for that matter. He would have to sneak back into the barracks after Marcus left. Marcus would, no doubt, issue an order for his arrest once Taras told his story, so getting into the barracks to kill him and then getting back out again would be tricky, but Gordian thought he could manage it.

He knew of an underground passage into Jerusalem. The zealots would have paid handsomely for such knowledge, but he'd kept it secret just in case he ever needed it. It would lead him under the city wall and right up to the floor of the barracks. Originally designed as an escape route in the early days of Rome's occupation of Israel, it had never been used. Through the years, and over many changes of personnel, its existence had been forgotten. Gordian had learned of it from his brother, but gods knew where his brother had acquired such an intricate knowledge of a complex built long before either of them was born. Probably from someone on the Council.

A seldom used storage room just down the hall from the infirmary hid the tunnel's entrance, and since Taras would no doubt be in the infirmary soon, Gordian felt sure his errand tonight would not take long. He chuckled to himself as he thought of the gift he would receive when he finished. Then he turned from the city and walked the three or so miles back to the door hidden in the dirt from which he and Taras had exited the tunnels.

Once there, he pushed his way through the door and headed down the halls to a chamber lined with fresh straw. He lay down in the soft, warm straw and tried to get some rest, knowing he would need it for the busy night ahead.

CHAPTER NINETEEN

"Centurion!" The shout brought with it the urgent sound of sandaled feet pounding through the hall. "Centurion! Come quick!"

Marcus cringed in his chamber. He knew from past experience the sound of running feet through the barracks accompanied by shouts of 'Centurion! Centurion!' never boded well. It usually meant he had to buckle on his sword and armor in a hurry and deal with some catastrophe or another. Today of all days he didn't need yet another distraction, especially since he was already very late for his meeting with the Sanhedrin. It sounded like he would be later still.

He flung his door open just as a sweaty, out-of-breath legionary raised his fist to pound on it. "What is it?" Marcus asked. "Are the Sanhedrin here?"

"No, Centurion. We found Taras."

Nothing could have made Marcus happier. *At last! Now we can get on with this.* "Excellent. Where is he?" Marcus was already buckling on his sword, ready for the walk to the Gardens of Gethsemane to arrest the man responsible for his brother's death.

"He's in the infirmary, Centurion. He's badly injured."

"The infirmary?" Marcus stopped midstride to turn and look at the messenger. He recognized him as a new recruit serving under

Gavros. His mind scrambled for the man's name. "It's Epidius, isn't it? What do you mean he's injured? How badly? What happened to him?"

"I don't know, sir. He was unconscious when I found him outside the city, and he hasn't said much since. He keeps repeating your name, as well as that of some rabbi. Jesus, I think. But that's all we can get out of him. He's very weak. I'm not certain, but he appears to have been tortured."

"Tortured?" Marcus's breath caught in his throat. He narrowed his eyes at the young soldier. "By who? Who would dare?"

Epidius paled. "I don't know, sir. There wasn't time to—"

"Never mind," Marcus interrupted, shoving past him. "I'll find out myself." He took to the halls at a dead run, not caring if anyone stepped in his path. About that he needn't have worried; any legionaries in the corridor who saw his face promptly made room for him to pass, and those who didn't were shoved aside as he passed by. None complained, of course. It was common knowledge among the men that further angering an already enraged centurion was not healthy.

Marcus stormed into the infirmary just as Justus, the physician, laid Taras on a raised platform to examine him. Justus was a small man, barely topping five and a half feet. His bald pate was bordered by the wild remains of his graying hair, which framed his ears in a tangled mass of tight curls. His faded blue eyes stared out from a mass of crow's feet and remained fixed on his patient as Marcus entered the room.

Without waiting for an invitation, Marcus walked right up to the platform and looked at his friend. His hands balled into fists at the sight of the legionary's dry, cracked lips and sunken eyes. "Taras, can you hear me?"

"He's not conscious, Centurion," the physician began. "He's hurt very badly. You should leave now while I—"

Marcus's gloved fist interrupted the doctor's admonition when it connected squarely with his jaw, sending him to the floor with a crash. The physician lay sprawled on the stone looking up at Marcus in stunned surprise.

"I didn't ask your opinion, Justus," Marcus growled. "Leave us. Now." Like most Romans, Marcus had little faith in doctors and medicine, viewing them as nothing more than charlatans who would as soon steal your coins as do anything useful to help you. The only reason Marcus suffered the physician's presence at all was because Tiberius, ever enamored of all things new and fashionable, had taken a liking to the "art" of medicine and ordered a physician to accompany all the troops of the Legion. But Tiberius wasn't here, and Marcus wanted the diminutive physician to know without doubt just who ran the barracks.

Justus apparently had no illusions about who was in charge. He scrambled to his feet and ran out of the infirmary, clutching his jaw in his hand and not looking back. *I probably broke his jaw,* Marcus thought. He'd be hearing about that from Pilate before the day was out. Marcus would deal with that when he had to. For now he had something much more important to attend to. He looked again at his fallen friend, who appeared as though he was already dead. Marcus examined the wide red welts around Taras's wrists and ankles. He'd been in the military long enough to know what that meant; someone had strapped Taras to the rack.

The thought turned his vision red as he tried to imagine who in the city would dare torture a Roman soldier. By the gods, whoever it was had made a huge mistake. Pilate would have no qualms about executing someone who treated his legionaries with such malice. *That is, if I let the bastard live long enough for Pilate to put him on trial,* Marcus thought.

He touched his hand to Taras's shoulder and gave him a gentle shake. "Taras, can you hear me?"

At first Marcus feared the physician had been correct. Taras was unconscious and unable to give him the answers he needed. But then his eyes fluttered open a crack, and he looked up at the centurion.

"Mary?" Taras whispered, so softly Marcus almost could not hear the words. "Is that you, Mary?"

"No, Taras. It's me. Marcus."

"Marcus?" At first he seemed confused, but then a flash of recognition lit his features "Marcus!" Taras's eyes flew wide open and he tried to sit up, but he only rose halfway from the bed before he fell backward with a grunt of pain.

"Lie still," Marcus said. "I can barely hear you, Taras."

"Thirsty… so thirsty."

Marcus reached for his flask. He popped the top off and poured some of his water into his friend's mouth. Taras took several large swallows, and Marcus pulled the flask away, fearing his friend would cramp up if he drank too much. "Better?" he asked.

Taras nodded, and even managed a weak smile. "Thank you."

"Who did this to you?"

"It was Gordian."

"Gordian? My Second?"

"He's not your Second anymore, Marcus." Taras shook his head feebly. "He's aligned himself with Jesus of Nazareth, and they are plotting to overthrow Rome in Israel. I heard the Nazarene talking about it. He plans to kill you. He—" Taras was cut off as another soldier entered the infirmary.

"Centurion?"

Marcus rounded on the intruder. "What do you want? Whatever it is, I am not available. Find Gordian..." Marcus trailed off as he though of Taras's words. *It was Gordian. He's aligned himself with Jesus of Nazareth, and they are plotting to overthrow Rome.* Was it possible? Or could it be the ramblings of a delirious mind? Taras certainly appeared lucid, and Marcus had come to trust his judgment over the years. "No, not Gordian," Marcus corrected himself. "Find Habitus and get him to help you. Do not disturb me again."

"But sir, it's the Sanhedrin. They sent one of their own to speak to you."

Damn it all! Marcus had forgotten about the Sanhedrin. Doubtless they'd been waiting for his arrival at the temple so they could all go to the Gardens and arrest Jesus. "Tell him to wait."

"I informed him you were busy, sir. He refused to leave. He said to give you this." The soldier held out a small piece of parchment, rolled and sealed with the symbol of the temple.

Marcus stared at the letter, not wanting to read the blame he knew he'd find there. Grunting, he took it, cracked the wax, and read the message. When he finished, he looked up at the legionary who'd brought it.

"Is the representative of the Sanhedrin still waiting?" Marcus asked.

The soldier nodded. "Yes, sir."

"Tell him I will be right out."

"Yes, sir." The legionary brought his fist to his chest in salute, then turned and left the room.

Marcus turned back to his injured friend, who had closed his eyes again. "Taras?"

No response. Marcus put his hand underneath Taras's nose, feeling for breath. When he was satisfied the man still lived, he removed his hand and leaned over. "I swear to you, Taras, I will find Gordian, and he will pay dearly for what he's done. Jesus, too. They'll both pay. For you and for Didius."

With that, Marcus turned and left the room. As he exited the infirmary, he spied the physician sitting on the floor nursing his jaw. It wasn't broken, after all. He supposed that was good news. "You, Justus. Get in there and see to Taras."

The man leapt to his feet and all but ran toward the room where the fallen legionary lay. Marcus grabbed his shoulder on his way by and forced the man to face him. "If he dies," Marcus said, "I'll see to it you spend tomorrow morning hanging from the cross, even if I have to make up a charge. I'll order my men to let your body rot on Golgotha until not even the vultures are interested in it anymore. Do you understand?"

Justus nodded, his eyes wide as saucers.

Marcus let go of his shoulder and walked down the halls to where the messenger waited. He had an appointment with the Sanhedrin, and by the gods it was time he kept it.

╬ ╬ ╬

Back in the infirmary, Justus noticed a slip of parchment on the floor. He looked to make sure his patient was still unconscious, then looked out into the hallway to see if anyone was nearby. *No one. Good.* He knew he probably shouldn't read an official message to the centurion, but his swollen jaw and injured pride demanded some small amount of satisfaction. Although he would never openly defy Marcus, he could take a small bit of enjoyment in doing so by covert means. Thus he opened the rolled piece of parchment and read the words written on it. There weren't many.

Centurion Marcus,

We do not need Taras to identify Jesus. We have another. His name is Judas. As I write this he waits for us in the city. Send word back with the messenger when you are ready to move. We await your reply.

Caiaphas

Justus gasped and dropped the letter back to the floor. Caiaphas! The high priest! He wiped the tips of his fingers on his tunic, certain he could feel the flesh burning. Justus wanted no part of anything between the Sanhedrin and the centurion. No good could ever come of such a thing. He would be much better off to pretend he'd never even seen the letter. He left it on the floor and went to tend to Taras, wanting more than anything to make sure the fallen soldier survived his wounds, for both their sakes.

CHAPTER TWELVE

Marcus arrived at the temple shortly after suppertime with six of his finest men in tow. It hadn't taken long to get there. His mounting rage at the murder of his brother and the torture of Taras gave him a great deal more energy than a man his age should possess, especially since he had not eaten anything since breakfast. A single thought forced his feet to action, lending a cadence for him to march by.

The Nazarene.

Over the last thirty-six hours, he had become Marcus's driving obsession. Ever since the morning of the previous day when he'd been forced to look upon Didius's severed head lying in the middle of the street, trails of spittle and the prints of several boots plainly visible on his brother's lifeless face, Marcus had been determined to bring the killer to justice. And although Malachi, the actual killer, was already dead, Marcus could still bring down the man who'd orchestrated the whole thing.

That man was Jesus of Nazareth.

Just thinking about the rabbi made Marcus's blood burn. His steps quickened as he pictured Jesus's hands bound to the crossbeam. First Didius and now Taras. And just when did Gordian become a traitor, anyway? How did such corruption occur in his ranks? It was all the Nazarene's fault.

Marcus fumed as he walked. Jesus had tangled with the wrong centurion. Marcus would see him dead before the week was out, strapped to a cross on Golgotha like all the other criminals in this wretched city. If Pilate wouldn't execute the rabbi, Marcus would do it himself.

Thus determined to see justice done for the sake of all those Jesus had killed or caused to be killed, Marcus marched up to the temple and demanded to see Caiaphas.

"You may not enter the temple," the Sanhedrin at the entrance said. "Wait here while I tell Caiaphas you have arrived."

Marcus hadn't wanted to enter the temple of the Sanhedrin and their ludicrous One God anyway, but he detested waiting outside. Still, to anger the Sanhedrin would be to anger Pilate, and he was not in any position to lose favor with Judea's Prefect. So, fuming at the delay, he found a spot to sit down and rest his tense muscles while he waited.

After a few minutes, Caiaphas exited the temple and walked over to Marcus. He fixed the centurion with a cold stare that told him all he needed to know. Caiaphas would work with him, but only because he had to. It was obvious to Marcus the temple priest would rather have dealt with Jesus on his own. He recalled once hearing Pilate mention something about the Sanhedrin not being allowed to put people to death. Ridiculous. Why have laws at all if you weren't willing to enforce them? *That's why they need us,* Marcus thought. That's why they needed Rome. They had no idea how to keep their population in line. Well, Marcus would show them. Starting with the Nazarene.

"Centurion," Caiaphas began, "you have come too soon. Judas has not arrived."

"Where is he?"

"I don't know. He should be along shortly."

Another delay. Didn't these people know how to do anything right?

"Is he late?" Marcus asked. "I was under the impression you and your brethren would be ready to go upon my arrival."

"He is not late," Caiaphas bristled, drawing himself up and squaring his shoulders. "He was to meet us after supper and bring you and your men to the Gardens. He will be here." Then Caiaphas looked behind the centurion to the group of soldiers he'd brought with him. "Is that all the men you will take with you?" He seemed nervous.

"Do you expect trouble?" Marcus did. He'd brought six of his best men, and had a further two score on alert should anything go wrong. "My men are strong, loyal, well trained and fully capable of subduing a single rabbi and his sheep. How about you, Caiaphas? Who will you send? More priests?"

Caiaphas' face reddened, but he said nothing more. Instead, he turned his back to the centurion and stormed away. Marcus smiled. He might not be able to go into the temple, but he could still trade words with the likes of Caiaphas. He doubted Pilate would even hear of the conversation, and it felt good to remind these Sanhedrin just who ruled Jerusalem. The Romans owned Israel. Every rock, every blade of grass, every bush. The people of Israel, especially the Jews, needed to remember that. Marcus was happy to remind them from time to time.

He instructed his men to wait by the temple, then he walked away from the gates and found a spot nearby where he could sit alone with his thoughts, and wait for Judas to arrive. Hopefully he wouldn't have to wait too long. Now that the time was near, he could barely keep his sword in its sheath.

He hoped the Nazarene refused to come quietly, and that he would get a chance to beat him a few times before the legionaries brought him under control. As Marcus watched the deepening gloom of the sky to the east, he prayed to each and all his gods that Jesus would force him to use his sword before the night was done.

I am coming for you, Nazarene.

☩ ☩ ☩

As the sun fell below the western horizon, most of Jerusalem's inhabitants sat at tables laden with roasted or broiled lamb, unleavened bread, dates, and in some houses, exotic fruits from the east. Much of the food had taken many hours to prepare. Families, free of the day's toils, laughed among themselves and conversations flowed freely from person to person. Here and there, however, the celebratory mood was marred with dark thoughts of the recent events in the city. From the wayward rabbi many had come to call the Messiah to the apparent murder of several Roman guards the day before, which promised trouble for everyone. Still, those patches of darkness were few and far between as the majority of Jerusalem's people concentrated solely on the vast amounts of food in front of them.

Underneath the city, in a rough stone chamber very few knew existed, Theron opened his eyes. He'd spent the day away from his chambers slumbering on a pallet of straw, wanting to be close to the city when he woke. Earlier, Simon had informed him of Jesus's pending arrest, and Theron didn't want to miss it. It wasn't quite what he had planned, but so much the better. Now he could actually witness the arrest and make sure nothing happened to jeopardize his plan. Now that dusk had finally arrived, he sat up, ready and eager for action.

There would be plenty of action tonight.

Theron stood and walked to the corner, where he donned his clothes. He looked down at the outfit he wore and was glad he'd had the peasant garb laundered. It would take too long and be too much trouble to find another peasant, kill him, and steal his clothes before he made his way to the Gardens of Gethsemane.

When he finished dressing, he checked his clothing over as best he could; making sure to tuck his new sword away in a secured fold of cloth. He wanted no more mistakes like the guards at the Middle Gate a few nights ago. True, he'd been clever enough to turn that to his advantage, but it galled him that he'd been detected so easily. Once satisfied his disguise would hold, he left the room and started down the hall toward the door that would take him to the surface. Then he would make his way to the Gardens, where Marcus would soon arrest Jesus.

There would be no escape. Theron meant to watch the arrest and make certain of the outcome. His carefully laid plan would come to fruition tonight, and damned if he was going to let anything derail it, not after everything he'd been through. Jesus would die tomorrow morning. Theron would see to it.

When he stepped from the tunnels into the cool night air, he couldn't help but smile.

I am coming for you, Nazarene.

In the Halls of the *Bachiyr*, at just about the same moment Theron stepped from his hiding place and walked out into the night, twelve of the thirteen oldest vampires in existence sat around a great obsidian table and listened to the plan of one of their subordinates. All around the table, heads nodded as the vampire who stood on the stone dais revealed what he knew, and what he planned to do about it.

"Theron has failed," he said. "Not only has he failed his mission, he has failed to protect the secrecy of our race."

"We know this already," Herris said. "Get to the point."

"I know where Theron will be tonight. I only ask the Council for permission to go there and eliminate him."

Several Council members laughed, while others simply shook their heads. The speaker on the dais fumed at their derision, but forced himself to remain composed. In truth, he hadn't expected the Council to think he could carry out such a lofty task, not really. It would have been nice if they hadn't laughed, though. He forced himself to remain calm. They could laugh at him now, if they wanted; they would stop laughing when he brought them Theron's head as a trophy.

"Surely you don't believe yourself capable of killing Theron," Herris noted. "The Lead Enforcer holds a tremendous advantage of power and age. You, if I recall, were only recently turned. Ten years ago, was it?"

"Eleven, Headcouncil."

"Ah, eleven," Herris replied with a smirk. "My mistake."

"I know it's not long for our kind," the vampire said, ignoring the obvious sarcasm in Herris' words, "but it was Algor himself who turned me. Theron is powerful, but he is not as close in blood to the Father as I am. There is power within my veins. Great power. His power." He pointed at Algor as he said this. "I *can* kill him. I ask only for the Council's permission to prove it."

The look on Herris' face spoke volumes about his confidence in the young vampire's ability to do as he claimed, but he said nothing to the contrary. Instead he deferred the issue to Algor.

"Well, Councilor?" Herris asked. "He's one of yours, after all. What say you?"

Algor sat in silence. The vampire in question felt the elder's gaze burn through him, searing away the layers of flesh and peeking into his heart. He knew the misshapen councilor searched for a weakness in him, and he also knew Algor would not find one. He was ready. He could do this. He'd been preparing for this moment for years. Tonight, the high and mighty Theron would finally fall.

"Very well," Algor said, addressing the Council. "If Headcouncil Herris has no objection, I say let him go."

"Are we all in agreement?" Herris asked the Council. When the rest of the Council indicated their consent, Herris turned to the young vampire, who stood on legs that nearly trembled from a mix of excitement and pride. "You are hereby given the task of executing Theron, former Lead Enforcer to the Council of Thirteen. The Father go with you in this, young *Bachiyr*. It will not be an easy task."

Herris pulled a piece of parchment and a quill from his robe. While the young vampire watched, Herris stabbed the quill into his wrist, drawing his own blood into the tip. He then wrote a message. When the scratchy sound of Herris' writing ceased, the councilor folded the message into thirds, then removed a stick of red wax from somewhere in his robes. He held the wax over one of the torches until it dripped, then he allowed a few drops to fall on the seam of the folded parchment. Lastly, he pressed a ring on his right hand into the wax, affixing his seal to the document and making it official.

Herris then tossed it to the younger vampire. "Here is the order for Theron's death. See to it immediately."

The young *Bachiyr* bowed his head. "Thank you, Headcouncil Herris, and my deepest thanks, as well, to rest of the Council. I will not disappoint you." With that, he turned and left the room, walking past the Lost One at the door without so much as a glance.

This was it! This was his big chance to prove his usefulness and skill to the Council. If he pulled this off, they might even make him an official Enforcer on the spot. Technically, he became an Enforcer the moment the Council of Thirteen ordered him to kill another vampire. But unless the Council held a ceremony to bestow the rank on him in an official capacity, no others of his race would recognize the title. But when he killed Theron, the Council would *have* to give it to him, and his stature among his people would double. No, it would triple.

He knew Theron would want to witness the arrest of Jesus, and he intended to meet him there and finish this business. First he had to meet with his brother, who had helped him cover up Theron's mistake. He supposed he should be thankful to the former Lead Enforcer. After all, his error had given him the ammunition he needed to approach the Council. Soon he would be rid of Theron, and would finally have the respect he deserved from his peers.

A smile lit his face in the darkness.

I am coming for you, Theron.

In the Council chamber, Herris fingered a missive he'd received earlier. Ramah, Second of the Council of Thirteen, had completed his business in the east and would return in a few days' time. Herris looked over to where Algor, Fifth of the Council, sat.

"Why did you let him go, Algor?" Herris asked. "There is no rush; we could have waited for Ramah. You know he has no chance of defeating Theron, no matter how eager he is."

"No," Algor agreed. "But it is for that very reason I sent him. Theron will kill him as surely as he did Ephraim."

"You desire this? To see your offspring slaughtered?"

"He is a fool, and an impatient one, at that. His ambition has tricked him into thinking he can defeat a *Bachiyr* of Theron's skill and power. I will not tolerate fools among my children. If he is so anxious to meet his demise, then let Theron cull the imbecile from our ranks before he does damage of his own."

Herris nodded. He'd been expecting as much from Algor. Still, it was a valid point. The young vampire had spoken rashly, and in his eagerness to gain some much wanted respect he'd thrown common sense to the wind and ended up assigned to kill a foe he could not hope to defeat. Such a lack of wisdom was not a desirable trait in a race that depended, above all else, on secrecy. But that still left a nagging matter for the Council to decide. "And Theron? He does need to be dealt with, after all."

"Let Ramah deal with Theron. He will return soon, anyway. He will likely foam at the mouth when he hears about the assignment."

"Agreed. Are we in concurrence?" Herris looked around the room. Eleven heads nodded back at him. It made sense. Theron was one of the most powerful of their kind in existence. Who would be qualified to capture and, if necessary, execute him? In reality only a member of the Council would prove strong enough, and Ramah was the only councilor whom Herris would send on such a mission. Damn him for not fathering any offspring, anyway. Still, it suited the Council's purpose to have so powerful an assassin at the ready. "Very well, then," Herris concluded. "Ramah will deal with Theron upon his return. It is high time he learned what it means to fail the Council of Thirteen."

Around the table, heads nodded. Herris dismissed the Council, and everyone filed out of the room.

Herris stepped through a door at the back of the chamber and into the halls beyond, making his way through the rough passages to an ornate, heavy door set into the wall. He pushed it open and stepped into a plush apartment, resplendent with treasures from all over the known world. Reams of purple cloth, gold statues from ages past, and even a few pots of rare eastern spices, although Ramah could not taste them. They were expensive; that's why he wanted them.

He crossed the room and sat in a solid gold, red-cushioned chair that Tiberius himself would have envied. Then he reached for a rope hanging from the ceiling behind him and gave it a swift yank. Soon after, a Lost One entered the chamber from the left entrance.

"Bring me a woman," Herris said. "A young one. And not from the public larder."

The Lost One bowed, and stepped out of the room, making not a whisper of sound as it went.

Once settled into his private chambers, he thought about the nights to come. Ramah would return soon enough, possibly as early as tomorrow night. Things looked good to Herris. Soon his Second would be back from his mission, a foolish vampire with an excess of bravado would be culled from their ranks, and Theron would be a Lost One. Perhaps best of all, Jesus of Nazareth, who'd been causing the Council so much trouble of late, would be dead.

Herris smiled. Things were looking up.

CHAPTER TWENTY-ONE

When Judas finally showed up at the temple, Marcus was not impressed. The man seemed frail and weak, as though a stiff breeze would carry him away and free him of the invisible burden stooping his shoulders. Judas's dark, sad face was framed by curly black hair and a shaggy, unkempt beard. His watery brown eyes lived under a heavy, worried brow and never stopped leaking. Marcus had tired of listening to his morose ramblings long before they left the city. He decided if he had to hear one more despondent whimper from his new informant, Jesus would not be the only one in trouble tonight.

"Can't you shut him up?" He asked one of the temple guards.

"He has betrayed his friends for thirty pieces of silver. No matter that it was the right thing to do; the man still bears the weight of his decision on his shoulders."

More foolish morality, not that he'd expected anything less from a temple priest. Marcus snorted. *No wonder Rome rules here.* He continued in silence, thankful at least that, noisy though the trip might be, he was finally getting somewhere.

When they arrived at the Gardens of Gethsemane they found a small group of people gathered there. One man spoke quietly to the rest, and the eyes of everyone present, save Marcus and those who came with him, gazed at the speaker in rapt attention. Marcus guessed the speaker to be Jesus. Most of the gathered crowd had tears in their eyes. To Marcus, the gathered men and women looked like they were under some sort of spell. Having never been to see Jesus speak before, he figured this was normal, and he was glad they'd come to put a stop to it. *If that is Jesus,* Marcus thought, *the man wields a great deal of power. It's good I brought soldiers with me.* The Sanhedrin were apparently of a like mind, for they began to close ranks. It didn't surprise Marcus to find the temple priests all held themselves separate from – and also behind – the armed Roman legionaries.

No one said a word, but the scant group of people slowly parted before Marcus's procession, allowing him to pass. He soon found his group facing off against twelve men, one of which was responsible for his brother's death. Most of them looked sad, but one man, a large, burly Jew dressed in sandals and a pale, coarse robe, stepped nervously from one foot to another. The man held his hand too close to his sword for Marcus's liking. *I'll have to watch that one,* Marcus thought.

At that point Judas stepped forward, tears glistening in his eyes and on his face. He walked up to a tall, willowy fellow in a white robe with a short brown beard and kissed him on the cheek.

"Judas," the man said, "this is how you betray me? With a kiss?" Like Judas, tears flowed freely down his cheeks.

That was the sign. Caiaphas had told him Judas would identify the one known as Jesus by kissing his cheek. Marcus put his hand on his sword.

"Are you the one called Jesus?" One of the temple priests asked.

Jesus nodded. "I am he."

"Arrest him," The priest told the others. When they stepped forward, the burly man took out his sword and swung it at one of the temple priests. The priest, not as well trained as Marcus's men, couldn't dodge aside in time, and the blow severed his ear. Marcus and his legionaries pulled out their own swords in response, and Marcus smiled. Jesus was going to make this fun, after all.

But Jesus disappointed him. He grabbed the burly man's shoulder and held him back. "No, Peter. Do no violence. I will go with them."

The one called Peter looked like he might argue, but at a second urging from Jesus he cleaned his blade and replaced it at his waist.

His smoldering eyes never left the gathered soldiers. Marcus kept his sword out, just in case, relieved to see his men did likewise. While Marcus was preoccupied with his men, Jesus reached over and touched the head of the temple priest who'd lost an ear. Several of the men nearby gasped, but Marcus was on the wrong side to see what happened. In truth he didn't much care, anyway. He had his prisoner. His brother would soon be avenged. Once he told Pilate what he'd learned about the Nazarene, the Prefect would never set him free. To kill a Roman soldier was one thing, to plot against Rome herself was quite another. Marcus was confident Pilate would order Jesus executed at first light.

"Shackle him," Marcus ordered. Two of his men rushed to obey, while the other four stood guard, their swords glinting dully in the torchlight. In moments, his men had Jesus bound hand and foot.

"Bring him," Marcus said. Then he turned and started the walk back to Jerusalem.

☫ ☫ ☫

Theron watched the whole thing from the edge of the crowd. Like Marcus, Theron didn't see what Jesus did to the injured man's head, and also like Marcus, he didn't care. He watched the armed force of temple priests and Roman legionaries led the Nazarene away in shackles. When they had gone far enough, he left his hiding place and started to follow them.

Even with Jesus arrested, he still had a few loose ends to tie up.

Marcus, for example.

☫ ☫ ☫

At about the same time Peter cut off the priest's ear, Gordian pushed open a small door in the floor of the barracks. He had to strain to do it; the door was located in a storage room and someone had placed a barrel on top of it. But somehow he managed to get it open just enough to squeeze through. Once inside, he moved the barrel off the trapdoor just in case he had to leave in a hurry.

Gordian then turned his attention to his uniform, making sure everything was in place. He didn't know if an order for his arrest had been given or not, but he didn't want to chance it by being noticed. His uniform should help him blend in as long as no one saw his face. The storage room was very near the infirmary, which was rarely guarded. He should be able to get in, finish Taras, and get out before anyone realized he was there. Once the deed was done he would return to the tunnels outside the city and wait for his brother. Tonight the two would truly be together again for the first time in eleven years. His separation from his twin had been hard on him. But after tonight it would no longer matter. None of it would matter. After tonight Gordian would be Second to no one.

He opened the door to the storage room and peered out. Just down the hall, he could see the open doorway to the infirmary. As he suspected, no legionaries stood guard. The smell of warm bread floated through the halls to greet him, reminding him he hadn't eaten all day. The kitchen staff was working late baking bread for tomorrow, which would be eventful. Ignoring his rumbling belly, he stepped into the hallway and walked to the room where the injured Taras unknowingly waited for death. *Now that you have passed along your message, Taras, your usefulness to me is finished.* This wasn't quite how Taras was supposed to die, of course, but it would do. Still, Gordian couldn't let his brother know of his improvisation, or he might take offense. He had assured his twin that Taras would be dead by morning. It was now well past suppertime, and he had no intention of letting a little thing like Taras's still-beating heart stand between him and destiny. The time had come to keep his promise.

When he arrived at the door, he poked his head into the room, which turned out to be larger than he'd expected, and was surprised to see not one, but two people inside. Justus sat at a small desk on the other side of the room from Taras. It had never occurred to him that Justus might still be in the infirmary. He hardly ever worked so late, and even then he would not miss supper. Why, then, was he still here?

Marcus. Gordian knew. Marcus must have threatened him. It was so like the centurion. Unfortunately, that did complicate things a bit. Nothing he could do about it, though. *Sorry, Justus.*

The physician had his back turned, and as Gordian entered the room, he trod lightly, stepping on the balls of his feet as he'd seen Taras do countless times. He'd removed his sandals earlier, knowing a little stealth might be in order, and now padded barefoot along the cold stone. As he advanced on the unsuspecting pair, he pulled a dagger from his belt; careful to slide the blade across the cloth of his tunic to ensure it didn't make any noise – another trick he learned from Taras. He drew his hand back and plunged the weapon deep into the back of Justus's neck, surprised at how easily the dagger sank into the man's flesh.

Justus gurgled and tried to turn around, but Gordian rotated the blade outward, keeping control of the dying physician's head and opening the wound further. Gouts of blood pumped from Justus's neck, spraying in every direction. It coated the bed, the walls, even Gordian's hands and arms, like a fresh coat of bright red paint. Some of it managed to spurt across the room and land on Taras's surprised face, whom Gordian noted was quite awake and alert. *And afraid. Good.*

Gordian smiled and pulled the knife from Justus's neck. The dead physician crumpled to the floor with a dull thud. Gordian paid the body no heed as he stepped over it and pointed his blade at the prone legionary. "Now, Taras. You have served your purpose."

"Why?" Taras managed to say. It was weak and barely audible, but Gordian heard it well enough. He shook his head. He would not waste time answering the ridiculous questions of a dying man. He walked over to the bed, holding his knife at the ready. He was only two paces from Taras when a shadow darkened the wall in front of him.

"What in the name of Jupiter? Gordian? What are you doing here?"

He turned to see Epidius standing in the doorway with a surprised look on his face. Epidius looked around the room, his eyes traveling to the bloodstained wall, the dead physician, and finally stopping to rest on Gordian's bloody knife. The young legionary's features twisted into an angry frown as he drew his sword.

"Traitor!" Epidius yelled, banging the hilt of his sword on his breastplate. "Traitor in the barracks! It's Gordian!" Epidius charged forward, his sword leading the way.

"Damn it," Gordian swore. He turned away from Taras and met Epidius's charge head on. The younger legionary had the advantages of youth, strength, and a longer blade, but Gordian had joined the Roman Legion ten years before his opponent was born. Experience and the tempering wisdom of age told him to wait. His young, hot blooded opponent would most likely go for the quick kill, and he was right.

As Epidius charged, he raised his sword in what Gordian recognized as a strike meant to push through his defenses, puncture his breastplate, and open a hole in his sternum to pierce his heart. He waited until Epidius's body was committed to the move, then he turned sideways while simultaneously stepping into the fight, his dagger hand leading the way as it shot upward from his waist. Thus instead of having his heart pierced by Epidius, Godian drove his blade deep into the younger man's side, just under his ribcage and into his lungs. It was a sound tactical strike that simultaneously ensured his opponent's death and prevented him from pulling enough air in his lungs to scream. Gordian pulled his blade free and watched Epidius fall to his knees, gasping and coughing blood.

"Boy soldiers," he said as Epidius raised a trembling hand to the wound. "Always forgetting their training when their blood is hot."

Epidius smiled at him, and for a moment Gordian could not think what the man found so amusing.

"I…didn't forget…*everything*." Epidius wheezed.

Gordian heard the shouting voices of many legionaries.

"I…sounded the alarm…first." Epidius coughed, and then smiled, his teeth stained red by his blood. "Enjoy Tertius…traitor."

Epidius's yell had apparently been heard throughout the entire barracks. Gordian could hear hundreds of sandaled feet tramping through the halls toward him. He wasted precious seconds trying to determine how close the soldiers were, and finally decided he didn't have time to cross the room and deal with Taras and still make it out before they arrived. He muttered a curse at the dying legionary, who had still somehow managed to thwart him.

There was no help for it. He would have to leave Taras alive for the time being. He ran out of the room and back toward the storage closet. He managed to get inside and close the door just as the sounds of angry soldiers reached the area. He lifted the trapdoor and stepped back into the gloom. He did his best to maneuver the barrel back on top of the door, no easy task from underneath it, and was finally satisfied. To any legionaries who looked into this room, it would seem as if the barrel had never been moved. He lowered the trap door to the ground gently, not wanting it to slam shut under the weight of the barrel and draw any unnecessary attention.

Just beyond the door to the storage room, he heard the angry shouts of at least half a dozen soldiers. They'd found the bodies of Justus and Epidius. The last thing Gordian heard before the trapdoor closed fully and shut off all sound was the command to move Taras to another room and place a guard at the door.

He cursed Epidius for ruining his plan. He only hoped his brother didn't find out until after he'd kept his part of the bargain. By then it wouldn't matter anymore, and Gordian could return to finish the job the following night, when he would be stronger and deadlier. Or maybe he and his brother would just leave. There were other places to be besides Jerusalem, after all. Carthage, perhaps, or even Athens. He'd always wanted to see Greece.

He sent up a prayer to any and all of his gods that his twin would not discover his failure until after he'd made Gordian a vampire. Then he walked down the passageway to the tunnels where his brother waited to introduce him to the world of moonlight and near limitless power.

CHAPTER TWENTY-TWO

Halfway between the Gardens of Gethsemane and Jerusalem, Marcus felt an unseen presence following his group. He caught small glimpses here and there; just shadows, mostly. Nothing he could lay a solid grasp on. But he hadn't made it through thirty years in the Roman Legion, eventually rising to the rank of Centurion, by ignoring his instincts.

"Fabian, Hirrus," he said, motioning to two of his men. "Slow down."

The two legionaries did as commanded, and when Marcus drew level to them he spoke in a whisper. "We are being followed. You two go on ahead. When you pass that bend, fan out. One of you go to the right and the other to the left. Walk about twenty or so paces from the path, then circle back around so we can surround whoever is following us. I will continue on and stay behind the group. That should drag whoever it is along behind me."

"Won't whoever it is recognize this as a trap, Centurion?"

It was a good point, but Marcus had that covered already. He pulled a scroll from his belt, handed it to Fabian, and smiled. His next words were spoken quite loud.

"You men, run ahead of the group and take this to Pilate. Do not let the Sanhedrin see it. It is for the Prefect's eyes only."

The two legionaries saluted, and ran down the path after the Sanhedrin. Marcus walked behind them at a much slower pace. There was nothing on the scroll of any importance, of course, but he hoped his shadow would note it and be fooled into thinking Marcus was alone. The centurion himself would not have fallen for such a ruse. Neither would Taras, but Marcus hoped his pursuer would prove less clever. He plodded slowly along behind the vanishing party, whistling a raucous drinking song and trying not to let his nerves show.

✝✝✝

Theron watched the exchange from the shelter of some bushes about twenty yards away. He saw Marcus and the two legionaries stop and heard Marcus order the two men to run and deliver the scroll to Pilate. When the two legionaries ran ahead Theron's lips parted in a wicked grin, his canines gleaming in the moonlight. He knew a ruse when he saw one. Marcus hoped to trap him. Theron thought about it for a moment, then decided to let the centurion have his trap.

He stepped from the brush and onto the path, making no effort to conceal the sound of his passage. His feet dislodged a number of pebbles and sent them rattling down a small slope. Marcus turned immediately, hand on his sword.

"Hail, Centurion." Theron said and started down the hill. In the weak light he could see Marcus's eyes narrow, probably trying to figure out who he was. Then recognition dawned on Marcus's face, and his stance relaxed. But, Theron noted, the centurion's hand didn't leave his sword.

"Ephraim?" Marcus asked.

"Yes, Centurion," Theron replied, and walked toward him. "I have been looking for you."

✝✝✝

"You are late, brother."

"I'm sorry," Gordian replied. "I had some last minute business to attend to."

"You kept me waiting too long, Gordian. The hour of Jesus's arrest has come and gone. I've missed my opportunity to deal with

Theron in the Gardens and now I'll have to hunt him in the city, instead. Tell me, what business could have been more pressing than ours?"

His brother's eyes narrowed as he spoke, and Gordian knew he was very, very angry at the delay.

"I'm sorry," he said again. "I had to be sure that Jesus would be captured. He's a crafty one. It required a few last minute changes of plan. A few words whispered in the right ears."

"And? Has Jesus been arrested, then?"

"Yes. Marcus left to arrest him earlier. He should be on his way back by now. Pilate will put him on trial him in the morning, and the prefect will almost certainly have him crucified."

"You're sure?"

"Yes."

"How can you be so certain?"

"Because Marcus believes the Nazarene was involved in several zealot attacks and a plot to overthrow Roman rule in Israel. Once Marcus passes his suspicions along to the prefect, Jesus is finished. Pilate will consider it treason of the highest order. Most likely, the Nazarene will die before the sun sets tomorrow evening."

"Good. Very good, brother."

Gordian stared at his twin in the flickering torchlight. A deep cold radiated from the walls of the underground chamber, and his skin began to prickle. The fine hairs on his arms stood at attention, and his breath came in pale white clouds. His body began to shiver, an involuntary reaction to the chill and a feeling he couldn't quite shake. Somehow the room, as well as the payment he was about to accept for his actions, suddenly felt profane. Unholy.

He shook the unwanted thoughts from his head. He would be with his brother again. After eleven long years of feeling like only half of himself, he would be whole. How could that be a bad thing? He should be overjoyed. His happiness should spill from him like a fountain, spraying everything in the area with his mirth and making this cold, dark chamber warm and bright. It was right. It was true.

Yet the feeling remained.

Probably just nerves. He had, after all, killed two men tonight. That was bound to leave him a little jumpy. But soon it would no longer matter. Soon nothing could harm him, not even time itself. He would be immune to the passing centuries. He smiled.

But what was taking so long?

"What of our deal?" Gordian asked. "Will you do it now?"

His brother turned to regard him, his face hard and frigid, the smile dark. "Yes, Gordian. Why not? Come here."

Gordian hesitated. Something about the look on his twin's face held him back, made him suddenly afraid.

"Are you…is everything okay?" He asked.

"Of course. Why wouldn't it be?" His brother walked up to him, and now Gordian could see the sharp points of his teeth flashing in the torchlight. He had known to expect them, of course, but seeing them still shocked him. For the first time, he began to comprehend exactly what it was he'd been offered in return for his services. He backed up a step.

"Are those…necessary?"

"These?" His brother smiled wide, revealing his fangs in all their grim splendor. "I'm afraid so, Gordian. This is what you asked for, after all."

"I…I think I've changed my mind." Gordian said as he backed away. "I think I'll just go back to the barracks, now."

"Oh, no, Gordian. I can't let you leave without your payment; it's much too late for that. You know all about us. The *Bachiyr*. The law of the Council is very clear on this." His brother took another step forward, his arms reached out to Gordian. The fingers ended in long claws. "Come, now. A deal is a deal, brother."

Gordian had other ideas. He turned and bolted down the hallway. His brother's laughter chased him through the dark corridor. *What have I done?*

He sped through the passages, looking for a place to hide. He didn't know where he was, his brother had only given him a cursory tour, but he knew the way out. He ran like mad for the doorway to the outside. He wasn't sure where he would go once he made it outside. By now word of his treachery would be all over the city. He would find no place within the barracks to hide and no one outside would aid a legionary who was also a murderer and a traitor. It wouldn't matter anyway. His brother would find him wherever he hid. The only place he could think of where he might be safe was the temple, and he was not allowed inside. He cursed his weakness and his brother as he ran along, knowing at any minute he would hear the sound of booted feet behind him.

⸸⸸⸸

Theron stepped to within five paces of the centurion before Marcus pulled his sword. "That's close enough."

At that moment the two men who'd run ahead stepped from the brush behind Theron and pulled their swords, as well. Just like that, Theron found himself surrounded by legionaries. Of course, the two behind him made more noise while they circled back than a drunken man in a pottery shop, but Theron pretended not to know about them. Just as he pretended to be caught off guard and afraid. He held his hands out in front of him to show Marcus he had no weapons.

"Is something wrong, Centurion?" Theron asked. "Have I done something?"

Marcus looked thoughtful. After a few seconds he lowered his blade. "No, Ephraim. Not that I know of." His look hardened, and he raised the blade again, "Or have you? Why are you following us? Last time we spoke, you were about to leave Jerusalem forever and go back to Sepphoris. Yet here you are, sneaking around and following an armed escort in the night."

"I only stayed behind to make certain Jesus was arrested and does no more harm to the people of Israel, Centurion. I wanted to see it for myself, or I knew I would never feel safe."

"So you admit to following us, then. Why didn't you announce yourself?"

"Would you, in my place? A Jew? Coming in from the Gardens of Gethseman after an arresting party and following behind armed legionaries? Would you have made your presence known?"

Marcus lowered his sword and put it away. "I guess not." He looked behind Theron at the two soldiers. "Stand down. He's not a threat."

The soldiers did as Marcus commanded, and Theron heard the sound of their swords sliding into sheaths. He stepped forward, and this time Marcus didn't try to stop him. Instead the centurion turned away and looked to the west, in the direction of Jerusalem. "You needn't worry, Ephraim. I arrested Jesus myself not even an hour ago. The fiend had my brother killed, then he tortured my friend, Taras, who even now battles for his life in the infirmary. I would have executed him myself had the Prefect granted me permission, but he refused. Not to worry, though, the Sanhedrin aren't likely to release him, and Pilate will most assuredly demand his death tomorrow once I—"

Marcus never finished his sentence. Faster than a snake, Theron struck him in the back of the neck with a clawed fist, slicing right through the throat and making it impossible for the doomed man to scream for help. Marcus gurgled and fell to his knees. Theron pulled his hand back, twisting it a little to make doubly sure the centurion would never rise.

Then he turned to the pair of stunned legionaries, who had closed to within arm's reach while Marcus told him about Jesus's arrest. Neither moved to grab their swords, and Theron was able to jab his right hand into the closest soldier's torso, piercing heart and lungs in one blow. The man wheezed as Theron pulled his claws from his chest, sending a spray of crimson into the night air that coated the vampire like a warm mist.

The smell of blood was strong, and it reminded Theron that he had not fed. To his heightened senses, the red mist in the air made it seem as though the whole world was made of the stuff. A few drops struck his skin and he could almost feel his body absorbing it like plants absorbed the morning dew. Hunger drove a hot blade into his belly. The lust to kill pressed in on him like a thousand pounds of stone, and it was only through an extreme effort of will he was able to let his latest victim fall and turn on the last legionary. By then the fellow had finally registered the attack. He fumbled for his sword with fingers that shook too badly to be useful.

Theron grabbed the last man's shoulders and pulled him close, like a lover. He sank his teeth into the soldier's throat, tasting the sweet flavor of the dying man's blood as it mingled with the sweat on his neck. He drank greedily, lost in the ecstasy of taking a life. Death whispered promises into his ear. This is what he lived for. Killing. Drinking. Living. For one sweet instant he held on and tasted the true nectar of the gods. His people had long ago found their Ambrosia, and he drank deep and long, filling his body with the unfortunate soldier's life.

Gordian saw the doorway ahead. No more than forty paces down the hall. Soon he would be outside. He stifled the urge to shout a prayer of thanks, lest his brother hear him. He ran as fast as his legs and burning lungs would allow, and when he made it to the door, he breathed a sigh of relief. He still didn't know where he would go once he escaped the passages, but anywhere was better than being trapped in the tunnels with his mad brother.

He pulled the handle hard in his eagerness to escape and leapt forward, only to crash his upper body into the solid wood, cracking his head. *Stupid!* He'd forgotten to unbolt it. He looked for the latch, but soon discovered the slides empty. The bar stood off to the left, leaning against the doorframe. Confused, he yanked on the door a second time. Nothing. He braced his legs to either side of the doorway and pulled with all his might, still it didn't move. Terror crept into his body as he realized the door was locked. Probably bolted from the outside.

No, there is no bolt on the outside.

Frantic, Gordian yanked on the door again and again, oblivious to the whimpering sound coming from his own throat. Why wouldn't it open? Why in the name of the gods couldn't he get out? He tugged and pulled and strained until his arms and back felt like they'd been filled with heated gravel, but still the door didn't budge.

"Open, damn you!" He said to the recalcitrant wood.

"It won't open that way, my brother."

Gordian whirled around, pressing his back to the door. There, not ten strides away, stood his twin. "Stay away from me. I want no part of this."

"It's too late for that, Gordian. Soon Jesus of Nazareth will be dead, and your hands are stained with his blood, as well as that of Archarius, Epidius and Justus, the physician. Yes, Gordian, I know about Justus and Epidius. Their deaths cling to you like cobwebs. I can see their phantoms hovering at your side.

"Curiously, I don't see Taras, which means he must still be alive. You failed, Gordian. Taras knows of the house in Jerusalem. He knows about the Lost Ones. He is a danger to the *Bachiyr* race. You had only one simple task: kill him. And you could not even do that."

"I was going to," Gordian said, too terrified to feel ashamed of the whimper in his own voice. "I couldn't fight the whole barracks. I planned to go back and finish him after our deal was completed."

His brother laughed. A sudden, sharp bark that speared Gordian and pinned him to the wall. "Did you really think I would share this gift with you? The Father take you, Gordian, you always were a fool."

Gordian slumped against the door with the realization that his brother had only used him for his closeness to the centurion; that he never had any intention of fulfilling his part of the bargain. Gordian felt the moisture building in his eyes. He'd betrayed everyone who had ever called him a friend, and the blood of so many was on his head, and all for nothing. He'd been a willing pawn in his brother's quest for notoriety and revenge. "Dear gods, what did I do?"

"You helped me, as you promised." His brother laughed again, and stepped to within an arm's reach. Gordian went for his sword, but the vampire was faster. He gasped as the thing that used to be his brother grabbed his throat and lifted him bodily off the ground. Stars burst into his eyes as his brother slammed his back into the door.

Gordian felt his airway blocked, and he struggled to breathe as white spots appeared in his vision. He brought his hands up and grabbed his brother's wrist, trying in vain to break the steel grip, but it was useless. He could no more budge his brother's hands than he could open the door on which his back rested. Before long, he no longer had the strength to hold his arms up, and they fell limply to his side.

His vision dimmed, and the last thing he heard before the world went dark was his twin's mocking laugh. "Thank you for your help, brother."

⚔ ⚔ ⚔

Once Theron drank his fill from the soldier, he tossed the corpse into the brush, where he hoped some lucky scavenger would find it and clean up his mess. He then checked on the legionary he'd stabbed through the chest. The man was already dead. The wound would be strange, but at least his body still held plenty of blood. No threat of being discovered there.

He then walked over to Marcus, and was surprised to find the centurion still alive, clutching at his ruined throat with both hands in a futile effort to hold his life's blood inside. Theron's well-aimed thrust had torn out the soldier's vocal chords. His hateful glare as he saw Theron could not be mistaken, however, and when the vampire knelt next to the expiring man, he answered the question he knew Marcus would ask if he could speak.

"Yes, Centurion. It was me," Theron said, certain Marcus would know what he meant.

Marcus *did* know, apparently. With more strength than Theron would have given him credit for, the centurion mouthed the name

"Didius" and reached over to his belt, trying to pull his sword free. Theron noticed the familiar jeweled hilt and laughed. He grabbed the sword and pulled it free of Marcus's grasp.

"I believe this is mine," he said. He lifted the sword high behind his head, noting with satisfaction the look of fear that bloomed in Marcus's eyes. He brought it down hard, the blade tearing through the flesh of the centurion's neck and digging deep into the earth underneath.

Marcus's head rolled free from his body, and Theron pulled his new sword from his sheath and tossed it aside, replacing it with his old one. He looked down at his tunic and frowned. The front of his peasant garb showed up bright red in the moonlight, soaked with blood. He'd never get into Jerusalem looking like this. He looked over at the soldier in the road. His clothes were likewise drenched, and would do him no good. Then he remembered the corpse of the soldier he'd drained. The uniform should still be intact and relatively free of blood. He stalked out into the brush, searching for the body. He needed clean clothes in order to get past the gate and into the city, and the soldier's uniform would be especially helpful to get inside the dungeon.

Theron meant to pay Jesus a visit.

CHAPTER TWENTY-THREE

Theron approached the barracks well after midnight. He'd timed it that way in order to catch the guards in the middle of their shift, hoping by this time the men would be so bored and tired they wouldn't pay much attention to those who walked through the gate, even at this late hour. As it was, of the four guards huddled around a small patch of earth, only one bothered to look up at the sound of sandals in the street. Seeing nothing more alarming than another legionary, he returned his attention to the ground where, Theron noted, the men played at a game of dice.

He walked between them and into the barracks with no trouble, and set about looking for the passages that would lead him into the dungeons. Fortunately he'd been held prisoner here the previous night, and he still had some memory of the layout of the place. He dared not ask directions, lest he give himself away. He didn't fear being caught by the legionaries, but the idea of having to abandon his mission before he could carry it out terrified him. At present, that mission had a familiar name: Taras.

Just before he died, Marcus told Theron that Taras lay injured and barely alive in the infirmary. Theron knew the infirmary was in the barracks, and since he wanted to go there to speak with Jesus anyway, it made for a convenient excuse to sneak into the place.

Now Theron could kill Taras and have his words with Jesus in a single trip.

It would be more prudent to go to the dungeons first, since killing Taras might set up quite a row and thus prevent him from being able to see the captured rabbi. So Theron wandered around the barracks, using his keen ears and eyesight to locate the passage that would lead him down into the bowels of the complex where, most likely, Jesus waited in the stocks.

It didn't take long. Soon he came to a stone corridor that slanted down, deeper into the earth. The dank smell of mold wafted up from the darkness. Mixed with it were the smells of burning coals, superheated iron, and blood. When he stopped to listen, he could hear the pleading screams of the men – suspected zealots, probably – whom the legionaries deemed fit to question echoing up the passageway. He pictured the pitiful souls in the dungeons; wretched prisoners strapped into the rack or held in the stocks as they begged for mercy, only to face the derisive laughter of their Roman captors. He smiled at the idea; he couldn't help himself. Mercy? He doubted the Roman tongue even had a word for it. Theron continued down the dimly lit hallway, following the sounds of pain to the dungeons below.

A short while later, the corridor leveled off and branched into two directions. To the left came the screaming Theron had heard earlier. From the passage to the right he heard a softer sound. Crying. Several people joined in the sad song, and every now and then a gruff voice would shout for them to be quiet or they would be next. Theron took this direction, and before long found himself approaching a chubby legionary at a wooden desk. The man had his back to him, and his head occsasionally bobbed on his neck as he nodded off.

Beyond the desk was a short corridor that ended abruptly in a stone wall. The air reeked of sweat, vomit and blood. Theron also detected the pungent odors of urine and feces, and he imagined the imprisoned humans would be in poor condition. The thought made him pause. What could the soldiers have done to Jesus already? He wanted to find the rabbi conscious and alert.

Theron noted several doors made of sturdy wood and reinforced by steel braces on either side of the hallway. Each had a tiny hole in the front, barely big enough to fit a fist through. Theron had found the right place. He cleared his throat, alerting the snoozing guard to his presence.

"What's your business here?" the legionary asked.

"Marcus sent me. I am to check on the prisoner Jesus of Galilee and make certain he is still alive. The centurion is most anxious for him to be brought before Pontius Pilate and face the ire of Rome."

The legionary looked him over briefly, then tossed a ring of keys to him. "Last door on the right. He's still alive, though I'd wager he rather wishes he wasn't."

Theron took the keys and smiled at the guard. "Oh? Have the Sanhedrin come to see him already?"

The legionary shook his head. "The Pharisees. They were in there for about two hours. Those bastards did a fair job of trying to kill him before his trial. I don't think they meant to, but they couldn't seem to control themselves. In the end two other guards and I had to force them to leave. Not that we care what happens to him, mind you, but as you said, Marcus wants him to face trial. Is it true he's leading the zealots? Anyway, the strange thing about it, no matter what the Pharisees did to him, he never screamed and barely spoke. He just sat there, quiet as a mouse. The only thing he said was something about paradise. I couldn't make it out."

"Thank you." Theron breezed past the talkative guard with a sharp smile. "I will see if I can get him to repeat it."

"Don't kill him, now. The Centurion will have my head if that one doesn't make it to trial."

Theron didn't answer, but the guard need not have worried. He could never kill Jesus, and he knew it. In fact, he doubted he could even touch a man of such strong faith. But he meant to see the man in the stocks, nonetheless. The Nazarene had cost him a good friend and a great deal of trouble. Now, before the Romans executed him, Theron needed to know why Ephraim had turned his back on his race. What about Jesus bred such disloyalty among people – and vampires, apparently – that they would betray their own kind to follow his banner above all others? Theron had to know. Then he could return to the Council and tell them what to look for, so something like this could never happen again.

He reached the door at the end of the hall and slid the key into the lock. After he unlocked it, he pulled the door open and stepped into the cell. There, shackled to the stocks in the center of the room, sat Jesus, looking up at him.

At first, Theron didn't recognize the Nazarene. The guard at the desk hadn't exaggerated; the Pharisees had nearly killed him. The bright glow of the man's faith seemed faint, somehow. It still shone in Theron's eyes, but it was muted; diffused, as though the beatings of the Pharisees had doused the young rabbi's faith with doubt or worry. His hair and beard were matted with blood, and his jaw and eyes were swollen and discolored. Dried blood ran from his right ear down to a point Theron could not see somewhere on the other side of the stocks. Beneath him lay a small pool of blood, and three of the fingers on his right hand stuck out from his palm at crazy, jagged angles, obviously broken. Theron had rarely seen a more ragged, pitiful sight than this wayward carpenter's son. He chuckled.

"I forget, Jesus," he said. "What is it your people call you? The Messiah?"

Jesus looked at Theron, his face sad, and said nothing.

"You let yourself be captured," Theron continued, "knowing what your fate would be. Your people outnumbered those who came to arrest you. You could have gotten away easily. Why didn't you? What good can your death do for you or your followers?"

Again, Theron received no reply. It soon became obvious Jesus didn't intend to answer.

"Of course. That would go against your words, wouldn't it? You couldn't very well preach nonviolence and forgiveness and then turn around and start a battle, could you? It looks as though you preached yourself into a corner, rabbi."

Still Jesus said nothing. Theron was fast becoming bored with the reticent prisoner. He could see no reason for anyone to follow the man. Certainly no reason for Ephraim, a longtime servant of the Council of Thirteen, to forsake all he knew for the wretched creature bent into the stocks before him. Theron swore under his breath, and spat in the dirt beneath Jesus's face.

"Well? Say something, Nazarene. Speak to me!"

Theron fought the sudden urge to drive his sword into Jesus's face. He'd gone through a great deal of trouble, and nearly died in a room not far from this one over the aggravation Jesus had caused him. The least the man could do was speak to him. Plead for mercy; call him a bastard son of a whore. Anything. But he kept his silence, and fixed Theron with a gaze that spoke of a burden too great for any one man to bear. Theron saw no anger or fear in Jesus's pale, moist eyes, only sadness. He leaned in closer, there was something strange about the rabbi's eyes, almost as if…

Theron gasped and took a step back, realizing what was odd about the Nazarene. There was indeed sadness in his eyes, a great deal of it. But Jesus's despair was not for himself, the vampire noted with surprise, but for Theron. It reminded him of the look in Ephraim's eyes just before he died. He shook his head in wonder.

"Ephraim must have been insane. Farewell, Jesus. Hopefully you find Paradise to your liking, though I doubt you will enjoy the trip." Theron laughed and turned to leave, determined not to waste any more time on fools and their followers. He reached out and wrapped his fingers around the handle.

"I know you, Theron of Macedonia" a voice behind him said. Not weak or soft, as might be expected, but strong. Full. Powerful. The resonance of it weakened Theron. "I know your kind well, *Bachiyr*."

Theron turned, but didn't take his hand from the door. Jesus's eyes bored into him. Their brown depths threatened to swallow the vampire whole. Gone was the trace of moisture from before. Gone, also, was the look of sadness. Theron stared in awe at the change that had come over the Nazarene. Jesus's face no longer grimaced in pain, nor did the sorrows of the world seem heaped upon his brow. Instead, he had assumed a peaceful, unearthly air, as if the goings on of the world outside were beneath him and meant nothing.

As he stood at the door, Theron noticed for the first time the air in this room lacked the foul odors of the others. It was pure, clean. He had no idea why that might be. To make matters worse the glow of the man's faith, so weak and dim only a few moments ago, now lit the entire room. Theron felt weaker than normal, and the strength in his legs threatened to give way. He fought back a maddening urge to run, screaming from the cell.

"You know me, Nazarene?" he asked. "Do you think so?"

"Oh, yes," Jesus said, "From the moment Ephraim first came to me. It was easy to see the taint of the one you call The Father on him. I pitied him, as I pity you."

"You are the one in the stocks, Nazarene, not me," Theron said. "You should save your pity for yourself."

"You have been lied to, vampire," Jesus said, a touch of sadness in his voice. "And you have been betrayed. You have lived a false life for a false purpose. Your people are nothing more than a ruse for an evil you cannot begin to understand."

Theron removed his hand from the door handle and stepped into the room, moving closer to the stocks. He approached with balled fists, ready to strike. His mounting anger gave him the strength to approach through the burning glare of Jesus's faith.

Jesus looked down at Theron's fists. "That is how Ephraim came to me, also. Like you, he came with an angry heart, ready to draw my blood. He knew the truth, and so do you. I can see it in your eyes. But unlike you, Ephraim was willing to listen. Oh, not to me, of course. Not at first, anyway. But to himself."

Theron froze, unsure of the Nazarene's meaning.

"He tried to tell you, didn't he? At the end?" Jesus asked. "But you didn't want to listen. Your elders have not been honest with you or your people. You have been manipulated for nine hundred years by beings a thousand times more deceptive and evil than yourself. You are meaningless, you know. Dust to those you serve. Less, even. Ephraim came to realize this. He—"

"To the Abyss with Ephraim!" Theron snapped. "He is dead. I killed him myself. *He* is dust, rabbi, not me. I am the Lead Enforcer and trusted servant of the Council of Thirteen. Unlike Ephraim, I will not fall for your tricks, Jesus of Nazareth, so keep your lies to yourself."

"Yes, Theron," Jesus replied. "I know of Ephraim's demise. The great Theron has slain him. Tell me, vampire, did it help? Did Ephraim's blood restore warmth and sunlight to your path? Or do you still walk in darkness and the chill?"

Theron didn't answer, but he didn't need to. Jesus answered for him.

"It didn't, did it? Nothing in your lightless world can restore that which you have lost. You will spend an eternity as you are now; cold inside, forever hating the life you can no longer possess. It is a pointless cycle of death that binds you. Ephraim knew this, though he could not admit it, and he came to me seeking the very same thing: salvation. I showed him it was not too late, and it wasn't. Not for him and not for you."

"What is that supposed to mean?" Theron asked. He tried to sound haughty, but the conviction had left his voice.

"Forgiveness," Jesus said, and a single tear fell from his eye and landed in the puddle of blood on the floor. "It's never too late to be forgiven."

"Forgiveness?" Theron whispered, and something inside him warmed at the thought. Until that moment, he hadn't realized he sought it, but upon hearing the rabbi's words, he knew them to be true. A longing for it haunted him, deep down where he had to look very hard to see it. But it was there. It hid, staring at him. Judging him. Always reminding him of the evil thing he truly was. He'd tried for centuries to drown it in blood, but it never went away.

The realization struck him like a physical blow, almost knocking him from his feet and forcing him a step backward. For the first time in hundreds of years, Theron thought about the many foul things he'd committed in the name of his people. Hundreds, perhaps thousands of lives taken, gallons of blood spilled both for amusement and to quench a thirst he knew in his heart to be an aberration. He remembered the taut, screaming faces of the people he'd tortured, their mouths stretched wide with pain. Their images surfaced in his mind's eye, accusing him, making him feel unclean. Foul.

Too much, he thought. He'd done too much evil. His soul, such as it was, would be forever tainted with the deaths of thousands. He held his hands up to his face, remembering the feel of them around countless throats as he squeezed the life away from so many. In the darkness of the cell, they looked red. Fitting, since they were stained with the blood of so many.

"It's too much," he whispered, not realizing he spoke aloud. "Too late."

"It's never too late," Jesus replied, "to seek forgiveness."

Forgiveness? Theron looked beyond his hands, to the torch on the wall. The flame danced and swayed, sending the shadows of the chamber reeling. Could it be true? He looked around the chamber, his eyes lighting upon the old bloodstains that the Romans had never bothered to clean up. The newer ones resembled a rust-colored moss. It looked like any number of rooms Theron had visited over the years. Many others just like this one, in which Theron himself had been the one to spill the blood. Countless victims, all crying for mercy but never receiving it. He'd listened to their screams and laughed. Could he really find absolution?

Not likely. Forgiveness was not for the likes of Theron. Jesus had to be lying, he *had* to be. Theron could never be forgiven, not by the rabbi's God, and certainly not by his victims. How could he? Theron could never even forgive himself.

"Damn you," he said. "Gods damn you, Nazarene. Enjoy your trip to Golgotha!" Blinded by his anger, Theron forgot the aura of faith around Jesus, and struck the captured rabbi with a closed fist. As soon as his flesh touched that of the Nazarene, a bright light flared around his hand and a tendril of fire leapt up his arm. Hissing, he snatched his hand back and smothered the flames with his cloak.

Once he extinguished the fire, he looked at his forearm. The skin of his knuckles where he'd come into direct contact with Jesus's flesh was burned and blackened. It felt like he'd dipped his hand into a vat of molten steel, and for a brief moment the pain clouded out all rational thought.

Then, slowly, the pain faded, but the skin of his hand remained charred. When he regained his clear headedness, he looked at Jesus through narrowed eyes. His legs buckled and he nearly fell. The touch of Jesus's skin had left him feeling weak and helpless, like he'd just been in a pitched battle and lost. He felt dizzy and disoriented, but mostly he felt angry. He again spat at the ground under the prisoner's head, and this time his spittle landed in the puddle of Jesus's blood. There was a pop and a sizzle, then silence. Jesus never took his eyes from Theron's face.

"It doesn't have to hurt, *Bachiyr*," Jesus said.

"You are wasting your breath, Nazarene," Theron replied, and took a step back. "You will die tomorrow. I will be here long after your bones have turned to dust and the world has forgotten your name." He turned his back on the prisoner and stumbled to the door. His fingers trembled as they wrapped around the handle.

Jesus's voice came from behind him. "Remember what I said, vampire. Forgiveness. It's waiting for you, but you must be willing to seek it. Even now it's not too late."

Theron didn't turn around. "Take your forgiveness to the underworld with you, maybe they will have need of it there," he said. He opened the door and stepped out into the hall, leaving Jesus to his fate.

╫╫╫

"What in the Abyss was that flash of light?" The guard asked as he rushed up to see to Theron. His eyes found the vampire's injured hand. "What did he do to you?"

"Nothing." Theron replied. "I was using a torch to try and get some information from him, but I used too much pitch and burned myself, instead. I'm fine. I'll stop by the infirmary when I leave here." The last wasn't a lie; Theron still had to deal with Taras.

The guard looked unconvinced, but said nothing more about it. "Too bad. You missed an interesting conversation with one of the guards stationed near the temple. He came in from his break to see

MCAFEE

Jesus. I wouldn't let him through since you were already in there, but he told me about a Passover tradition, and that Pilate might free Jesus tomorrow because of it. He even said—"

Theron's sword silenced the guard. He would have liked to use his claws, but the wound on his hand still burned, so he settled for cold steel. The legionary's eyes widened as Theron's fangs extended, and it was clear the man intended to scream. Theron twisted the blade as he'd done to Claudius, and the grimace that crossed the guard's face brought a measure of relief to his spinning mind.

You have been lied to, Vampire, and you have been betrayed.

He shook his head. Willing the unwanted thoughts to go away. He stood for a moment, staring at the dying guard. *This is who I am. This is what I do.* Theron growled, then yanked the blade free, watching as the man fell to the stone floor, his life ebbing away in a growing pool of crimson. He felt stronger, and he glared at the fallen soldier. *This is power,* he thought, *not forgiveness.* Yet even as he thought it, he recognized the small spark deep inside him that longed for something else. A return to the light. The thought filled him with peace, and it also paralyzed him with fear. He shut his eyes and forced such thoughts from his mind until the relative clarity of his anger returned. This was all Jesus's fault. He licked the points of his teeth as he watched the guard's blood spill away. He still needed to feed; the encounter with Jesus had taken a lot out of him. The soldier still lived, though only just. It would be easy enough to feed before going to see Taras.

"Good job," a voice behind him said. "Now let us out!"

Theron, shocked that he'd almost fed right in front of a human, whirled to see a haggard, filthy face pressed to the hole in one of the doors.

"Who are you?" Theron asked.

"Zealots, like yourself. Aren't you here to rescue us?"

Theron was about to tell the man no, and to enjoy his execution, when an idea occurred to him. *So, Pilate might let Jesus go, eh? Not if I can help it.* He looked up and down the hall. In total, it contained eight rooms, and at least three of them held prisoners whose faces pressed against the doors.

He still needed to see Taras. The guard's revelation that Pilate might pardon Jesus made the need even more pressing. These men would provide a perfect distraction. He unlocked every door except the one to Jesus's cell, and even let two men out of the stocks. By the time he finished he'd freed five zealots in all. Theron tossed one of them the dead guard's sword and carefully instructed them on how to get out of the barracks.

"What is your name, friend?" One of them, the one with the sword, asked.

"Ephraim," Theron lied.

"I am Barabbas," the man said, and saluted. Theron returned the salute with as much grace and severity as he could muster while thinking to himself the gesture looked ridiculous. "Go. All of you. God speed, now."

The zealots turned and ran up the hall, and Theron stifled the urge to laugh as he watched them run to their doom. The directions he gave them would send the whole group right into the legionaries' sleeping quarters. When the legionaries awoke and discovered five escaped zealots in their midst, the alarm would be loud and long. In the confusion it should be easy enough for him to finish his business with Taras.

Theron walked up the passage, looking for the infirmary. As luck would have it, he found it just as the zealots were discovered free of their cells. The alarm rang all through the barracks, and the two guards stationed outside the infirmary door, bored with their duty, left their post and ran to see what the commotion was about.

Theron entered the room and saw Taras lying on a cot against the wall. The man looked stretched and thin, weak as a babe. It would have been all too easy to kill him right then, but Theron's plan had changed.

Pilate might free Jesus tomorrow out of tradition. The guard's words came back to him. Passover. How could he have forgotten? If Pontius Pilate decided the next morning to let Jesus go free, Theron would be unable to stop him. After all, Theron could not go out into the sunlight. Damn it all, nothing about this assignment was going according to plan. Well, all that was about to change. Theron might not be able to stand in the sunlight and manipulate Pilate, but Taras could. Jesus would *not* be set free tomorrow, and Taras would see to it. He walked over to the cot and shook the sleeping legionary's shoulder.

When Taras opened his eyes and saw who'd awakened him, he tried to scream. Theron clamped his hand over the prone soldier's lips.

"Hush now, Taras, Theron said. "I won't hurt you." As he spoke, he pictured fingers in his mind; similar to those he'd used to charm Marcus the previous night. The fingers grew longer and longer until they extended to the legionary, then they wrapped around his head and held it in place, sinking slightly beneath the surface of the skin and burrowing into his psyche. Taras's heartbeat slowed to normal, and his breathing evened out. When his victim hadn't blinked for a count of sixty, Theron removed his hand from Taras's mouth.

"That's better," he said.

"What do you want?" Taras asked. "Have you come to finish me off?"

"Of course not. I just want to help."

"Help with what?"

"Seeing Jesus brought to justice, of course."

"Jesus?" Taras sounded confused, then his eyes caught fire. "*Jesus!* That damn zealot. Where is Marcus?" Taras asked. "I have to tell him about—"

"Marcus is dead," Theron interrupted.

"What? How?"

"He and a group of soldiers arrested Jesus a few hours ago in the Gardens of Gethsemane. On their way back into the city, several of Jesus's men attacked. They overwhelmed Marcus and two of his men, but not before the rest managed to escape with Jesus in tow. Angry at their failure, Jesus's men butchered the centurion. They removed his head and threw it into the dirt. Zealots, all of them. And Jesus is their leader."

"You are no better, whoever you are," Taras said with a surprising note of defiance. "I saw the real Ephraim's body. He carried a letter for Malachi. Warning him that people were coming who would try to kill them both. Ephraim's own seal was pressed into the wax. I also saw you enter the house near the Damascus Gate. The one with the demon inside."

Theron, stunned, couldn't speak. *He saw me enter the Gatehouse? He saw a Lost One?* He hadn't realized he'd been so careless. He hoped the Council didn't know. On top of that, Taras had seen the real Ephraim's body. No wonder the mind hold wasn't working as well as it should.

Thinking fast, he managed to come up with an excuse that, when combined with the influence he wielded on Taras's mind, he hoped would satisfy the legionary. "I don't know whose body you saw, but it wasn't mine. My ring was stolen from me three weeks ago while I slept outside of Jesus's camp. As for the house, you were meant to see it, and the demon as well. I knew you were following me. I wanted you to see the creatures this 'Messiah' has aligned himself with. Did you like what you saw?"

Taras, looking confused and afraid, didn't say anything. He simply shook his head.

"I thought not. Jesus must be stopped, Taras. Pilate doesn't know about Jesus's plans to overthrow Rome because Marcus didn't live long enough to tell him. So tomorrow Pilate may release him out of Jewish tradition. You must make sure that doesn't happen."

"But I can't walk. I can barely speak. How am I going to stop him?"

"I will help you. I can make you strong again."

A tear welled up in Taras's eye as he looked down at his ruined body. The knees and elbows were stretched beyond repair, or so it looked to him. Theron could read Taras's thoughts through the link between their minds, and he could feel the man's despair at what he thought were permanent wounds. Theron could have told him he would almost assuredly heal in a matter of weeks, but it suited his purpose for Taras to believe otherwise. He needed him on his side tomorrow, while the sun was up. It wouldn't hurt for the legionary to think he'd been spared by a miracle.

"You...you can do that?" Taras asked.

"I can, and I will. First you must promise me, no matter what it takes, Jesus will not walk free tomorrow."

Through their mental connection, Theron saw the image of Marcus form in Taras's mind, and he felt the pain of his loss along with the anger for those responsible. He could also see that Taras still doubted him, but despite his misgivings, the legionary desperately wanted to believe Theron's words. He wanted to believe he could be saved, and he wanted to believe the man who could do so stood in front of him, trying to convince him to save Rome, as well.

"Do we have a deal?" Theron asked.

After a few seconds' hesitation, Taras nodded.

"Swear it."

"I swear," Taras said in a harsh whisper. "On my life, Jesus will pay for his crimes. I will see it done if it's the last thing I ever do."

"Excellent, Taras. Then I will help you. Sleep now. When you wake, your body will be whole. Do not forget your promise."

Taras's eyes closed, and before a full minute passed he was in a deep slumber, enhanced to no small degree by the psalm Theron cast on him. When the legionary was fully asleep, Theron opened his mouth wide, revealing his razor sharp fangs. His bite, if he didn't use it to kill, would actually increase the human's healing abilities. The vampire's bite was the first step to creating a new vampire. The magic that kept him alive would seep into the human's body and make him stronger and faster to heal. It wasn't permanent. If nothing else happened to sustain the transformation the effects would wear off in about a month. But it would do for now. After all, Theron only needed one day.

He sank his teeth into Taras's neck, puncturing the artery just below the surface of the skin. The taste of blood sent a shiver through his body, and he couldn't stifle a moan. Theron needed blood. He needed a lot of it, in fact. His ordeal with Jesus had left him weak and drained, and his manipulation of Taras's mind had weakened him further. Only blood could heal and replenish him.

Despite the ache in his chest, Theron drank only a little. He needed Taras alive, and the man would need his blood and his strength for the day to come. Also, Theron's time ran thin, and he couldn't stay much longer. Already the zealot "escape" had been thwarted, and the guards were on their way back to their posts. He left Taras sleeping in peace and went out into the halls, where he soon learned the results of his plan.

The roused legionaries managed to kill one of the escapees and recapture three others, but one of the prisoners escaped. A baker named Matthew who'd just come to the city last week. He'd been scheduled for execution tomorrow, but now he might never be found. During the escape attempt the fleeing zealots killed over a dozen soldiers. One zealot in particular, a burly, hard featured man known as Barabbas, had put his sword through no less than five. Theron thought he recognized the name as the fellow he'd handed the sword back in the dungeon, but he couldn't be sure. His memory of those first few moments after his encounter with Jesus was cloudy.

Barabbas still lived, but Theron had a feeling the man would soon wish he didn't. Roman legionaries could make death seem a true mercy when they wanted; it was one of the qualities Theron's people most admired about them.

He left the barracks somewhat weak, but in a good humor, confident he'd set things right at last. Marcus was dead, Jesus soon would be, and Taras would help him see to it. Taras's words came to him as he walked away. *I will make certain Jesus pays for his crimes, if it is the last thing I do in this life.*

Taras could have no idea his proclamation would prove more prophetic than he imagined. The man was a loose end, after all. He would see to Taras's death personally tomorrow night. But for now he needed rest. He didn't wish to go back to the Halls; doing so opened up the possibility of running across a Council member, which meant he might have to take time to explain his plan. The Council would not approve, especially since it relied on letting Taras – who knew the location of the Gatehouse in Jerusalem and had even seen a Lost One – live for another day. They would want him to go back and kill the legionary right away, but Theron had other ideas. Taras still had a job to do.

Rather than face a debate and risk the disapproval of his elders, Theron elected to find another place to spend the day, which presented its own unique challenge. Where could he go? The tunnels below the city were the obvious choice because they were cool and sheltered from the sun, and Theron knew most of the nooks and crannies very well. Of course, Theron was not the only one who knew about them; the zealots used them regularly. However, that could work to his advantage.

After all, he still needed blood.

CHAPTER TWENTY-FOUR

Taras woke about an hour before dawn, his muscles sore from the long night on the hard stone bench of the infirmary. The soldiers who'd removed the bodies of Justus and Epidius, not knowing what else to do, had wrapped him in clean white blankets and left him alone, perhaps afraid to make things worse. Taras didn't know. His memory of the previous night was vague.

He grit his teeth together and braced himself for the pain, but it didn't come. Curious, he lifted his right arm and held it in front of his face, expecting to feel a sharp jolt in his elbow where the fat man stretched his tendons near to breaking. But there was no pain. And his elbow, far from the angry red, swollen mass of tissue he remembered from the day before, now looked normal and healthy. He closed his eyes, not quite willing to believe what they showed him. He counted to ten and opened them again, positive the view would be different. But nothing had changed. The tendons in his elbow were not stretched and swollen, his hand didn't tremble, and best of all, nothing hurt.

The previous twenty four hours were an eternity of suffering and agony. He vividly recalled the feeling of his joints popping out of place as the fat man pulled the lever, causing the two main sections of the rack to stretch apart. He shivered at the remembered fear and terror of knowing he would die there, his body literally torn in two. But the pain was gone; no trace of it remained to hinder him. Only the memory of the experience lingered to cause him distress.

But the torturer from the chamber wasn't the only stranger crowding Taras's memory.

Ephraim, he thought, remembering the man who healed his wounds. He'd claimed the body buried in Ephraim's backyard was another victim of the butcher Malachi. Taras believed him, though something nagged at the back of his mind. He felt he was forgetting something, but try as he might he couldn't grasp it. Like a dust mote in a sunbeam, it fluttered away any time his hand got too close. After a few minutes spent trying to capture the escaping thought, he gave up. It wasn't important, anyway. Not nearly as significant as the lack of pain in his limbs.

Ephraim had kept his promise; Taras felt whole and well. He laughed, giddy as a child with a new toy. It was true. The man had healed him. Completely. He'd saved Taras from a horrible, slow death. In fact, Taras realized with growing wonder, he'd never felt better in his entire life. He jumped out of bed and put his arms and legs through some exercises, marveling at how much stronger and faster his body felt now than ever before. It felt like someone else's body. A gift from Ephraim, perhaps. A stronger, better version of his old self to help with his task.

He stopped. His expression hardened as he remembered more of the previous night's encounter. This gift had a price, and now Taras must fulfill his part of the agreement. Jesus had to die. Today.

He ran to the armory and grabbed a uniform and a sword. The wide-eyed quartermaster in charge of provisions gave them to him without argument, amazed by his seemingly miraculous recovery. Taras thanked the man and left, headed for the kitchens, led by his grumbling belly. He would stop and grab some bread before he left the barracks. From there he would go and see the Prefect. Somehow, he would make certain Pilate didn't free Jesus.

After he spoke to Pilate and ensured Jesus's execution he would go visit Mary. Damned if it was daytime and damned if Abraham didn't like it. The last few days had taken him too close to death for his liking, and he would not waste any more time worrying about what Abraham might do. He would be with Mary, and the old man would not stop him. Not anymore. To the Abyss with Jewish law; tonight he would he would ask her to marry him, and tomorrow he and Mary would be on the road to Rome. All this and much more he decided on his way to see the Prefect.

But Taras never got a chance to talk to him. The sun was just peeking over the horizon when he arrived at Pilate's house to find a dozen heavily armed legionaries standing in a semicircle around the Prefect's door. They stood just outside the huge dwelling, barring the area in front of the house and keeping it clear from the many passers-by. Taras knew a few of the men, and noted that Pilate had chosen his guards well. The twelve legionaries standing around his front entryway were some of the best soldiers in Jerusalem. Taras walked up to one of them and asked to see Pilate.

"The Prefect isn't seeing anyone this morning," the soldier said, nodding his head to the street in a clear indication he was not interested in conversation.

"Why not?" Taras asked.

"Didn't you hear? Marcus the centurion is dead. A patrol along the road to the Gardens of Gethsemane found his body this morning. Someone cut off his head not far from the Damascus Gate. Fabian's body was also found, stabbed through the chest. Every man in the patrol that arrested Jesus last night said Marcus, Fabian, and Hirrus broke off from the main group and never rejoined them. Hirrus has not been found, and Pilate is furious. Because of this, and also the murder of the dungeon guard last night and subsequent escape of the zealot prisoners, he now believes Hirrus is a traitor to Rome. He also suspects there are others. Thus he will not allow anyone inside until the treacherous dog is found and interrogated, as well as any of his comrades."

Taras recalled Ephraim telling him about Marcus's death the night before, but he wanted to make sure he had his story straight.

"Marcus and Fabian? When? How did they die?"

"Last night, not long after they arrested Jesus. They must have been ambushed somewhere between the Gardens of Gethsemane and the Damascus Gate. Hirrus must have arranged for the three of them to become separated from the main group."

"So Hirrus is a zealot? Are you sure?"

"It seems likely, don't you think? In any case, Pilate believes it. He ordered his house sealed the moment he heard the news."

Something about it didn't make sense, though. "I can understand why they would want to kill Marcus," Taras said, "but Filius? why Filius? What was he to the zealots?"

The guard shrugged. "Wrong place, wrong time."

Taras thought about Marcus, noble Marcus, who'd always been the image of a good leader and friend, lying headless in the street. Just like his brother. He wondered if anyone had found footprints on Marcus's cheek, as well. Probably. The thought boiled in his mind, and heat spread all over his body, pushing sweat from his pores and causing his hands to shake. He longed to hit something, or someone. Anything at all would be better than this helpless frustration.

Taras maintained control by reminding himself that the man responsible for Marcus's death was in custody, and unless he spoke with Pilate the bastard might go free. He whispered a silent goodbye to his fallen comrade. He would grieve later, right now he didn't have time. He had to get in to see Pilate. If anything, Marcus's death made the matter more urgent than before.

"You have to let me see the Prefect," he said.

The guard shook his head.

"But I must speak with him. It's important."

"I'm sorry, soldier. Orders are orders. Only Caiaphas and a few temple guards are allowed to see the Prefect. No others."

Taras stood in front of the guard, not knowing what to do. He couldn't fight twelve of Jerusalem's best legionaries. He would have to find another way. Deflated, he turned to leave, but recalled his conversation with Ephraim. *You must promise me, no matter what it takes, Jesus will not walk free tomorrow.* He turned back to the guard. "What of the Nazarene Marcus arrested last night? What will happen to him?"

"Did you drown yourself in wine last night? By the gods, where have you been?"

"Just tell me."

"Well," the guard leaned close to Taras, probably trying to avoid hostile ears. "Pilate is under pressure from the Sanhedrin to have Jesus executed, but the Prefect has made it clear he has no wish to do so. In fact, he has publicly announced that he has no idea why Marcus arrested him in the first place. But the Sanhedrin are adamant the rabbi be crucified. So Pilate, in an attempt to compromise, has offered to let the people of Jerusalem decide the Nazarene's fate. Since this is Passover, Jewish tradition demands one condemned man be set free. Pilate will allow the people of the city to voice their opinion by putting Jesus on his balcony with another prisoner and giving Jerusalem the choice between the two."

"Who is the other prisoner?"

"Barabbas." The guard grinned. "The people of Jerusalem are not likely to cast their vote for the likes of him. In just a few hours Pilate will have his way, I'll wager, and those damned Sanhedrin won't like it one bit."

By the gods, the guard was right. Like all the legionaries in Jerusalem, Taras had heard of Barabbas. The man was a zealot who'd been implicated in the deaths of over a dozen Roman soldiers as well as a few other residents of the city, even a handful of Jews he considered Roman sympathizers. Marcus had tried several times to capture him, but the zealot was a slippery devil; always escaping against seemingly impossible odds. Marcus finally caught him a week ago. Just having Barabbas locked up seemed to put the entire population of Jerusalem at ease, Roman and Jew alike. Or at least it had until Didius and Claudius were found dead a few days ago.

Taras recalled hearing from another soldier that Barabbas had murdered several Romans the night before while trying to escape from the dungeon. Only the zealots would respect such a thing. The rest of the city feared him far too much to allow him to walk free. All in all, from the Prefect's position it was a clever move. He would not have to execute a man he considered innocent, he would rid himself of a dangerous criminal, and perhaps best of all, it would appear to all of Israel that he had made every effort to cooperate with Jewish tradition. Taras's respect for the prefect's mind grew.

But Pilate didn't know about Jesus's plans to overthrow Rome. Only Taras and Marcus knew, and Jesus's people had killed Marcus before he could pass along his knowledge to the Prefect, leaving Taras as the sole Roman in possession of such knowledge. He had to find a way to get to Pilate and tell him of Jesus's efforts to start a civil war. Barring that, he had to find a way to convince Jerusalem to vote to set Barabbas free.

But how?

"Taras?" A voice from behind him said. "Is that you?"

"Yes?" He turned, not knowing what to expect, but then he saw one of Pilate's guards step away from the house. The young recruit stood a foot shorter than Taras, with easy blue eyes and deeply tanned skin. His stocky frame and jovial features made him look soft, but Taras knew better. The man's name was Pavo. The two shared the same barracks and sparred on a regular basis, often going out for a mug of ale afterward. They weren't friends, exactly, but

Pavo was certainly no stranger, and in this case it pleased Taras to see a possible ally. "Oh, it's you. Hello, Pavo."

"Hello, Taras," Pavo said, "It is good to see you up and walking. I heard you were injured."

"It was not as serious as it seemed."

"So I see," Pavo replied, looking Taras up and down.

"I'm fine," Taras said, not wanting to waste time discussing his injuries. The less he had to explain, the faster he could get to his task. "Can you get me in to see Pilate, Pavo?"

Pavo shook his head. "I'm sorry, Taras. Pilate himself gave the order. No one is to see him until the traitor is found and executed. But Captain Arius over there has something for you." He nodded his head to the leader of the group. A captain who'd served under Marcus's predecessor.

Taras thanked him and walked over to the captain, where he stopped and saluted. "My name is Taras."

"Is it, now?" Arius grumbled. He scrutinized Taras for perhaps a count of thirty, then reached into a pouch at his side and pulled out a rolled sheaf of papyrus. "Here. This was found on Marcus's body."

"What is it?"

"I have no idea. It's addressed to you."

Taras took it and examined the rolled sheaf. *Taras* was written on the side in Marcus's bold, black script. The disk of red wax bearing the Centurion's official seal lay in two pieces, each stuck to the paper. He looked up at Arius. "The seal is broken."

"Pilate wanted to read it."

"I see," Taras replied. "Thank you, sir." He saluted the captain again, turned, and walked away, not wanting to read Marcus's last missive to him in front of so many others. *A useless gesture*, he thought. While Captain Arius had said Pilate wanted to read it, Taras held little doubt that several other pairs of eyes had read it, as well. With the seal broken, the information in the scroll became free game for anyone nosy enough to peek.

When he judged himself to be a safe enough distance from prying eyes, he opened the parchment. It was dated for the next day.

Effective on the date noted above, I Marcus Imbellicus, Centurion of the Fourth Barracks in Jerusalem, located in the province of Judea, hereby grant to Taras Aurelius, a legionary under my command, release of service to the Ro-

man Legion. Taras's discharge is honorable, and he is to be granted full rights and privileges as accorded thereof, including...

Taras blinked, then skimmed to the top of the document, wanting to make sure he'd read it correctly. *My release papers?* He looked to the bottom of the paper and there, on the lower left corner, was the Centurion's Official Seal. The papers were legitimate. Marcus had released Taras from his service to the Legion hours prior to his death. But why?

He thought back to his last conversation with Marcus. *I have a request to make of you*, he'd said.

Very well, Taras. Perhaps after you make your morning report? Marcus was smiling when he said it. Had he known what Taras's favor would be? Staring at the piece of parchment in his hand, Marcus's last official document, Taras knew he had.

Fighting back tears, he rolled the paper up and stuffed it into his pouch. He still had to do something about Jesus, but it would be several hours before Pilate brought the rabbi out to face the people. He desperately needed something good to lift his sagging spirits.

He turned and started walking to Mary's house, thinking as he went that he'd changed his mind; he hoped Abraham would not be home, after all. Taras was in no mood for the merchant's accusing stare, and he didn't want to have to hurt the man on his last day as a legionary.

Luck was with Taras that morning. As he neared Mary's home in the Upper City he saw her standing in the street twenty or so paces from her front door. She was engaged in conversation with another woman whose name Taras had never bothered to learn, and the two chatted animatedly over an ornate iron fence. When Mary spied him approaching she smiled and excused herself. She walked out into the street to meet him, and since she had her back turned she didn't see the glare the other woman gave Taras.

"Hello, legionary," Mary said. "Any new business to discuss?"

That was their cover for their daylight meetings. Taras was just an ordinary legionary talking to the lady of a wealthy household on matters of import. Mary thought the ruse had worked quite well in the past, and Taras didn't have the heart to disillusion her. Most of her neighbors saw right through it, but so far none of them had said anything. Most, like the woman at the fence, simply glared at Taras when Mary's attention was somewhere else.

But Taras had decided not to live this particular lie any longer, and he didn't hesitate. As soon as he was close enough, he wrapped his arms around Mary and kissed her, hard, right in the middle of the street. He heard the collective gasps of a score of people who witnessed the display, but he didn't care. He felt no fear or shame, and his elation at finally making their relationship public overshadowed the angry murmurs from the gathered Jews. If anything, Taras felt relieved to bring their love out in the open because it meant he would not have to sneak around to be with her anymore. Besides, tomorrow he would be leaving this cursed city forever, and Mary would be with him. The two of them would move to the outskirts of Rome and start their lives there, away from zealots and violence, away from death and her father, away from the judging eyes of those who disapproved, and far away from the influence of the Sanhedrin.

After her initial moment of surprise, Mary returned his passion. She put her arms around him and pulled him close. The two stood that way for several heartbeats, ignoring the muttered insults from the shocked observers.

After a few moments, Taras reluctantly pulled away. He looked at Mary's olive face, flush with pleasure, and he smiled. Then he ushered her into a nearby doorway, not wanting to be overheard or seen. He chose one that was deep and sheltered from the sun by an overhang. There he grasped her shoulders and turned her to face him. He longed to kiss her again, but first thing's first. "Is Abraham home?"

"No," she said. "He is still in Bethany."

"Good." He removed his arms from her shoulders and grasped her hands. She smiled at him, her eyes radiant and sparkling. Taras felt his heart ache just to look at her. His arms broke out in goose-flesh, and he almost couldn't speak past the sudden lump in his throat. "Marry me, my love. I can't stand this hiding any longer."

"Oh, Taras..." Her smile vanished. Her lower lip trembled as moisture collected in the corners of her eyes. "Why would you ask me this?"

"Don't you want to marry me?"

"Of course, but—"

"But nothing. I love you, Mary. Aren't you tired of hiding?"

"Yes, Taras, but you know the Temple will never allow it."

"I don't give a damn about the Temple. Look at this." He pulled his release papers out and showed them to her. "I'm leaving Jerusalem tomorrow morning, never to return. I want you to come with me. We will not need anyone's approval to marry in Rome. There is a small field I know of deep in the Roman countryside where olive trees and grapevines grow wild. Beside the field is a small cottage, just big enough to start a family. I have some money saved, and we will buy it. Or if not that one, then another. There are many such fields and cottages in the Roman countryside. None as grand as your current house, but it will be all ours, and the two of us can make it our own. That is the life that waits for us away from this wretched city." Taras swung his arm in a wide arc, indicating the whole of Jerusalem.

Tears built up in her eyes as he spoke. Her lips turned up, hinting at a smile. "Is this real?" She asked, pointing at the paper.

He nodded. "It is. I am free to leave anytime I wish. Will you come?"

She hesitated, and a single tear spilled from her left eye and rolled down her olive cheek. She turned to look at her father's house, not quite visible from where they stood in the doorway, and her shoulders slumped. His heart lurched in his chest. She couldn't do it. She couldn't leave her father, her family, and everything she'd ever known to follow him to a foreign country where she wouldn't even speak the language. He'd been foolish to expect it of her. It was asking too much. His own eyes began to sting with tears when she turned back to face him. He squared his shoulders, preparing his heart for the coming refusal.

"Yes," she said, crying openly now. "I will."

╫ ╫ ╫

Taras walked away from Mary's house with a renewed spring in his step that didn't diminish even as he was forced to push and shove his way through the growing horde of people making their way to Pilate's house. No matter how many times the crowd jostled him, or how many of them tossed insults his way, Taras's face beamed with a smile he could not contain.

She said yes.

Tomorrow, he and Mary would be well on their way to a new life together in Rome, and the Jews of Israel could scorn and insult some other poor soul. Before he left her house, they made plans to meet in the market square two hours after sunset. That would give the streets plenty of time to empty. He would have a wagon and a pair of draft horses waiting to carry them out of the city, and they would no longer have to worry about her father.

Taras just needed to take care of one last detail. He had to see to Jesus's execution. Seeing Mary and getting a much needed break from his day helped to cool his despair, but it hadn't given him any insight into how to go about fulfilling his promise to Ephraim. And so he began walking aimlessly through the streets of Jerusalem. A little less than two hours remained before Pilate would pronounce his judgment, and Taras had yet to come up with a plan that would ensure the Nazarene went to Golgotha. Time was running out. *Think, Taras! Think!*

He wandered the cobbled streets for almost half an hour, and soon found himself far away from the area of Pilate's house. This area spoke of less affluence and more hunger. The prostitutes of the city lived here, as well as the thieves and beggars. Of significantly more importance to Taras than the prostitutes, beggars, and thieves, however, was the fact that many zealots frequented the area, as well. To him, this fact alone spoke volumes about what sort of people the zealots were.

His mind weary from running around in circles, he stopped to sit, resting his back against a wall. It was no use. He could think of nothing that would aid him in his task. Dejected, he watched as scores of people walked by. He noted the shabby clothes and lean builds of many of the area's inhabitants as they went about their early morning affairs. Strange that it had never occurred to him before just how many poor lived in the city. Looking at the crowds as they walked by, at least half of them looked underfed or maltreated in some way.

Could that be right? He wasn't sure. His perception might be off, and he was certainly in one of the poorer sections of town. Yet even from these wretched hovels people spewed forth to cast their voices at the Judgment, which would happen in less than two hours. *They probably want to make sure they get a good view.* Taras wrinkled his nose. He'd never enjoyed crucifixions. Too long and boring for his taste. Granted, the victim suffered a great deal during an agonizing and slow death, but for a public execution, he'd take a beheading or a drawing and quartering any day. Both were fast, efficient, and quite a deterrent to would-be criminals. Something about having your arms and legs ripped from your torso seemed to scare people out of breaking the law, and what was the point of public executions if not to put the fear of justice into the hearts of wicked people? People, Taras mused, like Jesus.

Taras stood and paced along the cobbled street, walking through the impoverished sections of Jerusalem. The city's poor led hard lives. It was a pity they wouldn't get paid for their vote. Many of them looked like they could use a good meal.

Taras stopped in mid-step, and a man and woman walking behind him were forced to sidestep or bump into the legionary. The man swore at Taras under his breath, but he didn't notice, his mind was too busy turning over his new idea.

A pity they won't get paid…

"That's it!" Taras said aloud, startling the couple who'd just passed him. He turned and ran for the barracks, his plan forming in his mind as he went. The centurion of any barracks kept a safe hidden in his chambers. The safe would be heavy with gold and silver from Rome, which the centurion used to maintain his complex and pay his men. There would be a great deal of money there, as large groups of soldiers were expensive to house, train, feed, and clothe. With Marcus dead, his chambers would be empty. Taras knew the hiding place of the centurion's safe. More importantly, he knew where Marcus kept the extra key. It wouldn't be stealing, really. Marcus was dead, after all. And the money would go to see justice done for the betterment of Rome.

Jerusalem's poor would feast tonight, and Jesus would hang from a cross.

CHAPTER TWENTY-FIVE

Adonia jumped as a heavy fist pounded on her door. She'd just gotten word that Marcus, too, had been killed, and she wondered what dreadful news would come to her now. She looked at the door and decided this time she would not answer it. Far better to let whomever it was leave and take their ill news – and she was certain it *would* be ill news – with them.

Unfortunately, Opilio held no such compunction. Before she could tell him no, he ran to the door and yanked it open. There in the entry, framed by the morning sunlight, stood the dark silhouette of yet another legionary. The man, quite tall and muscular with the golden hair and ice blue eyes of a northerner, stepped through the doorway but stopped just inside, obviously waiting for an invitation.

"What is it, this time?" Opilio asked, his arms crossed over his chest. He scowled up at the legionary, looking unimpressed by his size or manner. "Is my other uncle dead, as well?"

The soldier at the door looked shocked to be addressed in such a manner. In truth, Adonia cringed at the disrespectful tone of her son's voice, especially to a legionary. Her husband's death had been a terrible blow to all of them, and losing Marcus so soon after had almost crushed the boy. The strain was taking its toll on Opilio's manners, which could be dangerous. Many legionaries could be very unforgiving if slighted, and she feared for her son's welfare if he could not control his temper.

But after a moment, the legionary smiled. The smile didn't reach his eyes, however, and Adonia noted for the first time how dejected and worn down the man's face looked. "You must be Opilio," the soldier said. "Marcus told me a lot about you. My name is Taras."

Opilio's entire manner changed. He dropped his arms to his sides and the scowl left his face. "You knew my uncle?"

Taras nodded, and Adonia moved to get a better look at him. She noted the sad look in his red-rimmed eyes as he said the name of her dead brother-in-law. It was a feeling she knew all too well. Her heart, which in two days' time had been broken twice, now ached a third time for another soul whose loss showed so clearly on his face.

"He was a friend of yours, wasn't he?" She asked from the other side of the small room. Taras looked at her from his place just inside the doorway. He nodded, but said nothing.

"Come inside, please," Adonia said. "Sit with us."

Taras entered the house and crossed the room. Opilio followed behind him after closing the door. When the three were seated in the front room, Taras looked back at the closed door as though afraid it would overhear him, then he spoke. His words were so hushed she had to strain to hear them. "I have news. Jesus has been captured."

"We know," she replied. "We heard the news from one of the street vendors who passed by on their way to Pilate's house. Pilate is expected to have him crucified in just over an hour."

"He may yet walk free."

"What?" Opilio's face turned a bright red. "Why would Pilate set that treacherous, conniving—"

"Today is Passover," Taras cut him off. "The Prefect is obligated to release one condemned prisoner. He doesn't know about Jesus's involvement with the zealots, and I can't get in to tell him because of the guards at his door. I have it on good authority that Pilate is going to let the people of Jerusalem decide. He will put Jesus on his balcony with Barabbas and let the citizenry choose which of the two men he will pardon."

"Barabbas?" Adonia asked, confused. "Isn't he the one who killed five legionaries in the barracks last night?"

"The same."

"No!" Opilio shouted. "No, if he does that, the people are sure to free Jesus. No one wants Barabbas loose in Jerusalem."

Her son was right. Earlier that morning Adonia overheard her neighbors talking about the zealot's near escape in hushed, fearful tones. The entire city feared him, since he seemed inclined to kill anyone he thought might support Rome. Everyone seemed relieved to know such a dangerous man was locked away. They felt safer. They, like Pilate, didn't know Jesus was the true danger. Her anger, which she had kept under control for far too long, finally flared to the surface. "How can that be? The man responsible for my husband's murder will go free? What a ridiculous tradition."

"It doesn't matter," Taras said. He pulled six large bags from his belt and plopped them on the table. Adonia heard the clink of metal as they hit. "I have an idea, but I will need your help. Both of you. There is precious little time."

Adonia listened. Taras's plan would work, of course. She felt sad and relieved at the same time. The people of Jerusalem might lose some of their integrity today, but at least they could make sure Jesus never hurt anyone else again.

Taras stood in the midst of a bustling crowd gathered in front of the Prefect's house. He'd been there for about an hour, going from person to person and placing a gold coin in every hand he came to. Before he released the coin, he uttered a single sentence to each hand's owner.

"Barabbas goes free."

Many people looked at him, confused. Still others handed the coin back and turned away, unwilling to be part of such a thing. But most only smiled, then nodded in agreement, and Taras relinquished the gold to them. He'd changed out of his legionary's uniform to better blend in, but he still stood out among the gathered crowd. Tall and fair haired, he'd always been easy to spot among the Romans, as well. Not many northmen served in the Legion. But Taras grew up hearing of the great empire to the south, and as a child he had dreamed of belonging to something so grand. When he was old enough and strong enough, he left the house of his father and journeyed to Rome, where he adopted the name Taras to blend in and enlisted in the military. At the time, Rome needed soldiers badly, and so he was permitted to join.

After a few successful campaigns, he'd been sent to serve under Marcus, and the centurion had seen the potential in him right away. Marcus himself commissioned Taras for Rome's elite group, sending him to Carthage to train with Rome's best and most devious killers. In a few short years Taras became one of the deadliest men in the Roman Legion, serving his country with love and pride. His loyalty, brains, and fighting skill made him very valuable to Rome, yet Marcus signed his release papers so he could start a new life. And now Marcus was dead. Taras reminded himself of that as he wandered through the crowd dispersing Roman gold, knowing it would serve a greater purpose in bringing his centurion's killer, one of the most dangerous zealot leaders in recent memory, to justice.

Taras loved Rome. He served her with all his heart and soul. He truly believed the gods favored the Empire and that divine hands guided Caesar's work on earth. The idea that Jesus meant to try and overthrow Rome sent his pulse racing and shortened his breath. How could a man seek to overthrow the gods? To even think such a thing merited death in Taras's opinion. And death was exactly what the Nazarene would get. Taras, Adonia, and Opilio had spent the last hour making sure of it.

While he went about handing out his murdered friend's gold, he heard many rumors spreading through the crowd. Some said Jesus claimed to be the Son of God. Others said he *was* God. Still others spoke of blasphemy and even treason. More than once, Taras heard the people refer to Jesus as 'King of the Jews.' Upon hearing this, he could not help but smile. Such a title would not sit well with Pontius Pilate.

He couldn't see either of his accomplices, but he knew they were out there, working the crowd closest to the Prefect's house. Like him, they handed out coins and told the people to free Barabbas. He just hoped, between the three of them, they would be able to buy enough votes to sway the rest of the people. It had been Opilio's idea to start at the front of the crowd. He reasoned that those men and women closest to Pilate would be the first ones heard when the voting began. Once the voting seemed to go one way, many of those left undecided would likely side with the majority. He was right, of course. People were like sheep. They would follow along with whatever the greater numbers seemed to want. He had to give the boy credit; it was a good idea, and it showed the boy's intelligence. It struck Taras as the type of thing Marcus would do.

When Pilate finally brought the prisoners out onto the balcony, Taras stopped handing out coins and turned to stare at the two men standing behind the Prefect. The crowd, which had been murmuring a steady din for several hours, fell silent. Taras tensed. The fulfillment of his vow hung on what the crowd would say next. Would the people he paid keep their word? Would those paid by Adonia and Opilio do likewise? There was nothing more any of them could do now. He waited, and listened.

"Citizens of Jerusalem," Pilate began. "I bring before you two men. This one," he pointed to Barabbas, "is a murderer who has killed many. While this man," he pointed to Jesus, "is guilty of no crime. Both have been sentenced to death, yet you have a custom of asking me to release one man from prison each year at Passover. If you wish, I will free the King of the Jews."

A few of the people, very few, could be heard shouting their agreement that yes, Jesus should go free, but they were being drowned out by the rest of the crowd's overwhelming chant:

"No!" They shouted, "Free Barabbas!"

"Crucify the false King of the Jews!"

"Kill him!"

"Free Barabbas!"

Pilate stared at the crowd. His jaw fell open as he gaped at them in wide-eyed wonder. Clearly, the Prefect had expected a different verdict. But as little as Pilate might care for the idea, the people of Jerusalem had spoken. He would find it very difficult to go back on his word now.

Pilate spent another full minute listening to the masses, perhaps trying to make certain he'd heard their wishes correctly. Then his expression soured, and he held his arms up to quiet the crowd. When relative silence ensued, Pilate again addressed the gathering. "Very well," he said.

He turned to the guards on the balcony and gestured toward the bound and gagged Barabbas. "Release him. Then take the Nazarene inside and make him ready."

Taras cheered along with the rest of the crowd. Finally, justice would be done.

╬╬╬

Taras watched from the front of a shop next to Pilate's house when Jesus was brought out. He'd had to shove and push his way through the crowd to get close enough to see Pilate's door, but it was worth every scratch and scrape. From the many bruises and cuts on Jesus's body, Taras guessed he'd been beaten by the guards. The Nazarene wore a crown of thorns on his head, and Taras heard one of the soldiers snicker about 'the King of the Jews.' Several long, angry red gouges marked his forehead where the thorns had torn a path into his flesh, and blood flowed from his hair and into his face, where they mixed with the man's tears. Truly, he was a pitiful site, but Taras was far too angry to feel any pity.

"Here is the man," Pilate said.

In response, Caiaphas and the Sanhedrin shouted for Pilate to crucify Jesus, but Pilate shook his head.

"You crucify him," he said. "I find this man not guilty of any crime."

There followed a discussion between the Prefect and Caiaphas that Taras could not hear due to the overwhelming noise of the crowd. He did manage to catch a few words: 'rebel,' 'king,' and 'Caesar,' among them, but the rest was lost in the overall din. By the effect on Pilate's countenance, the priest must have threatened to bring Tiberius into the matter. *That seals it,* Taras realized. Pilate would not risk Caesar's favor or his position as Prefect for anything. Certainly not for a single rabbi whom the people of Jerusalem had already demanded be put to death.

I did it, Taras thought. *I kept my vow.* Marcus, Didius, Epidius, Justus, and many others would be avenged. Jesus of Nazareth, leader of the zealots and orchestrator of the murders of Roman citizens, would soon die on the cross. Taras could now leave Jerusalem with a clear conscience, knowing he left it a safer place for everyone.

The soldiers led the Nazarene and two other prisoners away, beating him and spitting on his back as he carried his own cross to Golgotha. Taras watched the procession go with a remote detachment, wondering why he didn't feel as triumphant as he thought he would in the face of such a victory. Jesus's bent, bleeding body passed within a few feet of him. The Nazarene looked up, and for a moment their eyes met; Taras's hard blue eyes and Jesus's soft brown ones. Jesus's gaze held him rigid for the span of two heartbeats, then the Nazarene looked to the ground again as one of the soldiers prodded him forward with a crack of his whip. Taras jumped at the sound, unsure why he should suddenly feel pity for such an evil man.

He turned to Pilate, who wiped a cloth across his sweaty forehead with one beringed hand. Taras marveled at the number of rings on the Prefect's fingers. One of them, he knew, carried the Prefect's official seal.

Taras stopped short. The ring! That's what I missed. His conversation with Ephraim came back to him in a rush.

My ring was stolen from me three weeks ago while I slept outside of Jesus's camp. Those were the words Ephraim used when Taras confronted him with the letter. But Taras never said anything about a ring. He only mentioned that the letter was sealed with Ephraim's personal seal. Taras had searched Ephraim's house while Marcus watched the digging in the backyard, and there was another, larger seal in Ephraim's desk. How, then, had the man known the seal used for the letter was the one on the ring? And now that Taras thought of it, why would Ephraim write a letter to Malachi warning him to be careful if he thought Malachi was coming to kill him?

Now he knew what had made him feel so uneasy about Ephraim, and why a large piece of the man's story had seemed out of place. The ring and the letter on the headless body. In his joy at being healed and his eagerness to see Jesus executed, Taras had forgotten about both. But now he knew the truth; Ephraim was dead. The man who came to him last night was an imposter.

Likewise, his sudden clear headedness brought back the memory of his last few moments on the rack. He recalled how the voice that had spoken to the fat man sounded so familiar. He'd thought it was Jesus, but now he recognized it as Gordian's voice.

In that instant, Tara's anger and hate evaporated, and he was left staring at the bloodstained, bruised back of a man he'd helped to condemn to death. Jesus was no zealot. Taras had helped send an innocent man to Golgotha with a cross strapped to his back.

"Dear gods," he whispered, "what have I done?"

Among the raucous, bloodthirsty shouts and jeers from the people nearby, no one heard him.

CHAPTER TWENTY SIX

An hour after sunset, Mary grabbed her cloak and her bag. The time had come to leave. She'd been packing all day, but as she stared at the piles of clothes and mementos in her bed-chamber, she came to realize she didn't want any of them. She had no idea how large a cart Taras would secure for the trip, but she knew she couldn't carry all her things to the market district. Besides, they were part of her past. Taras was her future.

She walked away from her belongings and stood in front of her mirror. The dress she'd chosen for her flight to Rome was easily the most daring outfit she possessed. She had purchased it from a travel-ing tailor, who told her the style and cut were quite fashionable in Rome. But the dress, with its plunging neckline that revealed quite a bit of her breasts, proved so bold she'd never had the courage to wear it. Her father would beat her if he ever saw her dressed like this. Far from discouraging her, the thought brought a smile to her face, and a small thrill shot up her spine. True, her father would hate it, but Taras would love it.

She turned away from the mirror and stepped through her bed-room door. As she passed the door to her father's office she paused long enough to slide a letter under it. She'd written it earlier, and was careful to give no hint of where she was going. Despite Taras's reassurances they would be safe in Rome, she had her misgivings. Her father was a man of wealth and influence, and he would spare no resource to find her, especially if he thought she'd broken Jewish law and married a Roman.

She stood and walked the rest of the way to the end of the hall, where she descended the stairway into the main room. She turned and took one last look at the house, the only home she'd ever known. Nervous despite her excitement, her fingers trembled on the door handle. Did she want this? Could she really leave her father's house in the middle of the night?

She thought of Taras, and the life he would be giving up for her, as well. He loved Rome, and he loved the Legion. Until they'd met, those two things were his entire life. Now he was prepared to walk away from everything he knew. She smiled as she thought of his deep blue eyes. They'd shone so bright when he asked her to marry him. How could she have said anything other than yes?

Her fingers on the door handle ceased their nervous twitching. Taras wasn't afraid, and by God she wouldn't be, either. She turned from her house and stepped out into the night, thinking thoughts of a small cottage surrounded by olive trees and strong, golden-haired children. Mary floated down the street and never once looked back.

In a tunnel below the city, Theron awoke hungry. Although he had important business to attend to, like confirming Jesus's death and getting to the Nazarene's tomb for a souvenir to prove as much to the Council, he was forced to concede that a hungry vampire is a weak vampire. So, instead of looking for Taras, as he'd planned, he instead set off in search of food, walking through the dark streets on the city hoping for a lost soul. A beggar would do, or even a solitary soldier. Just something to keep his strength up for when he had to deal with Taras, who would, by this point, be much stronger and faster than an ordinary human.

He was on his way to the market district when he saw her. A lovely Jewish woman out all by herself at a time of day when most reputable women were asleep or tending to their husbands' desires. Her dark hair fell around shapely olive shoulders, which were free and visible for all to see, although the normal citizens of Jerusalem would have balked at showing even a hint of skin below the neck.

Likewise, the woman's blouse was cut far too low for a respectable Jewish lady. As a result her ample cleavage bounced and swayed as she walked, catching his dark eyes and making him hungrier.

Given her attire, as well as the late hour, Theron took her for a prostitute, possibly out looking for business or returning from one of her encounters. In his many years as a vampire, he'd met many such ladies of the evening. In larger cities, they comprised the majority of his diet. They were readily available, easy to lure to a secluded spot, and best of all, no one ever missed them.

Most likely, no one would miss this one, either.

╬ ╬ ╬

Taras made his slow way to the market district, watching his feet plod along the cobbled street. He was late, but he couldn't make himself go any faster. Elated as he was to be meeting his love and leaving Jerusalem, he could not get the day's events out of his mind. The crucifixion of Jesus hung in his mind like a stubborn cobweb, refusing to be swept away. Although he'd wanted nothing more than to flee Golgotha and forget his guilt, he forced himself to stay and witness the whole thing from beginning to end. Thus he watched as the soldiers, laughing and taunting, drove nails into Jesus's wrists, and he continued to watch as one soldier stuck a spear in Jesus's side. Taras stayed on Golgotha until long past the moment Jesus's chest stopped moving and the soldiers cut his limp body from the cross. He owed the Nazarene that much.

Taras wept the entire time. At one point Jesus's own mother walked up to him to offer comfort. Taras, ashamed, turned away from her. How could he face her after what he'd done to her son?

After Jesus's body was carted off by his grieving family, Taras left Golgotha. He toyed with the idea of staying behind to help entomb the body, but he didn't have the strength or the time. He was already late. He had to meet Mary in the market so they could leave. Taras couldn't wait to put this wretched city at his back. The place had taken Marcus, Didius, and Gordian from him, and now it had claimed his self respect, as well. The city of Jerusalem had stolen almost everything Taras loved. Now Mary was all he had left, but she would be more than enough.

When they reached Rome, he could forget about Messiahs and demons. There he could settle down with his new wife and start a family. In Rome, there would be no hill called Golgotha to remind him every day of his involvement in Jesus's death. Maybe then Taras could live with himself. He hoped so, not only for his sake but for Mary's, as well. She was leaving behind everything she knew to go to Rome and marry him. He owed it to her to be a good husband and never make her regret the decision.

In Jerusalem, with its gray walls and constant struggles, he doubted he could be that husband. But in Rome, with Mary by his side and Pilate, the Sanhedrin, and Golgotha far behind him, he thought he would be all right.

He wiped a tear from his cheek, one of many to fall from his eyes that day, and continued on to the market district. If anything in this life could lift the weight from his shoulders, it would be Mary's smiling face. He finally picked up his pace, anxious get to her and leave Jerusalem forever.

╫ ╫ ╫

Mary stood in the market square, alone except for her shadow, wondering where her beloved was. It was not like Taras to be late. She would have to chide him for it when he arrived, just a little, but she could never be angry with him. She just wanted him to hurry. Now that she'd made her decision, she was eager to put Jerusalem behind her. And, she had to admit, she was very eager for him to see her in this blouse.

She heard footsteps behind her and smiled, thinking Taras had found her. She turned around and held out her arms, ready to start their new life together.

But it wasn't Taras.

A stranger stood in front of her, silhouetted from behind by a torch on the street. His features shrouded in shadow, she could only make out the outline of his head, which was framed by shoulder length, curly hair. His clothes, too, were dark, and made not a whisper of sound as he approached.

She dropped her arms to her side, putting her right hand on the hilt of a knife she always carried with her, her one concession to the dangers of the city. Taras had insisted she learn to use it when they started their late night encounters. Until this moment she'd always thought it an unnecessary precaution.

Not anymore.

Evil rolled off the newcomer in waves, a dark blanket that billowed out like black smoke. She could feel it, writhing through the air between them and tainting it with a foul odor. Mary staggered; amazed that something so vile could exist in her city. What manner of being was it? She didn't know, and she didn't intend to find out. She pulled her knife from her waist and pointed it at the stranger.

"Stay where you are."

He chuckled and took a step closer. When he moved, he stepped further from the influence of the torchlight, and his face came into view. She could just make out the dark features of the stranger's face; the outline of his nose, the black hollows where his eyes glinted, even his faint smirk. But it was his mouth that caught her attention. Two fangs poked from his upper jaw, looking like the teeth of a viper in a human face. As a child in Jerusalem, she'd heard the legends, but she never believed them. The knife fell from her fingers and clanged to the cobbles below.

"*Bachiyr*," she whispered. The Chosen. Not a he, but an it. A demon. Something so evil it could not possibly exist, yet there it was. And it was coming toward her.

She took a step back, trying to put some distance between her and the *Bachiyr*. Her knife lay in the street beside her foot, but she didn't move to retrieve it. The knife would be useless, and she knew it. She could not fight the thing, not by herself. Escape was her only hope.

The *Bachiyr* stepped closer, still smiling and showing off its fangs. Its eyes flashed bright red, then faded into the shadows of its brow. She opened her mouth to scream, but no sound came out. The area around the two of them had gone deathly quiet, as though the creature had sucked all sound from the city.

She turned to run. It didn't matter which direction; she just had to get away from the thing behind her. She needed to find Taras, and fast. If anyone could fight it, it would be him. He must be nearby; they were supposed to meet here, after all. If she could just stay away from the *Bachiyr* long enough to find him, she would be all right. *Please, God, let me find Taras.* She turned to look behind her, to see if the *Bachiyr* was close, but the street was empty.

Distracted, she plowed right into the creature. Somehow it had gotten in front of her. It wrapped its arms around her body and drew her close. She fought it, beating her hands against its chest and face, but nothing she did seemed to harm the thing. It grabbed her wrists and forced her arms behind her back, then it maneuvered its body behind her and braced her in an awkward position with its leg. She was still on her feet, but overbalanced and unable to move. She opened her mouth in another silent scream, then felt a sharp pain at the base of her neck, just above the breastbone. The *Bachiyr's* teeth.

Fire coursed through her body, she tried to double over, but the *Bachiyr* held her rigid and upright. Desperate, she shuddered and fought and kicked at the thing's legs as best she could, stomping on its instep and driving the heel of her feet into its shins, but it didn't budge. If the creature felt any pain at all, it didn't show it.

Taras, where are you?

Her vision swam with images of Taras and small cottages. She saw their children playing underneath a grove of olive trees. She watched as Taras returned home from the market with a trinket for each of them tucked under his arms. He smiled at her; that dazzling, beautiful smile she could never resist, his blue eyes sparkling under the sun. They kissed while their children giggled at the display, but neither of them cared. They had each other. They'd made it. Despite all they'd been through; Messiahs and zealots, prefects and priests, centurions and murders, they'd made it. They'd left Jerusalem and her horrors behind them.

I love you, Taras, she thought sleepily. She was so tired. All she wanted to do was sleep.

"That's a lovely ring," a voice by her ear said. It sounded faint, but Mary knew it was her own hearing that was weak. She nodded and murmured her thanks, but the world went dark before she could finish.

‡‡‡

Taras arrived in the market district almost an hour late. Mary was nowhere to be found. Had she tired of waiting and gone home? Or worse, had her father returned from Bethany early and learned of her plan? Perhaps Mary was even now trying to find a way out of her father's house to meet him. Or maybe she was hiding somewhere in the market district waiting for Taras.

"Mary?" He called. There was no answer. He dared not raise his voice lest he wake others in the city or alert any nearby soldiers to his presence. Officially, he was not yet released from service, and Pilate, fearing zealot retribution for Jesus's death, had placed all the legionaries in Jerusalem on extra alert. Thus he should be out patrolling with his fellow soldiers. If they saw him outside, he could be charged with desertion. But there was no other way; he and Mary had to leave tonight, before her father returned in the morning. He had enough gold to buy his way past the guards at Damascus Gate, if need be, and his papers would be official tomorrow. With the only guarded border from Judea more than a week's journey away, he would not have any trouble leaving the provinces.

But first he had to find Mary.

"Mary? Are you here?"

He walked through the market, looking for some sign of her, but there was none. Perhaps she'd changed her mind. Maybe the thought of leaving her home and family had proven too much for her. She could even now be in her bedchamber, trying to forget their foolish plan and waiting for her father to come home.

No, he'd seen the look in her eyes when he asked her to marry him. She wanted to come to Rome. Something must have happened. Taras started in the direction of her house. If Abraham had indeed come home early and locked her away, Taras would have something to say about it. Trouble between the two of them had been brewing for months, if it boiled over tonight, so be it.

Taras walked along the market streets headed for Mary's house, thinking of the possible confrontation with her father. He was not paying attention to where he placed his feet, and before he left the market district he tripped over an object lying in the street and fell. Cursing, he picked himself from the cobbles and looked to see what he'd tripped over.

A woman's shoe.

He reached over and picked it up, feeling the first cold stabs of dread. It was a soft brown sandal, lambskin, sewn together with gold thread. Clearly made for the delicate feet of a lady of means. A lady with enough money that she didn't have to wear shoes more suited to labor. He turned it over and saw a tiny drop of blood on it.

"No," he whispered. "No, it can't be."

He shot to his feet. "Mary? Are you here?"

Please, Jupiter don't let it be hers, he thought as he looked at the shoe in his hand. He looked up and down the street, searching for any sign of her. A short distance away, a small flutter of movement caught his attention. There, at the entrance to an alley, a small strip of blue cloth flapped in the breeze. He ran to it and picked it up. Silk. Expensive.

Then he smelled it; the overpowering, copper scent of blood. It came from deeper in the alley.

Taras dropped the cloth and pulled his sword. He stepped into the alley, looking left and right. There were no torches here, and the light from those in the street only penetrated a few short paces. He paused, waiting for his eyes to adjust. About halfway down the length of the alley, he spied a bundle of blue clothing lying on the ground. He walked up to it, and the smell of blood grew stronger with every step.

When he got within a few paces he stopped. His sword fell from nerveless fingers and dropped to the earth with a clang. Taras didn't hear it past the blood rushing into his ears. He scrambled forward on his hands and knees, not believing his eyes. But he could not deny the long, dark hair or the soft olive skin. Skin that was still warm, but cooling.

He screamed, no longer caring if he alerted any legionaries to his presence.

He'd found Mary.

╬╬╬

In the Halls of the Bachiyr, a shadowy figure walked along the dimly lit stone passageways to the Larder. He knew there would be humans there, restrained and waiting for a hungry vampire to come along. This suited him, of course, because he just happened to be a hungry vampire. But then, he was always hungry.

Along the way he met a Lost One in the tunnels. The filthy creature dropped to its knees until he passed, its tattered robe bunched on the floor around its bony knees, along with several maggots that lost their footing and fell to the stone with a sickening plop. He paid it no attention as he walked by, the abject fawning of a Lost One was nothing to him; he'd grown accustomed to such treatment long ago. After he passed by the thing, it shot to its feet and scurried off in the direction of the Council Chamber, doubtless to let Herris know of his arrival. It didn't even bother to pick up the maggots.

After a short time he reached the door to the Larder and pushed it open. Four humans, a man and three women, stood naked in the flickering torchlight of the chamber. All four were bound hand and foot to the wall by thick chains. The cuffs had chafed the wrists of two of the women, and the angry red flesh underneath the metal testified to their desperation to flee. Doubtless they'd almost yanked their hands off trying to tug free of their bonds. Blood trickled from the wounds, but not quite enough to overpower the smell of urine, vomit, and feces that assailed him. He would have to speak to Herris about the condition of the place. Someone should at least wash the filth from the humans; maybe Herris could assign a Lost One to the task.

Filthy or not, food was food, and he stepped into the chamber. The humans stared at him with eyes wide as saucers. The man and two of the women started screaming as soon as he walked into the room. The third woman hung her head, either too tired or too dazed to struggle. She would be the easiest, though none would present a problem, chained as they were to the wall. He walked toward her.

Her heart picked up speed as he got close. He could hear it thumping in her chest like a hammer. She knew what was coming, then, but still didn't move. Perhaps she'd just given up, and was now ready to die.

That was no fun.

He turned away from the subdued woman and grabbed the man, who screamed even louder at his touch. The *Bachiyr* sank his teeth into the man's throat, gashing the huge artery just under the skin. He shook his head back and forth, enlarging the hole and spraying blood all over his face, the wall, and the three women. He drank long and deep, swallowing plenty but making sure a good amount ended up on the wall behind him. He wanted it to be messy.

When he was finished he turned to one of the women. He smiled, tasting the blood on his lips. She screamed again, long and loud, and he leapt at her. He sank his fangs into her throat in much the same manner as he had the man's, shaking his head back and forth and ripping the hole in her neck wider with each move.

By the Father, they tasted good! Forget the smell of human waste that permeated the very walls of this chamber, these prisoners were fresh. They'd probably just come in from the outside. Herris must have been expecting him.

He drained the woman and moved on to another, biting her throat and shaking his head in the same manner, leaving the woman who hadn't screamed as the last human alive in the room. By the time his third victim was dead, blood from three humans covered the wall, dripping down the chains and filling the room with its heady, metallic aroma. His face was covered in the stuff, and when he looked up from his latest victim, he noted the last human wore almost as much blood as he did. It splattered the wall behind her and matted her hair, pasting it to her head. It covered her face in a crimson mask and ran down her chest in rivulets, dripping to the floor below and landing on her feet, which scrabbled for purchase on the now slick floor.

This time she did scream at his approach, and wracking sobs coursed the length of her body as she alternated between screaming and begging for her life. He stepped up to her and stopped, his face inches from hers. She closed her eyes and grit her teeth, and he smelled fresh urine as her bladder let go. He reached up and touched his fingers to his cheek. They came away stained with the blood of his three victims. He pressed his bloody fingers to her forehead and dug his nail into her flesh. She screamed anew as he drew her blood. Using his fingernail like a blade, he carved a letter in his ancient language. The letter was meaningless, but the woman screamed even louder.

He leaned in, wanting to make sure she smelled the blood on his breath.

"Not yet," he told her. "But don't go anywhere, I may be hungry tomorrow."

He turned away from her and walked through the door, his hunger more than sated and his need for diversion satisfied, as well. She sobbed as he left, still begging him to have mercy, and he smiled as he wiped the blood off his face with his traveling cloak. Mercy? Where did the woman think she was? He chuckled as he closed the door to the Larder and resumed his walk down the stone passage.

Ramah the Blood Letter had returned to the Halls of the Bachiyr.

CHAPTER SEVENTY SEVEN

Theron walked through Jerusalem's empty streets, still tasting the whore's blood on his lips. He'd had to mutilate her remains to disguise the fact that her veins were almost empty, but he'd used his sword and not his claws, figuring the zealots would likely shoulder the blame. After all, Pilate blamed them for just about everything these days, why not a dead prostitute. He could do nothing about the wound on her throat, however. She'd struggled too much for him to make a clean kill. He paused to admire the gold and ruby ring he'd taken from her finger. Beautiful. Probably worth a pretty penny, too. He smiled and slipped it into a pouch on his belt.

Aside from his new treasure, the woman's blood restored him in the manner that only blood could, and he felt more like his old self. The back of his hand still bore a patch of blackened skin from where he'd struck Jesus, but a few more humans should help that to go away. Meanwhile, he had to check on the status of his mission. He left the New City and headed toward the barracks, hoping to find Taras.

Instead of Taras, however, he came across a stranger dressed in a coarse black robe, his face hidden from view by a hood of the same color. By the stranger's broad steps and rolling gait, Theron took it to be a man. The newcomer walked along the other side of the street, headed in the opposite direction, but when he neared Theron he crossed over. Theron tensed as he approached. There could be only a handful of reasons for one stranger to approach another in the middle of the night, and none of them were good. A zealot, perhaps? More likely a bandit. Theron waited, wanting to give the man time to get close enough. His death would be swift and silent; his blood would help cleanse the blackened skin from Theron's hand.

The stranger stopped about five paces away.

"Good evening, Theron," he said.

Theron recognized the voice. "Simon?"

Simon nodded and pulled back his hood, revealing his dark skin and short, curly black hair. "I've been looking for you."

"Why? And what are you doing in Jerusalem? Does the Council know you are away from your post?"

"They know," Simon replied. Theron thought he detected a hint of sarcasm in the other's voice. "They sent me to find you. Ramah has returned to the Halls, and the entire Council wants to speak with you."

"What? Why? I haven't finished my work, yet."

"They didn't tell me. I guess they thought a *mere clerk* would have no need to know."

Theron definitely caught the sarcasm in Simon's voice that time, but was too distracted by the news the Council wanted to see him to think much of it. What did they want? A thought came into his mind, then. Taras had been to the Gatehouse in Jerusalem, he'd even seen a Lost One. Did the Council know? Theron looked at Simon, noting the other's smug expression, and he had his answer. Of course the Council knew. They always knew. The Lost One had probably informed Simon of the intruder at the door. Doubtless the clerk had gotten a great deal of pleasure out of revealing Theron's mistake to the Council himself, damn him.

And damn the Council, too, for that matter. This mission was supposed to be a simple assassination, but it turned into a much more complex and delicate operation, and there were many factors involved of which they could have no knowledge. Did they have so little faith in his ability to clean up his own mess? Apparently so, for if Ramah had returned to the Halls, as Simon said, then there would be only one reason to pull Theron out of Jerusalem before his task was completed, and that would be to send Ramah in to finish where Theron left off.

The Father take them, this was *his* mission. Not Ramah's. This was Theron's chance to prove his effectiveness. He kicked at a stone in the street, sending it flying through the gray night air to smack into the side of a building.

He couldn't argue with the Council of Thirteen, though. They did what they wished and didn't explain themselves to anyone. Simon stood several paces away, his face still beaming with a self-satisfied smile.

"Let's go, then," Theron snapped, wanting to get this over with. He stepped around Simon and headed for the Gatehouse.

"Yes, let's…" Simon replied.

The slight edge to Simon's voice was Theron's first clue that something wasn't right. The second came a heartbeat later when the streets around him went suddenly quiet. Theron knew the effect; he'd used it himself a thousand times. A Psalm of Silence. He turned to face Simon just in time to see the vampire charging at him, claws extended and fangs bared.

Theron could have dodged the blow, and would have if he hadn't been so confused. Instead he let Simon barrel into him, taking only enough precaution to block the claws and keep them from stabbing him through the chest. When the clerk's body hit his own, the two tumbled over in the street, raising a small cloud of dust. They feinted and stabbed each other with hands made more dangerous by the sharp, bony points extending from their fingertips.

Simon scrambled about like a madman. Wiry and strong, he possessed an agility Theron soon discovered he could not match. But Theron was far stronger. In addition, he had been a vampire and a warrior for over nine hundred years. Simon was only turned eleven years ago, still an infant by the standards of their race. Theron rolled and tussled in the street with the clerk, waiting for him to make the inevitable rookie mistake that would decide the fight; it shouldn't take long.

He was right. Only a few minutes into the scuffle Simon failed to pull his arm back from a blocked strike right away, instead trying to force the blow. In that moment Theron had him. He loosed his hold on Simon's neck and grabbed his forearm. He locked his hand firmly around Simon's wrist, then twisted his body to the right and bent over at the waist, forcing Simon to roll with him or have his arm broken. Simon rolled, of course, and at the apex of the arc Theron sidestepped and slammed Simon face first into the street. With his opponent's face in the dirt, Theron rolled his legs onto Simon's back and braced the man's elbow against his stomach. Then he bent it backward until he felt the pop of Simon's joint as it broke free of the tendons holding it in place. Simon's arm went limp in his hand. The clerk would not be using it again anytime soon.

Simon opened his mouth wide and started to scream, apparently losing his concentration on the Psalm of Silence when Theron broke his elbow. Luckily Theron had cast his own Psalm around them. Otherwise the clerk's scream would have brought every guard in the city down on the two of them.

I could kill him now. It was true. He could, but then he'd never know why Simon turned on him in the first place. Was it because of Jesus? Surely not.

He grabbed the clerk's other wrist and dragged him into an alley. Once there he dropped the silence and bent down, putting his mouth right next to Simon's ear. "What is this about?" Theron asked.

Simon laughed at him. "The Council sent me."

"To find me? You said that already." Theron twisted the injured elbow until Simon's laugh broke in his throat. "Tell me why you attacked me, Simon."

"No, not to find you," Simon grunted. "They sent me to dispose of you. Headcouncil Herris gave me the order himself. The Council wants you dead, Enforcer."

Now it was Theron's turn to laugh. "Come now, why would the Council send you to kill me? Surely you are not that foolish."

"You are the fool, Theron. Your time is over. I will take your place as Enforcer, and the Council will forget your name long before your bones are dust."

You have been lied to, vampire...

Jesus's words came back to him, echoing in his mind. Theron shook his head, trying to clear the unwanted thought.

"No. Surely not," he said. And yet...

...and you have been betrayed.

"Burn you, Nazarene," Theron said under his breath as he tried to rid himself of the memory of his conversation with Jesus.

Simon used Theron's momentary distraction to kick him in the back of the head. Theron, surprised, lost his grip on the clerk's wrists and fell to the side. Both vampires shot to their feet at the same time, and Simon rushed at Theron, his good arm braced back for a jab with his clawed hand.

Theron had had enough. He sidestepped the charging vampire and stuck his foot in Simon's path. Simon, already committed to his charge, could not stop or turn aside in time and tripped over Theron's foot. As he tumbled over, Theron's hand shot downward and punched into the back of Simon's neck, his claws sinking deep into the other vampire's flesh. Simon hung there, impaled through the throat by Theron's elongated knuckles, and squirmed. Theron lifted him easily and brought him close. He clamped down on Simon's ruined neck with his fangs, giving himself a much needed drink while his victim flailed at him with his uninjured arm.

Simon gurgled and spat, but Theron wasn't worried; he'd torn the vampire's vocal chords out with the strike, and the only noises Simon could make while he died were a series of sputtering gasps. Soon, very soon, the clerk's struggles weakened, and soon after that they stopped altogether. Theron finished feeding and tossed the husk to the ground, feeling renewed strength course though him.

Once the fight was over, Theron tried to puzzle out what had just occurred, but it didn't make any sense. If the Council wanted him dead, they would have sent Ramah, as he was the only vampire in existence capable of killing him, barring the other members of the Council, who were above such missions. It just wasn't right. Why would they want him dead?

No, more likely it was Simon who wanted him dead, and when he realized he couldn't win he tried to distract Theron with the ruse of being summoned by the Council. That made far more sense. He looked down at the body of Simon, former clerk to the Council of Thirteen, and he could not stifle a laugh. Simon was a fool to attack him. the Council would know such an attempt would never succeed.

You have been lied to, vampire.

Yes. Lied to by Simon. Theron spat at the corpse, leaving a wad of red phlegm on Simon's chest. *You idiot,* he thought. *You deserved exactly what you received.* He didn't have time to bury the body like he had Ephraim's; he would have to leave it someplace where the first light of the sun could dispose of it. A rooftop, perhaps.

He bent down to pick up Simon's corpse and noticed the skin of his fist was still black. Strange, it should have healed with the intake of another vampire's blood, which was typically stronger than a human's. Theron pondered this oddity for a moment, then shrugged. Perhaps Simon's blood had been too weak. He was, after all, only recently turned. In any case, the wound didn't hurt, and he had more pressing matters. Like getting rid of Simon's body.

He reached down and grabbed the corpse by the arm and hefted it over his shoulder with a grunt. Theron carried the body to the nearest building, where he tied the hands together and put the loop of Simon's arms over his head. Then Theron climbed up the wall to the roof, where he left the body to wait for the dawn.

This done, Theron jumped lightly down to the street below. He still had one more piece of business to take care of before he could go back to the Council and claim his mission a rousing success. One last loose end to tie up.

Taras.

He stepped away from the building and walked up the street toward the New City, heading for the barracks.

CHAPTER TWENTY-EIGHT

Theron didn't make it all the way to the barracks. Shortly after arriving in the Upper City he passed by Ephraim's house, and there at the entrance to an alley just across the street stood Taras, leaning against the wall of a tailor's shop and looking at something in his hand. Theron was surprised to find him there, and assumed Taras must be waiting for him. He walked up to the blond legionary and smiled.

"Is it done?" Theron asked.

Taras looked up, and Theron saw a flash of something blue in the legionary's palm before he tucked it into his belt. "It is," Taras said, and Theron noted the despondent look on his face. "Jesus of Nazareth is dead. I watched him die myself at Golgotha."

"Excellent," Theron said. "Where is the body?"

"His family and friends are preparing it. They will entomb him shortly."

"Take me there." Theron turned and started to walk to Golgotha, thinking the Nazarene's tomb must be nearby. He hoped there would not be many people there, it would easier to take a souvenir.

"No," Taras said.

Theron stopped in his tracks and turned back to face him. "What do you mean, no?"

"I won't take you to his tomb. Mary—" Taras's voice cracked, "Mary wouldn't have wanted me to. I won't let you do any more damage than you've already done."

"Mary? Mary who? What damage?" Theron demanded. "What nonsense have you gotten into?"

"Don't say her name!" Taras's face turned bright red. "A murdering dog like you has no right to speak it."

"Murderer? What are you talking about, Taras? Have you been drinking?"

"You are not Ephraim." Taras's expression hardened. "I saw Ephraim's body. The head was removed, but I recognized the ring on his hand as the one used to seal a letter. A letter he'd written to Malachi. The letter warned that someone was coming to kill him."

"I explained that, already. My ring was—"

"Stolen? Yes. You did mention that. But I never said the letter was sealed with Ephraim's ring. I only said it had been secured with his seal. Ephraim had two seals, the one on his ring and a larger one in his desk. So how would you know which one he used to seal the letter, unless you had been there first and already seen it?

"I knew something was wrong with your story last night, but I couldn't figure out what it was. But as I watched Jesus led to his death, the memory returned to me. Why would you bury the victim of another man's murder? You wouldn't, of course. It would only make sense to hide a body if the murderer was you. And why would you write a letter to Malachi if he intended to kill you in the first place? It didn't add up. Do you know what I think? I think Ephraim wrote that letter to warn Malachi about you. The ring proves it. You killed Ephraim, and probably Malachi, too. Jesus was never aligned with forces of darkness, *you* were."

Taras shook his head. A tear spilled from his eye and rolled down his cheek. "Because of you, I helped put an innocent man to the cross. I watched him die. I owed him that much after helping to put him there. I saw what they did to him. It took a long time. His suffering and his blood are on my hands. I will have to live with what I've done for the rest of my life." Taras's face turned to stone, and he pulled his sword from his belt and advanced on the vampire. "But not you. You won't harm anyone else, whoever you are. I will make certain of that."

Taras lunged, and it was all Theron could do to step out of the way and avoid being skewered. The legionary had the benefit of strength and speed beyond his race, a gift Theron himself had given him out of necessity to speed the healing of his wounds. The vampire reached for the sword at his belt, then changed his mind and opted instead to use his favorite weapon; his claws. He felt the sharp twinge of pain as the bones in his fingers elongated, tearing through the skin of his fingertips and growing to about three inches long and an inch thick.

Taras took a step back at the sight, but he didn't run. He stared at the claws on Theron's hands for a moment. "Eight punctures," Taras whispered. "Didius's head was ripped from his shoulders… there were eight punctures in his throat…" He snapped his eyes up from Theron's hands to his face, and the vampire saw fire blazing behind the legionary's pale blue orbs.

"It was you!" Taras shouted. He raised his sword and leapt at Theron, his blade swinging in a wide arc meant to separate Theron's head from his shoulders. Theron parried the blow with the bony protrusions of his right hand, then launched his left at the legionary.

Taras, more agile than humanly possible, stepped to the side and managed to avoid Theron's swipe, if only just. At the same time he brought his sandaled foot up and into Theron's midsection. The blow loosened several items from Theron's belt, and one of his pouches went flying, spilling its contents into the street. The strength of the kick forced Theron backward a step, but his claws managed to draw three bright red lines of blood on Taras's arm in the exchange.

"Very good, Taras. I killed Didius. Ephraim and Malachi, too. I kill a lot of people, it's my job. But I couldn't kill Jesus. I couldn't even touch the man. To kill him I needed help. Roman help. Marcus was so angry at his brother's death he was ready to believe anything I told him. Once the Sanhedrin became involved, I knew my plan would work." Theron lunged, aiming for Taras's chest and hoping to pierce his heart and lungs with one strike. Taras deflected the blow with a downward slash of his blade and stepped away from the follow up strike of Theron's other hand. He ducked down and stuck his leg in the vampire's path, and Theron barely missed tripping over it and falling into the dirt.

"But you forgot about Passover, didn't you?" Taras asked as he launched an attack of his own, swinging his blade at Theron's legs. Theron jumped backward just in time to avoid having his left leg severed midway up the shin.

"Damn the Jews and their customs," Theron said. "I couldn't let Pilate set Jesus free." He launched himself at Taras yet again, trying to distract him with a swipe to the soldier's midsection and hoping to draw his guard down and bowl him over into the street.

"So you remembered me," Taras said as he ducked under the swing, falling onto all fours in front of the charging vampire. The move surprised Theron, who was unable to check his momentum in time. He tripped over the crouching soldier and fell sprawling into the street.

He rolled over and found Taras standing over him. The outraged legionary stared down the length of the blade he held to Theron's neck. "And what about Gordian?" Taras asked. "What did you offer him to betray the centurion? Silver? Gold? Power?"

This time, Theron didn't have to feign confusion. "Gordian? Who is Gordian?"

By the look on Taras's face, it was his turn to be confused. His sword arm dipped about and inch and a crease formed in the center of his brow. Theron took advantage of the moment to shift his leg into a striking position. He needed Taras distracted for just a few seconds longer. "What about you, Taras? You were so eager to help, weren't you?" Theron smiled, "How did you do it, anyway? How did you convince Pilate to execute Jesus instead of Barabbas?"

Taras's sword wavered, and his face lost some of its former steel. "That's not your concern," he replied, and drew his sword several inches backward. Theron could see the muscles in Taras's arm tense, poised for the killing blow. "Go to Tertius in ignorance, whoever you are."

Before Taras could plunge the blade downward for a killing blow, Theron kicked out with his right leg and connected with Taras's knee, which bent backward under the blow, the tendons giving way with an audible snap. Taras let out a pained yelp as he fell to the ground, dropping the sword and clutching his ruined knee with both hands.

Theron got to his feet and walked over to Taras's writhing form. He knelt by the fallen soldier, placing his knee on the doomed man's chest and pinning him to the ground. He brought his clawed fist level to Taras's midsection and pushed the tips into the flesh of his belly just enough to draw blood. Taras squirmed underneath him and tried to reach his sword, but Theron held him fast. "Where are they entombing the body?" Theron asked, driving the points of his claws in just enough to make Taras gasp in pain. "Tell me and I will make this quick."

Taras spat at him, and a sticky wad of bloody spittle hit Theron in the cheek. Theron frowned and wiped it off with his sleeve, then he drove his fist home. The curved, bony spikes tore through Taras's abdomen and dug into the earth beneath him. Theron entertained the notion of ripping the legionary in half and spilling his intestines out onto the cobbles, but decided to let the man bleed to death in the street instead. It wouldn't take long, but it would hurt a great deal. Fitting. He withdrew his hand, and blood welled from the dying man's belly like a crimson spring.

Theron stood up and looked at the dying soldier, who lay in the street holding his belly as though trying to keep his innards from pouring out of the holes. Taras tried valiantly to scream, Theron noted, but the only thing he seemed able to manage was a hoarse croak. "Thank you for your assistance, Taras," he said. "I could not have succeeded without you."

If Taras heard, he gave no indication. His head lolled over to one side. Theron thought he was dead, but his eyes fixed on a glittering object several inches from his face. Taras's expression changed from one of pain to one of confusion. Grimacing, he removed one blood-covered hand from his wound and reached out to pick it up. It was the gold and ruby ring Theron had taken from the woman. It must have fallen out when his pouch came loose. Taras's eyes squinted as he examined it.

"Mary?" He croaked, fresh tears falling from his eyes.

"Was that her name? Ah, yes… I see. She must be the one you spoke of a moment ago, the one whose name I could not utter, wasn't she?" Theron nodded to himself, then reached down and plucked the ring from Taras's trembling fingers.

"I'll take that," he said, unable to suppress a grin. "It's mine, after all." He put it into another pouch and then set about picking up the rest of his things from the alley floor. He thought about taking the legionary's sword but decided against it. He had enough to carry without donning a second sheath. Let anyone who might stumble onto Taras's body in the morning have the sword.

Theron turned his back on the gurgling soldier and walked out of the alley. With Taras's death, he'd tied up one more loose end, but now he had another problem. He still had to find Jesus's tomb. He'd planned on having Taras lead him there, but that was no longer an option.

Theron didn't regret killing Taras, the legionary had it coming to him ever since he took Theron prisoner and put him into the stocks, but the timing couldn't be more inconvenient. He needed to confirm Jesus's death with his own eyes, and without Taras to take him to the Nazarene's tomb, he would have to find another way of locating it. He pondered his options for a short while before realizing it shouldn't be too difficult to discover the tomb's location from the inhabitants of the city. No doubt the crucifixion would be the most popular topic of discussion among the people of Jerusalem tonight. Theron would simply listen in on the conversations of others, at their windows, if necessary, until he was able to learn what he needed to know.

He reached into his pouch and pulled out his map of the city, trying to determine the best places to go where he might overhear something useful. This time of night most people were asleep in their beds, the only people usually awake were the patrols wandering through the city and a few unsavory elements. Theron decided to check the area near the Roman barracks. With several taverns and brothels, it offered the most hope of finding someone useful. Theron studied the map to see if any places in particular sounded promising.

Suddenly a flash of pain tore into his back and the bloodied tip of a sword blocked his view of the map. The blade pierced his torso near his spine and emerged from his chest, cracking his sternum and spraying blood and ooze all over the parchment and his fingers. He grunted in pain and dropped the map to the street.

"This is for Jesus," a voice behind him said.

Fighting to focus through the pain, Theron realized he knew that voice. "Taras?" he croaked.

"And this is for Mary," Taras said. The blade twisted, much as Theron's had twisted in Claudius's chest several days earlier. Theron nearly screamed as the crack in his sternum widened, but he forced himself to keep quiet lest he attract more legionaries.

The pain drove Theron to his knees, and he gasped as Taras yanked the sword from his back and drove it through a second time, this time puncturing his side. Taras twisted the blade again, ripping and tearing the hole in Theron's gut. He fell to all fours as Taras yanked his blade free again. Blood poured from the two wounds to puddle underneath Theron in the street. Dazed, he brought one hand up to the wound in his chest and poked his finger inside the hole. The blade had pierced his heart clean through.

"Die, now," Taras said from behind him. "Die like Marcus and Didius. Like Claudius and Jesus. Die like my Mary; cut down like a dog in the street. May Pluto spit on your soul. I hope you—"

Theron heard a grunt behind him. His teeth clenched in pain, he turned his head to see Taras on his knees in the street, propping himself up with his bloody sword. The legionary looked too weak to stand, but his injuries didn't seem to ease his anger. His eyes bored into Theron.

"Die now, whoever you are," Taras said. "And go to the Abyss with the knowledge that I am the one who sent you there."

The smell of blood was heavy in the street. Theron tasted it in his mouth. Since it was his own blood, it did him no good at all. He couldn't use it to feed or to heal himself. Even so, he looked on as Taras cursed him, and a rumbling, wet chuckle escaped his lips. "No, Taras," he said. "I think not."

He grit his teeth through the pain and forced himself to his feet, watching as Taras's ice blue eyes widened in shock. He understood the man's confusion. By rights, his wounds should be fatal. They surely would have been if Theron was a mortal man. But Theron hadn't been mortal for over nine hundred years. The hole in his chest and belly hurt like fire, and he'd lost quite a bit of blood, but that was all. He would not die, though his pierced heart would take several days to fully heal.

Weak from loss of blood, he staggered over to the prone Taras, somehow managing to remain on his feet. He stood over the man, wearing a bloody smirk, and looked down at him, his chest dripping gore onto the cobbles. Taras, after a moment's surprise, tried to lift his sword arm for another blow, but Theron stepped on the blade, pinning the soldier's sword arm underneath.

"You cannot kill me, Taras," Theron said, his blood pouring from the open wound in his chest and splattering the cobbles by Taras's head. "You pierced my heart with steel. That is not good enough, my northern friend. Not good enough at all." He knelt by the dying legionary, scowling down at him. "But you have slowed me down."

He punched Taras in the face. A sharp snap reverberated through the alley as the legionary's nose broke. Taras swooned, and his head lolled to the side, but he recovered and raised his head to look at

Theron, one eye open and the other rapidly swelling shut, and spit at him a second time.

Theron punched him again, this time in the sternum. A burst of blood-flecked air issued from Taras's mouth, and the soldier's eyes closed. His head rolled to the side, and this time it stayed there. There was blood everywhere, so much that Theron couldn't tell how much was his and how much belonged to Taras. He looked the body over and nodded to himself. Satisfied that he had finally killed the legionary, he stood on shaky legs. A few drops of Theron's blood fell on Taras's face. He paid them no attention as he turned and walked away, leaving Taras's body in the middle of the street for the looters to find in the morning.

He needed blood badly, and his wobbling steps proved it. He probably should have drained Taras, but in his current state he wasn't strong enough to drag the body out of the city, and he couldn't risk leaving an empty husk in the street. He would have to catch someone closer to the tunnels, or better yet, *in* the tunnels. Zealots ran through the passages all the time, Theron need only pick a likely spot and wait. It shouldn't take long. But even with a zealot or two to feed upon he would need time to heal. Steel or not, his chest hurt, and a heart wound never healed quickly. Theron fumed at the delay, which would easily be several days, and cursed Taras's lucky shot. But he could do nothing about it. He would simply have to wait to learn of Jesus's fate.

Taras's body was found the following morning by a group of soldiers out on patrol. They were the first to locate his remains, and thus his sword and uniform didn't fall into the hands of any opportunistic thieves, as Theron had thought they might. The men carried his body back to the barracks, where the assistant to the undertaker pronounced him dead and set about readying the body for burial.

No time was wasted putting the body to rest. Habitus, the new centurion, was anxious to secure his authority and get people's minds off recent events, so he ordered his men to bury Taras that very day. The service was small, and only the centurion and a young legionary named Pavo spoke on Taras's behalf. They could not find anyone else to do so. Taras didn't seem to have any close friends, and few people showed up to wish his spirit well. One of the men who did attend (although it should be noted he didn't wish Taras's spirit well) was a portly, middle-aged merchant named Abraham, who proceeded to question every soldier he met about his daughter, missing since that morning. No one knew what he was talking about.

As the day wore on, the people of Jerusalem talked of the crucifixion and little else. The poor soldier who'd been found dead that morning was but a mere side topic in the events of the day. People would remember him briefly and mention it in passing, then return to the death of Jesus and the release of Barabbas. More than a few expressed concern about the dangerous criminal Pilate had set free, and openly questioned the Prefect's decision. Several of the loudest dissenters then went straight to a store, a tavern, or even one of the city's brothels, as they seemed to have extra money in their pockets.

As night fell on the city of Jerusalem, fewer and fewer people could be seen out of their houses. By the time the moon reached its zenith, Jerusalem's cobbled streets were almost empty; her people long in bed and the only folks up and about were the soldiers who had patrol. None of them ventured near the place where the dead soldier was buried, and why would they? Nothing ever happened there.

Yet on this night, when the owls hooted and the mice scurried through the grass in search of a meal, something *did* happen. Unknown to the city's inhabitants, the freshly turned soil of a new grave began to move. Bits of loose dirt tumbled from the top of the pile. Soon a pale, waxen hand rose from the earth, clenching and unclenching in the moonlight like a macabre lotus blossom.

CHAPTER TWENTY-NINE

It took Theron four full nights to heal himself completely, even after feeding on a pair of zealots who happened by. Four nights spent hiding in the tunnels under the city, oblivious to the happenings above, of willing the gaping hole in his chest to close and the muscles and bones to knit together. It had been a painful, debilitating experience, and the process sapped a great deal of his strength and blood, most of which went to repairing his damaged heart.

Even dead, his heart was the source of his life, and his continued existence depended on it being whole and healthy. Now that it was so again, he could venture out into the city to feed, which was a good thing. After four days underground and his exhaustive healing process, Theron was ravenous.

He wandered through the stone tunnels until he came to the exit, which lay hidden in the scrub brush just outside the city. He would try and take a traveler on the road, if possible. Someone walking the path between the Gardens of Gethsemane and the Damascus Gate, if one could be found at such a late hour.

Luck was with him that night. Less than five minutes after exiting the tunnels, he spied a man walking alone down the path. Theron prepared to spring, but as the man drew closer he noticed something odd. The man glowed. Not as bright as Jesus had, but the glow of the stranger's faith could be seen from ten paces away. With his left hand, Theron unconsciously touched the fingers of his right, which still bore a slight blackened look from his encounter with the Nazarene. He knew he would get a similar burn, albeit a less severe one, if he tried to prey on the person in front of him.

It was not unheard of, of course, for a human to possess such strong faith as to ward off one of his kind, but it was rare. Theron had been surprised to see the strong glow around Jesus, who'd been only the third such person the vampire had encountered in his nine centuries. But to find two in the same city? And so close together? Such a thing had never occurred before, at least not to Theron.

Common sense won out over his hunger, and he let the man go, hoping easier prey would happen by. He chalked the incident up to strange coincidence and settled in to wait for the next person to come along. What was one man, anyway?

Soon enough, a second person emerged in the dim moonlight. A woman this time. Theron gasped. She, too, glowed with faith. By the Father, how many such people could there be in a single place?

Theron let the woman pass unmolested, as well. When yet a third person walked along the path radiating a soft light, Theron could stand no more. He stepped out of his concealment and walked up to the stranger, wanting to test the man's faith and make sure he was not simply experiencing some sort of hallucination brought on by his low blood.

The closer he got, the more his skin curled and the hairs on the back of his neck stood on end. This was no hallucination. The man's faith was real. But how?

The man smiled as he approached, and Theron saw the purity of his emotions on his face. "Isn't it wonderful?" The man asked.

Theron, struggling not to bolt in his weakened state, could only stare in awed silence at the stranger. Not knowing what else to do, he nodded, hoping to at least get some information.

The man continued to smile, his eyes roamed upward toward the night sky. "I was in my home when I heard the news, and I had to go see for myself. Have you been? It's wonderful. He has risen. Just as he said he would."

"Risen?" Theron croaked. "Who?"

"Why, the savior, of course," the stranger replied, his eyes alight with wonder. "Jesus has risen from the dead. He will lead us all down the path of righteousness and into the Kingdom of God."

As the man spoke, a group of three more people emerged on the path. Theron noted with alarm that two of them possessed the same telltale glow. Between them, the third listened to the words of the other two with rapt attention. Theron could make out pieces of their conversation. Words like "Resurrection," and "Messiah" reached his ears. He realized with a start that all of the glowing men he'd seen so far had come from the same direction; the Gardens of Gethsemane. While he watched, the third man began to glow, as well. Softly at first, then increasing in intensity like opening a damper on a lantern.

The man apparently noted the confused look on Theron's face and mistook it for illness. "Are you all right, brother?" He asked, reaching with glowing fingers toward the vampire's shoulder.

Now Theron did bolt. He turned from the men in the street and ran for the Damascus Gate where, he was relieved to note, the two legionaries standing guard did *not* glow. He would have liked to kill one of them and have a drink, but there was no time.

Once through the gate Theron saw scores of people milling around the city, which was usually deserted this late in the evening. More troubling still was the number of people who possessed the same telltale glow. Everywhere he looked, glowing, smiling Jews dotted the crowd. Here and there he even spotted a legionary with the same affliction. He cringed as a small group of men, glowing like faint torches, passed no more than three or four paces from him. The effect of their faith in such close proximity sent a shudder through his body.

What in the name of The Father was happening in Jerusalem? This was far, far more dangerous than the single Nazarene. When only Jesus possessed such a glow, the situation was at least manageable. And when Theron had managed to have him executed that should have been the end of it. There should no longer be such a threat to his people in Jerusalem.

Yet here it was. Or rather, here *they* were. Scores of glowing men and women, their faith lighting the night like small suns to Theron's eyes, wandered through the city, unafraid of what might be around them. Just looking at all of them stung his eyes, and he squinted as he hurried down the street.

He had to get away from them and find some sustenance, so he wandered the streets, keeping his distance from any people he saw, until he approached an area of town that was largely deserted; the vicinity of the Temple. Here, at least, no strangers glowed. In fact, there were no people at all, which allowed him a moment to sit and think about this perplexing development.

Jesus has risen from the dead, the stranger had said. Impossible, of course. The only way to rise from the dead that Theron knew of was his way: the way of the *Bachiyr.* The way of the vampire.

He raised his palms to his head, trying to silence the wail of hunger rising in him, and saw again the blackened skin of his knuckles. He could not feed on those glowing bodies, and until the streets emptied, he would likely not have a shot at any others.

There was no help for it. He would have to go to the Council and tell them of the situation in Jerusalem. It galled him to know he would not be able to bring back a souvenir of Jesus's death as a gift to Herris, but the Council needed to know. Of all the things to befall his people in Israel, Theron could think of nothing worse than this. Somehow, someone had brought a tremendous amount of faith to the people of Jerusalem. But how?

Theron stood and, ignoring his hunger, started the walk back to the Damascus Gate and the small house that served as Jerusalem's portal to the Halls of the *Bachiyr.* But before he left the area around the Temple he spied someone in the street walking toward him. Theron noted with some relief the man didn't glow. The stranger was dressed in a long black robe that showed nothing of his face or stature, but his walk was calm and self-assured. He took a moment to study the newcomer, sizing him up for a potential meal. As he got closer Theron was able to see under the hood, and gasped when he recognized the man.

"Councilor Ramah?" He asked, and knelt to the cobbles.

CHAPTER THIRTY

"Do you know what is happening in the city, Councilor Ramah?" Theron asked from his position, kneeling in the street. "Have you seen the number of people with the glow?"

"*Do you know what's happening in the city, Councilor Ramah?*" Ramah mocked. "You should know, Theron. This is all your doing."

"What?"

"You arranged to have Jesus crucified."

"It was my mission," Theron said. "Given to me by Headcouncil Herris."

"Herris sent you to *kill* Jesus, not make a martyr of him."

"Martyr? What martyr? What are you talking about?" Theron nearly rose to his feet, but remembered in time to whom he spoke, and remained on his knees.

"Where is Jesus's body?" Ramah asked.

"His what?"

"His body. Where did you put it?"

"I'm sorry, Councilor Ramah, but I don't know what you are talking about."

Ramah looked at Theron for a long while. Theron stared back, confused and growing more worried with each passing second.

You have been lied to, vampire…

Finally, Ramah spoke. "You don't know, do you?" He chuckled. "Well, then. You should find this interesting.

"Your plan worked perfectly. Jesus was put to the cross and died a short while before sundown four days ago. His death was brutal, painful, and he died amidst rumors of being involved with the zealots. Pilate was pleased, the Sanhedrin were pleased, and the Council of Thirteen was pleased. But then, this morning, his body vanished."

"Vanished? What do you mean? How?"

"No one knows. By all accounts the tomb was sealed, but on the third morning following his death, a few women went to pay tribute. When they arrived they found the great stone that sealed the tomb had been moved, and the tomb itself stood open. There were no marks on the stone, and no one chiseled through the seal. It was simply open, and Jesus's body was gone. I had thought you took it, meaning to bring it back to the Council as proof of your success, but when you didn't appear I started to wonder.

"Then the rumors started. People claimed to have seen Jesus rise from the dead. There are even some who claim to have spoken with him. Can you imagine? They claim to have spoken with a dead man. It's not possible, of course, but that didn't stop a large number of people from believing it. The news spread through Jerusalem like fire, and before sunset thousands of people descended on the tomb to see it standing empty. In the last twelve hours nearly a quarter the population of Jerusalem has been swayed over to Jesus's cause, and the effects are still spreading. It is a disaster of the worst kind; the beginning of renewed faith in Israel."

"By The Father," Theron swore. This was serious. "Does the rest of the Council know?"

"Not yet. I have been looking for you for several hours and have not returned to the Halls. The Council sent me to find you when Simon failed to report. If I didn't find you tonight I was going to go back and tell them of the situation myself, but now that you have resurfaced, you can have the honors."

Theron grumbled. The Council would not be pleased to hear of this news. The only 'honor' he would likely find would be a severe reprimand. But he'd only been following orders. He'd been forced to improvise, true, but it couldn't be helped. All in all he thought he'd done a good job, considering the circumstances. By rights the Council should be pleased. Except for the damn glowing citizenry.

He prepared himself to journey back to the Halls when suddenly something Ramah said struck a chord. He stopped in his tracks and turned to face the Councilor.

"Wait, Councilor Ramah," Theron said. "You said you were sent to find me when Simon failed to report."

"Yes," Ramah said. "That is true."

"So Simon told the truth? The Council *did* send him after me?"

"You've seen him, then?"

"He attacked me," Theron said, a little defensive. "I killed him."

"Herris thought you might." Ramah smiled, obviously unconcerned about the news of the clerk's demise.

"Then why did Headcouncil Herris send him?"

"Didn't you read the letter?" Ramah's brows knit together.

"What letter?"

Ramah looked Theron up and down. Theron shifted from one foot to the other, uncomfortable with such scrutiny. He hated himself for being so nervous, like a child caught misbehaving, but he reminded himself it was Ramah in front of him. *Ramah.* The Blood Letter, himself. If he wanted to look Theron up and down, then by The Father, Theron would let him. To do otherwise was to invite a sure and swift death, and Theron knew it.

After perhaps a minute, Ramah completed his appraisal, and looked Theron in the face. "You don't have it," he said.

Theron shrugged, not having any idea what Ramah meant.

"What did you do with Simon's body?" Ramah asked.

"I left it on a rooftop for the sun." Theron replied. "By now Simon is a pile of ashes."

"Show me."

✝✝✝

Taras wandered through the grass and dirt, as he had the last three nights in a row, carrying a single bright red flower he'd plucked from somewhere near the Gardens of Gethsemane. He could no longer stand to be outside during the day. Ever since he'd awakened three nights ago, the sun burned him. His hand still bore the scars from that first morning. Every evening, he woke at sunset, and every sunrise he retreated to the shelter of a nearby grave. *His* grave. He'd been shocked to discover his name etched into the marker upon waking that first night.

He'd awakened to find himself buried in the earth and, after a few moments of panic and confusion, dug his way out. At the time, he was too busy escaping his earthen prison to notice the cold that crept into his bones, but once free of the grave he couldn't help *but* notice. Icy cold, like winter, settled into his limbs and chilled him to the marrow. But this was Spring; he should have been warm, even at night. No amount of huddling could make it stop, and no fire could chase it away. So to take his mind from the numbing chill, he walked through the Gardens and visited the tombs near the Mount of Olives.

His walks never took him into the city. He preferred to remain outside near the gardens, taking his company with the dead in the tombs nearby – one in particular – even if they weren't much in the way of companionship. He didn't want to be seen by any of the city's residents, knowing he looked frightful, but he guessed that's what happened when you died and came back.

Taras still didn't understand what had happened to him, but he remembered all too well the fiend – whom he still thought of as Ephraim even though he knew that name to be false – stabbing him in the belly with his clawed hand, and then punching him in the face until he lost consciousness. He thought he'd killed Ephraim when he stabbed him though his heart and gut, but he failed. Ephraim lived at least long enough to break Taras's nose and finish him off.

Taras looked down at his fresh tunic, most certainly a gift from whoever had taken Marcus's place as centurion. He lifted the hem between his pale fingers and examined the flesh underneath. The mark of Ephraim's claws could still be seen on his abdomen; four gaping holes that, for some reason, no longer bled.

For some reason, indeed. Taras shook his head at his own naïveté. The holes didn't bleed because he was dead. His blood, such as it was, no longer flowed through his veins.

He walked quietly along the path through the Gardens, thinking of all the wicked things he'd done in his life to deserve this fate. He'd hand delivered Jesus, an innocent man, to the cross, and aided a demon in killing not only the Nazarene, but also his friend Marcus and his beloved Mary. He knew something was wrong with Ephraim, yet he'd failed to act. He failed to protect her, and she paid for his mistake with a horrible death.

He would never forget seeing her body in that alley, torn to shreds by some foul thing. It had been all he could do to keep from killing himself on the spot. But instead of giving in to grief, he allowed a burning anger to fill him. First Didius, then Marcus, Jesus, and finally Mary. He'd tried to avenge them, but the holes in his belly testified to yet another failure.

Taras continued along the path, looking at his shoes and thinking his dark thoughts, for several minutes. Soon, too soon for his liking, he arrived at his destination. Another tomb. He didn't want to see it; didn't want to read the name chiseled into the marker. It wasn't the first time he balked. Some part of his mind tried to pretend it wasn't real, that he'd imagined the name. If he looked, he would have no such illusions. If he looked, any hope he had left would die yet again. But if he didn't look he would have to avoid the place for the rest of his days.

Nights, rather.

Numb, Taras raised his eyes from his feet to read the name etched into the stone.

Mary.

No tears came to his eyes. Tears, apparently, were one more thing denied to him, along with sunlight and companionship. But not love. That, at least, he could still feel. It burned through him, more painful than the sun and hollower than his own heart. The fact that he could not show his grief with tears somehow made it worse.

He laid the flower in front of Mary's tomb.

"I'm sorry, Mary," he said, and turned to leave.

"As well you should be," a voice behind him said. "Were it not for you, she would still be alive."

Taras whirled to see a large, middle-aged man standing behind him, a sword clutched in his trembling hand. Taras recognized him immediately.

"Abraham," Taras said.

"I knew your funeral was a ruse, Roman." Abraham said. "You filthy bastard. You just couldn't help yourself, could you? You butchered my beautiful daughter and now you've come to see where they put her. Come to desecrate her corpse, now?"

Taras stepped back, shaking his head. "I know you won't believe me, Abraham, but I loved Mary. I would no sooner have killed her than I would myself."

"Liar!" Abraham spat. "You took her from my home and gutted her like...like an animal. I saw the body. I saw what you did to her."

Taras noted the tears on Abraham's cheeks. Another reminder of all he'd lost. Did Abraham think he was the only one Mary's death had destroyed? "It's true," he said with as much calm as he could muster. "We were going to be married."

"Married?" Abraham's eyes narrowed, and his sword dipped an inch. "I didn't give my permission for you to marry her."

"And I didn't ask for it."

"It is forbidden for a Jewish maid to marry a Gentile."

"I didn't care."

Abraham stared at Taras, his expression going from anger to confusion and then back to anger. "Is that why you killed her? She wouldn't forsake her family and her people to marry you?" He spat on the ground at his feet. His eyes, wet with tears, bored into Taras. "She was too good for the likes of you, anyway."

"She didn't covet your blessing, Abraham, and she didn't care about your laws, either. Mary left your home of her own will. She and I were going to Rome, where she would be free of you and the ridiculous laws of your people."

"Save your lies for the devil, Roman." Abraham stepped closer, raising his sword. "You'll be meeting him soon enough."

"Abraham, please don't do this," Taras said. He took a step back, pulling out his own blade. "I can't be responsible for what might happen." Already he had noticed the pulsing of blood just under the skin of Abraham's neck. He could see the rhythmic rise and fall of the artery, and he could hear the blood flowing though it. It sounded to Taras like a cool fountain after a week spent wandering the desert. His grumbling belly lurched, and he doubled over in pain. He grit his teeth and noted something strange; his canines had grown. They were much longer than before, and sharper. He flicked his tongue over them and felt a sharp sting as they drew blood. The sweetly metallic taste of it filled his mouth like water to a man dying of dehydration.

And then he knew. He didn't have to be cold anymore. He didn't have to hurt any more. He knew how to fix his problem. Taras looked up at Abraham, who continued to advance on him with his sword drawn. Abraham's blood sang to him. A siren's song, begging Taras to act. To cut. To taste. To follow his budding instincts and feed. Gods, how he wanted it. No, *needed* it, and he had no idea why. Abraham's throat called to Taras, and he was too weak not to answer.

"No," Taras said, backing away. "No, please."

"Yes," Abraham replied. "You know what's coming, don't you Roman. Say hello to Lucifer when you arrive." Abraham lunged forward and swung his blade at Taras's throat, a blow that would sever his head if it connected.

But it didn't. Taras's hand shot up, his blade struck Abraham's with the loud ring of steel on steel. He stood to face Mary's father, towering over the older man. "I didn't want to do this, Abraham."

"No one *wants* to die, Roman," Abraham replied as he pulled his sword back and swung again.

This time Taras angled his blade so that when Abraham's sword clanged into his own it slid inward rather than stop short, knocking Abraham off balance. The maneuver also put Taras's free hand in easy reach of Abraham's arm. A more experienced fighter would never have fallen for the move, but Abraham was a merchant, not a soldier. A fact he no doubt realized himself when Taras's left hand clamped down on his shoulder and pulled him close.

"Let go of me you bastard!" Abraham swore. "Let go of me and take your punishment like a man, you son of a—"

Abraham's voice broke off when Taras brought the man's face up to his own. Abraham's eyes widened and his mouth clamped shut. Taras could feel him trembling under his hand. He heard the sound of steel on stone as Abraham's sword fell to the ground.

"Son of a what, Abraham?" Taras asked.

Abraham shook his head. "What are you?"

"I don't know." It wasn't a lie.

Abraham stared at Taras. Taras stared back at Abraham. The two stood that way for a full minute before Abraham broke the silence.

"Mary would never have married a demon like you."

Taras couldn't fight it anymore. What's more, he discovered he no longer wanted to. He gave in to the pain and let it take him down a path he never imagined he would go.

Taras snapped his arm inward, yanking Abraham close. He put his other hand on the side of Abraham's neck and forced his head into an odd angle, exposing his neck. Taras then drove his teeth into the man's throat, twisting his head slightly to make the hole bigger. A river of blood flowed into his mouth, and Taras's knees nearly buckled from excitement. He clamped his lips down on Abraham's neck and drew in as much of the stuff as he could swallow. Strength surged through him, and even as Abraham's struggles grew weaker,

Taras's arms, legs and torso grew stronger. The pain in his belly eased, and even the pain of losing Mary dimmed as his every sense exploded with rapture.

He didn't feel cold anymore. The dark no longer hindered his vision. He smelled the petals of the red flower in front of Mary's grave, and he heard the scuttling of a field mouse thirty paces away. Most of all, he tasted the warmth of Abraham's blood, sweet and coppery, filling his every pore with life and renewed energy.

Taras couldn't stop. He drank until there was nothing left.

CHAPTER THIRTY-ONE

T heron led Ramah through the city, dodging the occasional legionary and Jerusalem's glowing citizenry. They arrived at the building where Theron had left Simon's body the night before and climbed up the side. On the roof, He looked around until he spied a pile of clothes, covered in ashes, which lay unmoving in the still air. He pointed it out to Ramah. "There. That's where I left Simon."

Ramah wandered over and picked up the dead vampire's tunic. He shook out the ashes, which were all that remained of Simon, and handed it to Theron. "Did you search him?"

Theron shook his head. "I was in a hurry."

"Do it now."

Theron grabbed the tunic and felt through it, not knowing what he was looking for. He discovered a bulge in one of the inside pockets and reached inside. His fingers closed around something small and cylindrical. He pulled it out and discovered it to be a small scroll case. He opened it up and upended it, dropping a rolled piece of parchment into his palm. It was sealed with the red wax the Council favored, and emblazoned in the dollop was the seal from Herris' ring, marking it as an official order from the Headcouncil himself.

Theron broke the seal and unrolled the parchment, half expecting to find the order for his arrest, just as Simon has said, and was considerably surprised to discover the missive was for him, instead.

Dear Theron,

You will note this letter is addressed to you. We all knew Simon would fail in his task. He will not be missed. Our race is better off without his jealous and reckless ilk. We found the body of his twin brother in our tunnels, leading us to believe the two were working together on something. We believe the goal was to discredit and kill you. Obviously they failed.

Yet, you have violated the same law as Simon. By leading a human to our house in Jerusalem, you endangered our people. As Lead Enforcer, you know this sort of thing can not be tolerated. Therefore you must be punished for your lack of judgment.

But you have proven quite valuable to the Council over the last nine hundred years. Therefore, you are being given one final chance at redemption. Turn yourself in to the Council. Come this very night, and your punishment will not be as severe. Do not think to run from justice. You know Ramah will find you regardless of where you go. If you make this easy, your sentence will be less. You will only serve one hundred years as a Lost One. If you make us hunt you, Theron, your punishment will be one thousand years.

The decision is yours to make. We trust you will make the correct one and keep your honor intact.

Herris

Theron's hands shook as he finished reading. So that was it. The Council *did* know about Taras. He cursed and threw the scroll case to the rooftop. He'd been betrayed by his own kind, after all.

He stood still and silent on the roof, musing over this latest turn of events. How could the Council hand him so severe a punishment for such a minor offense as allowing a human to see the gatehouse and a Lost One. But there it was, in Herris' own blood. They had even sent a disposable servant to deliver the message, knowing he would not return. Theron knew the Council sent Simon to his death both to rid them of the annoying clerk and to show Theron they could be as devious as they were merciless. As added insurance, they sent Ramah immediately after, knowing Simon could never hope to kill Theron.

And that was just because of the incident with Taras. What would the Council do when they learned of the situation in Jerusalem? Theron had only to go to the Damascus Gate to see it was no longer safe for a vampire here, and according to Ramah the effect was spreading all over Israel. He had little doubt the Council would find some way to blame him, as Ramah did. What would be his punishment, then? A thousand years? Five thousand? Or would they simply kill him outright?

Of the three, Theron would prefer the last. He rolled the letter in his hands, stuck it in the pocket of his own tunic, and looked at Ramah. "They sent you to collect me." It wasn't a question.

"Of course they sent me," Ramah said, unknowingly echoing Theron's own words to Ephraim.

"But why? I would have returned to the Halls on my own once my mission was complete. Why send someone to collect me?"

"You can feel free to ask Herris when you arrive."

Theron knew better. Asking Herris why he did anything was tantamount to questioning his authority. Theron would spend the next ten thousand years dripping maggots from his bones if he were to be so bold.

"I suspect," Ramah said, "That they simply wanted to see what you would do."

So he was an experiment, now, a measure of the Council's hold on their faithful. Brilliant. Just brilliant. Bad enough to be disgraced, but to be used for the Council's amusement? It was humiliating.

Jesus's words came back to haunt him: *You have been lied to, vampire, and you have been betrayed.*

By The Father! He'd worked so hard for this. He'd come so very close to glory only to have it pulled away by a legionary and some anonymous, grave-robbing friend of the damn Nazarene. All his goals, gone in less than a week. A hundred years as a Lost One. It might as well be ten thousand.

He looked up at Ramah. The Councilor's expression was hard, his brow knotted. Theron was no fool; he knew he had no chance of escaping Ramah. That's why the Council sent him; they knew his presence would ensure Theron's cooperation. Knowing Ramah, the Councilor probably hoped he *would* run, just so he would have an excuse to kill him.

He looked around; noting the streets of the city had thinned over the last hour. The glowing bastards must have finally gotten sleepy and taken to their beds, meaning it would be a simple and fast walk to the Gatehouse by the Damascus Gate. Too short, most likely, for Theron's tastes.

"Well, Theron?" Ramah asked. "Shall we go?"

Theron bit his lip. He couldn't believe the words even as they came from his mouth. "All right. Let's go see Herris."

Ramah looked disappointed.

CHAPTER THIRTY-TWO

Taras stepped over the prone body of the dead soldier and walked through the Damascus Gate. Both the guards at the gate were dead. Taras had drank his fill from them and left their corpses in the street, much as he'd done to the three bandits on the road between the Mount of Olives and Jerusalem. Each kill made him stronger and faster, and he'd run most of the way, relishing the sting of the wind on his face. Now, as he entered the city, he felt more than strong; he was invincible. He grabbed a torch from the wall and a bucket of pitch from the guardhouse. Then he stepped through the gate and into the city.

The streets of Jerusalem stood empty around him. Taras cursed his luck even as he breathed a sigh of relief. If there were no people nearby, he would not be tempted to kill them. Not that killing was anything new to him. As an assassin in the Roman Legion, he'd always been dangerous, but never like this. Then he'd been a killer, but now?

Now he was a predator. A wolf in man's clothing. Taras, former legionary in the great empire of Rome, was no longer human.

He walked to the house where he'd first seen the demon-thing. He had no trouble finding it; he'd know the wretched place anywhere. This was where it all started to go wrong. Once he saw the demon, everything had changed. Gordian ambushed him and sent him to the rack. Taras recalled his escape from the fat man, and how the voice ordering his death had sounded familiar. He cursed himself for not recognizing the voice. If he hadn't been so dazed by pain, he might have saved the life of an innocent man. But instead Jesus died on a cross, and Taras's weakness helped to put him there.

Well, Taras wasn't weak anymore. He walked up to the door and pulled on the handle. Locked. No matter. Going inside hadn't been his plan anyway.

He walked around the building, pouring the bucket of pitch on the wooden exterior of the building. He started with the front door, wanting to make sure nothing could escape that way, then went to each dusty window and pasted the frames. He got some of the stuff on himself, as well, but paid it no attention.

Satisfied he'd covered all the exits with pitch, he walked around the house a second time, setting the doors and windows alight. The flames took to the pitch instantly, and the wooden house went up fast. A cloud of acrid smoke rose into the night sky, cutting it in half with a hazy gray line. The air above the building filled with sparks. Taras smiled and tossed the empty bucket to the ground.

Waves of searing heat rolled off the burning structure, forcing him to back away. He crossed the street and took cover in a nearby alley, watching to make sure nothing escaped the flames. He had to force himself to remain still when the people of the city started pouring from their houses, shouting and pointing at the blaze. He could smell their blood already. He could almost *taste* it. One man ran to the gatehouse to rouse the guards, and Taras heard him scream when he found the bodies.

Without clear leadership, the people who lived by the Damascus Gate took a long time to get organized, running and screaming like a gaggle of frightened children. Taras had to force himself to keep from running into their midst and picking them off one by one. So many people. So much blood. He gripped the side of a building, his fingers denting the wood, and braced himself against the mad wave of hunger that kicked him in the gut. He would not go on another killing spree. He would not.

But damn it all, he was still so hungry.

He somehow maintained his composure and sat back to watch the spectacle of the people trying to put out the blaze. Curiously, he noted some of them shone in the night, possessing an unearthly sheen like that surrounding the full moon, while others didn't. Taras had no idea why that would be, but for some reason the glow irritated him. Looking at them caused the hairs on the back of his neck to prickle. It didn't matter. All he cared about was the fire, and he watched as it devoured the cursed house where his life had begun to unravel.

I'll see you in the afterlife, Ephraim, or whatever your name is, he thought.

‡‡‡

Theron walked through the city, followed a few paces behind by Ramah. At this late hour most of the people had, thankfully, retired to their beds. Still, the occasional person could be seen here and there walking along the streets on some errand or another, but neither Theron nor Ramah stopped to feed. Many people possessed that same damned glow that Theron had seen earlier in the evening. *The beginning of renewed faith in Israel.* Theron shuddered. Ramah was right; this *was* a disaster.

As they neared the Damascus Gate, they heard a great deal of shouting and cursing. In addition, the sky above the area took on an orange hue. Theron caught a whiff of something in the air. He stopped and turned to face Ramah. "Do you smell smoke?"

Ramah stopped, as well. He sniffed at the air and nodded. "Something is burning."

"What do you think it is?"

Ramah said nothing, but motioned for Theron to keep walking.

Theron resumed his trek through the city. Soon they would be at the Gatehouse and it would be all over. Ramah would tell the Council about the new believers in Israel, and Theron would be a Lost One.

Theron clenched his fist at his side. A Lost One! How had he sunk so low? In less than a week he'd gone from the Council of Thirteen's most trusted servant to the lowest caste of *Bachiyr* society. It was all the Nazarene's fault. Everything was going fine until Jesus stuck his nose where it didn't belong. Now Ephraim was dead, and Theron would soon wish he were.

At least Jesus had suffered. By all accounts, the Romans had made his death particularly brutal. Crucifixions always were. Theron could take some comfort in that knowledge. Jesus was dead and would not trouble his people again.

Or was he?

He recalled Ramah's statement that several people claimed to have seen Jesus up and walking about. Ridiculous, of course. No one rose from the dead without the aid of the *Bachiyr*. Obviously it was a ploy by Jesus's remaining followers to create doubt among the Sanhedrin, and so far it seemed to be working quite well. According to Ramah, Caiaphas had sent scores of temple guards into the outlying countryside looking for Jesus, but they had found no trace of him. Caiaphas even petitioned Pilate to donate men to the search, but Pilate refused, saying he'd done his part and would have nothing else to do with the Nazarene.

In spite of his situation, Theron smiled at the thought. He tried to picture Caiaphas' face when Pilate told him no. The man probably turned purple with rage.

He rounded the last corner before the Gatehouse and it came into view. Theron stopped walking so suddenly that Ramah bumped into him.

"What is that?" Ramah asked. Then he, too, stopped in the middle of the street.

Both vampires stood and watched as dozens of men scrambled around the Gatehouse, each carrying buckets of water. Now Theron understood the nature of the orange glow over the area of the Damascus Gate. He watched as flames twenty paces high engulfed the structure, devouring it like a pack of hungry jackals.

"By the Father," Ramah said, his eyes reflected the orange glow of the flames.

"What do we do now?" Theron asked.

Ramah studied the burning house. "We will have to leave the city and travel to the nearest Gatehouse."

"But that's in Carthage."

"I know. We will have to secure a horse and cart."

"And a driver."

Ramah waved his hand, dismissing Theron's concern. "We will wait here a while. I don't want to be anywhere near the Gatehouse when the fire hits the portal."

Theron agreed, and the two skirted the area by the Gatehouse and looked for a place to wait out the blaze. Theron saw an alley across from the house, and pointed it out to Ramah. "We can wait there." Ramah nodded his agreement.

The two walked to the alley, but before they got within twenty steps of it, a man stepped out of the shadows and started walking toward them. Theron saw him and stopped, his jaw fell open and he couldn't help but stare. It couldn't be. By the Father, it *couldn't* be.

"You!" Taras screamed, and ran at Theron.

CHAPTER THIRTY-THREE

Theron had just enough time to get his hands up before Taras crashed into him and they both fell over into the street, raising a cloud of dust in the dry air. The two rolled around on the ground in a flurry of fists and feet. Taras punched and kicked and bit like an angry badger, and Theron had all he could handle to keep the legionary's hands away from his vital parts.

"I killed you," he said, grabbing Taras's wrist and holding his arm back. "I watched you die."

Taras growled something unintelligible and jerked his wrist from Theron's hand. Damn, the man was strong. Much stronger than he'd been the first time they fought. He was almost as strong as… as a *Bachiyr*.

"Oh, no," Theron said aloud.

He remembered the legionary lying on his back in the street, his face covered in blood. At the time, Theron never even imagined some of the blood might be his own, or that any of it would have found its way into Taras's mouth. But looking back, it seemed not only possible, but even probable given the amount of blood he'd lost when Taras stabbed him. He'd been so distracted with learning the truth of Jesus's fate, he didn't clean up his mess, and the result of his carelessness now stood in front of him, attacking him with abandon.

He had created another vampire, *without* the permission of the Council.

"Oh, no," he repeated. "Oh, no."

"That's right," Taras said, launching a fist at Theron's face. "You left me alive. But what have you done to me?"

Theron blocked the punch with his forearm, but could only curse and groan in response. If he was in trouble before, now he was a dead man. Until he saw Taras, Theron held out hope that maybe, just maybe, he could talk his way out of being turned into a Lost One, especially since Taras was supposedly dead, a loose end Theron thought he'd tied up. But now he'd be lucky if the Council let him live long enough to be turned into a Lost One. Once Ramah figured out the truth about Taras, he would probably kill Theron on the spot. All because he'd been careless and overconfident.

"Oh, no," he said again. It was all he could say.

Taras, his eyes blazing, continued to punch and kick at Theron, drawing a crowd. Theron blocked as best he could from his prone position, but he couldn't concentrate on the fight at hand, worried as he was about his tenuous future. Taras scored painful hits more often than not, and blood poured from several cuts on Theron's arms and face. Suddenly the legionary-turned-vampire flew away, his eyes and mouth wide with surprise. Theron looked up to see Ramah standing over him, a confused expression on his deeply tanned face.

Ramah looked from Theron to Taras, who lay in the street a few paces away, then back to Theron. "What is this, Theron?" he asked, nodding toward Taras. By this time, a crowd of people had gathered around the three of them. Some glowed, while others didn't.

"Ramah," Theron began, hoping to find some way to talk himself free of this mess. "It was an accident. I—"

But he never finished the sentence. Glowing or otherwise, the people in the crowd all seemed to have something to say.

"Look at that one!" One said.

"His teeth! Look at his teeth!"

"What are they?"

"Monsters?"

"Demons?"

"Don't get too close."

Then, in the worst moment of Theron's life, one of the gathered Jews uttered a single word. A word so damning that it finished his career as an Enforcer once and for all. *"Bachiyr!"*

The crowd fell silent for a pair of heartbeats as they digested the word, then they erupted in a cacophony of shouts and screams, and many of them ran. A few brave souls grabbed torches and swords, but even these failed to advance.

Sudden understanding lit Ramah's face, and the orange glow of the reflected firelight lent his eyes a smoldering air. His brows drew down, and his lips parted, revealing his canines. Theron knew, then, that he was a dead man. Ramah would carry out his execution right there in the street.

Theron scrambled backward, looking for an escape, knowing he would not find one. Ramah advanced on him, the Councilor's claws extended from his fingertips as he scowled his way forward. Theron's back touched something solid and immobile. Wood. He'd backed himself up against a wall. He could go no further. Ramah closed the distance in seconds, his hand raised for a killing strike. No words now. None were needed. Both men knew what the next few moments would bring: death. Theron braced himself for the blow that would finish him.

⸸⸸⸸

Taras rolled to a stop and shot to his feet amidst a small cloud of dust. He stared at the two creatures in front of him. The one called Ramah looked confused, while Theron - *So that's his name! Not Ephraim, but Theron* - backed away, muttering something about an accident. Then someone in the crowd shouted *"Bachiyr!"*

At the sound of the strange word, Ramah's face twisted in anger, and Taras saw the fangs glinting yellow in the firelight. Just like the fangs in Theron's mouth. *By the Gods,* he thought. *There are two of those things? Probably working together.*

Taras stared at the two *Bachiyr,* his rage mounting. This was their fault. And he intended to make them pay.

⸸⸸⸸

Just before Ramah swung, a wild yell erupted to Theron's right, and suddenly Ramah was bowled over by a crazed, writhing mass of yellow hair, deeply tanned muscles, and the shredded remains of a legionary's red cloak. The two tumbled several paces away from Theron, Taras screaming incoherently as he and Ramah rolled on the cobbles. Theron, dazed, rose on unsteady legs. He leaned against the wall behind him for support and watched the scene unfold.

Taras flailed at Ramah with both hands. Somehow, Theron noted, the legionary managed to grow claws, a skill that usually took time to learn, and he poked and slashed at Ramah over and over. Sometimes he scored a hit, but most of his attacks met with a solid block by Ramah, whose face twisted as he became more and more angry.

Theron knew an opportunity when he saw one. He didn't waste a moment as he turned away from the brawling vampires and sped toward the Damascus Gate, knocking aside any human who stood in his way, glowing or otherwise. He did receive a few minor burns from the humans whose faith shown on them like torchlight, but it was nothing compared to the one he got from Jesus. The difference between the two was like the difference between a small ember and a raging bonfire. It didn't even slow him down.

He ran through the Damascus Gate and into the Judean countryside, not bothering to look behind him. His legs blurred as he dashed down the main road, startling several travelers, and headed for the Gardens of Gethsemane. If he could make it to the Gardens, he could escape. Ramah would certainly hunt for him when he finished with Taras, but Theron knew many places in the local area where he could hide, and he was confident he could avoid the Councilor's eyes at least until the sun rose. He refused to think about what he would do after that until he was sure he'd gotten away. *Escape first, then make a plan,* he told himself.

He reached the Gardens of Gethsemane and turned to look behind him. The street was empty as far back as he could see. Theron gave a sigh of relief and sped away into the night.

╫ ╫ ╫

Taras rolled in the street with the one called Ramah for several minutes, punching and clawing with abandon. It soon became clear to him that Ramah was far, far stronger. Taras, having the element of surprise, was able to knock his opponent from his feet and had thus far managed to prevent him from getting his guard up, but he knew it would not last. Sooner or later Ramah would have him.

After a short while Taras began to tire. His strikes slowed and his balance wavered, and Ramah seized an opening and reached up with both hands to grab the legionary's head. Taras, no novice to battle, released the offensive and rolled with Ramah's hands, lest his head be torn from his shoulders. He rolled away into the cobbled street and jumped to his feet. But the damage was done; his advantage lost. Ramah, much faster than Taras's eyes could follow, closed the distance between the two and jabbed his claws into Taras's belly.

He screamed as his insides lit up with fresh pain. He'd almost forgotten what it felt like after devouring so many people. He squirmed and grabbed Ramah's wrist, trying to pull the claws from his gut, but Ramah's arms felt like steel. Taras's fingers, slick with his own blood, slid up Ramah's forearm, unable to get a solid grip.

Then a new pain hit his back. Intense, searing heat burned its way up his spine and to the base of his neck. Taras screamed anew, releasing Ramah's forearm and slapping at the pain that crawled up his back. Ramah likewise screamed, and suddenly the claws were ripped from Taras's belly, spraying blood in a wide arc on the dusty street. He watched as Ramah reached behind him in a frantic attempt to pat out a fire that had engulfed his clothing. All around them, a group of glowing Jews held torches in the air.

Taras's clothes likewise burned. The spots of pitch on his back didn't help, and flames licked up the side of his body. He dropped to the ground and rolled in the street, a holdover from his military training. The pain didn't lessen, but the fire on his back died. Gods, that hurt! He rolled in the dirt until he was sure he'd extinguished the flames and then he lay there, wincing and writhing in pain. In the corner of his eye he saw Ramah drop to the street and roll, as well. Soon that flame would be out, too. Would Ramah renew his attack on Taras? Would the gathered Jews set him on fire again?

Not tonight, he determined. Taras rose to his feet amidst shouts and curses hurled at him by the crowd. He stumbled, but managed to stay upright long enough to drive his claws into the throat of the nearest Jew. The man gurgled as his life spilled out of his throat, and Taras's knees nearly buckled at the smell of fresh blood. But despite his hunger, he did not have time to feed. He tossed the dying man aside and ran from the city, looking for a place to hide.

⸸⸸⸸

Ramah rolled on the ground, extinguishing the flames but not his rage. He stood up as a pair of humans, emboldened by the cowardice of Taras and Theron, approached with their torches held at eye level.

A ring of humans surrounded him, at least thirty of the vermin. Over half of them glowed with their newfound faith, and all but a few carried flaming brands.

Ramah's temper flared brighter than the torches. Theron was long gone, and although Taras would not get far, Ramah would have to battle his way through the humans before he could pursue, and that would take time. In a rare moment of indecision, he stood in place, trying to decide which of the rogue vampires to chase. The outlaw Theron, or the accidental and unsanctioned Taras. Both were equally dangerous in their own way.

The people at the gate made his decision for him. They closed ranks until they stood shoulder-to-shoulder, surrounding him in a thick ring of humanity. Ramah smiled and licked a stray drop of blood from his upper lip. They didn't realize it, but the humans had just given him a welcome diversion and a free vent to his rising ire.

He charged the group with his claws raised and ripped a bloody path into their ranks, spraying gore and viscera into the night air. The screams of the dying men reminded him of other fights, other nights like this one, centuries before. Ramah was no stranger to slaughter. He tore the throat from one man, the head from another, and spun to stick his claws through the chest of a third. Undaunted, they pounced on him en masse, but Ramah bit and cut and shredded his way through the wall of flesh and bone and tore his way through to the other side, drenched from hair to boots in the blood of his enemies. He still had time to run after Taras or Theron, but Ramah's bloodlust was up, and instead of chasing after one of the escaping vampires he turned around and dove back into the fray, cutting his enemies to ribbons as he went.

Of the thirty or so humans gathered at the gate that night, not a single one escaped. Ramah butchered every last one. Before long, reinforcements started to arrive, including several units of armored legionaries traveling in catch-and-kill formations. The alarm had gone out through the entire city of the fire and fighting near the gate, and it seemed the entire population of Jerusalem descended upon him. Knowing he could not fight off so many people, Ramah turned his back to the approaching force and sprinted through the Damascus Gate.

He'd lost Theron and Taras both, but he wasn't worried. Ramah the Blood Letter, Second of the Council of Thirteen and one of the original thirteen vampires, knew he had an eternity in which to hunt them down.

I will find you, he thought. *Both of you. If it takes a hundred years or a thousand, you will both face the Council's wrath.*

With that thought, Ramah turned north, headed for Carthage.

CHAPTER THIRTY-FOUR

Taras woke at dusk. His eyes, sharp though they were, took a moment to adjust to the darkness of the tomb. He'd been able to move the boulder aside with ease; the tricky part was putting it back from the inside. Then just before he laid his head down for the day, he'd prayed to every one of his gods, begging them not to let Ramah find him.

Apparently, Ramah hadn't. Taras wasn't surprised; he doubted anyone would look for him here. His big concern was that someone would come to the spot and notice the site had been disturbed, but even that worry was remote, given the circumstances.

Taras glanced sideways at the shrouded corpse that lay against the far wall of the tomb. He'd been unable to look at it last night, but now, with the moon rising and lending him strength, he found he could not keep his eyes away from it.

From her, not *it*, he amended. Even dead, she was still his Mary.

He shuffled over to her side and sat down, toying with the idea of ripping the shroud open so he could see her face. He dismissed the thought immediately. He'd already seen her wounds once; he had no desire to see them again.

"I'm so sorry," he said. He looked from her to the other corpse sharing the small space with him. Abraham, pale and waxen, stared up at the ceiling of the cavern, his unblinking eyes clouded over in death. Taras had hidden the body here just before leaving for Jerusalem last night. The gaping hole in Abraham's throat looked eerily similar to Mary's. He looked back to Mary, hidden underneath the soft cotton wrappings.

"The *Bachiyr*," he said. "That's what they call themselves." Taras realized with a start he'd almost slipped and said *we* instead of *they*. But so what if he did? What did it matter anymore? He was one of them, now, as well. He had only to look at Abraham's mutilated throat to prove it.

"Oh, gods, what did you do to me, Theron?" He asked aloud, recalling the name Ramah had used the night before. He dropped his hands to his face as he realized how far he'd fallen. By rights, he and Mary should be well on their way to Carthage by now, holding hands and making plans for their future family while a boat waited for them in the harbor. Instead, Taras sat in his dead love's tomb, with only her corpse and that of her murdered father for company. No tears, they still would not come, and without their cleansing power he found it impossible to release his grief. Thus he sat in the darkness of the tomb in silence, listening to the thoughts in his own mind. He almost wished he'd stayed behind in Jerusalem and let Ramah finish him.

Taras stood, hunched over, and made his way to the huge stone in front of the tomb. He placed his hands on it and pushed. The boulder moved easily, and he rolled it out of the way just enough to squeeze through the opening. Even in his grief he marveled at his newfound strength. He rolled the stone back into place and rested his head on it. He thought of Mary's beautiful face and sighed, knowing he could never return here; it would be a desecration of her memory.

"Goodbye, Mary" he said, placing his palms flat on the stone. "Goodbye Abraham."

No one wants *to die, Roman.* Those were the words Abraham used, almost the last words he spoke before Taras killed him.

"You were wrong, Abraham," he said. "Some of us want to die. Some would find it preferable."

"It's not beyond you, you know," a voice said from behind him.

Taras spun, yanking his sword from its sheath. It was too early in the evening; too soon after such a painful goodbye to kill again, but he would if he had to. When he saw the speaker, his mouth fell open and he dropped his sword.

"You remember me," Jesus said.

There stood the Nazarene, just as Taras remembered from the night he'd tailed Theron to the Gardens. That night, Jesus had not yet been arrested, and thus he didn't have the cuts and bruises Taras saw later as he was led to Golgotha. On the cross, his face was bruised and swollen, and numerous cuts and scrapes pocked his body. Now, however, the man's smooth, unblemished skin showed no evidence of abuse. The crown of thorns was gone, and Jesus's dark hair spilled over his thin shoulders and down his back. But the biggest change in the Nazarene, Taras noted, was the light.

Jesus glowed, similar to the people of Jerusalem but far more intense. Taras felt weak just looking at him. It radiated from Jesus like the light of the sun, and he had to squint his eyes nearly shut against the glare.

Taras blinked, thinking his own situation had driven him insane, but when he opened his eyes again, Jesus remained in front of him. "It's not possible," Taras said. "You are dead."

"As are you, if I'm not mistaken."

Taras looked down at his hands, so cold and lifeless, and realized he didn't have a reply. "I suppose you're right."

"Of course I'm right."

Taras remembered his part in the man's death, and shame filled him. He raised his eyes and looked at Jesus, so calm and serene in the moonlight. "Why are you here?" he asked. "Have you come to take your revenge on me, Nazarene? If so, please get on with it. I'm late; I should have been sitting with Pluto in Tertius four days ago."

Jesus smiled, and the light around him intensified so much Taras had to turn his head. "That is not why I came," Jesus said. "Your mistakes are not entirely your own, though you must still take responsibility for them. I hold no anger for you."

"Then why are you here?"

"To tell you it's not beyond you."

"What isn't?"

"You know the answer to that already, Taras." Jesus folded his arms and fixed him with a stern look, as though lecturing a dense child. "Your wish; it's not impossible. The Sun can do it. So can fire. If I'm not mistaken, the *Bachiyr* can also die by having their heads removed, and there are other ways, too. In other words, you have options."

"Options?"

"Yes, options. Allow death to find you, or spend eternity running from the other *Bachiyr*, killing and devouring innocent people. They will hunt you, you know. Ramah, in particular, will not rest until you have been destroyed."

Taras pondered that for a moment. He'd known about the Sun's ability to kill him; his burned fingers told him that much. But he hadn't been ready. Of course, at the time he didn't know the extent of what he would become, either. Was he ready now? Could he step into the sunlight, if it came to that? Could he willingly walk into his death?

A thought occurred to him, and he looked at the Nazarene. "But you're Jewish," Taras said. "How could you advocate such a thing? Doesn't it go against your beliefs?"

"Oh, I don't advocate either choice. Neither of them is very good, if you ask me."

"Then why tell me about them?"

"Because you needed to know you have them. You always have a choice. Your options may not be good ones, but they are always there, and it is up to you to choose one. That's the whole point."

"The point of what?"

"Free will, of course."

"What?" Taras sat on a small boulder by the tomb, his hand on his forhead. Free will? What did that mean? Was there any other kind? His head hurt, and he massaged his left temple with his fingers. "I don't understand."

Jesus smiled again. "That's all right. The important thing about having choices is to *know* you have them. Just remember, Taras, you are already dead. You should not, in fact, be here at all. But, since you *are* here, maybe you don't want to leave. It seems you haven't made your choice yet." Jesus paused and looked behind Taras, at the entrance to Mary's tomb.

"Then again," he said, "maybe you have." With that, Jesus turned away and walked down the path, headed in the direction of Bethany, taking his glow with him.

Taras was left in darkness as he sat by Mary's tomb – now Abraham's, as well – and thought about what Jesus told him. He did, indeed have options. But was he strong enough to do it? Could he face the sun and die, with honor?

He thought of the pain from last night when the crowd had set him alight. His back still burned. The only way to ease that pain was blood, which he craved even after speaking to the Nazarene. He thought of Theron, the *Bachiyr* who'd done this to him, who'd also killed Mary. If he died, who would bring Theron to justice? Ramah? Jesus? Anyone? Or would he simply roam the world, taking lives at will and causing more misery? But if Taras lived, would he be any different? He had only to reopen the tomb and look at Abraham's corpse to know the answer.

But, still…

Options, Jesus said. *You always have a choice*, and in that moment, Taras made his. *No,* he thought, shaking his head at his own cowardice. *No, I'm not ready. Not yet.* He stood, whispered a final goodbye to Mary, and started walking. *Here I come, Theron.*

He had no idea where to start looking, but he guessed one place was as good as another, and anywhere was better than nowhere. He broke from the road and stepped onto the same path Jesus had taken, but going the opposite direction.

☩ ☩ ☩

Theron woke in a cave somewhere east of Jerusalem. His body ached from his many wounds and the long flight from the city. He'd run until the sun crested the horizon ahead, and then he found this cave. Now, as he stretched his pained limbs, he thought it was not too soon to start running again. Like Theron, Ramah would be up at dusk, and he shouldn't be too far behind. Best to get moving as soon as possible. By now Ramah would have calmed from his initial anger and realized death was too easy a punishment for Theron, and would no doubt press the Council to have him turned into a Lost One for thousands of years. Just the thought of it sent a shudder up Theron's spine.

Theron checked his equipment, making sure his sword and boots were all in good working order. In one of his pockets, he found the letter he'd retrieved from Simon's tunic. He opened it and read it a second time, still not believing his eyes. But the cuts and bruises on his skin were proof enough of his dilemma. He knew the Council would hunt him down like a dog for turning a human into a *Bachiyr* without their consent. They guarded their members with a fervor bordering on fanaticism, only allowing a select few to join their ranks. No one was permitted to just go around creating more at their whim; only the Council had that authority.

He started to crumple up the letter and throw it to the ground, but instead he folded it up and placed it in the pocket of his tunic, wanting to keep it as a reminder. He knew he would be better off to do as Herris asked and return to the Council to face his punishment with honor, even given the new charges the Council hadn't known about when Herris wrote the letter. Except...

You have been lied to, vampire...

...except he pictured the Lost One in the house by the Damascus Gate. Could he go through that? Could he live such a miserable, humiliating existence? Rotting and festering for centuries while his flesh was eaten alive by swarms of insect larva? He imagined himself in the tattered robe, serving the vampires in the Halls: tending to their whims and cleaning up after them when they finished in the Larder.

"I can't do it," he whispered. He could not make himself obey Herris' request. He stepped out of the cave, his hunger driving him to hunt. He needed blood, and it seemed he no longer had to worry about using any restraint. What did it matter anymore? Why should he care if bodies were discovered drained of blood when he finished with them? The Council already wanted to kill him, or to turn him into a Lost One. Why should he care about their laws now? To the abyss with them.

He left the cave and loped down a rough mountain road, heading away from Jerusalem and into the countryside. He hoped to come to a small village or town before daybreak. Tonight, he would feast, and the Council of Thirteen be damned. Oh, they would catch him eventually. Theron held no illusions in that regard. Sooner or later Ramah would track him down and then, if he survived, Theron would spend the next eternity or two as a Lost One.

...and you have been betrayed.

The words came, unbidden, into his mind. Jesus was right; he *had* been betrayed, by his own people. Theron examined the flesh on the back of his right hand, which remained charred and blackened from Jesus's touch.

"Damn you, Nazarene," he sswore, kicking at the dusty street. "None of this would have happened if not for you."

He again found a small measure of satisfaction in the knowledge that Jesus had died horribly on the cross. Nailed to it, or so he heard, left to die a slow and painful death under the seething Israeli sun. But it wasn't enough. Because of Jesus, Theron's own people had turned against him. After hundreds of years of loyal service, he was now an outcast. The Nazarene was probably laughing at him from beyond the grave.

Well, he would have the last laugh. Theron would use his skill and power, unequaled in *Bachiyr* society except among the Council of Thirteen, to hunt down every single human who called himself a friend of the fallen rabbi. Their deaths would be horrible. Theron would put them through all the suffering the Council meant for him. He would rip their organs from their still-living flesh and savor their screams like wine.

When he finished with Jesus's friends, he would hunt down those who had heard the Nazarene speak and do the same to them. Then he would go after anyone those people had spoken to about Jesus. It would take a long time to finish, but time was all Theron had left. If it took him a thousand years or ten thousand, he would eliminate all traces of Jesus's life on this planet, washing it away in a river of blood until no one remained who'd heard the name of Jesus. He would continue his quest until humanity had lost all memory of the carpenter's son from Galilee or until the Council caught him.

Whichever came first.

He looked up at the moon, shining from the heavens, and shook his fist at it.

When he returned his eyes to the road, he spotted a caravan stopped up ahead. Half a dozen horses stood tethered to trees at the side of the road, and four wagons surrounded a small fire. Clearly, the drivers had made camp for the night. Theron walked up to the wagons, not bothering to hide the sound of his approach.

"Hello, traveler" a man said from beside the fire. "Have you come to join us? We have food and a pallet. You are welcome to share our dinner."

Theron recognized the speaker. Filius, his name was. A Roman legionary. Or at least he used to be. He recalled the night Taras led him through Jerusalem bound hand and foot. Filius had accosted him, even struck him. Apparently Filius had traded his legionary's uniform for a simple, coarse robe tied at the waist with a short piece of rope. Theron noted the man possessed a faint glow, but it would not be strong enough to protect him. Not tonight.

Theron smiled and stepped into the ring of wagons.

Dinner, indeed.

EPILOGUE

Just outside the city of Caesarea, 103 A.D.

After following the scent for nearly an hour, Ramah the Bloodletter, second of the Council of Thirteen and their primary assassin for over four thousand years, stepped through the splintered door and into the small home. Nestled into the hills of the countryside, the house was not easy to find. The gray stone had been allowed to grow moss, and the structure itself seemed to squat into the earth, its roof just peeking over the ground. If Ramah's suspicions about the place were correct, it had been built that way on purpose, lest the Romans discover the place and crucify whoever lived there.

Ramah's hard brown eyes probed the darkness of the interior, noting with stern displeasure the coagulated blood sprayed along the walls in arcs up to ten feet long. A demolished table lay in a corner, the broken body of a middle-aged man in a blood-spattered white robe sprawled over the shattered remains. The man's shredded neck could not support his head, which lolled to the side at an angle no living man could attain. Glazed, empty eyes stared up at the ceiling from a face that was only just beginning to collect a swarm of flies. The man had not been dead long. A few hours, at most.

As he walked through the house, he noted several other corpses among the broken furniture and other household items. All were in similar condition to the first, including the torn remains of two small children. He could not even tell if the two little ones were boys or girls, such was the devastation their killer had wrought on their tiny bodies.

He shook his head as he continued through the house, looking for a sign that would tell him for certain he was on the right track. He knew this to be the work of a *Bachiyr* like himself, but he needed confirmation that it was the one he sought. At this point the slaughter could be the work of any one of a number of renegade vampires, the Father knew there were plenty of them these days. He had to make sure he was following the right one. In truth, it didn't matter much. Ramah would kill whatever vampire committed these acts regardless of whether or not he or she was his intended target. Whoever did this had left too many clues, too many possibilities for the people of the nearby town to guess the true nature of the savage murders. As such, he would have to raze the place when he finished his search.

He wandered through the building several times, but could not find what he sought. More than a little irritated at himself for wasting valuable time, he started to leave. He was almost to the door when he stepped on a metal ring in the floor. He frowned. How had the ring escaped his notice earlier? Had he not felt it beneath his boot, he might have walked out of this place and never known it was there. He reached down to grasp it and sure enough, a section of the floor came up, revealing a stone staircase leading down into the earth.

Ramah walked slowly down the stairs, knowing already what he would find. His hunch was confirmed when he came to the bottom and found a large stone chamber. A central aisle cut through the middle of the place, bordered on either side by the remains of several wooden benches. At the head of the aisle, on a slightly raised area, stood a small wooden altar. Emblazoned on the front of the altar was the simple silhouette of a fish, symbol of the new religion sweeping the world. The symbol was smeared with blood, as though the killer tried to cover it up.

The air here was thick with the heady scent of blood and clouds of buzzing flies, but his attention was drawn to a question scrawled on the wall behind the altar, written in the blood of the victims. He smiled when he read it; it was all the proof he needed.

Next to the message, the killer had drawn a black hand on the wall. Ramah had seen the same mark many times in the last seventy years.

He turned and examined the rest of the room. Amidst the clouds of hungry flies, he counted at least a dozen more bodies. He smiled in the darkness as he took in the macabre scene. The Christians, as they called themselves, must have been right in the middle of one of their secret worship ceremonies when the killer came in and sent them to their Promised Land.

Judging by the ferocity and brutality of the killings, as well as the writing on the wall, it could only be one vampire; the same one Ramah had been hunting for seventy years. A fugitive who went out of his way to s out these Christians and kill them as horribly as possible, then leaving without bothering to cover up the deed.

"I have you now, Theron," Ramah said aloud, the words echoing against the stone walls of the makeshift tomb.

THE END

Acknowledgements

33 A.D. had a lot of help getting all the way from my brain into your hands, and those people need to be recognized for the wonderful, helpful people they are:

Many heartfelt thanks to author (and awesome cover designer) Jeremy Robinson, for helping me at every stage of the process and for so much more. Author Aprilynne Pike (Ahem, #1 NYT *Bestselling* Author Aprilynne Pike, that is, heh heh) for believing in me even when I didn't believe in myself. Author Jon F. Merz for the advice and for offering to read the manuscript. My friend and fellow author Liz Strange, who never stopped believing in this book and told me to stop worrying. Tyhitia Green for her faith and constant encouragement.

My beta readers, who read everything and told me in no uncertain terms (and none too gently) what they liked and what they didn't like, which is exactly what I needed: Apryilnne (got you in here twice!), Susan Parker, Joy Terry, Stacey Suttles, Alice Loweecey, Jaycinth, Rosemary Parker, and the many members of my family who dared to read a pile of loose papers and offer their opinions: Julie and Mike Newton, Mike and Peggy Jordan, Adam Jordan, and Steve Nelson.

Also a huge shout-out to all the folks at Absolute Write for all the advice and for picking apart my work. The sheer volume of information on that website is of incalculable value to any writer.

Most of all, I've got to thank my wonderful wife, Heather, who put up with a lot of nights in front of the television or working out all by herself while I got lost inside my own head. Thank you, Hon, I love you very much.

About the Author

Author Photo by Heather McAfee

David McAfee was born in Lakenheath USAFB, England, and spent his youth traipsing about the globe with his military family, soaking up the cultures of faraway places like the Philippines, Turkey, Spain, and California. When David was in his tweens, his father retired to Texarkana, Texas, which David still considers home.

He started writing at the tender age of six, albeit on a much smaller scale, and today his work can be found in at least one horror magazine.

David currently lives in Tennessee with his wife, daughter, and a whole herd of small furry animals. He enjoys writing, motorcycling, and spending time with his family. *33 A.D.* is his first published novel. He can be reached at Monkeyfeet73@yahoo.com and can be visited on the web at mcafeeland.wordpress.com.

CPSIA information can be obtained at www.ICGtesting.com
Printed in the USA
BVOW061816101211

278071BV00006B/73/P

9 780982 630709